Cover Art by Ashely Jurgens @wolfandbearr

Cover Design by Elliana Maggetti

Developmental and Copyedits by Kay Morton @kmortonedits

Beta Editing and Reading by Kalina Tyne

Inside Art: @qetsu_art @ @pangolin2b

For trigger warnings, see last page.

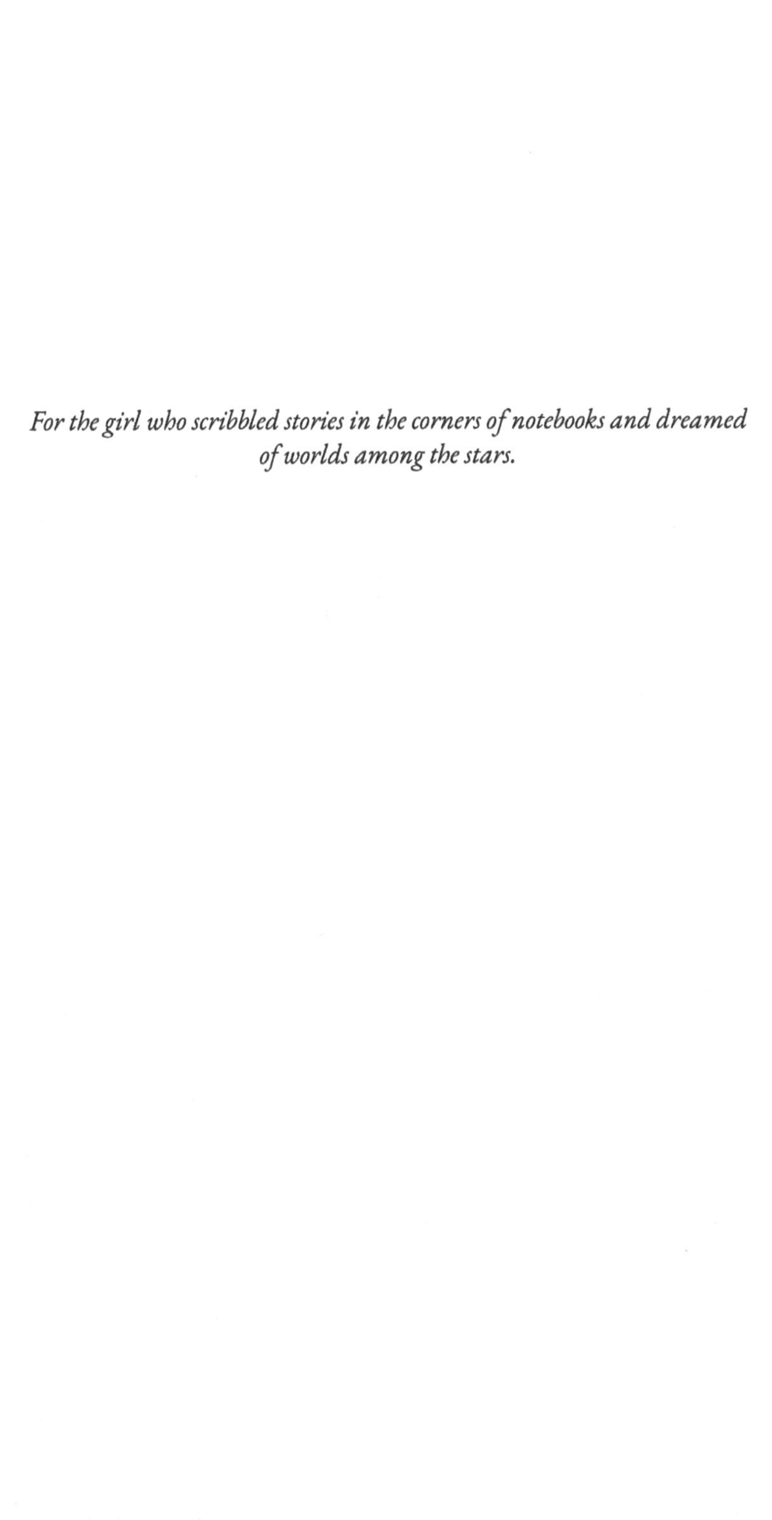

*For the girl who scribbled stories in the corners of notebooks and dreamed
of worlds among the stars.*

THE TALES OF THE HOLLOW

E.R. MAGGETTI

THE TALES OF THE HOLLOW

enchantment realm prequel novellas

book 0.5

E.R. MAGGETTI

Content Warnings

- Mentions of death of parents or siblings on and off page.
- Mild gore and violence
- Harassment from a drunken man
- Please note these are Adult Fantasy Novellas and contain adult themes. Not meant for younger audiences.
- This is an open door romance with low spice.

THE ISLES
THE ASH MOUNTAINS
THE HOLLOW
DRAGONIER FOREST
THE FAE LANDS
THE OPEN LANDS

EVANTHIA
KINGDOM OF LORIENNE
THE RED MOUNTAINS
NIVARIA

LONG LOST KINGDOM

part one

CHAPTER 1

Kyeria

F ollow the stars west, they will guide you home. Kyeria could hear her mother's voice over the pounding of her own heart. Her own feet pounded into the forest floor beneath her, matching her heart rate. If someone looked at her life—a life comprised of going village to village, moving from one kingdom to the next with a new name, a new story— she wondered if they'd think it a sad one. She lived only two, maybe three winters in each place before needing to move on. Before the humans saw she didn't age like them, or became suspicious. She was fae in a land that had killed the last ones on this continent, pushing her people back to their holy island. On this continent, Kyeria wore many faces, a merchant's daughter selling at the local markets, a barmaid, a seamstress, or traveler, among other things. But she wished for a slower life, one where she could just be, where her magic could be free and her heart calm.

"She's headed towards the mountains!" a shout behind her brought her crashing back into reality. She leaned against the trunk of a giant oak, catching her breath. She was on the run, *again*.

Kyeria couldn't see the stars now, not under the dense canopy above her. The trees grew thicker ahead. She couldn't see the mountain peaks from below the canopy, but she knew that the mountains were due west, and west meant home. Her heart sang, beckoning her in that direction. The galloping of horses made the ground tremble. A burst of birds took off from a tree nearby at the incoming noise. She stilled. One deep breath and she focused on clearing her mind of her own thoughts and taking in those of the trees.

"The leaves, follow the leaves," the trees whispered. The wind made the loose strands of hair whip around her face, and she saw a trail of red and orange leaves, flying along a band of wind directly into the mountains.

"Beware the ash, child of the trees. it comes from above," the wind howled.

She took off, weaving between the trees to stay out of sight from the soldiers coming after her. They wouldn't follow her into the mountains. No one would. It was not only uncharted for the Evanthians, but tales of dark and twisted fates lie ahead. The Ash Mountains were off limits to humankind, and the only fate was a cold death should they try to enter. But Kyeria did not have human blood as the ones who hunted her did.

She whispered to the Goddess Luna to grant her passage and broke past the last line of trees of Evanthia and into the Ash Mountains. Her magic reacted in turn, making her fingertips burn with a dull awareness, as if she was passing through a magical barrier.

The wind herself pushed Kyeria in the correct way, weaving in and out of the base of the mountain, climbing small areas until a small river revealed itself and she felt the relief wash over her. Kyeria turned, looking behind her to see only a dense field of trees. She was rather high up in the mountains now. Resting against the trunk of a tree she bowed her head in thanks to the Goddess Luna. She felt the life in the wind die down as she rose. Her magic calmed—signaling safety.

Kyeria was on her own now, in uncharted lands with only her memories of her mothers stories to guide her. But she was used to being on her own in an unforgiving land, surrounded by humans who despised her kind and thought them a kind of demon due to their magic and longer life spans. It was ten years ago when the great war ended. Her kind had lost, pushed back to the Fae homelands, situated on the far west on an island. Lush and full of life, water flowed freely there. The wind sang as it danced through the valleys and mountains. She could feel the magic here under her feet as she could in her own village back in the Fae lands. She knew magic lived in the Ash Mountains from the stories from the neighboring kingdom of Evanthia and from tales that spread through her homeland. However, experiencing it for herself felt like a sort of reverence. She let her hands rest on the root of the tree and felt the ground hum under her.

"Child of the trees," the wind whispered again and her hair pushed forward, making her look up. There seemed to be a valley with some caves in the sides of the mountains. She pushed her own magic into the roots leaving white flowers dusting the ground as her offering back to the earth. The wind gently flowed past her, brushing her skirts up and pushing her feet along. Kyeria pushed her red locks behind her ears and headed for the caves. The river was glistening, birds sat in the shallow waters and a sharp glimmer of light caught her eye. She narrowed her gaze and followed the odd light burst. Then the sun hit just right revealing a true form; peeking from behind the far tree on the opposite side of the river was a light sprite. Kyeria smiled and held out her hand, magic hummed from it and small flowers burst around the ground where the sprite sat on a small tree branch. The sprite seemed delighted by the small act and danced in the flowers before meandering over to Kyeria.

"I am Kyeria," she said in the language of sprite. The sprite glowed in delight.

"Child of the trees, the wind whispers of your arrival." She smiled. Light sprites were mostly a gathering of white light but if they permitted you close enough you could see faint outlines of their shapes. Her small wings beat quickly as a hummingbirds did.

"I am Ember." Her small hand rested on her chest. "You may rest here now." She flew ahead and Kyeria followed the sprite into the cave, guiding her to a nook inside of the cave where she was able to see out and watch. Kyeria wasn't sure what dangers the mountains held. She was grateful for this shelter.

"Why are you so far from the islands, Miss?" Ember asked, perched on a rock. Kyeria sat down, and folded her hands in her lap with a small sigh.

"I have not seen my own lands since before the war," she answered.

"The moon has passed many times since then, I fear your kind is not common now, but it seems the mountain recognizes your magic," Ember spoke, her voice soft and airy.

"I went into hiding when the war ended," Kyeria replied, trying not to let memories of the war flood her. She was young but the Fae were taught to fight as soon as one could hold a sword up. Many with magic were needed in the great war, and Kyeria possessed not only the magic of the earth but the ability to heal. It was rare to hold two classes of magic, let alone to have two such powerful ones, so she had gone to the front, proudly following her people into war.

It was bloodshed, her mind filling with the screams of her people, too young to understand such pain. She had woken in a field herself, must have been assumed dead since she had been covered in blood and alone. Kyeria spent the next ten years in hiding, keeping her hair long and she covered her ears with wrappings over her hair and ears. She had worked and wandered from village to village since. It wasn't until the outskirts of Evanthia that she had been exposed by someone she had trusted. and when the guards came for her in the night, she did what she knew best; she ran.

"You hold much sorrow," the sprite said sadly. "You will be safe here, but beware the skies and the shadows, this is the gods' land afterall."

Kyeria woke to a strained humming. Her magic was stirring. The ground was buzzing with signs of danger. She quickly stood, the sky was dark, and only the small dim lights of sprites lit the river along with the moon. She tucked two daggers into her corset and left her bag behind.

The wind whispered through the leaves. Something was wrong. Something from this land was in danger and calling out. Kyeria's magic was blessed upon her by the Goddess Luna, as all earth magic was. She was familiar with her senses being heightened in the forests; preferring to dwell in them. She weaved through the trees, down the mountain to the edges of the border of Evanthia. She walked until the sun was cresting in the morning, Kyeria's bare feet following the humming of the earth directing her to where Luna guided her. A small burst of dim light glittered past her.

"Hurry miss, someone has found an egg, you must help," Ember begged.

"What kind of egg?" Kyeria replied in a whisper.

"From the skies, miss." She followed along at Kyeria's shoulder, keeping her light barely visible; sprites could manipulate light to their liking, rendering them seemingly invisible if they needed to be.

She heard the shouts of men, a deep voice spoke through the dark forest, giving orders. She recognized them, as they all wore furs and their eyes were voids. They were clearly traveling, armed and searching for something. Which could only mean one thing.

Raiders.

She despised raiders, they stole and cheated their way through the continent. Kyeria had a few run-ins with them, they prayed on what looked weak. She, however small and dainty appearing, was not weak.

The wind cried out as they reached the edge of the rocks. A winding trail of vines led her to follow a trail that climbed up what seemed to be a small hidden cave entrance. Kyeria's magic fluttered again, assuring her that this was where she was needed. Ember fluttered next to her, her light dim so human eyes could not see her. Wings beating as fast as a hummingbird.

Kyeria placed a hand on the leaves below her, feeling into the soil, letting her magic cast out a net searching for other magic. There, in the back of the small cave, was a beacon of magic, she could sense the beginnings of life, an egg, unhatched. Goddess above, she knew with certainty it was a Dragon egg. Ember whispered next to her, "From the sky miss."

Kyeria knew this was rumored to be sacred land. She recalled the earth's warning: *"Beware the ash, child of the trees. it comes from above."*

This was Dragon territory.

"See these marks, this is it," one of the men said pointing to the carvings in the far right corner of the stone. It was hardly visible, but the marks read in an old elvish language. Her mother called it the language of the gods, and it was rarely spoken and only written in sacred lands. Her mother had passed down the knowledge as all Fae did with their children. The language of the gods, the words of the Dragons, the sacred scribe.

Her mother spoke frequently of the Dragons, great and terrible beasts. They were the center of many tales. Incredibly strong and rare beings that lived for great ages. Eggs only hatched every few centuries. The younglings were protected fiercely as was the will of Luna. It was deeply rooted in the Fae histories to protect and revere the Dragons. Kyeria pressed on, Ember taking to the trees above, her small translucent wings beating silently.

There were three men, much larger than Kyeria herself. Two had swords strapped to their backs, the other had laid down his sword and pack on the ground and was pawing a hand over the carved marks in the cave entrance. While the entrance itself was hidden in an array of vines, the elvish words explained a path. She prayed to Luna that the third man did not have knowledge of the language or the ability to read it.

Kyeria steadied her breath, making herself a wraith. She slid behind the next tree, around some rocks and behind a bush where the abandoned pack lay with the sword next to it. It was a bigger sword than she was used to but she didn't have any weapons on her other than two small daggers which would not be enough to take down three large men, and she didn't want to get close enough to need to use them in combat. Kyeria put a hand to the earth again, pushing her magic into the soil and growing branches far to the right as a distraction.

One of the men spotted it and shouted, making the others look. Two moved towards the new growth and the unarmed man stayed by the carvings in the stone but watched the other two. It gave her enough time to shoot her magic towards the cave, reinforcing the entrance with strong branches, impossible to move past.

"Heavens above!" one shouted.

"Show yourself, mistress of the trees!" the second one shouted.

"Do not tempt fate to anger the Goddess," the third argued back to the other men.

"No Goddess of mine, you fool," the first shouted back.

"Show yourself!" the second shouted again. Kyeria sweeped up the sword and charged at the unarmed raider. A grueling scream pierced the air as the metal pierced his fleshy middle. She quickly pulled the sword back and whirled as he dropped. The other two brutes were on her in a second. Magic spilled from her as if dancing after so long of standing still and unused. Kyeria's magic was like a well, it could be used up and depleted if she used too much, but it had been years since she had used more than small pieces, and at this moment she felt limitless.

8

Vines climbed up and wrapped around their feet. One slashed at the vines with his sword and broke free, advancing on her. Kyeria only had a breath to grab the dagger sheathed on her thigh and twist out of reach, throwing the dagger. The polished silver handle was gleaming as the dagger embedded into the man's skull. Blood streamed down his face and she swung the borrowed sword again, stopping him for good this time. The third man had broken free of the vines next and attacked. He was faster than she had anticipated and he quickly gained the upper hand. He swung skillfully and the tip of the sword grazed her arm. She hissed in pain, the sting of metal shooting through her.

Her magic splintered at the touch of steel. Kyeria recognized it as the venom fuzzed with her magic, smothering it. The steel of Enith had a poisonous effect on the Fae. Her arm felt heavy where the steel had bit into her skin. Kyeria slid past him, to his fallen raider and plucked the dagger from him, throwing it precisely to hit the last man in the eye; he fell back. Long enough for her to use her second dagger for close combat. One slash. Then the second one, deeper than the first. She willed her last bit of strength into lifting the sword and plunged it into his heart. Then Kyeria collapsed.

Her breath was ragged. Her vines and roots retreated back into the earth where she had willed them to grow from with her magic. Her magic, it was being sucked out and out from her very being as if the earth was taking it back. The wind picked up, and Ember was frantically fluttering near her, whispering words that Kyeria could not understand. The wind was whipping Kyeria's hair now. She whispered her sorrow to Luna and prayed no raiders were left lurking and the egg would be safe. She had failed. This land begged for her to help and she had failed.

Her magic was seeping back into the earth, small dark blooms erupted from the soil as the blood from her arm dripped down and met the earth. The wind viciously slashed at her, as if trying to wake her but Kyeria's eyes were heavy. So heavy. Time passed oddly, she heard voices —maybe Ember had called for other sprites. Then footsteps. Kyeria swore she heard footsteps, but the little sprite could not do such a thing. Her magic was only a whisper now, and the wind was just the wind, no guidance or words floating. She knew then that she was dying. Kyeria thought of her mother, of being reunited with her people who had been left on the battlefields. The fae did not fear death, they celebrated the end of this life and the beginning of the next. Her lungs burned now, her breaths more labored as the venom spread through her.

The ground shook under her, so violently she pried her eyes open as much as she could, a darkness covered her, followed by a chill that raked through her body. Her magic hummed faintly, a distant echo diluted by steel that had pierced her. It wasn't darkness she felt, but a shadow. She blinked, struggling to clear the fog of sleep from her vision, and blinked again, her mind wrestling with the impossibility unfolding before her.

Scales. There were scales—massive, shimmering, and impossibly close. They were like polished armor, reflecting the soft light in a myriad of muted, steely hues. Her heart raced as she slowly shifted her gaze upward, her breath catching in her throat.

Above her, impossibly close, was a dragon. Not a distant legend or a figure from tales told around a campfire, but a living, breathing god of myth, hovering in the space above her. Its eyes, deep and green like ancient forests, fixed on her with a mixture of curiosity and timeless intelligence. The dragon's wings, enormous and folded tightly, created a canopy of shadows over her. Her entire world seemed to narrow to this single, breathtaking moment. Dragons were equivalent to the gods according to her mother's stories—powerful, untouchable. She had never believed she would see one up close, let alone with such intimacy. The air around her thrummed with the dragon's presence, each slow, deliberate beat of its wings sending ripples through the very fabric of reality. She swallowed hard, trying to process the enormity of what she was witnessing.

The dragon's gaze remained steady, its presence conveyed a silent understanding, a deep acknowledgment of the awe and disbelief in her eyes. For a few precious, suspended moments, she was caught between the realms of disbelief and wonder, staring up at the living embodiment of myth and magic.

"Child of the trees, you have saved one of our own at the cost of your own life," a deep old voice spoke into her mind. The breath wholly left her lungs. She remembered the stories her mother weaved into her bed time stories, that the ancient Dragons could walk through minds. Kyeria wasn't sure if she was hallucinating, being this close to death's door. She pushed her thoughts out, hoping the Dragon could hear her.

"It was my honor," she said in her mind.

"Miss!" Ember's voice fluttered to her, carrying along a cup made of leaves. "Water from the sacred lake, it will heal you," she explained, tilting the cup into Kyeria's mouth. The effects were quick, Kyeria's vision cleared fully. She felt the magic tickle at her limbs, and the angry slash down her arm closing, her body healing.

"My land thanks you for your kindness," the Dragon hummed in her mind. Kyeria pulled herself up to her knees, looking up at the Dragon.

"It was my honor," she said aloud and bowed her head.

"You are not of this land, the wind whispered of your arrival."

Kyeria's wide eyes took in every scale before her, in awe of the being before her. "I thank you for the passage, I am unsure my fate should I have not made it past the forest edge."

"I am Fendiah, the elder." The Dragon slightly tilted his grand head in greeting.

"Kyeria," she replied out loud, holding a hand to her heart and bowing.

"Kyeria of the trees, it has been many cycles of this sun since I have seen one connected to the land as you."

"Yes, I fought in the great war and have been hiding since the last of my people were erased from this land." Her eyes were deep with sorrow as she spoke, still visibly weak from venom that had torn apart her magic moments ago. She felt again like she had on the battlefield ten years ago. Weak, alone, and left in an unfamiliar land.

Fendiah let out a huff at this, the trees leaves around them shuttering with the movement. He was silent for a moment, his golden-yellow eyes staring into her very soul. Black scales rippled down his neck, catching the light and glimmering.

"Kyeria, child of the trees, I grant you passage and safety in our home as thanks for sacrifice and protecting our most valued hatchling." The Dragon looked towards the cave, his massive wings moving. Kyeria held back a gasp. She had been testing fates by running into the mountains. Passage through the Ash Mountains was impossible, stories had been spun that anyone who entered would wither to the winds. The Dragon stretched his wings out ready to take flight. But he paused.

"Passage—*if* you bring the hatchling with you across the trek and deliver it to the winter-haired heir. He alone will bring the young one to where we rest."

"Of course, it would be my honor." Kyeria bowed as Ember rested on her knee glowing brightly.

"You shall take them, little sprite," the Dragon said before taking off into the sky. The beat of his wings shuttered the earth below her. The trees swaying out of the way. "Well that was something," Ember giggled. Kyeria looked down to her perched on her knee, her form coming into full color. She glowed bright. Her long waving blonde hair, a dress made of leaves, and white wings that fluttered.

"Off we go!" She smiled and flew towards the cave. Kyeria pushed down her hand and tested her magic, she could feel it replenishing. So she pushed her magic into the earth, making the vines fall away from blocking the entrance.

"Ember!" Kyeria called after the sprite. "Who is the winter-haired heir? And what village?"

"Oh miss, it's the most wonderful place, only those who have been in that land for ages know of it, but if Fendiah commands it then so must you go!" She smiled brightly.

"And the heir?" Kyeria pushed as they walked into the cave. The light was swallowed up, only the small light the sprite emitted guided their way.

"The Dragon prince!" Ember squeaked. "You'll see! This way miss!" Kyeria kept walking deeper into the cave as the ceiling got lower and lower. Kyeria had to crawl to the last section, a small egg the size of her palm lay in a bed of leaves and vines. The Dragon egg glowed a deep pink and purple, scales surrounded the outside. It was the most beautiful thing Kyeria had ever seen.

"Well aren't you just stunning," Kyeria whispered to the egg. She swore she felt her magic stir when she touched the egg.

"We must get back into the mountains now, miss!" Ember buzzed near her. Kyeria nodded and carefully cradled the egg in one hand and used the other to push herself out of the small space until she could stand again.

Kyeria pushed aside the hanging vines at the face of the cave. She fastened her clothing to hold the egg snug to her chest so her hands were free. Collecting her two daggers from the outside, she called upon her magic to bury the raiders, and the ground opened and vines and grass grew over their lifeless bodies. She left the swords there as well, letting the roots take them deep into the earth. Not to be seen or used again. Kyeria's hand rested on her heart, her magic felt like it was waking up again, the water from the lake leaving an odd icey tingle shooting through her veins. Her magic jolted in response, her well of reserves were filling back up at a rather fast speed.

"Let's go," Kyeria said to the sprite. Ember let her light glow in approval and led the way back to where Kyeria had spent the night, near a river of water. It was close to the high sun when they arrived and Kyeria felt her body dragging.

"Rest now, we can continue when your magic settles." Ember saw Kyeria's skeptical look and added, "Sprites can sense magic!" Kyeria walked to the water's edge. Her magic bristled at the acknowledgement of the lake. She could feel their own magic—the lands, this lake. She assumed it was just a small glance of the magic that lay in the Ash Mountains. Kyeria let the air fill her lungs, resting a hand on the egg. She whispered, "Don't you worry, you will be just fine, little one."

A day had passed. Kyeria followed Ember through the mountains, resting in caves or under trees along the way. A small river flowed near them, calling Kyeria to it. A familiarity making her magic hum louder in her ears, as if the magic that flowed down the banks was the same that flowed in her veins. The wind danced along with them singing as it went, she could hear it all, the wind, the trees. Kyeria seemed to have magic overflowing at the seams. Leaking back into the earth and leaving trails of wildflowers in her wake. The water from the lake had not only healed her but brought her magic back stronger than it had ever been on this continent. Ember giggled at the new flowers as they littered the ground. Kyeria couldn't fight the smile tugging at her lips as well. Her heart felt at ease in this land, safe and welcome. She pushed her hair back, revealing her pointed ears. She had needed to hide herself for so long, but not here. Here she could feel magic in the soil, a true form undiluted by the blood of war elsewhere.

"We are close now, miss!" Ember fluttered back to Kyeria who smiled.

"Ember, you must call me by my name."

"But miss!" Ember exclaimed like the most scandalous thing had been said.

"I am not of noble birth, and my people are no longer on this land, I am simply Kyeria."

"If you insist," Ember replied, her voice seeming reluctant.

As they continued on their trek, Ember told stories of the Ash Mountains, and the villages of The Hollow.

"The Hollow," Ember explained, "is much smaller than the kingdoms you're familiar with, but it holds a unique significance. This is the realm of those who have long served and protected the forests and mountains of the Dragons. Centuries ago, they settled here to revere the Dragons as their gods and care for the land. They constructed a grand temple for their worship and a castle for the Guardians—a royal family entrusted with the sacred duty and magic of protecting this land. The Hollow is surrounded by rugged, treacherous terrain, and a magical barrier. It is a wonder how you were able to get through, though I suppose it has something to do with you not being a human! An ancient magic surrounds us here, reaches to the edges of the Ash Mountains, and the Dragioner Forest."

Ember shined brightly talking about the castle. She said she had never been inside, but the sprites helped to serve as messengers for the heir. The Guardian heirs were royalty in The Hollow. There were three in the line to the throne currently: the king and his two grandchildren. Kyeria had questions bursting from her, this new and exciting land that her magic felt so calm in was unlike any other. She tried to ask Ember more about the heirs but Ember only blushed and smiled before saying, "You'll see, Miss!"

CHAPTER 2
Kellian

"Why are you so fucking stubborn?" Aura's voice broke the pleasant silence of Kellian's observatory. He was hunched over piles of scattered papers on the ground surrounded by sketches of the stars and texts from the ancient libraries in the castle. White hair casted down in messy waves hitting below his shoulders, half pinned back and pulled into a bun. His angular jaw was flexed in concentration despite his sister's distraction.

"What could I possibly have done now, dear sister?" Kellian asked, not removing his eyes from his task at hand.

"Oh, stop dreaming about clouds or whatever it is you do." Aura stood leaned against a large looking glass pointed to the sky. Kellian was still focused on his work, she was tapping her foot impatiently—her training boots still on from the sound they made on the floor.

"You know that is not what I am doing," Kellian dismissed her with a sigh. He had been studying constellations for years all for a greater purpose than simply the stars in the sky. Aura knew this, but was choosing violence on this bright morning.

"What do you want, Aura?" He looked up, meeting her golden eyes, identical to his own. His sister was pure fire bottled up into a small physical form of a human. She threw her hand in their air.

"It is half-past sunrise, on the twelfth day, Kellian! We are needed in the temple in less than an hour!" She was fuming.

"And why, pray tell, are you yelling at me while you are in your training leathers?"

"You take longer than me," she huffed.

"I do not," Kellian's expression softened, it was nearly impossible for him to actually hold any resentment for his sister. He pulled his head up from his journals, running a hand on his neck and letting his shoulders relax.

He had been up here for too long. It was too easy for him to get lost in his research and love for the stars. He could chart them for hours, logging information and sketching as much as he could from his travels and scouting. The morning light casting through the windows above was draped over in shadow as a Dragon flew over the castle.

"Shit," Kellian murmured, clambering to his feet. "I'm going! Happy?" He scowled at his sister. Aura stayed leaned against his looking glass bigger than her body with a satisfied smirk on her pale features.

"Delighted," she smirked and walked out the door.

By the time Kellian entered the outer room of the temple he could hear the clambering of villagers inside who were there to pay respects to the gods. Aura swept into the room after him. Training leathers and dirt were long gone, replaced with a long blue gown. She was every bit of grace and elegance as their mother had been. Kellian knew he was a mirror image of his own father, stern and iron faced but had the same winter hair of his mother and sister and golden eyes of his father and grandfather. But their parents were long past gone and it was just Aura and Kellian to head the temple offerings of twelfth day.

"Grandfather said a traveler is in the forest," Aura whispered as advisors and other castle attendants filtered through the room. Kellian's sharp gaze narrowed on his sister. *How was it possible for someone to get past the borders? Even more so, who could this person be for the magic of the borders to allow them to pass.*

"Elaborate," his voice was a low growl.

"A woman," she shrugged, pausing before lowering her voice further, " Fae."

Kellian whipped his head to meet her eyes. Wide-eyed in shock, he wished to know more, he *needed* to know more. No one was allowed into the Ash Mountains—magic would stop any human. But Fae were not on this continent, not since the great war. When two of the biggest human kingdoms had won, they forced all Fae back to their islands. It was a death sentence to be on the continent and be Fae. Here in The Hollow, it was a little more complicated. Protected by the land and the magic of the Goddess Luna herself, his people were closer to Fae than human. Descendants of Ariella, the Goddess and warrior of the skies, touched this land with her magic many moons ago. Her children were the first Guardians, the first Dragon princess and prince, as Kellian and Aura were now. It was what they were born for, to continue the legacy of the Guardians of The Hollow. To keep the holy land safe and hidden.

"Grandfather," Aura's calm voice brought Kellian back to the present. "He said to meet her by the lakes."

"Since when do we just agree to safe passage to The Hollow?" Kellian snapped, running a hand through his hair, disrupting the neatness of his tied back hair, freeing the long white strands to fall around his eyes.

"Hush now," Aura scolded. "I will do this, you must go now." And with that she turned, the skirts of her gown swinging as she pushed open the doors to the throne room. A quiet fell over the villagers as she entered.

Kellian admired his sister's grace and how she commanded with such ease. He dreaded his duties as a Guardian at times, but Aura was different. She was kind and soft with the villagers, listening to concerns and finding solutions for the smallest of issues. Kellian would rather be anywhere but in grand rooms and making diplomatic appearances. He slipped out the door to his left and took a back path through the old gardens—his mothers' gardens. Slowing his steps he breathed deep, taking in the lavender in bloom that reminded him of his late mother. Aura was so much like her it hurt sometimes to look at her too closely. He was sure his grandfather felt the same, after losing his only daughter.

The wind whipped against Kellian's skin and he looked up to find a grey elder Dragon flying low, landing in the field outside the gates. He picked up his pace and walked out of the gates to the Dragon. Bowing after he approached, he waited for the Dragon to speak first.

"There is a woman waiting by the Great Lake to speak with you. I

have granted her passage to the village and safety here as long as she needs. She holds the hatchling egg of Venille's last line." The Elder Dragon's words spoke in Kellian's mind. Kellian nodded and bowed his head again. The Venille line was thought long-lost, the last egg hatching when he was very young. Most Venille Dragons migrated and stayed in the west where there was permanent winter. The last to hatch never returned, as most did not, and the Guardians had thought the line was gone.

"Aura informed me to meet this woman by the lake," Kellian replied and paused thinking over his words. "You feel she can be trusted?"

"*Yes, she is a child of the trees. They speak fondly of her, and one of the sprites has become quite attached. She saved the egg from raiders on the east end of the mountains. She gave her life, only that of the holy water saved her. For this we owe her a life debt,*" Fendiah, the elder, spoke with finality.

"As you wish." Kellian bowed and Fendiah took off into the skies once more. Kellian steeled his feet to the ground bracing against the strong winds. He gathered supplies and strapped a sword to his back, and began the trek to the Great Lake.

By the time Kellian reached the lake, it was almost night. Kellian knew he and the strange woman would need to set up camp by the lakes before traveling back to the Hollow. A woman that had somehow fought off raiders and saved a Dragon egg, all on her own.

Kellian climbed the last part of his path before the lake revealed themselves, surrounded by rocky mountains and trees. The meadow grasses stretched long, wildflowers blooming boldly this season, and a few caves scattered, their mouths facing the lake. By the waterbank, in a slightly tattered white flowing dress draped over her shoulders, was a woman with striking red hair and pointed ears. She was barefooted, eyes closed and hands on the ground, as if rooting her in place. She turned quickly, as if suddenly aware of a presence and her green eyes collided with his. A sudden painful jolt ripped through him, and a wrinkle formed above her brow. Kellian let out a breath. He stopped at a nearby tree, keeping a distance between him and this fae woman.

"The Dragon spoke of you," she said. Her voice was melodic, heavenly, dripping like honey. Kellian nodded, trying to shake himself out of his own personal haze.

"That was Fendiah, our Elder. He sent me to find you."

"These are Dragon lands then?" she asked, a small glimmer of light floating near her shoulder. She leaned down to it and a small smile played on her lips.

"They are," Kellian answered, still standing on the edge of the rocks by a grand oak tree, waiting and drinking in the sight of this stranger.

"And you are?" She tilted her head slowly to the side, she seemed to be analyzing him as well.

"They call me the Dragon prince," Kellian smirked and pushed himself off the tree. She looked almost startled at the title. As was his intention. "And you are?"

"Kyeria." She had a bit of a shy smile unfolded onto her lips, head still tilted and obviously listening to the whispers of a sprite who was concealing herself.

"Show yourself, sprite," Kellian ordered. The glimmer of light solidified and fluttered over to him. His stern facade cracked when he saw Ember forming before his eyes as she let herself be seen.

"Ember," he nodded. Ember glowed a little brighter in greeting. She, like other sprites, had worked as a messenger for the heirs and royal family.

Kellian turned back to Kyeria. "We need to stay the night here, it's the safest option. I will escort you to the village at dawn," he explained, walking towards the woman. Kyeria simply nodded, gathering her belongings into a worn bag, slung it over her shoulder and gathered a pile of branches and leaves, walking with confidence to the nearest small cave. Kellian was momentarily amused at her thinking this would be enough items to make a fire to keep them warm, but his eyes stayed trained on her as she continued. She settled on the cave floor, pressing her hands to the ground, producing a spark of fire and tossing it into the small pile of wood logs.

Kellian marveled at the small magical act. He had never seen anyone use magic so easily, let alone this type of earth-based magic. There had, of course, been witches in his village, healers and an oracle. All people in The Hollow had a type of magic flowing through their blood lines, but fae born of the island were much different. His grandfather had once explained that all Fae took their magic from the land, but only one type of magic took form the strongest during early development. Then the Fae were cast into their respective magical training—earth magic, fire magic, air magic, and healing magic.

"Ember says you were quite the hero," Kellian broke the silence as they sat by the fire. He was trying to focus on the fire instead of her. But his eyes betrayed him and flicked up to her nonetheless. Kyeria shook her head, and reached into her bag. She ever so gently pulled out the Dragon egg. The scales of the Venille egg were dark, gleaming purple where the firelight caught.

"The magic of this little one called out to me," she said, placing it on the ground between them. As she stared into the fire Kellian studied her features. Her hair was twisted and pulled back, but small fire-colored strands escaped and curled in different directions. Her eyebrows had a small crease in them, as if she was deep in thought.

"It is of a very rare line, sacred to us here in these lands," Kellian offered her a small truth, laying a hand on the egg.

"It is powerful." Kyeria turned from the fire and looked up to him. "I can hear *and* feel the magic humming off of it."

"You can sense magic?" Kellian asked.

"My magic is that of the earth. In a way I can feel the magic this egg is putting off into the earth, because everything is connected. The wind, the soil, the water, the essence of Luna herself." A far off look glazed over her eyes and Kellian wondered how long it had been since she had been home, in her lands. The great war was over a decade past. Kellian could not imagine what her life had looked like while surviving on this continent since the war ended.

"These mountains are teaming with it," she said, looking at him again.

"With what?" Kellian asked dumbly.

"A strange magic," she whispered back.

They sat for a time in silence. Kellian hesitated to offer up information to this new woman, though he found it surprisingly difficult to hold back his words. He realized he felt at ease around her, comfortable, more so than he had expected. Though it was impossible to tell if her intentions were good and honest after knowing her for mere minutes, something in his soul insisted they were

The sun had long since set and the only light was that of the fire burning lowly in the cave, encircled by dim embers. The stars were out, and Kellian was drawn to them, as he always was. He looked out to see Kyeria sitting just outside the cave on a ledge, looking out onto the lake.

She could hear his soft footsteps, but her mind was far from her body, focusing on the earth beneath her, the calm winds and steady stream of lake water lapsing into the shore below her. Her mother taught her that meditating was one of the easiest ways to tune into one's magic. Kyeria was enveloped in a small amount of warmth and softness. She distantly recognized it as a blanket.

After finishing her meditation, Kyeria returned to the cave. The sheltering walls made it much warmer inside compared to the chilly winds outside. Kellian was sprawled on the ground, using a bundle of fabrics as a pillow, and he was softly snoring in his sleep.

Kyeria wondered about this Dragon prince. He seemed guarded but kind, proud of his people and of The Hollow. His white hair tumbled around his face, making his golden eyes seem so bright. She felt overwhelmed looking at him, as if something in her veins hummed the way her magic reacted to the wind or the tree speaking to her.

Kellian explained more about this hidden land, how it was magically protected and humans could not pass into the Ash Mountains from a spell cast long ago to let them wander endlessly at the edge of the mountains. Kyeria assumed that this was how the raiders found the cave with the small egg hidden inside, that the magical border had, at a time, gone out further and the forest had been protected farther as well. Kellian had explained that over the years, the boundary of the spell had pulled closer, leaving the egg at the very edges instead of safe, deep within the Ash Mountains. It was shocking to Kyeria to hear of an ancient spell faltering when she could sense the magic was that of Lunas—where her own magic lived. Kyeria kept this thought to herself however; there must be other entities at play that she was unaware of.

She sat watching the cave entrance. Ember had left, promising to come back in the morning, and curiosity sparked through Kyeria's veins. She wanted to know if there were more sprites hidden throughout the continent, or if they kept in existence only here in the valleys of the Ash Mountains.

Kellian let out a grumble before his eyes cracked open, landing on Kyeria. He pulled himself to a seated position, his voice ragged with sleep as he said, "I'll take the rest of the watch, get some sleep." Kyeria's shoulders were low, hanging with tiredness, as she walked to where he had been resting. She laid a hand down on the earth and brought a small pillowed shaped bundle of leaves and grass up.

"Nice trick," Kellian grumbled, walking to the entrance of the cave and sitting on a rock that looked out to the lake and valley. Kyeria pulled the blanket over her and let her mind wander. She wondered why he was staying watch; if this place was protected from the humans then what was out there to harm them. It seemed as though many of the bedtime stories her mother would tell her were true in these lands. Those of Fae myths and legends. She knew of the Dragons but never imagined seeing a sprite in her lifetime until Ember flew right up to her. She believed them long since gone from the lands. Kyeria drifted off to a soft sleep, dreaming of home, of her mother whose golden eyes and flaming hair matched her own, and the stories she would share with the village children, the tales of a long lost land where Dragons roamed free.

Her bones rattled with awareness, awoken by her magic as a shutter of a warning rang out. The wind howled and in her sleep ridden daze she couldn't make out much of the wind's words until she saw Kellian missing from the large boulder at the front of the cave, and suddenly she heard the wind warning, the trees shrieking. One word.

Run.

She picked up her pack and sword, letting her hands drag over her waist to feel the daggers still attached under her layered cloak. Tucking the egg safely in her pack, she took off. Kyeria tried to slow her heart pounding in her ears to focus on her magic and listen to the earth itself.

Something was here, something dark like a shadow had descended into the lakes. She weaved behind the rocks and to a large tree trunk. Pressing her hands into the tree and closing her eyes, she sensed two presences that were unfamiliar to her.

Just as her eyes snapped open, she felt a third presence—a figure in light armor with long, flowing white hair and a distinctly female form. Kellian's scream pierced the air, a raw cry filled with genuine fear that cut through her, making her experience his anguish as though it were her own.

A black haze spread across the area of trees where she had just seen someone pass through. Kellian was sprinting, his eyes wide with fear and his sword drawn. He moved with an unnatural speed, beyond what she would have expected from someone who appeared human. Desperate to help, Kyeria cast her magic, letting it weave through the trees. As she reached out, she detected another presence, cloaked in a darkness so profound and terrifying that it made her blood run cold. Her magic surged into the earth, causing vines to erupt in an attempt to restrain the mysterious figure. However, her efforts proved futile against it. She felt a deathly grip emanating from where the figure stood. The mist coalesced into a menacing beast that ripped the vines apart easily.

Kellian spun around, his eyes locking onto hers with a mix of emotions she couldn't fully decipher. They were wild and pleading, as if his fear extended beyond himself to include her. He pointed urgently toward the lake.

"Kyeria, get to the lake!" His voice was filled with desperation. Kyeria shook her head and sprinted toward him, sword drawn. For a brief moment, his eyes softened, understanding her need to help and not stand by. The beast of shadow lunged at Kellian. Kyeria felt the air leave her lungs. It struck, and he tried to swing his sword out in defense but he was on the ground. With an unfamiliar shriek, a white haired woman arose from the shadow, and light burst out from her hand and into the beast, making it crash into the trees behind it, shadows splintering apart back into the cloud of shadow. The woman ran to Kellian, hands clutching around his head, blood was soaking through his shirt now.

24

"I can help!" Kyeria was running to get to him. The woman looked at her, golden eyes untrusting, white hair braided back from her face. She looked like Kellian; a warrior. Terrifying and beautiful.

"Please, let me help." Kyeria whispered to the mysterious woman. A loud noise from afar came at them, making Kyeria's heart stutter. The shadow was forming back into a beast and charging toward them. The woman looked torn, pure agony on her face at the idea of leaving Kellian but knowing she needed to advance on the beast.

"You are the child of the trees?" she asked quickly. Kyeria nodded and that was enough for the woman to blink out of eye shot and rush towards the beast, her light as her defense.

Kyeria pulled open Kellian's white tunic shirt and let her hands rest on his skin, pushing her magic in. His skin was warm and threaded with muscle. She felt a tremble go through her own body. Looking at Kellian this closely, his eyes were sealed shut, wrinkles forming around his eyes in pain. The wound slowly sealed and she felt his rickety breath even out under her hands. Kellian's gold eyes cracked open. They were identical to the woman who was throwing light at the monster.

"You were supposed to go to the lake," Kellian grumbled.

"Why would I do that?" she insisted. His brow furrowed.

"It is magical, the shadow beast cannot enter there," he answered. Kyeria looked behind her at the still lake under the moonlight, and had a thought. She was overwhelmed at the realization that Kellian had tried to protect her. She closed her eyes to push aside the feeling, focusing on the issue at hand. She could feel her magic pulling her attention behind her, the wind brushed her hair back as well. The lake.

"It cannot touch the water?" she asked. Kellian shook her head. "Then we must get you there."

Kellian shook his head towards the blur of white hair and light fighting the shadowed beast.

"I will not leave Aura's side." He pulled himself up with great pain and took up his fallen sword.

Kyeria whirled around to see Aura fall, and Kellian charged at the creature with a scream. Kyeria pushed the wind to spread the beast apart, making the shadowy form splinter. The beast screamed but always came back to the shape of an untouchable shadow creature, snarling, claws slashing at them. Aura dipped and rolled out of the way of a slash, narrowly avoiding a hit. Kellian muttered some words and his sword began to glow dimly. He swung and this time the metal hit the shadow beast and it made it shrink back with the hit.

The water, the lake is magical and the beast cannot touch it.

The trees whispered out to her:

The lake.

The lake.

The lake.

Kyeria reached out, pulling the last of her magic and throwing it at Aura and Kellian. The water followed her magic, accepting her will for it to move, and a wave crashed on them. A curdling shriek came from the beast and it vanished into a cloud of steam. Splinters of it running away on the wind, leaving them there in the aftermath of the fight. Aura and Kellian stood drenched in water, swords in hand and mouths agape in shock where the beast used to be.

"What the Hel are you?" Aura gasped slightly out of breath, arm bleeding. Kellian's eyes met hers again, swirling with questions. The two white haired not-so-human humans looked back at her, matching golden eyes and beauty.

"It cannot touch the water." Kyeria shrugged and walked over to them. "Hello, I'm Kyeria." She touched her chest with a hand and smiled gently at Aura.

"Fuck." Aura let out a breath. "I think I am going to like you." She brushed off the extra water from her armored corset and sleeves and put a hand on Kyeria's shoulder in thanks, then began walking north. Kellian watched her closely, clearly uncertain about her magic and abilities. He gave her a grateful nod before following Aura. Kyeria shook her head and trailed behind them. Kellian retrieved his pack from the abandoned cave, extinguished the small fire, and then returned to where Kyeria stood. He reached out, lifting her heavy pack off her shoulder and slinging it over his own. His fingers brushed her neck, sending a shiver of electricity down her arm. Their eyes met once more, and she saw a storm of unspoken emotions in his gaze. He simply nodded, his voice deep and weary. "Thank you."

He then led the way, and the three of them headed north. As they walked, Aura began to recount tales of The Hollow. She shared stories of sneaking into the woods for days on end, only to be pulled back by her brother or grandfather with stern warnings not to wander off. Now, with a shadow beast lurking in the lands, such freedom was no longer possible. Despite the gravity of their situation, Aura carried a brightness and ease in her demeanor.

"How long has this beast been roaming?" Kyeria asked.

"Since the last winter solstice," Kellian spoke for the first time in the hour they had been walking.

"Do you know where it came from?" Kyeria continued. She saw Kellian shoot Aura with a look, sharp eyes and a stealed mouth. Aura simply rolled her eyes.

"We are not certain. I have theories, of course, but nothing of substance; Kellian here doesn't approve of my theories, that is." Aura flipped a dagger over her fingers aimlessly as they walked.

"I would love to hear them." Kyeria sent a small smile towards Aura who returned it easily. Kellian went on scowling, his mouth contorted into a thin line as if holding back from speaking.

"Your Hollow sounds very familiar," Kyeria mused. Kellian's eyes darkened. He was deeply protective of this land and his sister, that much was blindingly obvious.

"My mother used to tell stories about a land with Dragons and a magical lake and a hidden kingdom," she continued. "There were old Fae tales about people with magic unlike our own. Not called from the Goddess Luna, but another. That Dragons were gods and there were those destined to guard them and serve them." Another look passed between Aura and Kellian she could not decipher.

"The Fae Islands were told to us to be quite beautiful, and are also in some of our fables," Aura offered. "Not to be too forward, but how are you here? On this continent? How could you have come in from the east and not the west?"

"I came over with my people in the Great War. All were needed," Kyeria said simply, her truth that hadn't been spoken in such a time.

"It's been a decade..." Aura trailed off. "And you've been *here* since the end of the war?"

Kyeria nodded.

Kellian's eyes met hers for the first time since the lake. Those deep golden eyes. They bore into her own, truly an intimidating experience.

"Yes. On my own," Kyeria clarified. She could anticipate the questions from them wondering how a Fae could be here and for so long and if there were more. There were not though. Only her. Who woke surrounded by so much death, long forgotten and assumed dead like the rest of her people. She had crawled and crawled, only twelve years of age, until she felt land under her again and not rubble and Fae. She saw only destruction in the then abandoned field. Smoke from fire that had died and not one living soul. When she reached into the soil, a deeply sad mourning was there, a cry for the people, the people who loved and cherished the land, who lived in peace with it. She couldn't sense a living being for as far as her magic could reach.

She knew she was alone. In a land that hated her people and slaughtered them. She was deep in what is now known as the Open Lands. What once was Fae territory was now barren, nature refusing to grow in solace and mourning, in respect for the lives lost. At the time, she found the nearest trees and climbed as high as she could and stayed tucked in the leaves and branches for days before wandering to the nearest village. Her wild hair had covered her ears and a kind villager had taken her in for a time. But that had been a lifetime ago. For the past ten years, she had moved from town to town, hiding her ears and casting her bright eyes downward. Her softer features, unlike the sharpness often associated with Faes, helped her blend in with humans more easily.

"I cannot imagine," Aura said sadly. "We owe you greatly for your kindness and for protecting a hatchling, and with the shadow beast." She smiled, stilling her dagger and pocketing it. "You will stay with us, in the castle." An audible intake of breath to her left came from Kellian.

"The castle?" Kyeria's eyes widened.

"Yep." Aura pointed. "Right there," she said, and peaking out of the trees were the tips of a stunning castle, stone walls draped in vines. She heard the water, felt it in her bones before seeing it. The river had led to another small meadow where a lake stood, and in the distance was the castle propped up on a small hill, surrounded by an intricate gilded gate. They walked up to the gate, stone pillars on either side, vines wrapping around and around. Aura seemingly tapped the gate and it let out an iron creek before unlocking. She pushed it open and strutted in. Guards came over, muttering to her in hushed tones. A tall dark haired one with a red cloak nodded to Kellian before walking with Aura, who was half his size down the path.

"Kellian, show our guest to her new home!" Aura shouted behind her and continued walking away deeper into the keep. Kyeria stopped, taking it all in. A second passed and a gruff noise signaled Kellian's presence before his body crashed into hers. Kyeria was propelled forward, dirt ground ready to greet her before a warmth wrapped around her waist, strong and rather large hands steading her and placed firmly on her side and one on her stomach.

"Sorry," Kellian mumbled before dropping his hands. Kyeria brushed her hands on her dress and simply shook her head as if to say, *not your fault.*

"We did not have much time to prepare, Fendiah only alerted me of your arrival right before a meeting. With the beast roaming, I thought it more important to get to you then prepare a room," he explained as they walked into the castle.

"I rather doubt you'd be the one preparing a room." Kyeria's words were out of her mouth before she could think better of keeping her words to herself. Kellian looked rather shocked.

"No, I suppose not," he replied. They ascended the grand staircase and meandered through several corridors. The castle, a majestic structure of weathered stone, had walls lined with tall, narrow windows that allowed the sunlight to pour in, casting warm, dappled patterns across the floor. The stone, both rugged and regal, seemed to absorb and reflect the light, creating a play of shadows and illumination that highlighted the castle's ancient, enduring beauty.

"Well I'll certainly get lost here..." she trailed off looking up at the very tall ceilings. Paintings in golden flecked frames hung on every inch of the walls as they walked. "These are stunning."

"Yes, my family has harbored the arts for centuries in The Hollow." His voice was soft, matching his eyes as they took in the same paintings she was admiring.

"Your room is here." He stopped in front of a red cherry wood door covered in carvings of intricate patterns. He opened the door to reveal a large room, gauzy curtains catching in the wind over floor to ceiling windows that lead to a small patio. It was far from the nicest of rooms in the castle, but one of the few that was habitable.

"This is–" Kyeria started before feeling very small. She shouldn't have this room, fit for someone of regal birth, someone important, but certainly *not her.* "There must be a smaller room, you might need this. It is...so grand." The words quickly tumbled out of her mouth.

"You don't like it?" Kellian asked, sounding almost offended. She whirled to face him, the small shock evident on his face.

"No!" she gasped. "It's breathtaking, but it's too much! I don't need this, and I certainly don't deserve it. Goddess above, I've rarely even had a bed of my own." She babbled on, struggling to find the right words to convey her sense of unworthiness.

His eyes softened with understanding.

"We don't have many guests," he said gently but with a tone of finality that brokered no argument. "This room will be yours." As a prince, his words carried weight, and she could only manage a soft "Oh" in response. He gave a brief nod before turning toward the door, pausing in the frame.

"There's extra clothes in the dresser, a bath in that room there, I'll be back before the sun sets." His arms were crossed, his white hair tousled and streaked with gray from their journey. Half of it was pulled back, but several strands had come loose, framing his face and falling into his eyes. Kyeria took a moment to truly observe him. He was tall and broad, and his fighting prowess, evident from their encounter by the lake, was unmistakable. His intense gaze was fixed on her, as though he could see right through the carefully constructed façade she maintained.

She smiled and bowed her head. "Thank you, I cannot begin to express my thanks," she said gently. He didn't offer a smile in return, but nodded all the same before leaving and closing the door behind him.

Kyeria released a long-held sigh and stepped into the adjoining room. There, at the center, stood a grand copper bathtub, its surface kissed by the steam of warm water, inviting her weary body. Her aching muscles ached for the comfort it promised. She noticed salts and delicate glass jars lined on the ledge, each labeled with promises like "to calm" and "to heal." With a sense of relief, she poured both into the water before disrobing—peeling away her chermis, her tattered, mud-stained dress, and her boots. As she sank into the soothing embrace of the bath, she let out a sigh that seemed to release a decade of burdens. Here was a room all her own, a bath to ease her weariness, and a refuge where the shape of her ears was no longer a threat. For now, she would let the rest unfold in its own time.

CHAPTER 4
Kellian

There was a naked woman on the other side of the wall from where Kellian sat and that fact was repeating in his mind. A woman whose eyes alone had made his feet falter and his heart pause, like something deep in his soul recognized her. The Hollow was a hidden realm, safeguarded by an array of powerful spells that kept its borders secure from intruders. Only the Dragons ventured across these boundaries, soaring high above the land. The inhabitants of the Hollow were deeply committed to their land, their families having upheld a centuries-old promise to nurture and protect it.

Kellian raked a hand through his hair and let himself fall back on his bed with a groan. What was to be done about the girl with hair the color of a sunset simply arriving on their land, and now living in the room next to him. A knock on the door shook Kellian out of his thoughts. He rose and walked to the door, opening it slightly. A flash of dark hair flew by him after pushing the door open and slipping past him into his room.

Esmeralda. She stood tall for her little frame, nearly as strong-willed as his sister, Aura, but not nearly as terrifying. Her brown eyes bore into his. Her dark, curly hair framed her face in a wild, untamed halo, and her maroon dress and robes added a touch of regal elegance to her otherwise disheveled appearance. She stood with her hands on her hips.

"The magic let in someone from the outside." She looked like millions of equations were calculating in her mind. Kellian nodded.

"I felt it, right away. At the easternmost border on the Evanthian side. She was clearly distressed. I could feel the spell accept her." She shook her head and paced in front of the hearth. Kellian let his tired body slump into one of the chairs in front of the hearth. A deep olive velvet and massive chair, a matching one next to it, both propped in front of the hearth.

"Esmie," Kellian tried to interrupt her but she kept going.

"This shouldn't have happened, until today it shouldn't have been possible. I read through the scrolls, the ancient spells and findings, even the Book of Niem. Nothing. Kellian, nothing." She stopped pacing and faced him. The fire from the hearth that was burning bright was shimmering behind her, and her shadowed shape looked rather intimidating for her only being half his age and size. He simply cracked a smile.

"Didn't know of any spells that could stump you, Esmie."

"Oh shut it." She glared and let herself fall into the chair next to Kellian's.

"Respectfully..." she started and gazed into the fire instead of at the friend she'd known all her life. "What the fuck," she finished, and was met with a deep rumble of laughter from Kellian. As if the stress and anticipation of the last two days burned right off of him.

"What's she like?" Emeralda looked to him again, their eyes meeting and her shining with curiosity.

"She has magic, the trees, the wind, the earth itself seems to listen to her."

Esmeralda sat back, eyes aglow in awe. "She's Fae?" she asked. Kellian nodded again.

"And how did she get here, how has she survived?"

Kellian filled her in on what he knew, that Kyeria was brought over to fight in the war at a young age, and was left here alone, her kind hated and none left alive on the continent, the rest retreating to their island, and her left behind in an unknown land. That Kyeria came through the border where the spells lay, unharmed; as if the magic of this land knew her and accepted her. That she then went back out and saved an egg, a Venille egg that had been past the shrinking borders. And lastly, that Fendiah had then offered her safe passage, guided by a sprite to the lake and waited for Kellian to arrive. Once he had, the shadow beast Aura had been tracking and how Kyeria had saved them and about her magic.

"And she is to stay here?" Esmeralda questioned when he was finished.

"Fendiah has already declared it. In the castle, and that she is to be kept safe."

Emeralda simply nodded, letting the information sink in. "If she possessed magic and the gift, she might be useful with the borders."

Kellian looked to Esmie in interest, nodding. It was something he could ask after she was settled in.

Esmeralda went into discussing some new research with him,pulling out some papers and a book, pointing out weak areas on the map. They walked to the library together to do more research.

Esmeralda was the last of the winter witches, from a long line that served the crown faithfully. While Kellian himself possessed no magic, he found great interest in the history of magic and the skies and stars. He could spend hours in his tower, surrounded by looking glasses that stared into the night sky and piles of books, maps , and new charted stars from his own travels. Esmeralda was a healer. It was rare for anyone from The Hollow to possess magic other than the witches, which were dwindling down to just Esmeralda herself. Her grandmother passed not but a few years ago after dutifully advising and helping to protect The Hollow, the forest, and the mountains. Esmie learned as much as she could in the time given to her, but the magical borders began receding only within this decade, her grandmother had not finished her research or practices on the border magic before her own health declined. She was far too young to have the burden of protecting The Hollow in terms of magic, but she was the only one who could.

By dawn, Kellian had realized they'd been huddled over research all night in the dimly lit library. He rose to stretch his limbs. Esmeralda was deep in the oldest sections of magic-related books. The library was a vast cavern under the castle, spanning below a few levels, with an endless supply of books on histories, magics, and lore littering the shelves, as well as some modern literature brought by their own people who had gone out on their own travels. Only a small number of people from The Hollow ever ventured past the wards protecting this land. The magic happily accepted them back within its protection when they returned.

Emeralda was sitting on a bench covered in furs for comfort, her dark curls now pulled in all directions, falling over her shoulders loosely. Her robes, thick to fight the cold of the underground library, billowed around her. Kellian knew she could be down here for days, forgetting the necessities of eating and seeing daylight, her mind wrapped in the words of their ancestors.

"Enough for today," Kellian announced, snapping his book closed. Her head popped up, eyes glossy from the trance she had been in. Esmie had described before that her mind seemed to completely jump into what she was reading and play it in her mind like it was happening in front of her. Kellian never knew if it was a part of her deeply rooted magic or just how she experienced the world.

"I suppose," Eseralda sighed. She set down the book gently next to her and rose, her deep red skirts draping around her. She tugged at the dark robes around her as if suddenly feeling the great chill of the libraries. They parted ways, both agreeing to meet in the dining hall.

Kellian returned outside Kyeria's door, just next to his own. He wore a fresh linen shirt and wool trousers, his hair damp and pulled loosely half into a bun to keep out of his face. He let out a sigh, preparing himself, and raised his hand to knock. But when he expected his knuckles to wrap on the wooden door, they only met air.

The door had swung open, Kyeria looking up at him. She wore a black dress that draped over her shoulders and hung loosely. Her hair was loose, waterfalling down behind her shoulders. Kyeria had been stunning when he first saw her, all bright haired and half-covered in dirt as she was, but beautiful nonetheless. But as he looked at her now, at how beautiful she was, a painful feeling ripped through his chest. He did his best to shake it off as Kyeria looked at him, eyes round and questioning as he stood in the doorway forgetting how to form words.

"Would you like to join us for dinner?" he asked, his voice hoarse. Gods, why was he struggling to string together a sentence in front of her.

"Or I can have food sent up to you if you prefer..." he paused again and added softly, "I understand this can be a lot to take in." Her eyes softened and creased as she smiled.

"You mean the entire kingdom no one knows exists and is protected by a magical barrier that doesn't allow anyone in except, apparently, me." Kyeria replied, Kellian could only nod, offering a smile in return. *What was he supposed to say?*

"Well I am dressed for the occasion, so lead the way, *prince*." Kyeria smiled brightly but not with her eyes. Her smile was forced, like she was sizing up a potential predator.

"You'll meet Esmeralda at dinner. She's family, in a way," Kellian explained as they walked. Kyeria fell into step with him. He trained his eyes forward.

"Anyone else?" She asked looking curious.

"Aura."

"Your sister."

Kellian nodded, "Yes."

"Has she always possessed magic?" Kyeria asked. Kellian smiled.

"No, she was very sick as a child, and our parents traveled outside of The Hollow to find a cure. They returned with the nectar of a special flower, one so rare it had only really been told of in our histories but not seen. It possessed a drop of magic from the Gods and could heal any illness."

"So she has god's blood?" Kyeria gasped. Kellian smirked at her awestruck face.

"In a way. She has the ability to use light, bend it almost. We don't entirely understand it since it is not common to have that kind of magic in The Hollow."

They rounded the corner to a hallway filled with gold speckled columns and grand doors. Passing through them they stepped into a hall with tall mirrors on the walls opposite entrances to balconies and windows flanked by rich drapes. Kellian paused at a smaller redwood door and held it open. Inside was a hearth, a few large wooden tables, and chandeliers hanging filled with lit candles. Aura and Esmeralda sat at a set table, filled with food. Their smiles were bright, sharing something with each other, when Aura turned and beamed at Kyeria.

"There she is!" She walked over to Kellian and Kyeria, Esmeralda following with a soft smile.

"This is our new friend, Kyeria." She motioned to Esmie, "This is Esmeralda, our resident witch!"

"Hello," Kyeria's voice seemed small. Kellian looked at her in surprise. While Kyeria was kind, she had a fiery spirit and it was shocking to see her making herself small. But he assumed it was in part to how young Esmie was. Esmeralda gave a cautious smile.

"Pleased to meet you," she replied.

They sat and began their meal, Aura talking animatedly about the shadow beast, Esmeralda speaking up to correct facts and share her own knowledge. Kyeria listened closely, her eyes shining with intrigue. She seemed comfortable with the women, even offering up her own thoughts. Aura explained that she had been tracking the beast for months, and Esmeralda shared how she thought the beast was 'eating' magic and therefore draining the magic borders. Kellian sat back, drinking his wine, observing them and their harmonic manner.

"Where will the little hatching be taken?" Kyeria asked, referring to the egg that she had rescued. Aura seemed to fully trust Kyeria, she had a great sense about these things, which put Kellian at ease as well. Anyone who chose to save a Dragon egg from raiders deserved his trust.

"We have ancient caves here under the castle, where the eggs are kept."

"The magic is strongest here at the center of The Hollow," Esmeralda explained. Kyeria nodded.

"Yes, I can feel that." She smiled. Esmeralda's eyes glowed with delight.

"You can sense magic?" she asked. Kyeria nodded. "Your magic is blessed from Luna?" Esmeralda continued, met with another nod from Kyeria. The Goddess Luna was the Goddess of the earth, also called The Mother of all nature by some. She blessed the land and could also curse the lands, make them prosperous or barren. Kellian had seen the barren lands of the continent cursed by the goddess, and he wished that fate on no one. There was no wrath like that of a goddess.

"Can you sense mine?" Aura asked, delighted at the possibility, pulling Kellian's attention back to the women.

"I can sense a magical essence but it is very different from how magic usually presents." Kyeria shook her head. "But I am mostly familiar with the magic of Luna, not of the Old Gods."

The three went on talking, the conversation flowing, at ease with each other. Aura was obviously pleased to have another female around.

Kellian sat back and let his mind wander. He wondered what the world was like beyond The Hollow. It had been some time since his last visit to the far lands—he was needed here. They had sent scouts every few months, the last group headed east to Evanthia. Their brutality was growing under the current king, and Kellian knew another war was brimming between Evanthia and the Kingdom of Lorienne to the south. He wondered when the next great war would be and if that would be the one to push The Hollow out of secrecy, forcing them to protect their land and their magic. But that fate was decided by the Dragons—a complicated string of rules and traditions.

Kellian turned back into the conversation as Esmeralda reached out, swiping a thumb over a cut on Kyeria's shoulder, healing it. Kyeria beamed.

"My mother was a healer," Kyeria's eyes creased, a real and true smile there, but sadness lingered in her eyes. Esmie reached out a hand and laid it over Kyeria's in understanding. Esmeralda's own parents had left this land to assist in the great war. Any in The Hollow were free to leave, only bound to never speak of this sacred land. Some chose to not stay in safety but go and help in the war. Many witches aided the Fae. Most did not return.

"My family, we are all healers at our core, the winter witch's legacy is to protect and care for those in need." She smiled sadly, her eyes glistened. "My parents left The Hollow to aid your people." Kyeria's eyes widened. "I was very young, put in the care of my grandmother, but many witches from other lineages left as well." Her eyes flickered to Kellian's. He simply nodded. Aura's eyes were downcast.

"We sent aid and helped many return to your lands after the war. The ones close enough for us to get to," Aura added, her eyes flicking up to Kellian as well.

"I heard of this on the northern side of battles," Kyeria said softly.

"Why were you brought to the front?" Aura asked, making Kellian suck in a breath. Such a blunt question to ask someone she hardly knew but Aura said it kindly, her intentions simply of curiosity. It was obvious she greatly liked Kyeria.

"Aura," Kellian warned. Kyeria looked over, meeting his eyes for the first time since they had first sat down.

"It's alright," Kyeria assured them. "I think it is not much to share my story after receiving your protection." Kellian nodded in acceptance and she continued, "Most of my kind are blessed with magic, but that of one magic from one god or Goddess." Aura and Esmie nodded, knowing this of the Fae. "I, however, have two magics. Both from Luna." She smiled at Esmie, "My earth magic is strongest. I can sense living beings connected to the lands. I can grow and decay at will with Her blessing." The group nodded, being familiar with this magic class.

"Luna is also the Goddess of healing," Esmeralda said. Kyria nodded. Kellian and Aura shared a glance, remembering their encounter with the beast and how Kyeria had stopped Kellian from bleeding out. Kellian felt his body react, remembering how her magic swept over him on the forest floor that day.

"It was possible but very rare among our people to have two classes of magic. Only certain lineages experienced it, normally much higher in power. We were a family of simple merchants, not of any power or royalty. But my parents served to protect the land and it was our duty to fight in the war, and my two magics were too invaluable to be left on the homeland."

Kellian's heart clenched and he spoke for the first time then, "You were a child." His eyes searched hers. Gold and green collided.

"It was an honor to serve," Kyeria whispered back. She seemed tired now, like reliving her history had drained her. Kellian stood, making everyone look at him.

"It is late, we should retire," he announced. Aura and Esmie stood nodding and whispered their goodnights to Kyeria, thanking her for sharing her story.

"I will walk you to your room." Kellian held out his arm to Kyeria. She simply slid her own hand into his awaiting arm.

"It is brave to share your story with people you hardly know," he said as they walked into the hall. There was no judgment or harshness to his voice, only true and honest thought.

"I have been on the run for ten years. I have not been able to trust anyone since I was on my island." She looked out towards the windows as they passed them. The sun had set and the moon was high in the sky.

"But my magic, I can sense intention, the air shifts. And you..." she trailed off. "Esmeralda and Aura are good." She said it simply, as a statement she was sure of.

"Can you tell when people lie?" he asked.

Kyeria let out a small laugh. "No it is not like that, but my magic recognizes magic and can sense its trueness or good intent. You all have a type of magic, this whole land is teeming with it. And it is honest and true in nature," she said with certainty. "And you are the first people to not want to kill me as soon as you knew me for Fae." She looked up to Kellian. Her eyes gleamed, the light of the moon shone off her red flecked hair. Kellian again was at a loss for words as her beauty washed over him in this striking and severe way.

"I have never wished to be deceitful about my life, but in order to survive I had to conceal who and what I am." She looked back outside. "But you...all of you, seem rather unbothered by my kind and my magic." She paused and took a steeling breath. "I would like to help, or work, in any way I can. Fendiah has offered me safety, something I have rarely known, and for that I am eternally grateful for and I intend to earn my keep here."

"You need not work. If Fendiah declared you live here and be protected then it will be. You saved us an invaluable heir to one of the most powerful Dragon families, you have earned your keep and then some," Kellian replied. They rounded another corner, Kellian could see the matching dark wooden doors of his own and Kyeria's from where they were.

"But I would like to, I might be able to help with the borders. I recognized its magic when I walked through. I think it is similar to my own."

"In what way?"

"From Luna herself. I asked her for passage and she granted it to me. I turned back for the hatchling and when I entered again, the magic there—whatever deep and ancient spell protects these lands—it hummed a song, one from old tales said in the Fae Lands." Kellian let that information wash over him.

"Do you have a library?" she asked. "I would love to see if there are connections between the Fae lands and their tales and of this Hollow."

"We can go tomorrow. At first light, meet me here and we will go to the hatchlings first, then the library. Esmie would love to show you around there and push me out of the way. I have some things to attend to later in the day so she can help you look for anything you might need."

Kyeria let her hand slip from his arm, her fingers brushing his exposed skin sending a shiver through him.

"I'll see you at dawn then," Kyeria replied before walking to her door and muttering a "Goodnight Kellian," and Kellian's own heart stuttered at his name on her lips. She hadn't before used his given name, and those letters on her lips shot electricity through his veins.

Kyeria found herself growing fond of the small family of The Hollow. Ember visited her often on the grounds around the castle. Aura walked with her during the day showing her the gardens, the training grounds, and telling her about the beast they encountered and how she's been tracking it. Aura talked about how Esmeralda was certain the shadow beast was sucking the magic away, which was making the borders shrink, leaving some lost Dragon eggs vulnerable outside of the protection of the border. Raiders had taken to the forest and edge of the Ash Mountains and tried to find Dragon eggs. Only one had been successfully taken years ago and since then, Kellian had been taking treks to find and bring back any beyond the borders.

They had walked for quite a time, Aura pointing out her favorite spots as they went. They ventured to a winding river beyond the castle gates, and Ember buzzed with excitement and a new message for the Heirs before she was off again. Aura promised to take her into the village soon, and spoke excitedly about the markets. They parted ways and Kyeria went back to her room. She had been wearing a linen tunic borrowed from Aura and when she returned to her bedchamber, the tunic and clothes she had arrived in were gone, a black gown hanging in the closet. Much to her dismay, the dress was stunning. But she felt like she was wearing something much too nice for the simple dinner Aura had mentioned earlier. She spent time in front of the grand mirror in her room arranging the fabrics just right, even spent time on her hair, twisting pieces back and out of her face, letting her curls fall down her back. She sensed Kellian at the door before he knocked. He, like Aura, held an odd form of magic. One she did not recognise. It was different from Aura's; all magic was unique to the one carrying it, having their own signature on it. But Kyeria would have expected Kellian to have the gift of light as his sister had, and surely he would have used that rather than a sword when fighting the beast by the lake.

When Kyeria swung the door open she was slightly stunned to see Kellian looking so formal. His white hair was now as bright as Aura's, pulled back and a few pieces framing his face. It was shoulder length, unlike how the Evanthian's wore their hair in a short militant style. His golden eyes seemed brighter in the light of the sunset streaming into her room.

They went to dinner and met Esmeralda. Kyeria was so deeply excited to meet another witch, it had been so long since she had been around one, and she could feel the familiar magic radiating off of her. They were immediately engrossed in conversation. Kellian was rather quiet during the dinner, sitting at the head of the table, candle light surrounding him. When they left the dining room, her hand holding onto his arm, he was again content to talk. She was shocked at how trusting they seemed. Obviously Fendiah's word was law here. She was not surprised as Dragons were that of Gods in their own rights.

With the promise to meet at dawn, Kyeria changed into the night dress that now hung in her closet, letting herself melt into the large bed, layers and layers of the softest fabrics, surrounded by a small army of pillows. Kyeria had never known such luxury. She felt a great sense of calm here, the land at peace with her arrival, she slept better than she had in a decade.

Waking before the sun, Kyeria walked to her wardrobe which was surprisingly empty. A small knock on her door made her spin around on her heels. A small older woman fluttered in, her white hair in a long braid, a soft smile settling on her face as she took in Kyeria. In her hands was a small stack of folded clothes.

"Hello Dear," she greeted. "I am Miss Bells. I had your old clothes washed and fixed where they needed to be. Aura had me grab some extra items for you as well." She set them on the edge of the bed.

"I will send out for more soon; the village market opens back up today," she chirped and started making the bed and arranging things in the room. She then pulled two small vials from her pockets and sauntered over to Kyeria,

"His highness said you were fond of baths, so I have brought you more oils!" Miss Bells held out her hands holding the vials. Kyeria tried to stop the deep blush but her cheeks flushed nonetheless thinking about Kellian even mentioning that to the sweet Miss Bells.

"Thank you!"

"Not a problem, Miss." She turned and her hair shifted from covering her ears. Pointed, like Kyeria's were. She let out a gasp,

"You are Fae." Kyeria was stunned, unsure how she didn't, or couldn't, sense any magic on Miss Bells. Miss Bells smiled.

"That I am." Her eyes creased. "It had been a time since I have seen any new Fae on the continent."

Kyeria nodded, a little too shaken to speak; she always assumed she was the only one left. After waking with the only heartbeat in that awful field.

"How long have you been here?" Kyeria asked.

"My family has been here for many decades. We settled in the isles before the great war, but we were a traveling bunch."

"You don't have magic?"

"No, I am from the Mien line," Miss Bells replied. Kyeria knew of the Mien's; they were families of Fae born without any magic classes. Usually tradespeople and travelers, those who kept the markets bustling, bringing in new items from other lands.

"Are there any other Fae here?" Kyeria whispered, eyes curious.

"None that look like us," she answered. "I do not know for a fact, but I gathered from my time here that some are far removed, but nonetheless from Fae lineages, a strange magic surrounds many people here."

"I have worked in the castle for many years now. The highnesses carry a strong magic. You might have sensed it by now."

"Is it a secret?" Kyeria asked.

"Not exactly, but not my own story to tell." Miss Bells smiled. "But they are good, kind people here. You will find your place soon enough. Now, I must be on my way but if you are needing anything at all, I help run the day to day here in the castle." She tapped her hand on the dresser next to her and left the room.

Kyeria walked over to the new clothes slightly in a trance at meeting someone of her own kind here in this hidden kingdom. Pulling on new clothes, Kyeria sat on the window sill waiting for the sun to rise. She felt Kellian's presence before she heard his knock on the door. She brushed off her clothes and made her way to the door where she was met with a soft smiled Kellian.

"I know you want to see the libraries, but first would you like to come with me to drop off the new hatchling?" he asked. She nodded quickly and they walked down the hall and down the great stairs, passing a grand ballroom and the throne room bustling with people. They rounded another corner and a grey haired man smiled at Kellian, reaching out a hand to say hello.

"Kyeria, nice to see you again. I hope you are finding The Hollow to your liking," the man addressed Kyeria. She felt taken aback-— essence was so deeply familiar but she had never met this man before. She tried to form words but instead her mouth hung agape, her magic swirling around her, trying to find the connection.

"Grandfather," Kellian greeted. His soft golden eyes were an exact match to Kellian's. She noted his grey hair was brighter than that of old age—white like Kellian's and Aura's. His skin was rugged and worn from age and weathering. Deep lines creased around his forehead and eyes.

Something passed between Kellian and his grandfather before Kellian nodded.

"I'll let you be on your way." His grandfather looked again to Kyeria. "I would love to properly introduce you to The Hollow. We shall have a ball, to welcome you to our corner of the world." Kyeria bowed her head.

"I am honored, your highness." Kellian's grandfather simply waved a hand with a calm smile and continued on his way through the stone castle. Kellian reached out a hand to touch the small of Kyeria's back and led her on. They continued, and still Kellian's hand stayed, and she could feel the heat of his skin through the fabric of her clothes. She tried to keep her breathing even, her heart calm. But it was nearly impossible.

"Your grandfather," Kyeria broke the silent trance they had been in as they walked. Kellian, as if remembering himself, let his hand drop and folded them in front of him. "He seemed so familiar," she whispered, looking ahead. Kellian nodded.

"The old ways, the runes and protection spells have all deemed you worthy by letting you enter the borders that protect The Hollow," he started. She looked at him, his eyes steeled and serious. "My grandfather is Fendiah," Kellian spoke and Kyeria's ears were filled with white noise, her magic swirling in her, recognising and approving of this knowledge, the pieces all fitting together.

"Your grandfather," her eyes snapped to him, "is a human."

"He is." Kellian nodded. "It is a form he can take."

"And he can also be a Dragon?"

"My family are known as the Guardians of The Hollow—the Guardians of Dragons. Long Ago, old magic was cast to bind our family line to the Dragons, so that some in the family would be able to take the form of a Dragon," he explained. They were now in a dark hall, and had traveled down many stairs. It was cold here. Torches burning bright lit the hallway and a grand doorway stood at the end of the hall.

"These are the ancient caves, their systems run long and far within The Hollow. This is where we bring hatchlings to keep them safe, it is also where the Dragons rest." He held out a hand to motion her forward.

"Are they of your relation?" Kyeria asked, dazed with this new information.

Kellian chuckled, "No."

"Okay." Kyeria simply nodded again, all she was able to do, slightly overwhelmed at this information.

"Your sister?" Kyeria's feet stopped her. Kellian shook his head,

"She is human. Only human," he clarified. "Aura was sick as a child, as I've mentioned. We thought she had passed down the gift to shift into Dragon form as our grandfather has. It is a fickle magic, only manifesting in those worthy of such a gift close to the gods. Aura, we think she ought to have been the one chosen but when she became so sick, her body was too weak, and the gods decided she was not to be chosen as such and her role would be that of a Guardian, to protect the lands and the people."

"Magic being earned by those worthy is a common way of thought among many lands and people. The same can be said of the Fae lands. Not all possess magic, some are given other roles, still important in their own ways."

"Similar to Miss Bells, who I assume you've met by now," Kellian said. Kyeria smiled.

"I didn't think I would ever meet one of my own on this continent again." She looked to the grand doors. "This place is something of pure magic."

Kellian hulled open the grand doors. There was a large hearth in the middle, blazing bright and lighting the room. About a dozen people were gathered around, and beyond them was a lifesize stone statue of a Dragon, as large as Fendiah had been in Dragon form. It made Kyeria feel small.

"This is Alleron. The great god of Dragons," Kellian spoke as they walked towards it. He pulled a lit torch and dipped it towards the feet of the stone Dragon. Fire erupted around Alleron, surrounding him in flames. The heat and light blinded Kyeria.

He spoke of the history of Alleron, how he had traveled to these lands, and established The Hollow, the Dragonier forest, and the Ash Mountains of Dragon territory. How he established that no mere human would step foot on these lands to harm or hurt their kind, and a kingdom would be created to guard these lands and caves to harbor and raise hatchlings in safety.

They walked farther into the caves into smaller rooms. A few people dressed in plain tan garbs with thick ropes tied around their waists tended to something small in baskets of straw and hay. Kyeria craned her neck to look into a basket, and an egg the size of her own forearm sat, surrounded by small torches of light.

"Your highness." One of the attendants bowed to Kellian. "The lanelle hatchlings have been moved per your request. We have a separate area for the newer eggs, so we can assess their development."

"Thank you Anwar." Kellian nodded, then said to Kyeria, "Anwar is one of the oldest caretakers in the caves. He oversees all the eggs, and has even seen multiple born in his lifetime."

Kyeria smiled. She could feel the magic surrounding Anwar. He was more Fae than human, but not fully Fae—his ears were not pointed like hers. Though he must not be bound by a human lifespan if he had seen multiple Dragons hatch. For as the stories told, it was decades or sometimes centuries between Dragons coming into this world. Eggs could sit dormant for hundreds of years.

Kellian pulled his satchel over his shoulder and pulled out the shimmering egg Kyeria had saved. It felt like months ago now, rushing into the mountain and past the borders into safety. The moon had only cycled a few times since that day.

Kyeria's own magic jolted awake at the presence of the familiar egg. She wondered why it reacted so to this particular egg but not to the others in this room.

Anwar reached out to take the egg gently. "It is a great honor to have recovered a Venille heir Dragon egg," he said looking at Kyeria. "We have heard of your great act from Fendiah himself, but to see an egg from this line when we thought them lost for such a time..." he trailed off, his eyes looking glassy and far away. "Thank you, dear one. Thank you."

"It was my honor to assist a Dragon." Kyeria smiled. "I was raised on great and wondrous stories of this land that you call The Hollow. I am honored to have helped in any way. Luna herself guided me here, granting me the ability to help." She bowed her head after speaking her Goddess' name, as did Kellian and Anwar.

"Peace be to Luna," Kellian and Anwar muttered.

"This hatchling feels very active," Anwar said, looking at the egg in speculation. He walked to a table, a few lights and bottles strewn across the thick wooden top. Kellian and Kyeria followed. Anwar raised his hands and circled them around the egg, muttering in a language Kyeria was not familiar with. A golden Aura surrounded the Dragon egg, the light pulsing. Kyeria felt her magic tingling in her fingertips. She looked down to see a gentle glow around her hands. Kellian was staring at them as well. Anwar finished his ritual and looked to Kyeria.

"The hatchling has seemed to have bonded with you," he said simply, as if it wasn't a life-changing statement.

"What?" Kyeria tripped over the word. Kellian's hand reached out to steady her.

"Could you lay your hand here?" Anwar asked. Kyeria placed a hand on the egg. She could feel a pulse, strong and true. The egg shook and Anwar sucked in a breath.

"Blessed be to Alleron, it is almost time," Anwar whispered.

Kyeria snapped to Anwar. "The egg is going to hatch?" She tried to keep her alarm at bay. Anwar met her eyes, soft and in awe.

"It is a long process, but this is how it starts. We must honor its arrival." Anwar smiled brightly, clasping Kyeria on the shoulder,

"You are a wonder, Kyeria, child of the trees. Your presence pleased Alleron and the gods have blessed us with a new arrival. We must begin preparation." Anwar flitted about, and suddenly more people were buzzing around. Kellian's steady presence beside her rooted her to the ground. She felt a small pressure on her back—his hand again. He nudged her forward and they left the room with the hatchlings to Anwar and the other caretakers.

"We must tell Fendiah of this great honor." Kellian's eyes creased, his lips parting into a real and genuine smile, and it was the most beautiful thing Kyeria had ever seen.

"You are truly a gift." Kellian reached out his hand and cupped her cheek. Kyeria felt her world tilt, everything suddenly so intense and overwhelming. Kellian's golden eyes glowing so bright they burned.

Days went by, and Kyeria noticed Kellian appearing in her attempted routines throughout the day, as if drawn to her as she was to him. She didn't quite know her way around the castle yet, but his constant companionship was rather comforting as he walked her from place to place. In the early mornings, Kellian would walk her to the library to meet Esmeralda. During some days they would walk the lengths of the castle together, lost in conversation, sharing stories. He seemed to note the things she liked, like how she made tea with Miss Bells, then had tea waiting for her the next morning at the libraries, or that she had gone so long without the simple pleasure of a long bath and how she was enamored with the aromas and elixirs they had for them here. Later that week, new ones had been placed, lining the shelves in her washroom with small handwritten labels. The lavender one was quickly becoming her favorite.

Whenever they walked together, he was alert, stopping her before she'd stumble over the cobblestones in the garden, as she was too busy taking in the flora to pay attention to where her feet were stepping. She was so deeply taken by the nature that surrounded the castle, the gardens in particular. On sunny days, they walked through them together, sometimes he'd even reach out and brush a stray golden-red curl from her face, electricity jolting through his fingers as he skimmed the skin of her cheek. She felt a tug inside her very soul, as if she needed to be near him, that she started asking him to visit the Dragon caves under the palace with her every morning after breakfast, finding excuses to be near him.

They would walk together after their visits. He always seemed talkative when it was just the two of them, like her essence pushed away his broody air and let him be at ease. She asked about his tower and he talked and talked. He asked about her homeland and memories of it and she would get lost in the old stories of home. They spent a week like this, the escorted walks through the castle, for meals, or to see the gardens or nearby land outside the castle gates. Kyeria could find her way around the palace just fine by now, but she never said as such.

One particularly cold night after dinner she stood by the windows in the dinner hall looking up at the stars. They were to hold a ball at the full moon, a few weeks from now. Fendiah had been attending more dinners than he used to, seeming to enjoy Kyeria's company as the rest of them did. Kellian had mentioned how the King stayed in Dragon form frequently, as they had a kingdom that was hidden and peaceful, Fendiah began leaving kingly duties to Kellian, preparing him for when soon, he would be King. The little mismatched family sat at the table, a grandfather and his heirs, a witch, and a fae who stumbled into this world. Kyeria found herself happy here, almost like she may have found a home.

After meals were had, stories and drinks were shared, slowly most retired to their rooms for the night. When only Kellian and Kyeria remained in the warm candle lit room. The tension clogged the room, floating around the two of them. As she stood at a window, taking in the night sky and the thousands of stars, she felt him walk up behind her. Felt the warmth of his body just inches from her own. Featherlike touches of his breath on her neck.

"That is the draconis constellation," he muttered, edging closer to her. He reached past her, his arm bushing hers and pointed. "The Dragon." His breath moved the strands of her hair resting against her cheek as he spoke. She took a short breath in, heart leaping into her throat at the proximity.

"They say it appeared after Alleron passed on from this earthly land and he watches over us now," Kellian continued. Kyeria could turn and her lips would be inches from his own. The pull to him was overwhelming, as if a trance of a song could lull them together. Instead, they kept stealing moments, near touches as they walked or Kellian pointed out paintings or stars, and stolen glances across dinner tables or royal halls.

"You study the stars, up in your tower." It wasn't a question, she knew it to be true.

He took the hint in her words. "Yes," he muttered. His lips were almost touching her ear now. She slowly spun to face him, their lips inches apart. Her eyes caught on his lips and tipped up to his own. Gold meeting green. For a moment they stood there, the pull in her chest thrumming alongside her heartbeat.

"May I see?" Kyeria's voice barely a whisper. Kellian looked down his nose at her, tried to keep his heart rate even, his heated gaze calm. It was a futile effort. He was so deeply overtaken with her. He couldn't get the fiery haired fae out of his mind, felt like a string connected her to him, tugging him along. Day and night, no matter the time.

The walk to the tower was slow, whispers of touches along their whole walk, until they reached a landing on the spiraled stairs up to the tower, with a window and a stone edge where the moonlight pooled in. Kyeria's hair lit up under the moon and Kellian figured his did as well.

He wanted to mesmerize this moment, this shade of red on her cheeks, how her hair glowed and her eyes were soft.

As she missed a step looking out the window, one hand already resting on her back tightened and slid to her waist, grasping there. Kellian's other hand steadying her laid on her stomach. She tried not to react, but a small gasp broke free despite herself. He could see her eyes betraying her. Heat laid there. She leaned back into him. Then he was pushing her against the stonewall of the stairs.

"Careful." His voice was low and gravely.

"Did I make you nervous Kyeria?" he asked leaning in, his breath tickling her cheek. She straightened.

"Nothing makes me nervous," she shot back.

"Nothing at all?" he said, his lips inches from hers again. His gaze hitched on her lips before it flickered up to meet her eyes. Her own eyes dashed down, a blush speckling her cheeks. His hand was at her chin, tipping her head up.

"Eyes on me, love," he breathed. Her eyes snapped up, colliding again with his.

"Kellian," she whispered his name, and that's all he heard, his mind was loud, begging him to lean in, only an inch, and brush his lips against hers.

"I wanted to see the tower," Her soft words pulled him from the daydream.

"If that's what you want, love." He replied, voice low. A small shuddering breath released as he spoke. A sly smile formed on her lips, she reached out and took his hand, electricity buzzing through him and they walked ahead up the last few steps. Kellian pulled out a key from around his neck that was hanging on a chain and unlocked the door. She walked in and stared at the grand room. Much of the tower was glass, with panels towards the top with handles, able to be opened. Vast windows sprang up from the floor, meeting with the wooden beams and glass of the roof. The exposed stone had paintings covering them, blues and golden constellations.

"This is beautiful," she muttered, taking it all in. She heard the door close and felt his heat return behind her.

"It is." Kellian loved his tower, and wished to spend all his days here. The views were incomparable, the glass domed ceiling let in wafts of daylight during the day and held a perfect view of the stars at night. Small vines twisted around the stone pillars, a pink flower just starting to bloom. Kyeria's eyes twinkled, taking it all in. He watched her, *entranced*.

He was desperate to know what her lips felt like, if her skin was as smooth as it looked. He felt like he could spin out of control at any moment. If there was one thing Kellian did not like, and rarely experienced, it was being out of control. His whole life had been dedicated to staying calm, collected. A steading breath, and he let the feeling of ice spread through his veins, cooling the fire.

"Would you like to see the map of the isles? It is one of my favorite places outside of the Hollow, I have spent a lifetime charting it."

With a tilt of her chin, she smiled sweetly, "I would love to see."

They spent hours there, talking, Kellian pointing out constellations. They moved to a large cushioned seat, leaning back and looking up through the glass domed ceiling. Kyeria spoke of home, a single tear leaking out and quickly brushed away by his thumb. Hours later, she had drifted off to sleep on his shoulder. Kellian felt his heart in his throat, looking at her. Her face so serene in sleep. He let himself drift off next to her on the oversized seat. Much like many nights when Kellian slept in his tower after charting the stars, they fell asleep together in the same spot.

CHAPTER 7

Kyeria

Kyeria had spent her entire life sensing the magic around her, feeling it in her fingertips, her bones—sometimes she even felt it wash down the roots to the ends of her hair. It tingled, pulsated, electrified her skin and surged through her body like blood. But the feeling in her now, the feeling of lying peacefully in Kellian's arms—it calmed her, quenched her completely. After a lifetime of running, she could finally be still.

She was half aware of the warmth of his arms wrapped around her, the comfort and security that enveloped her, unsure if the familiar scent of him was only a dream.

A cool breeze washed over her, and she cracked an eye open to see the curtains flanking the sides of the great windows of the tower blew gently in the morning wind. Her mind was fizzy with sleep, she squeezed her eyes shut again and buried her head into the warmth beneath her to block out the bright sun and cool breeze, earning a deep rumble of a laugh beneath her.

"Good morning," Kellian's deep voice filled the space, his face pressed into the crown of her head. *His voice. His voice was heavenly, like pure crackling honey.* She could stay here and drown in it.

"Morning," she muttered. His fingers brushed over her cheek, pushing the hair away.

"We fell asleep talking about the stars?" she asked, pulling away slightly to look at him. Kellian nodded with a soft smile.

"Seems we did."

"Breakfast?" She asked, pushing herself up and stretching her arms up. She caught his stare and tried to keep the blush from rising. To no avail, the heat rose to her cheeks and she ducked her head to hide it again. It was all a bit of a dream, talking so late into the night that they fell asleep and waking in his arms. Feeling so calm and at ease with him, in a way she had never felt with any other male.

"I'm afraid not," he muttered, his lips brushing her forehead with a soft kiss. "I need to leave today to survey the west before the ball." Kyeria felt her heart drop a little but she nodded.

"For how long will you be gone?" she asked, trying to keep the disappointment from her voice, she had grown used to his daily companionship. *What would her days look like with him gone?*

"A fortnight," he sighed. She felt the disappointment deepen. He reached out tilting her chin to him.

"I'll be back soon, *love*." Her breath caught at the name. She tried to slow her rising heart, he had called her *love*. *Goddess above, give her strength*. Kyeria wanted to lean in, past this invisible barrier, and kiss him. She searched his eyes, would he want that as well?

Kyeria instead bowed her head in a nod of acknowledgement.

"Be safe."

"Always." He smiled, cupping her cheek before rising.

Kyeria also had much to do—researching with Esmie, and her vow to help Aura in the forest to track the shadow beast. Part of her wished to stay right here, in the warm cushioned seat the size of a bed, wrap herself in his arms and finally kiss him. Let her lips linger on his and melt into this tortuous pull she had towards him.

She could've stayed right there, for quite some time, and been content. Maybe more than she had ever been. Kyeria couldn't stop herself from wanting more. More time with him. More whispers of touches every morning and night.

But Kellian left as the sun came into view and morning broke fully. He walked her back to her room, leaving her with a chaste kiss on her cheek, promising to be back as soon as he could. Kyeria took a luxurious bath with the potions left by Miss Briggs, cooling and calming her tired limbs. She dressed for a day of travel and bounded out of her room in search of another white haired royal. Kyeria finally found Aura on the training grounds sparring with a soldier. A few other soldiers milled about, watching and seemingly betting on the outcome.

"Good Morning Kyeria, welcome to the show," Aura yelled out over the clang of metal hitting metal. Aura pivoted out of the way of a blow.

The man Aura sparred with had short brown hair, dark and falling around his face. His skin was two shades darker than Kellian's or Aura's —he looked not from this corner of the continent at all. Kyeria realized he looked like the people of the outerlands, where the land was mostly sand, where no trees lived and the sun beat down all day. He must be the trainer she had mentioned: Nox.

Aura spun. She kicked and her foot collided with the back of his knees, making him fall. She moved at such a speed, Kyeria could hardly keep up. Suddenly, the tip of Aura's sword was pointed directly at the man's chest. He yielded, kneeled below her, and raised his arms in defeat. The small crowd cheered, and she heard some saying they knew Aura would win and that Nox needed to fight harder.

"Hello, dear friend." Aura wiped at the sweat on her forehead.

"Are you tracking today?" Kyeria asked. Aura nodded.

"You coming?" she asked, sheathing her sword at her waist.

"If that would be okay." Kyeria nodded. Aura waved her to follow. Nox fell in step with them.

"A weapon of choice Miss?" he asked, his accent heavy on every word.

"Bow and arrow if you have it," Kyeria responded as they entered the training ground's weapon room. He brought her a leather-wrapped bow with intricate engravings on the wood, as well as a quiver of arrows.

"How long will you be out for this time?" Nox asked, looking to Aura. She shrugged.

"Towards the Lione River starting past the Pellon Village," Aura said, grabbing a few extra daggers and slipping them into pockets on her leather corset. Aura had explained to Kyeria that The Hollow was made of many small villages, all centering around the castle. Magic, of course, filled the whole of The Hollow, but was at its deepest and most potent in the center where the castle stood

"Alright, watch the rivers end, we've had reports there," Nox warned.

"If you're so worried, just come with us," Aura sighed. Much was going unsaid between the two, Kyeria could sense that much. But she stayed quiet as they packed a small rucksack for Nox to carry and headed out past the gates and into the Dragonier forest.

They walked for miles, until they had their first clues. A deep dark rot was forming. Kyeria could feel it before she saw it. The trees whispered out to her:

Danger.

Danger.

Danger.

They pressed on, ready to face that danger head-on. Kyeria and Aura learned vital information about the shadow beast that afternoon. It was phased by Aura's light magic the most. Could rip through the vines and any earth magic Kyeria could throw at the Helian Beast. She grew vines up to trap it—it simply did not budge. They escaped with few wounds. A gash on Aura's arm that Kyeria healed after they lost their trail and the beast continued farther down the river. Nox muttered curses at the venomous effects of the gash, regardless of Kyeria's healing powers. Some of the venom had sunk into Aura's skin and she was a bit green from it; Kyeria was not fond of this new revelation—that even her healing abilities could not fully heal a strike from the shadow beast. Once they neared the castle, dark grey wings beat above—Fendiah was back from a flight. Kyeria felt at a loss, this shadow beast being so much of a mystery but her want, her need, to help this place and these people. Aura had already rushed inside to find Esmeralda, wanting to relay new info for more research. Kyeria looked forward to spending the hours in the library with them later on, being steps closer to how to rid the land of this succubus.

CHAPTER 8
Kellian

*It is said, in the time of Alleron, that those possessing the great magic
would act as vessels. Vessels to hold the blood of the Dragon gods. That they
may be given the great honor to fly alongside the Dragon gods. Of this line
shall those be chosen, destined to guard the holy land of Dragons. Not of
every generation, but those worthy will be among the Gods. Serving and
blessed. After great research it has been noted that this sacrifice from the
Galanis line shall have another soul, tied with a soul thread, destined to
meet. Destined to protect the Dragon lands.*
-The Book of Niem

TWO WEEKS LATER

Kellian was half-listening to his sister. She was seemingly
trying to mimic the chirp of a hummingbird as she paced around
Kellian's tower. He was reviewing notes from the night before, charting
the skies.

"Kellian you cannot, under any circumstance, stay hidden in this
tower any longer. The rite and rituals are to take place tomorrow night!"
Aura scowled. "Are you even listening to me?" She slapped her hand
down, covering the page he had been writing on, no doubt smearing the
edges of his last written words.

"Aura, please," Kellian grumbled. "Go back to the forest. Your
energy is better used hacking at a beast than at me."

Aura scoffed. "I'll have you know, Kyeria and I tracked the beast
east, towards the Lione River."

58

Kellian's head snapped up. "Kyeria went with you?"

"Gods above, have you not heard a single word I've said? I know you were busy—overseeing the western border for the last few nights—but please bring your mind back to your body." Aura scowled.

"Dear sister, can you not see I am making note of that trip now."

"You have been holed up here for too long, you are done now," she declared.

"Is that so?"

"Yes." Aura's arms were crossed, her face twisted in petulant annoyance. She looked like she had when they were much younger. Hated taking orders, hated being told what she couldn't do, and forced everyone to pay every ounce of their attention to her and her plans.

Kellian let out a defeated noise. "Gods, fine. Lead the way."

"Don't you huff and puff at me, brother. I know you wish to see Kyeria after your time away. Plus we have a whole ball to celebrate her," she chatted as they started down the stairs.

"It is not a ball for *her*, it is for the hatchling. A ritual, to honor the gods."

"Of which would not be possible if not from a certain red haired maiden." Aura's eyebrows were high, her eyes sparkling with the joy of tormenting him. Kellian knew if he rolled his eyes anymore at his sister he would simply lose one.

"Shut it," Kellian cursed, right as a certain red haired Fae woman walked around the corner with Esmie. Kyeria almost tripped over herself seeing Kellian and Aura.

"Kellian!" Kyeria squeaked. Kellian held a smile at her startled expression. Her hair was particularly wild today. She wore a loose white dress that bellowed around her hips and a green corset lined with little delicate leaves. A golden necklace sat on her neck. He recognized it, of course—it was an emerald necklace, like the ones Esmeralda loved to make.

"Kel!" Esmie burst into a smile and ran forward, throwing her arms around Kellian's middle. He let out a huff as her small body collided with his catching her before she toppled them over. Kyeria's eyes drifted to the floor.

"I haven't been gone that long," Kellian chuckled. Esmeralda, being much younger, was irrevocably attached to Kellian and Aura as if they were her own siblings.

"Long enough," she lectured. Kellian smiled down at her, patting her head.

"Kyeria." He nodded towards her. Her eyes lifted again and she bowed slightly to him.

"How was your trip?" Her voice was small and unsure—he did not care much for it as such, he was used to the blunt and brave woman who spoke her mind.

"Informational," he responded, and looked to his sister. "Aura says that the ball has been set. As a guest of honor, you should go into town. The Hollow seamstresses can fashion you something special."

"Oh that's–" Kyeria started, but was cut off with Aura waving her hand.

"Oh perfect!" his sister practically shouted, latching her arm around Kyeria and dragging her away. Esmie stayed behind.

"How far did you fly?" Esmie asked, her eyes glowing with curiosity.

"The west end, near the isles. New constellation this time of year." He smiled at her interest. "Have you been enjoying Kyeria being here?" He asked sincerely as they walked out onto a balcony overlooking the gardens.

"She's lovely," Esmie mused, "We've been studying some of the old books in the library. She knows a great deal about runes from her family. I think I have a few ways to strengthen the borders as they are, but ultimately the beast seems to be consuming the magic."

Kellian pushed a hand over his face and through his hair.

"Are you excited for the ball?" he asked, shaking off his worries and focusing back on Esmie, who more than anyone deserved a night of fun at court. She had known too much struggle in her short years.

"Oh yes!" she practically squealed. "Miss Briggs made me the lavender gown, it is to die for!" She smiled and began picking at flowers on the vines that grew up the balcony. Plucking a flower off its stem, she pushed it into her mess of black curls.

"I wonder what Kyeria will wear," she mused. Kellian's heart sped up. He knew Kyeria dressed up for a ball would surely be the death of him.

"This is maybe the nicest thing I have ever laid eyes on, let alone worn," Kyeria said, looking at herself in the mirror, running hands over the golden silk fabric of her dress. It had long sleeves and was sheer around her collar bones, sparkling brightly under the moonlight. Tonight was the ball in honor of the new hatchling. Some rituals of the old gods were to be performed, which she was told was a grand event. Aura sat on Kyeria's bed, Esmie next to her, feet swinging.

"You look beautiful." Aura smiled.

"Like a queen," Esmie murmured, earning a tap on the shoulder from Aura next to her. Kyeria let out a nervous breath, steadying herself.

"Kellian, is he–" she started.

"He's a part of the ritual. He started his part this morning with the priest, caretakers, and grandfather," Aura explained.

"And you... are here because?" Kyeria asked, wondering why Aura, a royal herself, was not participating. Aura waved her hand.

"It's awfully boring." She jumped to her feet, golden satin gown pooling around her. "Tonight's the fun part!"

She tugged Esmie off the bed and slipped on her shoes. The three of them walked to the grand hall where the staircase descended into a ballroom. Music wafted through the palace, as well as loud chatter from guests and pops from bottles opening and clinks of glasses. Kyeria had never seen anything so grand. She walked down the stairs arm in arm with Aura and Esmeralda. People smiled and nodded, giving small bows to Aura as they passed.

"Seems we're a little late—the hatchling ritual starts soon!" Esmie whispered, running off out the open doors to the terrace where the gardens and a large lawn laid. Chandeliers hung from trees, torches lit the way—even the outside was as gold and glimmering as the ballroom.

A great wind burst through the courtyard, and Kyeria's hand went to her chest in awe as a great grey Dragon landed—Fendiah. But then another followed, one almost as large and vast as Fendiah, but this one was white—shimmering white. She blinked a few times, magic washing over her in the same familiar way it had when she met Fendiah in human form.

"It is time for the great rite of a hatchling, to be born of fire and emerge to join the ranks of the Dragons as declared by the gods themself and blessed by Alleron," the voice boomed through the courtyard. She recognized it as Fendiah's.

"My heir will present hatchlings to you, the kingdom of The Hollow destined to serve and protect Dragonkind."

The white Dragon stepped forward, the earth shuddering under its step. The Dragon king's heir. A burst of flame erupted from both of the Dragons, onto where the Dragon egg sat on a raised pedestal surrounded by a low flame.

Cheers erupted around her. She and Aura were standing rather close to the front, with no one in front of them. The heat from the blaze warmed their faces.

Suddenly, a small Dragon emerged from the flame. Larger than she expected to see come from the small egg. Surrounded by tendrils of magic swirling around it, a dark Dragon with purple and pink glittering scales so dark they were almost black came forth.

"Blessed be to Alleron," whispered every person in attendance. She turned looking around her, at the people of The Hollow. But her awe-stricken trance was disturbed by a deep familiar voice shouting her name, Kellians husked voice was raw with fear as he screamed.

Kyeria turned trying to find him, but her vision blurred and the very air burned around her. The last thing she saw was the new hatchling and their glowing eyes boring into her own before she was consumed by flame.

LONG LOST KINGDOM

part two

ART BY: MARIA @QETSU_ART

CHAPTER 10
Kellian

THE DAY OF THE BALL

"Grandfather, shouldn't Aura be participating in the ritual tonight?" Kellian asked. He wore formal attire, draped in rich blues and greys, golden embroidery feathered along the lines of his sleeves.

"I do not wish to put her safety at risk. She will be with the other humans," Fendiah replied with a stern voice as they walked into the ancient caves beneath the castle. There was no room for argument, but Kellian felt himself bristle at it nonetheless.

"She is as human as I am," Kellian argued, fighting the urge to raise his voice. Aura was no fragile being, having proved her strength over and over, but grandfather insisted on keeping her in a glass cage.

"You," he turned his piercing gaze, meeting Kellian's, "are no human." Fendiah shook his head, greatly disappointed in the disrespect of the sentence alone.

"Nor is Aura. We are Guardians first." Kellian's tone matched his grandfather's, sure and certain. Fendiah nodded, accepting the words of his grandson.

They continued the day of rituals, preparing the hatchling egg. He felt it stir in his hands as the priests chanted. They honored Alleron, the great Dragon god and gave offerings. The day pressed into night, and the land was aglow in a golden fire sky. Deep red and orange painted across it, the gods and goddess themselves greeting the new dragon's arrival. Tonight the new hatchling would be presented to the Hollow in their ancient tradition: a birth by fire.

Kellian stood next to his grandfather Fendiah, in his Dragon form under the deep night sky. The guests, villagers, and hundreds of people in their court were gathered around. Music danced through the gardens, lit lanterns glittering, illuminating the space. It looked like pure magic. Kellian remembered his mother telling him about the royal garden parties. It had been so long since one had been held on the castle grounds like this. It was fitting, of course, as it had been quite a time since the Hollow was blessed with a dragon hatchling. He had noticed Esmie running through the grounds by the flash of her night colored hair and chocolate colored skin, ribbons trailing her as she went. Her wild hair was tamed tonight, undoubtedly by Miss Bells. Guests were chattering loudly, torches lit a pathway to the open lawn, lighting the night around them. Even the sprites were fluttering around, enjoying the festivities.

Kellian tried to steady himself, but was filled with an unease eating through him, even the dragon bristled. He had still not yet laid eyes on Kyeria. Nor his sister. His mind wandered as the festivities slowly moved out to the great lawn. The people of the Hollow ready for the ritual and the honor of bringing the Dragon into their home and land. His eyes scanned the crowd again.

He felt her before he saw her, like lightning striking down—Kyeria was there. A long golden gown adorned her every curve. She was a vision, pure and true and *his*. He felt it rip through him, a primal feeling to growl out the words *'mine'*.

The Dragon rumbled. The ground shook. Guests began to quiet themselves and gather around the altar, and bells chimed to announce the start of the ritual. The priests and priestesses chanted, surrounding the altar where the Dragon egg laid. Their hoods were up, masking their faces, and their chants had a drug-like effect over the people of the Hollow, only leaving Kellian, his grandfather, and Aura unaffected. Aura was at Kyeria's side in the front now, but Kellian noticed as something snagged Aura's attention in the dark. Unaffected by the hymns, she snuck away. Fendiah grumbled, noticing the act alongside Kellian.

Brushing off his sister's antics, he peered across the castle grounds again, finding the familiar soft eyes of Kyeria's. She was transfixed, as everyone looked to be, though her eyes did not dull like the others, but were shining instead. Her copper-dipped hair glowed in the firelight—she looked like she was being lit up entirely by firelight from within. Kellian felt his heart thrum, deep and true.

With a final clang of bells, Kellian stood his ground, digging his feet solidly into the earth. Fendiah reeled back in dragon form, his dark grey scales nearly black in the night, the firelight only barely gleaming off the edges. It was time. Birth by fire. The egg sat on what could be described as an altar. An old tradition of the Guardians, a golden nest made of steel and iron surrounded by hay that stayed lit. After the hymns faded, silence enveloped the crowd. Only the night surrounded them, the swaying of the trees and the bristling of the leaves.

Fire erupted from Fendiah towards the egg in an exhale, and the priests around the altar started the hymns up again, louder then, and the people began to whisper, "Blessed be to Alleron."

Kellian barely had a moment to see the Dragon erupt from its egg over the flames, deep red and black, glittering scales, because the little Dragon did the impossible. It stopped immediately, and faced the crowd —the very front where Kyeria stood. An unfeasibly large burst of fire erupted from the small Dragon's mouth. In a flash, Kellian's feet loosened from the ground and he was running. He screamed, bellowing out Kyeria's name. The people scattered.

"Kyeria!" His voice felt raw, guttural and filled with pain, his skin was burning, but that was impossible of course, an heir could not burn by Dragonfire. But he felt it, the prickling of fire on his limbs, climbing up his neck. Fear encased him, the blood quickly leaving his face he realized. She was burning. He could smell it then. Charred flesh. And something in him snapped. He had to move faster. The claws and wings turned back into that of a man, the mist surrounding him parted and his bare feet were pounding into the earth as he ran to her. He threw himself in front of her. The flames consumed him fully.

Finally, the pain stopped. He realized it was *her* pain, *her* skin burning, and he could feel it like it was his own until he stood between the new Dragon's flame and his woman.

People were screaming around him, he could barely hear over the chaos. A familiar beam of light was shining but Kellian could not place from where, he could only keep himself wrapped around Kyeria's body, shielding her to block the flames. Kellian held Kyeria so tightly, so close that he felt he could barely breathe. But air wafted into his lungs just fine—it was her. He was crushing her, he knew he was crushing her, he had to stop. But the scent of charred skin, the image of her burnt being was etched into his mind. He couldn't tell if it had stopped or if it was a nightmare playing on a loop in his mind. It wasn't until soft hands touched his shoulders.

"Kel." The voice felt millions of miles away.

"Kellian, let the girl go, lest you injure her further." Fendiah's voice boomed, even in his mind. It shook him out of his trance.

Kellian blinked, again and again, taking in the woman before him, limp in his arms. Kyeria's fiery red hair was covered in soot, singed at the ends. Her arms—Kellian eyes scanned her, and he had to hold in a gasp —Kyeria's arms were red, blistering patches of her skin were missing entirely, burned in a way only Dragonfire could. Dragonfire was unlike any other, it was not meant to be and could not be healed like any other wound, and the burns snaked all the way up her chest and neck. His golden eyes closed, his breath coming in gasps. Like the world was closing in on him. He couldn't lose her, he could not lose this woman who had barreled into his life, magic filled and destined. He imagined a world without her in it, a world where she was torn from him, by something as poignant and awful as Dragonfire.

Kellian felt like he was dying. Like someone was ripping out his very soul.

"Please, please, wake up," he gasped, his voice raw and cracking. His hands cupped her cheeks. "Kyeria, open your eyes, love."

"Kel." Again the soft touch. He looked to find Esmeralda. The deep sorrow splayed across her face struck Kellian numbly, all his energy was so focused on the lump and unconscious woman in his arms. He could not spare his worry on Esmeralda. The girl who had become family, who he was meant to protect. Because her skin was unmarred, her gaze was sure and steady. As his should be. She was calm, albeit eyes glassy and face sullen.

"Let me help, Kel. You have to let go." Her voice was soft, sympathetic. Kellian also felt the presence of his sister kneeling next to him, hand on his arm. She was a calming balm to him, as she had always been, one of the only ones to be able to pull Kellian from the brink of panic in the most dire of circumstances. He had reasons to get up, people who relied on him. He had to move, he had to let go—he was crushing her.

"Kellian, let go," Aura said, her voice stern. He released a breath and let go, laying Kyeria on the ground. Esmeralda moved to her quickly and hovered her hands over Kyeria's body, assessing the damage. Her magic glowed in her finger tips, but Kyeria's skin hardly changed, still burned and angry and red.

Esmeralda paused, fear dancing on her brow. He knew she had never seen him like this. He was always strong, always stoic, always sure. He watched her eyes soften even further as she spoke again, "I'm so sorry Kel, I'm not strong enough to heal Dragon fire." She shook her head, her tear-filled eyes now fixed on his.

"That's alright Esmie, let's get her inside the castle, grab your potions and balms. She will heal." Aura commanded everyone around, the bright light was gone now and as the haze of the moment was passing, he realized his sister must have used her light to stun the young dragon. She was moving so fast, a blur of white light seemed to be buzzing around them, directing people quickly and gently. Aura moved with the grace of a royal, she held her head amidst the chaos and a fleeting thought made Kellian wish he could handle hardship the way she did. Head on.

He took in his surroundings, the people had scattered, only few lingered and servants helped any that were harmed. The castle is hard at work to right the wrong. It had been so long since that last ritual of a new dragon, but this was not how it ought to have gone. Fendiah's hand grasped Kellian's shoulder, shaking him from his thoughts and back into reality. But reality was fuzzy, his vision was tunneled, only able to focus on the crumbled and burned girl in his arms. Kellian dragged his stinging eyes up towards Fendiah. He distantly realized he must be crying, his eyesight was glassy. His grandfather's creased brow and age lines bore down at him.

"Are you able to carry the girl?" Fendiah asked. He was offering to help, to carry the physical burden for his grandson, Kellian realized. But nothing could tear Kyeria from his arms at this moment.

Gathering himself and the onslaught of emotions ripping through him, feeling the burns on Kyeria's skin like they were blistering on his own arms, up his chest and neck. He could feel it all. This strange connection was screaming at him deep in his soul. But he rose, legs a heavy weight on his own body. He lifted her, holding her as gently as she could, hoping to not have hurt her further. This was his burden to bear.

"Where is the Dragon?" Kellian growled.

"Your sister was able to stun the youngling, and the priests have moved it back to the caves," Fendiah informed him. Kellian nodded. He couldn't understand why this had happened, why the youngling had thrown fire towards Kyeria, how even it could produce that much fire. But he couldn't solve that mystery tonight.

As Kellian carried Kyeria into the castle, the deep wooden doors felt larger than ever. The light from the candle lit chandeliers blurred with the rest of Kellian's vision, and it was muscle memory that took him back to Kyeria's room.

Aura began fussing as soon as Kellian laid Kyeria on her bed. She called for Miss Bells to fetch tonics, salves, and balms. Esmie was busy making healing potions, and Fendiah was away, attending to the new hatchling.

Kellian couldn't get his limbs to move, he simply sat next to Kyeria, feeling himself sink into the mattress under them. He held onto her hand like if he let go, her lifeline would fade into the ether. Esmie returned, juggling three potions. She tipped each back into Kyeria's mouth, holding it open to do so. Kellian jolted at a gasp that rang through the quiet room but Kyeria's mouth and eyes stayed sealed shut despite the potions. Miss Bells also returned and handed Kellian a new canister, he assumed with more balms to try and ease the burns. They smelled so strongly of pine and mint, it overwhelmed him. He was reminded of when he found her, covered in the scent of the woods.

"Hold this," Miss Bells said, features pinched in focus. Bringing in warm clothes and water, she began cleaning the wounds. Miss Bells had always excelled in healing, not that she possessed the magic, but she was a careful caregiver, who could focus on the injured with such precision. While she was gentle and kind on any given day, the way she handled the room was with a fierce determination. Kellian had always respected this from Miss Bells. She meant business and no one would be getting in her way, He stayed by Kyeria's side through it all, as Miss Bells cleaned each open wound. He forced himself to watch, the ghost of the burns still on his own flesh.

He stayed—even as the girls left, even as the candles burned away, he remained by her side. Hands intertwined.

CHAPTER 11

Kyeria

Kyeria woke to a soft breeze. She tried to open her crusted eyes but her body protested. Her limbs felt heavy, fingers numb. Then her mind slowly and painfully took in her surroundings, eyes still sealed shut. Her thoughts were thick and hazy. She took a deep breath. pine and smoke from the hearth surrounded her. Her heart began to race, pounding on her chest.

The smoke.

The darkness.

It had consumed her. Wholly and terrifyingly.

There were flashes of night and shadow, fire and soot choking her. The shadows were closing in and Kyeria tried to pry open her mouth the scream, but her eyes were sealed shut. She tried to orient herself, the breeze was familiar and a heavy presence was with her. Kyeria's heart raced, was she in danger, was something trying to get to her. But she felt again, a deeply familiar presence, dousing her soul in a calmness. Kyeria took a moment to grasp at the strings of reality. She pushed her body to react, trying to reach for her magic, in turn her eyes slowly opened.

It was night. She felt crisp air floating through her room, whisking in an earthy scent, like it was about to rain. She blinked away the sleepiness, unnerved by the heavy feeling of her eyelids and muscles. One blink, two blinks—there was Kellian, his presence like a warm fire, soothing her nerves. He was *real.* She wanted to reach out, to touch him, to confirm she was here and safe. But her body felt heavy, even blinking felt drugged, like long crashing waves that kissed the sand and wished to stay there.

Kellian was asleep, eyes closed and a wrinkle between his brows, slumped in one of the deep green velvet chairs that usually sat in front of the hearth. It was instead moved next to her bed, his massive frame sinking into it, hair disheveled, clothes wrinkled. Kyeria took in the room, with the windows open she could see the stars were bright, light streaming in from the moon and the castle seemed very quiet. As she came back to her senses, she felt the stinging of pain crawling up her arms and neck. She winced as she shifted but a small faint ball of light fluttered near the window distracting her. Kyeria squinted, wondering if her eyes were betraying her. The form took shape before her eyes, revealing the long flowing blonde hair and a dress made out of red leaves.

Ember.

"You're awake!" She fluttered closer and Kyeria nodded, not yet trusting her voice.

"Are you okay Miss Kyeria?" Ember's voice seemed small and afraid. Kyeria tried to swallow, but the dryness in her throat made her cough a bit. Kellian stirred. Ember's eyes darted to the mass of man sleeping in the chair. Her wings glowed in the moonlight.

"I was so worried! I was far in the south of the forest when the news arrived to us!" Ember fussed, her little eyes swelling with tears. "He has not left your side, Miss." She smiled sadly at Kellian. Kyeria looked at him again, the wrinkle between his brow had smoothed, but his body looked worn. There was ash on his arms and neck, as if he had stayed rooted to her side, confirming Ember's words.

"Yesterday he yelled at the servants! It was a bit startling, as his highness is usually so calm!"

Kyeria tried to move her arms but hissed out in pain. They were wrapped, from her palms to her shoulder, both arms. And gods above, they hurt. Hazed thoughts cornered her vision. She knew where she was but it was night and she wasn't sure how long she had been here at all.

"Be careful, miss, Dragon fire is slow to heal!" Ember cried out, her small voice frantic.

An onslaught of memories hit her. The night of the ball, the glasses clinking, and noises of a filled castle grounds. Then heat and fire and so much pain. Kyeria tried to shift through the fragments. The smell of burnt ends filled her sense of Kellian, his voice raw and screaming for her. The memory rocked through her like a wave crashing violently on the shore. But it was still only shattered pieces.

Her eyes flashed to Ember and she tried to convey with her eyes, *"What happened?"*

Ember's face flushed with sadness. "The new hatchling mistook you for that of the heir blood, only they are immune to Dragon fire. His highness raced to you, I am told he moved so fast across the field but the Dragonfire had already reached you, if he had not used his own body to shield the rest, goddess above, I do not know what would have happened."

Kyeria let out a small gasp, her lungs constricting. She raked her eyes over Kellian's body. He looked in fine condition, no burns visible, only lingering ash on his skin.

"The fire cannot hurt him, don't worry miss," Ember assured her. Kyeria swallowed again, and tried to muster her strength to speak, but only a gasp and a raspy note came out. He stirred again, seeming to be surfacing from the deep depths of tired rest, as if the confirmation of her being alive was enough for him to wake. After a moment, his eyes bore into hers the next time she blinked. Kellian bolted upright, seeing her eyes open and on him, unraveling himself from his slumber on the chair so quickly, the large chair almost toppled over entirely. He was by her side then and reached for her. He took her hands in his and she felt her magic respond, buzzing through her limbs. *Thank the goddess,* she thought, comforted deeply by the presence of her magic, though it ran low. It felt as if every reserve left was being used to try and heal her wounds.

Kellian blinked a few more times as if not believing his eyes, he swallowed and her eyes zeroed in on the movement before he opened his cracked lips. Then a door swung open and Esmeralda and Aura flew in, in all their wondrous chaos.

"Oh, thank the goddess!" Aura burst through the door, her hand flying to her chest as she stopped in the doorway, stunned to see Kyeria awake. Esmeralda peeked over Aura's shoulder holding a steaming cup and smiled brightly. *She loved them,* Kyeria thought, *so well and truly loved them.*

"How are you feeling?" Esmeralda asked, moving around Aura and coming to Kyeria's side. Kellian's hands left hers, giving the girls room.

The absence of Kellian's touch felt like ice water washing over her, without his warmth. She glanced at him as he seemed to emotionally and physically withdraw. Her thoughts clouded in worry before Kellian's expression softened as if responding to her nervous thoughts themselves. Kyeria was stunned at the intuitive nature he held, he seemed to understand her emotions so clearly. Her nerves responded, calming slowly at his steady presence, reminding her she was okay, she was grounded.

Kyeria refocused on Esmeralda. Her curls were tied back into complex braids, and she undoubtedly knew Aura had done them as the white haired princess had braided back the top of her hair and let the rest waterfall around her shoulder. Gold jewelry was weaved into some of Esmeralda's hair, and her cheeks were flushed as if she had been running through the castle herself grabbing ingredients for the potions in her hands. A golden potion swirled in an odd shaped bottle, and Esmeralda held it out.

"For the haze." Esmie offered the vile. Kyeria tried to focus her eyes on the vile and Esmeralda continued, "I had to keep you asleep for longer than your body wanted to be, to let it heal. Dragon fire is something fierce to try and heal, but my grandmother had a few journals on her own trials with it. I brewed as many potions as I could from her directions. The one to keep you asleep dulls your magic a little, puts you in a dreamscape. You might remember some of those dreams in the coming days, but don't be too alarmed. They were only dreams, and your body much needed the rest and time to heal." Esmeralda's soft eyes bore into her own, searching. Kyeria blinked a few times and nodded slowly. She felt odd, her body felt heavy and cold, laying like a weight on the soft mattress. A swish of a blue gauzy dress caught Kyeria's attention to see Aura pushing in front of Kellian.

"I'm sure you have a million questions, so here's what we know." She lightly tapped her fingers on the wooden end of the bed to a rhythm trapped only in her head. Kyeria let the rhythm sooth her, made herself focus on the soft touch of the sheets under her fingers, the familiar four poster wooden bed, the breeze from the window kissing her skin gently. As if to say, *you are okay.*

Kyeria refocused her eyes on the golden ones of Aura before her. A delicate smile lay there, one she had watched Aura use when talking to many people of The Hollow, an open kindness. She was so bright, it sometimes hurt to look at her as it did Kellian. Aura and Kellian had this light about them, each very different, like their essence were these different balls of light that burned different colors.

"You have been asleep for a week," Aura began slowly, waiting for the information to hit Kyeria. She swallowed and tried to clear her throat. She pried open her dry lips and tried to speak again but it was like one of her childhood dreams where she would try to scream and nothing would come out. Her heart rate picked up, she felt too heavy as if she was awake but trapped in her body. Panic washed over her, her eyes flashing to Esmeralda then Aura, then finally landing on Kellian. He was watching her so closely while keeping a seemingly purposeful distance from her. She could feel the terror was over her features, unable to mask the emotion fast enough, she felt him move to her side again before seeing he was steps closer. His closer presence was like a balm of relief. His expression was as if to say, *you are okay, you are safe.* She swore she could almost hear the low husk of his voice saying the words to her in that moment, but his lips were sealed shut, the same worried crease in his brow as he took her in.

"Don't be alarmed! Talking might take a few days. Your mind is awake, but your body will be slower to come back to you," Esmeralda soothed.

"Take this one." She nudged the bottle in Kyeria's hand, but while her fingers flexed on the bottle, she couldn't seem to lift her limb. Aura glanced down to the bottle and laid her hand on Kyeria's fingers.

"Let me," she said, and took the bottle, holding it up to her lips. She tipped the bottle back to her and Kyeria swallowed the sweet potion. It tasted like honey, and cleared her mind a bit. She could sense her magic more, she sighed with relief—it was there, dimmed at the bottom of her well, but it was there.

"Next, the hatchling is one of the strongest new Dragons we have ever seen. Esmeralda and I have been studying old texts in the library and we have found some information on this line of Dragons. They would fire-bath their bonded riders. In this time, fae still lived on the continent, and some were chosen by the Dragons, to be their bonded rider or magical counterpart. However, these fae were a part of the ancient people who were tied to the Dragons, therefore immune to the Dragon fire, similar to how Kellian and I are the Guardians. We do not have all the answers. But we are working on it." Aura paused and glanced at Kellian, who was standing stone-like next to her.

"And most importantly, we," she glanced around, "are so relieved you are okay." She reached out and squeezed Kyeria's hand. Kyeria felt her eyes welling with tears but still felt so disconnected from her body.

"I'll leave these for you. We have a meeting with someone in the village who has more knowledge on healing Dragon fire burns," Esmeralda said, squeezing her hand and standing. Aura nodded, leaned in to kiss Kyeria's cheek and nodded to her brother before walking out with Esmie.

The door clicked shut and Kyeria stared at the ceiling. The golden swirls that decorated each shape were painted on each curve of the stone ceiling. She traced them with her eyes in an attempt to calm her heart. Kellian cleared his throat and she felt the bed sink next to her, then a warm hand on her cheek. It wasn't until she noticed he was wiping away a tear that she felt herself crumble. Her vision blurred as tears took her sight. She felt like she had been stuck in an odd dream with a lingering fear trying to consume her for days. It must have been the dreamscape from the potions, she thought. But Kellian being here, feeling his warm hand, his real living being next to her, was such a relief she felt like she was gasping for air.

"You're alright," Kellian murmured into her ear. "You are safe."

Then she realized he was holding her. She wasn't sure when he had started but one arm was around her and the other was cradling her head to his neck. He whispered words into her hair and she couldn't move a muscle, and her tears were streaming, her vision still blurry. But she was alright. She was safe.

Kyeria wasn't sure how much time had passed, laying there peacefully with Kellian, when she drifted off to sleep. Real sleep, where only oceans and mountains on her fae islands greeted her in dreams. Her mother's voice called to her. She turned, noticing the sand under her feet.

"My darling." Her mother's voice was like the sweetest of tunes to her ears.

"Mother?" Kyeria's voice cracked and her feet began moving, running into the arms of her mother.

"Hello child, look how you have grown." Kyeria's mother had golden red hair like her own, swept up and braided back. She wore blue and gold

spun robes and the light gleamed off of her so brilliantly. Kyeria's eyes watered just looking at her.

"How are you here, Mother?" she asked, her voice feeling so young.

"It is but a dream, my sparrow," her mother replied, her hand cupping Kyeria's cheek. Her mother had called her a little sparrow the first time she found her daughter high up in the trees along the river behind their cottage. Kyeria had asked, "What is it like to fly, mother?" and wished on the flowers in the meadow to be a bird.

"Why are you here?" she asked instead, her mother nodded as if approving of the question.

"Your magic is at peace here." Her mother noted, "you have made it to our home."

Kyeria shook her head. "No mother, I am in a land called The Hollow, on the continent, far from the island." Her eyes were watery but she looked right into the light of her mother.

"You have found your other half, sparrow." Her soft eyes were gleaming.

"Who?" Kyeria asked.

"You know not to whom your soul bound is?" her mother asked, looking concerned. "I can feel the bond from you, you have been with them," she added. Kyeria shook her head, trying to clear it. Her mind was swirling. Why had her mother said this was our home? Where did she mean? In this odd dreamscape? In this swirling other reality?

"Mother? Where is our home?" she asked, trying to free herself from the fog. It was tumbling around them, creating a cavity between them.

"Where my people bound themselves to the land, to honor and protect. Ours with those of the Galanis line."

"What do you mean?"

"We took to the land, them to the skies. The Guardians, my sparrow, you are bound to them. Soul tied, generations past." Her mother's voice felt farther now. Kyeria was reaching out through the fog, the stars behind her mother and the light was dimming.

"Mother, please!" she called. "Stay with me!"

"Go back to your people my darling. You are safe there, go back to your Guardian."

She drifted away and the dream was overtaken by fog flipping the dark sky for that of a bright one. Her feet were on soft, familiar soil then.

Kyeria looked up and a Dragon flew ahead. Then a slow blink, this reality slipped through her fingers and shifted. A woman with hair as white as Aura looked down at her now.

"Why is Aura not going to be one of them, mother?" a voice asked. It was not her own, but that of a young boy. The woman smiled, her blue eyes gleaming.

"She is well and alive my dear, for that I will thank the stars and sky every night. The honor will fall to you now, as one of the Guardianchildren will be the Dragon heir. The goddess came to me in a dream and made it so," she replied, her blue eyes gleamed. "It will all make sense soon, my love. The goddess will anoint you with the ability to take Dragon form in your twelfth year, later than any have before, but I have all the faith in you, my son."

"What is it like to fly?" the little boy asked.

"Endless." The boy's mother looked off to the sky to watch the large grey glimmering Dragon flying above.

The world swirled again, and Kyeria was once again thrust into night, stars gleaming. She could see a tower high up in the castle. It looked so familiar to her, as if her very bones recognized it. A boy sat at a windows edge, his feet dangling off a ledge hundreds of feet above the ground. His eyes looked sunken, clouded. Brows creased and seemed to take over all of his small expressions. Dull unpointed ears poked out from his white hair that was cropped close to the nape of his neck. As if the whole world was sitting on his shoulders, he sat on that edge, as if one strong breeze would let him fall down the stone tower walls, to the open castle grounds below.

The cool wind blew by, whispering to her, "Go home child of the trees, it is time now."

The next time Kyeria woke, the fire was burning low. The velvet chair that had been next to her holding a tired white haired prince, was now neatly back in front of the hearth. A pot of steaming tea was set on the nightstand, with another potion bottle and a note in Esmie's scribble saying, *"Take this, then drink the tea. For the burns and the pain."*

She tested her fingers and arm, flexing each finger individually. Then when she was sure her arm was strong enough, she picked up the tea cup and raised it slowly to her mouth. The warm liquid spilled down the front of her as her hand shook, and she gasped in shock from the heat and dropped the cup. She stared at the porcelain, shattered on the ground in a million pieces.

"I've got it," a deep voice broke her trance. Kellian was there, a cool cloth then laid on her brow. He had walked right over the shattered glass, the sound of cracking under his feet. He had wanted to get to her first, she realized. His warm hand pressed the cloth to her brow until she closed her eyes. She heard Kellian moving around and when she opened her eyes again, a small broom was in the large hand of Kellian. Silently, he cleared away the shattered teacup. After he was done, he squared his shoulders towards her, a serious expression locking into place. But his eyes were soft, always soft.

"Do you want to try standing?" he asked. She looked at him in mild shock. She just dropped a tea cup after trying to hold it for longer than a moment, now he wanted her to stand?

"Esmie said it's good to move if you can to regain your strength," he explained quietly. She swallowed and tried to speak, a cracked attempt at "Okay" left her lips. Kellian smiled softly, eyes glancing at her arms and ever so slightly wincing. He walked over to her and held out his hands. She looked at him quizzically. Not being able to speak was quickly becoming infuriating. She wondered what was going on in his mind, if he was mad at her or the situation or even the little Dragon.

"Come on," he encouraged, pulling the covers back. Her long navy blue nightgown crumbled around her knees, and the satin and lace trim tickled her skin. Kellian reached over, scooping his arms beneath her knees and bringing her forward, legs facing him and dangling off the soft bed. She looked up, took as deep a breath as she dared to and put pressure on Kellian's hand, pushing her body to stand. She immediately felt she was falling, her knees like liquid, useless and weak.

"I won't let you fall," he said gently, his breath brushing her ear, his hands firmly grasping hers, an anchor to hold on to. Kyeria straightened her back with great difficulty and let Kellian hold her up. Her head held higher, she tried again.

"Good," he encouraged. He took a step back from her and she tried not to look panicked. She pushed her leg to move, and it was the most ungraceful movement she had ever made, but Kellian was there, holding her weight up. They did a few more of these exercises before Kyeria felt exhausted and Kellian helped her to sit on the bed. She looked angrily at the bed, hating to be confined. Hating not being able to move her own limbs or voice. Kellian looked to the pillows and fluffed them for her so she could sit up. He guided her to lay back, and pulled the covers over her legs again. He didn't say much that day. His eyes were clouded with something Kyeria couldn't recognize.

Days passed and Kellian came every morning to help her stand, take a few steps and stretch her muscles. She could move more and more each day. Even her voice was getting stronger. The burns remained, like fresh wounds refusing to close. But twice a day Esmeralda brewed her tea and potions to keep the pain at bay and the wounds from getting infected. Aura accompanied Esmeralda, helping redress her wounds or bringing Kyeria small gifts. Aura would come back from the villages or on her treks with new items, bounding into the room to show her.

Kyeria was coming to see Aura and Esmeralda as the sisters she had always wanted. They were constant companions, distracting her with research or making her laugh until her belly hurt. Kellian was a constant most morning unless royal duties conflicted. While he had been ever present, he seemed reluctant to be fully here with her, as if he was holding himself back. It was a deep type of frustration to not be able to simply voice her concerns, to ask him what was going on inside his mind. But even when her voice was returning, albeit cracked and raw, she put off asking, suddenly worried about the answer. So instead their mornings were quiet as he helped her stretch her sore muscles, and gain her strength. The touch of his warm palm on her back, or the light hold on her arms, she drank in every moment. While the words were few from Kellian, the presence was consistent. While he had been there every morning, when she woke the day before she was met by Miss Bells and a cup of tea instead of Kellian.

Kyeria woke again this morning and found her room empty. She tried to hide her disappointment on the second day Kellian did not appear at dawn, when Esmeralda and Aura instead came through the door together a bit later. He had been gone for two days now to the eastern border villages and she felt his absence so deeply. Like someone had carved out a piece of her chest and simply taken it with them. It was an odd feeling, Kyeria was so used to being on her own, but this small family she had tumbled into made her feel things she didn't think she ever would. Despite everything, here, she felt safe and loved and cared for. Something she thought she would never again.

Miss Bells set up trays of sandwiches and brought in new books from the library and took back the ones Kyeria had finished that morning. The tea helped her throat, and her words were less cracked, her magic was sifting through the damage, and her body was coming back to her. Esmeralda helped her walk around the room in Kellian's absence, stretching her sore limbs, and Aura was rambling about how infuriating Nox had been at training yesterday. Esmie sent Kyeria a knowing look and she held in a giggle, biting her lip hard.

"I mean does he need to be so insufferable?" Aura groaned, falling dramatically into one of the wingback chairs in front of the hearth. Dirt shook off her boots onto the table as she kicked her feet up, and Kyeria winced at the mess. Esmie only rolled her eyes before setting her hand at Aura and making her remove her boots off the table.

"Are you still having nightmares?" Esmeralda asked gently after settling back into the wingback chair. Kyeria had been plagued with restless sleep lately. When she did sleep, she tossed and turned with nightmares. When she woke in the dark, she felt trapped, and the weight of her inability to talk and move the way she used to was at its heaviest. The terror would wrap around her so deeply, pulling tight on her throat, around her lungs, around her whole being. She had mostly brushed them off, but Kellian had found her sometime last week in the middle of the night. He said she had been screaming, heard her cries from across the hall and thought she was dying. He had rushed to her, taken her in his arms and muttered a few soothing words. They were a balm to her terror, slowly coaxing her back to reality. Again, Kellian was there, his ever solid presence acting like an anchor for her to hold on to, keeping her above the waves of her nightmares.

"Some," Kyeria responded to Esmie's question. Aura and Esmeralda shared a look, making Kyeria ask, "Why?" She furrowed her brow and slowly eyed the two women, wondering what they meant by it.

"Well..." Esmeralda basically sang her response. "Do you feel up to visiting my potions room?" Kyeria nodded happily. Aura had to help her, but they slowly made their way.

The room was warm and dimly lit. Books were scattered around, candles burning. They sat Kyeria in a soft chair, and began moving aside piles of potions, books, and piles of collections from Esmeralda clearly looking for something. Kyeria waited for an explanation; a few minutes passed before Esmeralda paused and turned to explain herself.

"We made you a gift," Emeralda said sweetly and continued rummaging through the piles around her. Kyeria looked at Aura who nodded with a ghost of a smile, like she was trying to bite back her excitement at whatever it was Esmie was looking for.

"You had been having nightmares," Emeralda said, "and you mentioned you sleep with the fire burning even if it is blistering hot outside, just so you'll have some light, so you know what is real and not real." Esmeralda emerged empty handed again from behind another pile that sat taller than the small girl. Kyeria took the time to take in Esmeralda. Her earrings clinked with her quick movements and a shimmer pulled her eye to an amulet around her neck in the shape of a starburst. She had begun wearing the jewelry she would make, it made her seem so much older, not the mere sixteen years of age she was, six years younger than Kyeria herself. Esmeralda was dressed in her usual red robes, the color of a ruby in the night, deep and dark. A leather corset wrapped around her middle. That seemed new, Kyeria noted. She was used to Esmeralda wearing the looser clothes of the younger people of the Hollow. But Esmeralda seemed to be dressing more maturely now, as if shedding a layer of being. She moved with a sense of grace about her, a more elegant way than her usual clumsy manor. In a blink of an eye she had grown so much.

"Not that one, not that one," she muttered, still rifling through stacks of things in her tower. "Oh!" Esmeralda exclaimed and ran across the room. On a wooden table sat a white candle in a golden candlestick holder, there was a handle and a plate that connected to the pricket holding up the candle. Small vines were etched into the gold. The white candle, while lit, was not melted at all.

"This," Esmeralda held it out and whispered a spell, lighting the candle, "is for you."

"Esmeralda and I have been reading through her grandma's spell books, and we found one to enchant items with one's power," Aura explained.

"So I enchanted you a candle with Aura's light, so that it will never burn away." Esmerada's smile was so sweet and soft, Kyeria fought the tears begging to escape.

"So you'll always have light," Aura spoke up gently.

"And you'll never be in darkness," Esmeralda added. Kyeria picked the candle up, running a thumb over the intricate etchings of the holder. She was stunned into a bit of silence. Kyeria had never mentioned the details of the nightmares, only that she had trouble sleeping if it was fully dark, a silly childhood fear turned paralyzing. The healing potions she had been given to keep her asleep after the dragon fire burns, made those small trivial fears into horrid monsters of nightmares. Maybe she had mentioned the dark to Kellian, or he had noticed, and this sweet family of the Hollow had put a gift into motion.

Kyeria felt so seen, she knew to be loved was to be known. And these two women, they meant the world to her, she saw them, she knew them, as they saw and knew her. This family, they had taken her in at The Hollow, made her feel welcome and warm. Without being able to form the words, Kyeria crushed them both into a hug before muttering, "Thank you, thank you, thank you." When she pulled away she looked over the candle again, the energy radiating off of it was different than that of a natural flame, so she dragged her fingers over the flame but no burn touched her skin. Magic filtered through her skin instead.

"Oh also, the fire can't hurt you. Since it's Aura's light, it is only manipulated to look like flame, then we bound it to the candle itself. Granny Winter's spell book is very interesting," Esmeralda said happily. They sat in silence for a while, Kyeria so overwhelmed with her emotions, of feeling like she had a home, after so much of her life was spent alone.

"I brought some new texts today on the forming of The Hollow," Esmeralda announced one warm morning. "You might find this one rather interesting." Aura and Esmeralda had bound into her room, like many mornings as of late.

"What is it?" Kyeria asked, brow lifting.

"About the Galanis line and how they are magically tied to the Dragons." Esmie helped Kyeria to the second chair that sat in front of the hearth, identical to the one Aura slouched in.

"There's some inscriptions here, I was hoping you could translate it." Esmie handed a red leather bound book to her. Kyeria opened the old pages and sipped on her healing tea. Aura drifted off, tired from training early, most likely from before the sun rose. Esmeralda sat at the window seat, a matching red book in hand.

"This is the old language," Kyeria spoke after reading a few pages. Esmeralda nodded.

"Yes, but it's different, I can translate most of the common letters of the old language, this one I couldn't make sense of," she replied.

"It's a dialect of sorts..." Kyeria trailed off.

"What does it say?" Esmeralda looked over to her, holding her place in her own book with a ribbon and setting it aside.

"I don't understand..." Kyeria whispered. Emeralda was at her side.

"This here, this is my mother's family name." Kyeria let her finger trail over the old name, *Greenburrow*. It was even written in the old language the way her mother would sign her letters. The memories were so faint now, but she remembered her mother sending letters to a sister who lived on another island. Ana Greenburrow. Kyeria's mother always spoke so fondly of her. But in the old fae culture, when married, the woman leaves the land of her people and joins the land of her husband's. So her mother had boarded a ship and traveled to the southern end of the great fae island. The holy land of the fae. But her family was not from the great fae island. Kyeria knew this but had been missing pieces of her own family's history. Broken shards of memories resurfaced, but she was a mere ten years when last she saw her mother. But her family name had been Greenburrow. The Greenburrow women had been ripe with earth magic, stronger than many other who were blessed with the same form from the Goddess Luna

"It says that the Greenburrow line worked in the land, helping with magic ley lines. The Lake, the one in the mountains, is on connecting magical ley lines, that's why the magic is so strong there. Many ley lines cross within the boundary of The Hollow, under the water sources. The streams that go through the castle grounds come from The Lake, which is what makes the magic so strong here," Kyeria noted.

"I thought your people were merchants and artists?" Esmeralda asked.

"My father's, yes. Not my mother's. They were magic weavers for their towns," Kyeria explained.

"What is a magic weaver?" Esmie asked.

"Family lines with stronger magic. Many had more than one elemental magic, as I have that of the earth and healing. My mother had the same. Her family was rather important, actually, to the kingdom. They ensured the magical balance of northern lands, their earth magic was some of the strongest of the islands."

"What does this say?" Esmeralda flipped to a marked page half way through the text and pointed at a specific line. "It looks so familiar to me."

Kyeria's eyes found the letters and her breath hitched.

"The Winter witches," Kyeria whispered. Aura sturred and glanced up at them both hunched over a book. Their old language talked of the Winter's and the Greenburrow's working to build a land on the magical ley lines, to ensure safety for the Dragons, giving them a breeding ground that was holy and protected. Thus the Hollow had been created.

"What did I miss?" she asked, rubbing her golden eyes, her white braided hair coming loose from its form.

"This ancient text I found on the farthest level of the library has my family name in an old fae language," Esmeralda said, stilling.

"And mine," Kyeria finished and met Aura's eyes who sat gap-mouthed staring at the two of them.

CHAPTER 12

Kellian

I t has been many days since Kellian felt his heart stop beating. Days since he threw himself in front of Kyeria and held her hard enough to bruise her burned body. He paced his room at night, visited Kyeria every dawn helping her regain strength again. But the days before she woke, when she lay still as stone in that bed after the Dragon fire had consumed her, Kellian refused to leave her despite his sister insisting he needed to rest and feel the fresh air on his skin. He told her to leave him alone, pried open a window in Kyeria's room, and sat back down in the chair he had dragged over to be by her side.

Once Kyeria had awoken, he felt himself take what felt like his first breath in days. But then the guilt crashed into him. He had failed to keep her safe—a Dragon, his own kind, had harmed her. Kellian couldn't make sense of it. But as Esmeralda threw herself into research, and Aura into training, Kellian turned most of his attention to his royal duties. Other than his morning visits to help Kyeria, he was buried in work. Fendiah had taken flight and would be back at the end of the month. Fendiah had gone to the Isles, to convene with the Northern Dragons and to inform the council of a new Venille hatchling.

Aura began taking some of their royal duties, helping to lessen the weight on Kellian's shoulders. She was up before him most mornings to get in training and then in her royal robes, meeting with councils and visiting villages by midday. Any of her free time was spent with Kyeria and Esmeralda. Kellian, however, busied himself during the day and found himself not being able to sleep and would instead take long flights at night to settle his mind.

Today was no different. He was walking the halls after a meeting with an advisor. The last two days consisted of enough royal duties to keep him from visiting Kyeria in the mornings. It had only been two days but his fingers itched to touch her soft skin, and he was convinced being near her was an addiction at this rate. Kellian wore a perfectly embroidered tailed jacket, the golden thread twisting into vines and leaves. It reminded him of her. Everything did. Kellian felt a tug deep in his core like something was calling to him. He rubbed his chest, unfamiliar with the feeling. His mind wandered to the bright light outside, where the flowers in his mother's gardens were in full bloom. *Kyeria would love to see it*, he thought.

Another tug.

Kellian passed another dozen windows and felt his feet take over, guiding him to the hall his and Kyeria's chambers resided in.

Soon his knuckles were tapping on her door and he heard her gentle voice float over to him. "Come in."

Kellian pushed the door open. She was sitting in her bed, and she looked so small surrounded by pillows, with a book propped in her lap.

"Oh!" Kyeria startled, taking in his presence, obviously expecting his sister or Esmeralda. He smirked at the surprise on her. She quickly ran a hand through her hair and adjusted her loose dress. "I wasn't expecting you."

"Would you like to go for a walk?" he asked. Her eyes gleamed at the idea before sadness invaded her green eyes again.

"I don't know that I can," she muttered. Kellian felt his heart shutter at her defeat. He would turn over the world to make it better, but he knew her magic ached to be outside, so today they would make that happen.

"I'll take you," Kellian said with a finality that seemed to shake her.

"I am not dressed," she countered. Kellian halted his walk to her and turned towards the closet, pulling out a long wool coat and a scarf.

"For the chill," he explained, bringing the items to her. She pushed herself up and swung her legs around, her feet hitting the cool ground. She could take a few steps on her own now, as her strength was returning. Her skin seemed brighter and Kellian assumed her magic was resurfacing as well. Kellian didn't say a word, just began helping her into the coat and buttoning it to keep her warm. When the skin of his fingers brushed her arms, he tried his best to not let his expression change, but it was like a shot of electricity right through his veins. Touching her was like his own personal drug. Kellian took a steading breath and pulled the scarf around her, gently reaching and pulling her hair out from beneath the scarf.

"Is it really cold enough for this?" she asked, her eyes twinkled with amusement, as if catching on to him being worried about her.

"Cold enough," he grunted. Kellian couldn't stand the thought of her being too cold, or hurting, or being anything but okay. The least he could do was make sure she was warm on a walk. Kyeria looked like she was trying to hold back a smile.

"Now what?" She looked at him in question. He responded by leaning in to her.

"Hold on," he said, before he lifted her into his arms easily. One arm wrapped around her waist, the other under her legs. He tried not to touch the worst of the burned areas he knew were littered along her body.

"So by walk, you meant carry?" Kyeria let out a small smile and Kellian felt himself smiling back. He was so relieved she was seeming more like herself again.

He walked out of the bedchamber across the hallway and to his own door, pushing it open with one hand. Kyeria's cheeks reddened.

"Why are we in your chambers?" she asked, looking down. He loved the way her cheeks reddened.

"I have a short cut to the gardens."

Her eyes shot up to meet his. Goddess above, he loved her eyes. He could get lost in them.

"You have your own path to the garden?" Her eyes were alight with excitement and Kellian felt the adrenaline from making her smile simmer through him. He nodded and walked them to the large windowed doors he always had open. Once outside, they met a stone staircase with an intricate iron railing.

"This is stunning," she whispered. It was, Kellian knew this. The view from his chambers of the gardens were some of the best. His room was high above them with his own personal set of stairs leading to the gardens. A guard stood at the bottom of the stairs and nodded at Kellian as he passed.

"Will you be carrying me the whole time?" Kyeria asked with a smile on her lips that made Kellian's insides warm.

"If you wish it," Kellian offered, but he looked ahead. "But I have a spot I quite prefer where we can sit if you don't mind going further," he explained. There was a patch of meadows past the main paths, a river cut in through, and a large willow tree and some tree stumps he had cut down over time to make into a long bench. It was one of his favorite spots inside the castle gates. Many hours had been spent there, as a younger man, hiding from royal duties, and now he came out here for silence and reprieve. The water was calming and always called to him.

Kellian walked, Kyeria in his arms. Her muscles had relaxed, he could feel her letting go of the tension, the fresh air bringing life back into her. As she closed her eyes the wind swept by, catching up in her loose hair. A smile crept on to her features and she relaxed into him even more.

Once they arrived at the willow, he gently set her down on the bench and sat next to her, his arm propped behind her in case she needed it.

"This is beautiful," she breathed. Her eyes flickered to his and they seemed clearer. Kellian could feel her pull. The want, if not need, to be closer to her, to have his lips on hers. He steeled his expression and looked out to the water streaming by. They sat in silence for a while until she reached her arm out and rested her small hand on his thigh. Electricity shot through him from the small touch.

"Thank you," she said. Kellian blinked, looking down to her.

"It's nothing," he replied. "You had been in the room too long." She nodded. He knew she needed to be outside, with the wind and the trees and the soil or grass under her feet.

"My magic feels more alive than it has in days," Kyeria muttered. She held out a hand, letting her fingers move in the wind. She focused and raised her hand. Small wildflowers bloomed around their feet. Branches rose from the soil, twisting and forming a table out of it in front of them. She leaned forwards, her elbows resting on the new table made of branches and vines. Little blossoms bloomed around the edges.

"Nice trick." Kellian smirked. She looked at him, remembering the first time he said those words the day they met.

"What has happened with the hatchling?" she asked after many moments of silence.

"The hatchling is in the caves, it is fine," Kellian supplied but Kyeria sighed, looking out to the water.

"What is wrong?" she asked. Kellian was a bit surprised she saw past his calm reply.

"It's quite odd actually, the hatchling seems very fatigued and sad, hasn't moved from its nest, won't let any of the keepers touch her."

"Her?" Kyeria perked at the information. "What's her name?"

"She has not spoken to anyone. Refuses to." Kellian ran a hand through his white hair. It was loose, neatly brushed and tucked behind an ear revealing piercings. She reached up and her fingers traced the bar of metal through his ear.

"This is new." She tapped the earring. It was a symbol of bravery—certain piercings were a gift, earned and fought for. Fendiah had awarded him with it for saving Kyeria, but he felt deeply conflicted instead of proud. It was an honor to save the life of one in need, but guilt of putting her in danger at all tugged at him nonetheless.

"I would like to see her," Kyeria announced. She pushed herself up from the bench, her hands grasping the table for stability.

"Excuse me?" Kellian shot back, standing to help her. She sent him a glare.

"I will see her." She squared her shoulders. Kellian could see she would not be dissuaded now that the thought had solidified for her. He simply nodded.

"As you wish," he simply replied. She pushed her legs forward, taking a few wobbly steps. Kellian followed, giving her the space to do it on her own. Each step seemed more secure and confident until she was at the river's edge. The water wading at her feet, she looked to the sky, closing her eyes.

"How does the water greet you?" Kellian asked. Her magic was such a blank slate for him to understand. Utterly different and new and endlessly interesting.

"That there is a beast eating at the magic of the land," she muttered. They knew that. "That there is new life here." She placed a hand to her heart. Palm outstretched across her scarf. "That I am safe here," she whispered. He pulled closer to her.

"Always," he whispered, he was trying to give her space but staying away from her was nearly impossible. So he stood behind her, close enough to smell her flowery scent and reach out. A finger wrapping around a strand of copper locks.

"You are upset," she noted but didn't look at him or move out of reach. He dropped his fingers nonetheless.

"There is much to be done, and things I cannot change," he replied.

"You think it is your fault," Kyeria pointed out, lifting an arm and glancing at the blotchy red skin peeking from under the bandages. She saw in the corner of her eye the grimace that raked through him.

"It is," he replied. "Hatchlings are unpredictable, it has been decades since the last one. But in my lifetime, a fae has not been present during the hatching ritual."

"You couldn't have known." She sighed and turned to him. Reaching out, she placed a hand on either side of his arms.

"But I should have known not to risk anything." He closed his eyes. "Not when it comes to you." His eyes were still closed when a ghost of a kiss was placed on the corner of his lips. His heart quickened, the same electricity charging through him, then he leaned in. Finally taking what he had been holding back. He kissed her like he would lose her, like she was his air, his reason for existing. Because she was. She was everything. Her almost dying had shaken something deep in him. He felt so protective of this sunlit woman. Like he would do anything to keep a smile on her lips and her heart light and loved.

Kyeria pulled away, resting her forehead on his. He tilted up and laid a kiss on her forehead before settling back into her gaze.

"Wounds heal." Her eyes were searching his, trying to convey how important it was to her that he did not blame himself. Kellian closed his eyes, let out a sigh, and nodded.

"I would like to meet her today," Kyeria said again, her voice confident and certain. Kellian nodded, in awe of her yet again.

"Okay."

Kyeria had refused Kellian's offer to carry her again. She insisted she needed to gain back her strength, and promised to take it slow. Her arm was looped into Kellian's, relying on him to stabilize her as her legs moved. She seemed more confident, her strength coming back into her body, like being outside made her magic wake up, like her fae healing was finally catching up.

They walked back into the castle.

"It is a far walk, are you sure?" Kellian asked again,

"I am perfectly fine. I have a royal Dragon to meet."

"They're not exactly royal," Kellian corrected.

"How come?"

"The royals, we exist as the Guardians, to protect the great lines of Dragons. The Venille line, which the hatchling is from, is one of the very first Dragon houses. The Venille line creates some of the most astonishing Dragons. They're faster and stronger than the others. With more authority as well. A Venille is first in line to be the head of the Dragon council," Kellian explained. She nodded along as they walked.

"You should know, Venille have different powers as I mentioned. Many from that line of Dragons have the ability to take human form."

"Like your grandfather, the king?" she asked.

"Fendiah is a human first, a Guardian first, then blessed with the ability to shift into Dragon form. The Venille's are Dragons first, but possess the power to take human form. But they are very much Dragons, with more power than any of us Guardians could ever hold."

"Is Fendiah the only Draconis?" she asked. Kellian grimaced. This was a truth he should have shared earlier.

"No," was all he managed to reply before they were in front of the large doors fronting the Dragon caves. He could see the question in her, he thought maybe a part of her knew already, that the pieces had already fallen into place. She was rather good at that, but he knew he owed it to her to formally tell her even if she only suspected.

"Ready?" he asked, turning to the doors into the caves. She nodded, steeling her shoulders, her head held high.

There she is, Kellian thought.

CHAPTER 13

Kyeria

The Dragon caves, while dark, were lit warmly with half-burned candles covering the floors and on the walls held by iron sconces. She felt her magic hum, jittering awake. Kellian led her slowly to another room. Long draping fabric hung from the stone walls, and a large bed of straw with red blankets lay in the middle of the room. It was, however, empty. Kellian sighed and turned. Sure enough, a small black Dragon with purple and pink and black reflective scales flew overhead, much too close, and landed in front of Kyeria. Kellian took a small step in front of her, claiming her from the Dragon.

"*You have come,*" the Venille Dragon spoke. Her voice was feminine and sweet.

"Hello, I am Kyeria." Kyeria smiled and bowed her head.

"*I am Ameline.*"

"Do you know your syers, Ameline?" Kellian stepped forward. The Dragon ignored him. His eyes bored into the side of the Dragon's head and horns.

"*You are hurt,*" the Dragon announced, taking a step forward, but Kellian matched the step, putting himself between the two.

"It's okay," Kyeria assured.

"She is hurt from the Dragon fire," Kellian answered.

"*Guardians are not able to be hurt by Dragon fire.*"

Kellian shook his head. "She is not of the Guardian line."

"I am fae, from the lands of NorHaven," Kyeria replied. Her magic was alight, buzzing so loudly she could barely hear her own thoughts. Kellian moved further in front of Kyeria.

"You are not my Guardian, prince," the Dragon spoke, casting him an angered look.

"I do not understand," Kyeria spoke, looking Ameline in the eyes. She was small, and her scales looked like they were made out of blood under the firelight. Ameline rose to her full height then, standing nearly double the height of Kyeria and a head taller than Kellian.

"Ameline." Kyeria squared her shoulders. "I am new to this land. I do not know its customs and am slowly learning its history. It is an honor to be in your presence." Kyeria stepped in front of Kellian and bowed her head. Ameline in turn bowed her own head, leaving Kyeria feeling like the air had left her lungs. Kyeria knelt to the ground and pushed her magic into the stone. Ameline had a feline way about her, and she let out a content purr at the magic.

"You are that of the earth," Ameline stated, looking directly at Kyeria.

"I am," Kyeria replied.

"My line has not been here in centuries. Long we have slept. Only a few eggs remain. I am the last here in the Ash Mountains," Ameline explained. *"My ancestors, we are not connected to the Galanis line. We are instead tied with the fae folk. Much older in name and history. We are bonded with those of a specific line of fae folk—yours. The Greenburrow family were bound to the Venille line centuries ago, as the Galanis line was bound to be guardians."* Kyeria glanced at Kellian. An unreadable expression laid on his face. Kyeria reached for him, taking his hand and squeezing it once. He looked over, his gaze softening.

"You will not harm her?" Kellian asked.

"It was never my intention. Those who are bonded are bathed in Dragon fire, this is how it is done. The same way we are brought into the world is how we claim what is ours. There should be no pain, only the mark of the Dragon and their bonded." Ameline turned to Kellian. *"I do not wish to insult you, prince. But I do not answer to you or the Galanis line. The Venille Dragons are of their own laws."*

Kellian nodded. "I would never assume to rule over any dragon." He bowed his head, then continued, "Have you taken flight?" The Dragon shook her head.

"Not yet," she replied and looked at Kellian closely. "I should like to go with you when you are back in your Dragon form."

Kyeria's head snapped to Kellian.

Dragon form.

Kellian's golden eyes looked to Kyeria's in worry. He simply nodded. "I will leave you be, if that is what Kyeria would like."

Kyeria's head felt fuzzy. She didn't love being this far underground, felt as though the sky and the wind were so far from her, it felt suffocating. But she took a breath, steading herself and nodded to Kellian—she was okay. His eyes lingered and he walked out of the room of caves.

Kyeria was left with the Dragon the color of night and blood staring at her.

"*How hurt are you?*" Ameline asked gently. Kyeria didn't know it was possible for a Dragons tone to soften, and yet it did.

"I will heal." Kyeria shook her head. "But my magic shut down, slowing the healing. There is not much known of Dragon fire effects, as it usually causes fatality." Ameline nodded, dropping her head again.

"Tell me about the Venille Line," Kyeria asked.

"*Let's go outside,*" Ameline said. "*I hate it down here.*"

Kyeria smiled. They both needed the sky and the wind and the open land. Anwar wandered over, and bowing to Ameline he presented a leather harness with holds on the side and top.

"This is a rider's seat," he explained. "Do you feel strong enough to hold on if I show you how?" he asked. Kyeria's eyes went wide. She shook her head—no, she did not feel strong enough to ride a Dragon, the thought itself, seemed unreal. A dragon rider, she had never heard such a thing.

"*I can not fly carrying a rider quite yet,*" Ameline answered, as if reading her thoughts. Kyeria eyed the Dragon in question.

"*I can read your thoughts, yes,*" she replied again, making Kyeria still. How was that possible?

"*You are my bonded rider,*" Ameline said. "*Anwar cannot hear me right now. I am only projecting to you, and not the both of you.*"

"*How do you do that?*" Kyeria thought instead of speaking.

"*I will teach you. Anwar will put on the harness. Hold on to the side and I will walk you. The night of the ritual I fell into a sleep alongside the time you slept. But when I woke, Anwar explained what happened and that you were burned heavily. So I had him make a rider's seat to assist you before you and I are able to fly,"* she explained.

Kyeria felt her chest warm, taken aback by this gesture. Ameline looked to Anwar and nodded. He came forward and began fitting the rider's seat to Ameline's scaled back. After, they walked through the caves, until sunlight was streaming through and stone and dirt turned to a grassy meadow, a bright sky and few clouds hanging above them. Large pine trees littered the corners of the meadow. Ameline guided them through before pausing where the sun hit them unobstructed before curling her tail under and sitting in the meadow. The long grasses peaked around her, and as Kyeria sat, small flowers sprouted up around them. Her magic was happy, humming brightly, the trees were singing gently, even the wind felt at ease, as if everything was just right. Kyeria with her feet on soil, surrounded by nature, with a small Dragon whose eyes were closed, head tilted to the sky, the wind whisked by in response.

Welcome home, the wind sang.

"So, you and I are bonded," Kyeria said slowly. Kyeria didn't really know much about such a thing. She knew the Galanis line were fated to be the Dragon Guardians, long ago binding the souls of the Galanis line to be able to protect and serve with the Dragons. This Kyeria had come across many times in the texts she and Esmeralda had combed through in the library.

"*Yes,*" she said simply. Ameline began to explain about how hatchlings can live for centuries in their eggs, slightly aware of the life around them, but time moves differently for them, as they are magically protected. So while her body was smaller and she looked like a baby Dragon, she was really over one hundred years old. Kyeria asked so many questions, and her mind felt clearer out in the meadow. It seemed like Ameline knew this would be. The Dragon looked as content as Kyeria did out in nature. Kyeria laid back and looked at the sky, the few clouds floating by.

"I wonder what it is like to fly," Kyeria said with her eyes closed, focusing on the wind floating by them before peering over at Ameline.

"*I have a feeling you will love it,*" Ameline purred. She swore if a Dragon could smile, Ameline was smiling. Kyeria took in her appearance. In the sunlight her scales had more red and some deep purple hues, glowing in the daylight.

"*I had some scales shed when I was sleeping—very common for new hatchlings. I had Anwar save them for you. It is custom for the bonded to have armor made of their Dragon. Nothing can pierce Dragon scales but a Dragon itself. And on my honor, as your bonded, I will never engage to hurt or harm you."* Ameline bowed her head, the red and black scales glimmering under the sun. Kyeria breathed in the sweet wildflowers and let her hands push into the earth. The wind responded.

"You have a very strong magic about you," Ameline commented.

"Do you have magic?" Kyeria asked.

"Not like your own. I have Dragonfire, and will be able to shift into human form if I wish soon. I can sense magic, but in human form I will not be as strong or able to protect us as I can in Dragon form," she replied. Kyeria turned her head, looking at the Dragon again.

"You said Kellian can fly." It wasn't really a question. Kyeria felt her heart lurching, pounding at the truth that hung in the air. Aura wasn't able to become a shifter, the magic passing over her due to her illness as a child. But their grandfather was one, so maybe the magic jumped back to Kellian. She wasn't sure she understood why or how, but how had she not noticed?

"He is of the Galanis line. They take the form of a Dragon," Ameline said as if it was a common fact.

"Does it ever skip generations?"

"It does not," Ameline replied. *"Kellian's father was able to take Dragon form, so does his grandfather Fendiah. There is a gap for me; the last of the Galanis line that I recall hearing about was a queen named Ophelia."*

"The Dragon Queen, yes." Kyeria nodded. She had read of Ophelia, the great-great-grandmother of Kellian and Aura. A few paintings were centered around her in the castle, Kyeria had searched out the texts from her time, as Ophelia's closest confidant was a descendent of the Winter witches who served at her side and helped create the magic that kept the Hollow safe and kept the humans and outside world away, and seemingly someone from her own line of the Greenburrow's as well. That ancestor would have been the last Dragon rider. Kyeria listened to the wind, the trees, the earth beneath her and she couldn't ignore a truth nagging at her now, so she said it out loud, let the wind and the trees, the earth and her Dragon hear them.

"Kellian is a Dragon,"

"He is a shifter, no Dragon," Ameline replied, sharp in her words.

"Sorry," Kyeria muttered back. She didn't want to offend Ameline, she was simply trying to understand. How could she have gone this long around him and not known? Though a part of her mind, of her soul pulled at her. Somewhere deep inside her, she knew. The magic that enveloped Kellian was unlike any other, and far too similar to that of his grandfather's for it to be a coincidence.

They stayed in the meadow until sunset. Talking and getting to know another. Ameline explained some of how the bond worked and helped her practice blocking off her thoughts. The magic was easy for her, simple compared to her own. As if willing it made it simply be. So they laid in the meadow, Dragon and Dragon rider.

Esmeralda came to collect Kyeria from the caves that night, helping her walk back to her rooms. Kyeria shared what she learned and Esmeralda promised to find more information about the Venille Dragon line in the library for them to read through. Kyeria could tell she was buzzing with excitement. Esmie loved any excuse to dig into the library, especially the farthest floors with the oldest documents.

Aura was out on a tracking mission with Nox and wouldn't be back until tomorrow. Kyeria could walk again, albeit not far, but it was something. She was ready to not be trapped here any longer. She itched to explore, to fly. Once back in her room, she was greeted with a warm fire already burning and a washroom that held a steaming bathtub. She knew it was Kellian who sent a servant to have them ready, and her heart warmed at the thought. He had seemed withdrawn after the night of the ball, as if he was afraid Kyeria would break with any sudden movement. And while Kyeria appreciated the care, there was nothing she hated more than feeling weak. She survived Dragonfire after all, she had a bonded Dragon—she was anything but weak. She washed away her doubts, her frustrations, and fear with the water. Miss Bells appeared to help her after some time had passed and she was grateful for the assistance. Miss Bells had a way about her, and being fae, Kyeria felt so deeply comfortable with having someone from her homeland around. Few words would pass between them sometimes, but the steadiness of her, the way she treated Kyeria, was a great comfort.

Kyeria went down to the caves every day to visit with Ameline. They entered into a routine of walking to the meadow, Ameline recounting the history she knew to Kyeria and Kyeria filling in the gaps with what she had learned through her research with Esmeralda. A week passed like that, her voice was strong again, and only a hint of soreness remained in her limbs. The burns were healing, albeit slowly, and likely to leave scars. But Kyeria did not mind it, for they were her markings, that she was Dragon-bound. Claimed by fate, *a Dragon rider*.

It was the middle of the night when Kyeria woke for the fourth time. She twisted and turned in her sheets, the cool air was wafting through the night and the wind was restless. She felt her magic hum, she felt as restless as the wind itself. Kyeria could not shake the feeling, the awakeness of her mind. She closed her eyes again and tried to settle herself. Thought of open fields, and golden sun rays warming her skin. Of her future and fate here. Her mind continued to wander, refusing to quiet.

Cracking open her eyes again, she stared into the starry sky. The moon was high and bright, lighting the night. Kyeria threw off her blankets and let her bare feet drop to the cold floor. Dressed quickly in simple training clothes and boots before walking out her room, down the halls, and out to the back gardens. She had the route memorized by now, her feet moved easily without much thought, taking her to the dragon caves outdoor entrance. The large stone carvings that revealed the cave entrance was ahead, flaming lights on either side. A monk stook guard at one end and as Kyeria walked through her favorite meadow that separated her from the caves, she spotted her dragon.

Ameline's scales looked black under the moonlight, making her seem like a shadow in the night.

"You're awake," Ameline commented, turning her head to Kyeria.

"Couldn't sleep," Kyeria responded, running a hand through her copper hair.

"I think I am ready," Ameline said after a beat of silence. Kyeria paused and looked to her Dragon.

"To fly?" she barely whispered. And Ameline responded in her mind.

"To fly."

Exhilaration ran through Kyeria. One of the monks had fitted Ameline with her rider's seat before going back to the caves. Kyeria now stood looking at Ameline, fitted and ready to take flight. For the first time, together.

"Are you ready?" Kyeria asked, trying to bite back her smile.

"Are you?" Ameline asked back. Kyeria only smirked in return earning a contented Ameline who looked just as eager. Kyeria climbed up Ameline's front leg, swung a leg over the leather seat, and let her hands fall to the small hand pieces on either side.

"Volano." Kyeria commanded in old elvish.

Fly.

Kyeria's grip tightened on the rider's seat as Ameline passed the lower clouds and shot past them. The moon's light guided their way among the dark sky. The stars were gleaming and so clear past the clouds, Kyeria now understood Kellian's fascination with them. Why he spent hours charting them and figuring out how to use them to navigate your way through the realm.

The stars went on for as far as she could see, different arrangements and clusters. Ameline stretched her wings, the dark purple scales glowing under the bright moonlight and stars. Kyeria's magic rushed through her, tingling at the end of her fingers. It was content here. Up high above the clouds on her dragon. Ameline didn't say a word while they flew together, as if also soaking in the experience.

When they landed again in their favorite meadow, Kyeria felt like she was floating through the grass as she walked back next to Ameline. She walked her back towards the mouth of the cave, a goodnight muttered into the wind before she headed back to the castle.

Kyeria let the moonlight guide her back through the trees. She walked slowly, happy to be among them, the wind was happy tonight, the trees content. This land was so magical, she hoped to spend her lifetime here. She pondered how different her life was not that long ago, making the decision to run into the mountains that were sung about, and warned about the horrors of trying to enter them. All the lore that flitted across the realm in warning to never cross the Ash Mountains. And here she was among the very trees just past the mountains. Her wandering thoughts stopped when she heard a twig snap nearby. She paused, holding her breath. Kyeria had been so in her head she had barely even paid attention to her surroundings. Who would be up at this hour? This early in the dawn that it was practically still the night?

When she cast out her magic however, a familiar essence was just beyond the next few trees where the palace gardens began.

"Aura?" Kyeria whispered through the night.

"Goddess above, what are you doing out here?" Aura asked, rushing towards her. Kyeria moved from behind the trees blocking her, a wide smile sitting comfortably on her lips. She took in Aura, in training clothes she could have sworn she saw her in yesterday. Her normally perfectly braided hair was in a slight disarray. Kyeria bit her lip.

Oh.

"What were you doing?" Aura asked, raising an eyebrow.

"What were *you* doing?" Kyeria bounced back at her. They both eyed each other before bursting out into a fit of giggles. They walked back to the castle together and Kyeria beamed recounting her first flight with Ameline to Aura. They walked, arms linked until they reached two halls. Kyeria waved goodnight, walking down the hall that held her own chambers and Kellian's. But instead of opening her own door, she stood outside Kellian's.

She hesitated. There were no guards out tonight. The ones patrolling were likely not back yet, so she reached out to the doorknob and twisted. Shockingling, it turned and she slipped inside.

Kellian did not stir until she slipped into the bed. Pulling the covers over her and curling into him.

"Are you alright?" Kellian whispered. She hummed her response, leaned in and kissed his lips. Half asleep he pushed into her in response.

"Go to sleep," she whispered back and let herself drift off. Her mind finally still and calm.

|| THE TWELFTH MOON OF SPRING ||

· · ·

"When are you headed out next?" Kyeria asked Aura at dinner with everyone, the next night.

"Day after next, Nox can't come though so I might postpone, since this one disapproves of me going out alone." She pointed her fork accusingly at Kellian.

"Because if you are dying, I would rather someone around that can drag your ass home," he grumbled, pushing around the food on his plate. Aura smirked—she loved getting under his skin. Kyeria bit her lip to hold back a laugh and shared a look with Esmie instead, who recklessly let out a giggle. Kellians eyes snapped up.

"Do you both have a problem with me worrying about my sister's life?" he asked glaringly, but Kyeria knew he didn't mean it. The soft glimmer in his eyes told her differently.

"What if Kyeria goes with you?" Esmeralda offered, met with Kellian slamming his own fork down on the table.

"Absolutely not," he growled. Kyeria shot him a glare.

"I can speak for myself." She squared her shoulders and Aura smirked.

"Yeah," Aura added. "Then she can drag my ass out of so-called danger."

"She is still recovering," he snapped. "This is not a discussion."

"Excuse me?" Kyeria tried to hold back the gasp. " Once again, I can speak for myself, and you, Your Royal Highness, do not speak for me." Kyeria felt her chest filling with unsteady breaths—she was not going to be told by anyone what she could or could not do. She had been stuck in her rooms for far too long. She was restless, she needed to go, to be helpful, to do something, anything.

"Aura, I would love to accompany you on the next tracking." Kyeria sent a blinding smile towards the princess, who smirked at her brother knowingly.

"Absolutely not," he said standing.

"Oh relax, brother." Aura laughed. "I am only tracking, not interfering with or confronting the beast. We are tracking the movements and how the magic of the borders reacts to it. We will stay at a safe distance, there is practically no danger."

"It is a beast we know little about, sister, and I would rather the woman who has just begun being able to move around the castle without having to stop and catch her breath not be in further danger."

"Kel," Aura sighed and stood at the other end of the table. "I think we will do as we want." She turned and walked out of the door. Kyeria nodded and continued on eating her food. After moments of uncomfortable silence, Esmeralda excused herself, and it was only the two of them, sitting, eating silently in the grand dining room.

"What is really going on?" Kyeria asked softly, breaking the silence. Kellian's shoulders fell.

"I–I was out, on a scouting flight, and the monster is stronger than we understand, and while I know you are capable, seeing you—" He paused and met her gaze. "Seeing you hurt again, I don't think I can bear it." He closed his eyes. Kyeria stood and walked over to his chair, kneeling down and resting her forehead on his.

"I am okay," she whispered. "I am here."

His hand gripped the back of her head holding her to him. He let out a shaky breath. She pulled away and looked at him levelly.

"Is this why you've been distant?" she asked.

"I have not been–"

"You have," Kyeria cut him off. "You've been shut off, I've seen you every day Kellian, but your eyes rarely meet mine. You are keeping yourself at arm's length and I cannot understand why. What have I done?" she asked, pity nowhere in her tone.

"You nearly died," he said, his voice cracking. "I held you in my arms and you did not breathe Kyeria, and I felt my own heart dying, I can't explain it fully, I—" he fumbled.

"I know," she whispered. "Your soul has known mine," she said, quoting an ancient poem.

"You—" He looked up. "You have heard the Goddesses Proverb?"

"I have been reading," she said, sitting in the chair next to his. "Have you heard of soulbonds?"

"Yes," he whispered, "my mother would tell us stories as children. That there are people whose souls know each other for more than a lifetime, that they find each other in each, sometimes early, sometimes too late, but they are pulled together, bound."

"When I first saw you—" Kyeria shook her head. "My heart... it felt like something deep in me snapped, like the entire world shifted on its axis."

"I felt it too," he said, reaching for her. "But—" he began, and

Kyeria could feel her heart stutter. He had been so far, so distant, she didn't want him to pull away, she needed him.

"No, Kellian." She took his hand in hers and squeezed. "We cannot run from this."

"You were hurt because of me. I could have kept you safe. It's my fault." He sagged, shoulders slumped like the weight of the five kingdoms laid on his shoulders.

"Come back," she whispered. "Come back to me." Her voice was raw, so deeply vulnerable. She held back a tear from slipping out as Kellian pushed forward, crashing his lips to hers. After so many days, weeks without his touch, it felt like breathing again, like air being pushed into her lungs. He slid a hand around her back, tugging her body close to his. When he pulled back, he looked to her with darkened eyes,

"I could never leave you, not if the weight of the world was tying me down, I would move the Heavens and this earth, swear to any gods or goddess. Do not fear, my love, I will never leave. My soul is yours."

"Kellian," she gasped, crashing her lips to his in return. Kellian devoured her, holding her like she would wither to the winds if he let go. He pulled her up, pushing the dishes and letting them clatter aside, and sat her on the large wooden table.

"Not touching you has been torture," he said, voice gravelly and raw. She pushed away, letting herself catch her breath, resting her forehead against his. His chest was heaving heavy like hers, like trying to come down from a high.

"Kellian." Kyeria sobered herself. "When you go on flights," she began, keeping her eyes shut, "you're not riding a Dragon are you?"

A beat of silence passed. "No," he finally said.

"Why didn't you tell me?" she asked, feeling small.

"It is not a secret," he said and she shook her head.

"It is not spoken freely," she rebuked. He sighed, his warm breath hitting her.

"It was meant to be Aura," he said.

"The magic had passed me, but the goddess herself blessed it upon me on my twelfth birthday," he started. "My grandfather was elated. After the passing of my parents, and none of the heirs being able to shift, he was worried—about what it meant, for the magic binding us here. What it meant for the kingdom and the treaties we have with

Dragon kind." His hand drew non-existence shapes on an exposed part of her thigh, the fabric having been pushed up during their romp.

"My father was a golden one, they are rare and typically of a royal bloodline, that or the greybacks as Fendiah is."

"But you are white," Kyeria said. She had filled it all in, all the pieces had fallen days ago. She had asked Ameline, but she insisted it was not her information to share.

"Yes." He nodded.

"At the Ball, you were right there," she said.

"Yes, I watched it happen. I shifted and ran to you as fast as I could." He swore under his breath. "That night—" He swallowed. "That night is something I will not forget. I never wish you to be in harm's way." Fingers tightened on hers. "But this life, it is not meant to be safe. We are intertwined with Dragons for goddesses sake."

"As am I, Kellian." She let her hand rest under his chin, tipping it up to her. "I am bonded with the very one. She will not hurt me, she never meant to." Her chin wobbled with emotion and he nodded.

"I know that, logically I know that. But–"

"But you are placing all of the blame of that night on you, when it didn't have much to do with you at all." She said it kindly, but firmly. "Kellian, Ameline and I are bonded, it was written in the stars long before I was on this land, long before even you. The bonds of a Dragon and fae are ancient."

"As are those of the Galanis and the Dragons," Kellian added, his eyes seeming somber.

"As are you. I appreciate your care, and all you have done." She took a steading breath. "But I have survived on my own for a decade. I am Fae, not human. I am not fragile bodied or minded. I am capable of taking care of myself. And while I am thankful to you, your people, and your family, I will not be caged."

"Kyeria." Kellian paused, his brows creasing and genuine sadness filled his features. "I would never wish for you to feel as such."

"I will be going with Aura on tracking missions, I will be flying soon with Ameline. I will be fine," she said softly.

"I never wish to hold you back, please know that," he said, and Kyeria nodded. "You are free to do as you wish, always." His gaze softened. "I only ask I can be by your side when you'll let me." He smiled.

"You could have just said you were feeling left out of tracking missions." Amusement laced her words. If Kellian's soul truly yearned for hers the same way hers did for him, she did not doubt his worry came from a place of honesty.

"I never wish to be parted from you," he said, eyes softening. Kyeria paused, really looking at him. His eyes gleamed at her, full of pure adoration, and something else forming, something she couldn't quite identify. She felt the pull, the soulbond in the deepest inner-workings of her tugging and dragging her to him. She leaned forward, placing a soft kiss on his lips.

"Well now." She sat up straight and pushed herself off the table, her heels hitting the stone floor. "I would love to formally meet the white Dragon, your highness."

"Right now?" Kellian looked caught aback.

"Mhm." She smirked.

"As you wish." He took her hand in his, raising it to his lips, and led them to the gardens outside. Candles and fire lit the path, but unnecessary, as the moon was full in the sky. There was an essence of wonder floating through the castle grounds. The air whispered to Kyeria as it floated by, the trees were humming. Kyeria felt her shoulder relax, easing the weeks of tension from healing so slowly, from being in her room for so long. The crisp night air was a welcome feeling on her cheeks. She had tied her hair back in a braid, but the pieces framing her face were free and flowing in the wind. She let herself smile—she and the wind were happy, this land was so deeply content. Here, where magic was free and the land was respected and cared for. Kyeria tilted her head up, gazing at the stars. Silver and golden ones stood out to her, in a long sword-like shape.

"That is the north sword constellation." Kellian pointed to where her eyes were locked. "The last star is red and points north. You can always orient yourself that way." His hand squeezed hers.

"Neat trick." She smirked, remembering their first night they met in the cave, when he had commented the same thing to her lighting a fire. It felt like a lifetime ago now. Before she even knew what this land was. Before she laid eyes on the stone castle with flowering vines climbing most of the towers. Before Aura, and Esmie, when she thought she was destined to wander, to never find a home.

They continued their walk to the far east end of the grounds, beyond Kellian's mothers garden to a grand lawn. He let her hand go and put distance between them. She tried to contain her excitement, but her fingers tapped on her skirt, and she could feel her magic seeping into the earth. The wind picked up, delighted in receiving the magic.

"Are you ready, love?" he asked with a smirk. He knew her small movements, the tap on her fingers while she tried to contain the excitement. His gaze zeroed in on them. She beamed back at him, eyes creasing, and nodded. He stripped off his shirt, tossing it aside. Kyeria did her best to keep her heart calm, but there wasn't much use. The moonlight glistened off his skin. Small scars ran, connecting a large one on his chest. She had traced it that night in the tower. But he had yet to share the journey that led to it.

He kicked off his shoes and smiled wickedly before raising his arm in a mist of shadow. Her breath caught in her lungs as the human form of Kellian disappeared, and from the mist, a gleaming white Dragon stepped out. He was enormous, towering over her. He knelt his head down to meet her, closing the space between them. She reached out a hand as she would do with Ameline and set it on the scales between his piercing golden eyes—the exact same eyes he had in human form, twin to his sisters and grandfather. It was the one physical feature that remained in this form, and she knew it would be his distinguishing factor aside from the white scales. He was magnificent. He bowed his head down further and shot a look over his shoulder. Leaning down, his tail swished, pushing a gust of wind towards her, making her hair fly back. She let out a laugh and shook her head. Her magic hummed deep in her chest. She felt it reaching out, swirling out around her, invisibly wrapping around them. Kellian shivered and his golden eyes bore into hers.

"*Want to go for a ride?*" the voice appeared in her head, the same familiar low thick tone she knew so well.

"You are in my head," she said out loud in disbelief.

"*I am.*" The Dragon form of Kellian's body shook as if he was stretching a long-needed muscle. She wasn't fully surprised at this, since the other Dragons could mind-speak, but this felt different, as if a thread of the soulbond itself.

"*How would I stay on without Rider's gear?*" she asked, confused.

"*I won't let you fall,*" he said simply. His wings rose and slowly came back down, the wind whipping at her again.

"Okay," she said, slightly uncertain and walked towards his massive leg.

"Just climb up," Kellian said in her mind, amusement lacing his words.

"Yes, that looks very easy." She shot him a playful glare and began climbing. With some effort she situated herself on the back of the Dragon.

"Ameline and I have not flown yet, she is still too young," Kyeria said, feeling the nerves settle.

"Then think of this as practice," Kellian replied. His voice in her head made chills erupt on her skin. It felt so deeply personal, and her magic swelled at the feeling, accepting it happily.

"Practice," she muttered to herself. "Seems easy enough."

"Hold on tight," Kellian said before his massive wings began to move. He took off gently and slowly. She held on as tight as she could, horns placed in the perfect spot for her hands to wrap around and hold onto.

"Have you ever had someone do this before?" she asked silently, projecting her thoughts to him as she had done with Fendiah in the past.

"Never," he replied, his tone thick. Adrenaline shot through her as he picked up speed. They were not too high above the castle, gliding towards the mountains. She could see a few castle attendees and guards walking the grounds, and they looked so small from up so high. The light in two of the towers was bright, candles burning even in the windows. Kyeria found the red glow of a lower tower window and knew it was Esmeralda in her workshop. She smiled at the thought.

They flew past the castle, and into the Ash Mountains. Gliding over the lower peaks, Kellian flew higher and higher, Kyeria's heart picking up speed alongside the height.

"There's the lake, where I saw you for the first time." His words broke through her racing heart beat, immediately calming her. Below them was a great and glimmering lake, surrounded by mountain rocks and the mouths of caves. She smiled at the memory.

Flying was the most freeing thing Kyeria had ever experienced. Seeing the world from such a high vantage point was surreal. They only flew for a few minutes, Kellian insisting that he didn't want to go too high without a rider's seat for Kyeria. After Kellian landed, she climbed off of him and he shifted back into human form. His smile was so broad and bright it was blinding. He reached out an arm and tugged her to him, kissing her deeply.

"Your highness! Your highness!" A flutter of light bursted towards them. Kyeria recognized Ember from her rosy glow in the night.

"Ember, are you alright?" she asked immediately.

"Oh yes! But um—" She paused. Kellian placed a hand lazily on Kyeria's waist, holding her to him, sending a chill through her.

"Lady Esmeralda sent me! It's about that beast!" Ember shook her head as if disapproving of the existence of said beast.

"Tell us." Kellian's expression sobered.

"She said she found a potion recipe in one of the ancient texts that can make one's power stronger. If Aura's light can be amplified, then no darkness should survive it."

"Where is Esmeralda?" Kyeria asked after her gaze darted to Kellian. If they could finally rid the land of this shadow beast, then they could work to restore the magical barrier, to keep the mountains and sacred land safe.

"There's another message," Ember whispered. Kyeria nodded her on. "Aura has left."

"What?" Kellian's voice boomed. Kyeria's arm reached out to steady him.

"What do you mean, Ember? Why?" Kyeria's voice was even and sure.

"There are raiders, your majesty. On the eastern border of the Dragonier Forest. She had gone to protect the border."

"Of fucking course she did. Not bothering to tell anyone."

"She told me!" Ember spoke up, little hands on her glowing waist.

"Did Aura have anyone with her?" Kyeria asked.

"Obviously," Kellian sighed, running a hand through his wind blown hair. Kyeria looked to him then spoke in her mind, wondering if he could still hear her in human form.

"Care to share what that means?"

He cleared his throat, a look of shock passing his face for only a sliver of a moment before he said out loud, "Nox would be with her, or he would be defying direct orders."

"Kel–" Kyeria's voice turned soft, worrying for her friend. "What orders?"

"He's her personal guard." Kellian waved it off like this secret was nothing. Not knowing of the feelings Aura was obviously harboring for Nox, how she spent all her free time training with that one specific high guard. Aura only thought him in charge of her training. She thought he enjoyed going with her tracking. She had confided such in Kyeria.

"She doesn't know this," Kyeria stated rather than ask.

"No," Kellian said, face steeling. "We must go get more information from Esmie about this potion." He dropped his hand from her waist and began walking away. Kyeria spun on her heel, shocked at his dismissal, and looked to Ember who only shrugged.

"Do you know the way they went? Which path?" Kyeria asked the light sprite.

"Yes Miss, I can take you." She smiled, knowing that was exactly what Kyeria intended to do.

"Meet me in the training court in a few minutes." Kyeria nodded and ran after Kellian.

"You think a potion will be the key to all of this?" Kyeria asked, slowing to match his pace. Kellian nodded but did not answer.

"We have had more border issues in the last year than we have had in decades. The border is shrinking and the Evanthians are traveling farther and farther into the Hollow territory. The magic of this land seeping into theirs, the ramifications of something like that—" He paused. "It is unknown and it is powerful, and not something Evanthia should ever have. Not with the Mad King on the throne, and certainly not fueling their land. He had witches on his council, while magic might be outlawed in those lands, your own kind hunted if found, he had his own."

Kyeria lost her footing, tripping over her own feet at the information.

"He—" she stuttered. "The Mad King has those of magical descent? In his court?"

"No—not his court." His eyes dropped to the stone floor as they crossed the doorway into the castle. "They are not free, they are under his every will and whim."

"Kellian—" she gasped. "How do you know this?"

"We have spies in the court." Kellian shrugged, again like this was simple unimportant information.

"Goddess Above, the Mad King, the one that this very place is protected against has enslaved fae and witches and Goddess knows what else?" She was yelling now. "And you haven't done a thing about it?"

"It's not that simple, Kyeria." He was too calm for this.

"Of course it is!" she yelled back. "Those are my people, Emeralda's people, *your* people."

"I have a plan in place," he said, stopping and turning to her, "but the borders shrinking puts that plan in jeopardy. The kingdom cannot have resources split right now. We are doing everything we can to get them out, and we have aids in place to keep them as safe as possible given the circumstances. Kyeria, my love, I will go to the ends of this earth for my people." His voice was steady and stern. The confidence eased Kyeria's worries a fraction, but she spent the rest of the walk to Esmeralda's potion room rambling off questions.

She learned that about five years ago, Kellian found out that the Mad King of Evanthia had stolen three witches, two fae women, and a guard from the Hollow itself. They had been on a small materials trip to the small western Evanthian villages, to visit some of the witches who lived in the woods. They had their own magical barrier, weak compared to the one that guards the Hollow, but enough to avert the gaze of passerbyers. Unless they were looking directly at the house, they could not see it. The house had been surrounded by so many trees it was nearly a maze to get to it. But raiders found them out and accepted an egregious amount of gold in return for outing the witches to the royal guard who brutally took them all into custody. A light sprite had been notified and followed them. A group of the light sprites sneak messages back and forth now, keeping Kellian informed. It is nearly impossible to penetrate the Evanthian castle, but Kellian has a knight there undercover.

While most of the walk was filled with this information reveal, the last minute was a swollen silence. Kyeria tried to put together all the pieces, trying to figure out what could be done to get them out. She could not imagine what the past five years had been like for them, trapped in enemy territory.

Once they arrived at Esmeralda's room, they found her hunched over a glass jar, buried between glowing potion bottles, golds and green and purples and blues, some looking like they were mid-movement, others were as dark as an angry sea.

"Esmie," Kyeria greeted. She popped up, nearly knocking over the glass bottle in front of her, a small spoon in her hand dripping with translucent liquid.

"Oh!" she startled, her dark curls were tied back haphazardly. Her long golden earrings in place and her red robes with half burned sleeves.

"Are you alright?" Kellian asked zeroing in on the sleeves, his gaze sweeping over her for any damage, but her dark skin was unmarked, and free of any burns.

"Oh yes! I just mixed up a potion earlier! Put in the fire leaf instead of lyre leaf!" She waved around a deep red leaf. "They look nearly identical and I must've forgotten to label the jars the last time I was foraging for the pair," she explained, wiping her forehead and leaving soot behind.

"Ember found us."

"Oh thank the gods, I sent her over an hour ago!" she exclaimed.

"We were busy," Kellian said simply, making Kyeria's cheeks flush.

"Did you hear Aura ran off too? That girl, sometimes I swear she just jumps into action before even telling anyone, I only caught her in full armor as she passed my door." Esmie looked rather concerned, her brow was furrowed and the bags under her eyes were more evident then Kyeria had noticed in the past.

"Ember said something about a potion?" Kyeria asked gently.

"Oh! Yes." Esmeralda spun and dug through the sky high cabinets behind her, pushing aside journals and scraps of paper before moving to two other piles and a grey leather bound book with gold embellished writing on the front was in her hands. She cleared room on the table and opened it.

"Here, this is an old edition of the Winter Witches Magic Helms, one that has since been rewritten by someone maybe two decades ago, but this original version dates back to when the magical barrier was put in place, during the Dragon Queen's rule." She pointed to a sketch of a beast and the small writing next to it.

"Here." She tapped the golden and worn page. "When they were first creating the borders, forming the magic and connecting the pieces around the Hollow, they encountered a being that fed off the magic. As the border is many pieces intertwined, they had to build it in stages, and the beast was eating away at it. It is said to have taken on a shadow-like form, growing larger and darker. Giving off a dreary cold feeling when near. Consuming the magic into itself and draining the land under its feet. They mixed two rather common potions together but added in a Merstone gifted to them by a friend, which made the potion change entirely. Thus giving the user of the potion an unlimited amount of amplification of their magic. I think, based on how the Beast reacts to Aura's magic, that if hers is amplified, it would ultimately destroy the beast. The light burns away the magic the beast has consumed, and it will wither away back to harmless shadows." She snapped the book closed when she was finished reading. "So all we need is a Merstone," she announced.

"And what is a Merstone?" Kyeria asked.

Kellian huffed. "Only a rare gemstone that must be gifted by a mermaid of the isles. One stolen will curse your family for generations, and one taken under persuasion will either kill or deeply injure you. It can only be given of free will and good intentions." His voice was rather annoyed for finding out the solution for a beast plaguing his kingdom.

"And?" Kyeria pushed.

"And requesting an audience with a mermaid is not exactly easy." He rested his arms on the table as he leaned over it to point at a map next to them. "We are here." He tapped the forest and mountains and a green area to the west of them. "The isles are here." He tapped just north, where many small islands scattered across the northwest side of the map.

"West," Kyeria whispered. There were other islands charted, a large one to the far west on its own. She pointed. "These are the fae lands." It was unmarked on the map, only a sketching of the mainland.

"Where are you from?" Esmeralda gazed at her in wonder. She turned, picked up a pen and tipped it in ink. "The fae lands?" she confirmed, and Kyeria nodded and watched as Esmie wrote the title in stunning script on the unnamed island.

"Do you have ships?" Kyeria asked, eyeing Kellian. They were not near the ocean. A large body of water lay southwest, but the northern seas were a trek away from her understanding.

"No." Kellian shook his head. "But I know someone who does—who owes me a favor." He smirked. "To the isles then?" he asked, eyes gleaming with anticipation towards Kyeria.

"And Aura?"

"As long as Nox is with her, she will be well," he said simply. Kyeria scowled.

"I will send Ember to check on them. If they need reinforcements, they will be able to get to them quickly."

"Send them now," Kyeria insisted.

"The soldiers?" Kellian's brow rose.

"Yes," she said firmly.

"As you wish." He smiled. "Pack your bags, my love, we are going on a quest."

"I'll pack you some essentials," Esmie announced, fluttering around her workshop and grabbing handfuls of leaves, salves, and a few potions.

"Make sure you keep this one dry," she started, holding up each resource while she explained to Kyeria. "These leaves when wet can be placed over a wound. This potion will make you invisible for an hour. This one is a healing elixir and will numb pain and quicken your healing. I only have one made, so use it *only* if necessary."

Kyeria nodded along, making mental notes on all the information. Emseralda piled them together and pulled out a red velvet pouch to stow them inside. "Keep this close to you," she said firmly.

"Please be safe," Esmeralda said, squeezing Kyeria's hand as she passed over the small bag of magic.

"Always." Kyeria smiled and squeezed her hand back.

CHAPTER 14
Kellian

Kellian found Ember on the training grounds. He beckoned her over to explain the new mission and told her to go check on Aura and Nox, and send other royal messenger sprites to get reinforcements as well. She nodded happily, asked about Kyeria—whom Kellian promised was okay—and then went on her way.

Kellian made his way back to his rooms. The moon was high in the sky and it was well past midnight. He found a large traveling bag and filled it with some clothes, a warm blanket, supplies, and other necessities. He then headed to the kitchens to get three days worth of rations for their trek to last through the land before they would reach any water. He sent another light sprite with a message, to a Captain Grim, the High privateer of all the seas in the northern waters and beyond, to ready passage for them. Kellian cursed himself for needing to contact Grim.

Grim ruled with an iron fist, an the illusive pirate lord of the black tide fleets that ran the trades and dark markets across all the seas. Many had never even seen his face. He was untouchable from the kingdoms— they even paid him to keep the passages open for trade. His fleet was well over the hundreds now, fully manned by those of the Nivarian Island, or most commonly called The Pirate Rock. Kellian had known Grim since childhood, as he too was from The Hollow. It was a lifetime ago now and Kellian shook off the memories.

A knock hit his door, a soft tap in a melodic pattern. *Kyeria.*

"Ready to go, your highness?" Kyeria smirked. A matching leather bag hung on her shoulder, weighing her small frame down. Kellian reached and slipped the bag off her arm and whispered, "I told you, I'd follow you anywhere." His breath tickled her cheek and a blush grew over them. She took her fingers and drew his chin towards her, kissing him deeply.

"Where you go, I go." She nodded, filling him with a sense of calm.

"We will take horses, one each, and travel to the outer edge of the Hollow until we hit the sea. It is a day's journey to hit water," he explained.

"Alright." Kyeria turned and began walking away. Kellian admired her ability to greet any challenge with her head held high. Kyeria wore brown trousers and a dark leather corset lined with golden leaves embroidery. He wondered if she had added that herself. Long sleeves covered her arms, which still bore the remnants of the burns. A heavy wool cloak rested in her arms. He was glad for her knowledge of living in the woods, and being on foot. While he tried not to think about those hard years on the run, he admired who she was now because of them. How strong and unflinchingly sure.

"How is the wind tonight?" he asked, falling into step with her. Her bright smile reached him quickly.

"No warnings in the north," she confirmed after a minute of silence once they reached the steps outside. They walked to the training grounds, meeting a stablehand. Kellian's horse was as black as the night sky, with a dark mane to match. Kyeria's was a very sturdy brown mare. He had requested one of the strongest riders for her, not taking any chances.

"We will need to travel through the night. The Northern Gates are a bit different than other parts of the border," Kellian informed Kyeria as they mounted the horses.

"How so?" she asked, receiving a smile from Kellian and knowing eyes.

"You'll love it," he assured her.

They rode for hours through the night, letting the silence envelope them. Only the wind and the trees shuffled alongside them, Kyeria smiling here and there in reaction to them. He wondered what it must be like to be so attuned with nature the way she was. While Kellian held the ability to take the form of a dragon, he held no other magic. From the first time he shifted, he wished his ability to conjure fire would translate to his true self.

The sun had not broken the horizon yet, but the sky was brightening as they approached the Northern Gates. He knew the timing was perfect. Right as the sun broke over the horizon, golden light gleamed towards them, then the gate—seemingly invisible without the light of dawn—was aglow. Golden spires twisted in all directions, forming an arch. A purple bloom was sprouting—so rare, it only bloomed where magic touched that specific border of The Hollow.

Kyeria gasped, her hand rested on her chest as her gaze bore into the gate, taking in every detail. She dismounted her horse and fell to her knees, both hands palm down into the grass. Kellian chuckled and dismounted next to her.

"This—this is wondrous." She beamed. "The magic here, it is so bright and full," she said, looking up to him. She brushed her hands off and stood.

"These flowers," she began reaching for them, her finger barely touching a petal and the color changed to a bright blue.

"They are the flowers of the dawn, the Aura flower. Is this your sister's namesake? I had read about them but never seen them. My mother would tell us stories of flowers that only bloomed at dawn that held a form of magic in them, but in person—" She paused her stream of consciousness.

"My mother," Kellian began, clearing his throat, "she was given the seeds, after a happenstance, the witch told her to plant them where all the light of dawn could reach them unrestricted, and that if any magic need be strengthened it could be planted near." A ghost of a smile passed his lips. " When my mother worked to put the magic border in place, to protect the Hollow from the surrounding wars, she planted this one at the farthest border, one that reached towards the ocean, so that we may not be in danger from attacks on the northern side."

Kyeria took his hand, squeezing once, then twice, then a third time.

"You have yet to speak much about her," Kyeria replied.

"She was the most selfless woman I have ever known. I am proud to be her son," Kellian stated, squaring his shoulders. "We must go now, while the dawn light hits the gates is the only time we can pass it on foot."

Kyeria reached for the reign of her horse, and began walking into the gate, Kellian behind. The usual cool touch of magic brushed past Kellian as he passed through after Kyeria. He shook off his shoulders gently, then remounted his horse. Kyeria followed suit. They rode for a short amount of time before resting for lunch. Tying the horses to a nearby tree, they sat on a higher spot, overlooking the grassy meadows and beyond was the sparkling sea.

"We will rest here, Grim will be here at dusk." Kellian pulled out food from his pack, and they ate. Kyeria spoke of her mother more, moving Kellian to speak of his own more freely. He had loved his mother, but her death was difficult for him to speak of. He wished he could talk to her, wished she wasn't taken so young alongside his father, wished Aura had known them as she grew.

"What is bothering you still?" Kyeria asked as the sun sank lower, the day pressing on. He leaned back, pulling her to him and kissing the side of her head. She let out a small laugh, nuzzling into him. Her small hand pressed on his chest, finding a necklace laying there.

"When did you get this?" she asked.

"It is a family symbol." He flipped it over in his hand, an intricate design with a raven in the middle stood raised off the golden pendant.

"That is not the Galanis symbol." She shook her head as her thumb brushed over the raven.

"No, my mother's." He smiled sadly. Her hand reached up, cupping his rough stubbled cheek. He leaned into it. His eyes opened golden and bright and he was about to speak when a shriek cut through the trees, Kyeria jolted up.

"*Are we past the magical barrier?*" Kyeria asked through the bond.

"*Yes,*" Kellian answered and stood slowly, reaching for his sword. It was a twin to Aura's but even larger, a golden gemstone in the hilt, signifying the Galanis line. Kyeria pulled a short sword from her back, using her other arm to pat her leg ensuring her daggers were in place.

"Get behind me," Kellian ordered. They stayed low, but the fire and the horses were a giveaway, they could not pretend they were not here, not now.

Shadows moved through the trees, Kyeria pushed out her magic like a web, sensing three sources.

"*I count three,*" she informed him down the bond. Kellian nodded up towards the far trees, she saw another, high up in the trees, something glimmered. Four, then.

Then with a shove she yelled at Kellian, "Get down!" Arrows flew through the air. Kyeria was so shocked she barely rushed her arm up to block the arrow with a dense screen of vines. She let it crash back into the ground then took a fighting stance, short sword out, and glimmering magical vines wrapping around her other arm.

She felt a presence slightly behind her and with a swish she grabbed the dagger at her thigh and spun, launching the dagger. The dagger hit its target, a grunt and a curse before a woman revealed herself.

Raiders.

She was dressed in raiders clothes, mismatched armor and clothing, and stolen goods.

"You bitch!" the raider screamed and lunged for her. Kyeria swung again and blocked a hit with her sword. She threw her magic, vines exploding from the ground and wrapping around her ankles.

"Good try." Kyeria smirked, and walked forward, unarming the woman and leaving her tied up in thick vines. She could hear Kellian fighting off what felt like two men. She stalked forward, around a tree, keeping to the shadows. And just as she was about the lung forward towards one of the raiders, a hand wrapped around her neck, covering her mouth before she could scream.

"Not so fast, missy," a man hummed, slamming her against the tree.

"Let her go," Kellian boomed. His voice was unrecognizable, filled with fury. She had seen Kellian fight, she had seen him train, delegate, and rule, but this, this was different.

"You better pray to all your gods, because I will end you if you so much as leave a single mark on my woman." His voice was feral, growling even. Kyeria's eyes were wide.

"Behind you!" she screamed down the bond as another man advanced on him. Kellian spun, their swords only meeting each other twice before Kellian struck him down. Kyeria tried to use her magic but the man holding her quickly pinned both her hands with one of his. Holding them down. She had to have her hands to cast. She bit down hard on the hand over her mouth. The man cursed and his hand fell. She spit out the piece of flesh from his hand. It always was an effective way to get an unwanted man off of oneself. She smirked to herself,

unsheathed another dagger and sliced at him. But the man was faster and slashed her side; she let out a guttural sound before falling.

"Careful now, miss," the raider snarled and grabbed her again, holding her back to him, a knife on her throat. Kellian froze, the two men he had been fighting were down, lifeless crumples onto the ground, their blood seeping into the earth. While her face stayed blank, Kellian could feel an icy tendril down the bond from his soulbound. Knowing it was the loss of life and the earth's reaction causing the coldness to wash over her.

"Move another step," the raider growled, "and I'll slit her throat."

"I'd like to see you try," Kellian snarled. Kyeria had been working her hands free, slipping one off and shoving at the man. He let out a grunt, but her attempt was futile, the wound on her side was deep and not healing fast enough. She tried to spin out of his grip, slashing her body. She screamed out, bit down on his arm, and the man squirmed under her.

"You're a feisty little thing, huh, lass?" the raider snarled in her ear.

"I want your horse, your gold, and your bags," the raider announced.

"Fuck you," Kellian spit out.

"Or your lass here will bleed out on the grass." His grip tightened and Kyeria let out a gasp at the air being squeezed out. She couldn't breath, her eyes were watering as his grip became tighter and tighter wrapped around her neck.

"Fine," Kellian spoke loudly and dropped his sword to the ground. The raider's grip loosened and Kyeria coughed, her lungs on fire. Kellian saw red. He wanted to rip the man to shreds for laying a hand on her. On what was his.

"See we can be civil after all," the man said. "Stand over there," he instructed Kellian and dragged Kyeria with him, knife cutting at her skin, a thin trail of blood left behind. She winced at the stinging pain.

The raider turned his back, but Kyeria kept her eyes on Kellian. She shook her head at him, signaling him. But his eyes, once golden, were black. His features contorted. Fury overtaking every essence of his body,

He moved so fast Kyeria gasped. She had never seen any human move like that, but Kellian was closer to fae than human, he was stronger and faster, could see farther and hear farther.

The raider's grip was off her and he was on the ground in less than the time it took her to blink. Kellian plunged the sword down his neck. He pulled the sword free, his wild eyes found hers, and slowly the black haze faded and she was greeted again with the gold she loved so much.

"Are you alright?" he said, his voice raw.

"Yes," she whispered back. He nodded and wiped his sword on a spare piece of fabric before placing it back in its holder again.

"I—" she started, but Kellian pulled her to him. His large hand pressed the back of her head, holding her there.

"You're okay," he muttered. She dipped her head into the crook of his neck, letting out a sigh as the scent of him washed over her. She pulled away, eyes searching his and leaned forward kissing him, both hands on either side of his face. But the moment was cut short when an awful screech filled the air, making Kyeria jump and spin around.

But Kellian knew that awful squawk anywhere.

A large black raven was diving directly at them.

"Hello Lucius." Kellian glared at the black eyed raven.

"Time to go." The raven's voice sounded like the shadow of death, deep and awful. It never sat well with Kellian.

"Who are you?" Kyeria sat up, getting closer to the wretched creature. Kellian placed a hand on her arm to stop her. "You are not alive," she stated, head turning as she analyzed the creature,

"Quite right Ma'am, but rather rude I must say." Luci's eyes narrowed. "Who are you?" The words were strung out, sounding like creaking wood, but Lucius' head turned as well, matching Kyeria's.

"You are not of this land," Lucius squawked.

"No, I am from the fae lands," she said, brushing her hair back and revealing her pointed ears.

"Yes," the raven replied, looking as thoughtful as a bird could possibly look. "We must leave now. Follow me." And he took off into the sky. Kellian sighed deeply.

"I fucking hate that bird," he announced as a squawk reeled in the distance. Good, he hoped that damned bird heard him.

"It is not a bird," Kyeria said, watching it circle them high above in the sky. "It is most definitely not a bird." She shuttered, and Kellian had half a mind to sweep her up and ride back to the castle, abandoning the mission all together. Just wrap his arms around her and stay there, not worry about anything else.

While Kellian packed up their small camp, Kyeria walked around picking some flowers, wrapping them in a long vine and pocketing them. She then reached out her hand on a tree, it shook in response to her magic. Lucius flew out of it sounding annoyed. It brought Kellian deep enjoyment.

"Watch it, witch," Lucius screeched.

"I am no witch." Kyeria glared. Her voice was stone. "I am derived from the goddess Luna herself. I honor all living things and *you* are not living."

"I am living-adjacent," Lucius said, landing on a rock.

"What are you?" Kyeria sounds angry, like seeing something that was basically made of death itself went against everything she knew and honored.

"You shall see," the bird chirped. The raven drew its wings again. "Time to go."

Kellian cleared his throat.

"Something is wrong with that raven," Kyeria said to him, taking the reins to her horse out of his hands with some force.

"Oh I know," Kellian muttered to himself. They rode their horses down the hills and across another meadow, getting closer and closer to the sea. Lucius screamed from above as they went. *Kellian really hated that fucking bird.*

They came around one last bend of trail before a steep cliff was between them and the sand below. A scarcely skinny path lay there big enough for one person, but no horse. Kellian rolled his eyes, taking his and Kyeria's bags down and rolled the reins up into their saddles.

His voice boomed. "Go home," he said and his hand whipped in the air making both the horses take off in a gallup back the way they came.

Kyeria stood at the small path looming ahead of them. She squared her shoulders, pulled her cloak tighter against the harsh winds, and began to walk. Kellian did the same. Twin bags crossed over his back. Doing his best to focus on Kyeria and not the raven circling them from above. Kellian had already zeroed in on the small ship sitting not too far off the shore. An even smaller raft in the sand, the shore crashing near it. A dark figure in the shadows under the cliff side.

Grim.

He was sure Kyeria could sense him. Magic meeting magic would unceremoniously make.

"Captain Grim?" she asked, letting her voice drift on the wind as she walked the sand. Grim pushed himself off the rock he was leaning on and slowly walked towards them. The swagger of a pirate lord and too much confidence. Lucius circled before flying down and landing on Grim's shoulder.

"Hello, my Lady." He bowed his head slightly and held out a hand. She shook it and pulled it away, reaching into her pockets for the bundle of wild flowers she had collected. She held it out in her palm.

Lucius made a soft noise, the only soft noise Kellian had ever heard the bird utter in the long years of knowing him.

Grim slowly smiled, his dark features, shaggy dark hair, black as night eyes and tanned skin from living aboard a ship stared back at Kyeria.

"You are fae?" he asked, gazing back at her after looking at the flowers.

"I am." She nodded. "As you are," she announced. Grim bristled. Kellian of course knew this fact, but it was a closely guarded secret of Grims.

"You—" he started.

"I can feel the magic of Hades on you," she explained. He nodded and opened his own palm. Shadows erupted from it, small tendrils of it, they weaved into the air around him and towards the flowers. They tickled her palm and while Kellian would have retracted his hand, Kyeria simply smiled.

"An ancient offering of peace." Grim's voice was deep and gravel-filled. The flowers dissipated into the shadow tendrils and dissipated.

"Is he your familiar?" Kyeria asked, nodding to the raven on his shoulder. Grim nodded, eyes dark.

"Yes," he replied. Kellian knew of them only through stories. It was rare, but in old tales fae from the fae lands, commonly the wild fae, would be able to conjure a familiar. A piece of one's soul or being projected into an animal of any form. Grim's was a raven, its feathers the exact hue of his hair.

Kellian cleared his throat, his eyes were narrowed on Grim. And Grim turned slowly to him, meeting his eyes, head held high.

"Brother," Grim greeted Kellian. He could feel Kyeria stiffen next to him.

"Grimwald," Kellian said lowly.

"Gods, do not call me by that name."

"It is the name our mother picked," Kellian shot back.

"Goddess rest her soul, dear brother, but it would be Captain Grim."

"I am not calling you that."

They stood in a standoff, eyes fiercely glaring. Kyeria watched them, even Lucius was silent.

"Would you like a passage to the Isles and an audience with a princess of the sea or would you prefer a long walk back to your stone castle?" Grim looked fierce, shadows trickled from his fingers, as if coming directly from the tattoos that covered his forearm and hands.

Kellian knew better.

"Fine, Grim." He conceded.

"Good enough." Grim smirked and turned an easy smile on Kyeria. Kellian's clenched fit twitched, wanting to punch his idiot brother right there.

"After you, my lady." Grim held out a hand, Kellian cursed at him and side stepped him to be next to Kyeria. He has one of those glimmering sneaky looks like he did when they were young. Kellian and Grim were not, however, raised together. Grim was the child of his mothers by one of her courtesans. It was no secret that his parents had them. They chose time together and apart but after producing a legitimate heir to the kingdom, things shifted. Grim was younger than Kellian but older than Aura. It was no surprise that Grim was not of the Galanis line, with his dark hair and features in direct contrast to Kellian and Aura's pale skin, white hair, and golden eyes.

Grim was raised by his father in a far away village. They had met a few times through the years but Grim was harsh by the way he was raised. And while Kellian hadn't seen his brother in some years, he seemed rather the same; a sly confidence radiating off him, with questionable intentions. Perhaps hardened by the years at sea but still full of his dark light, eager to be an annoyance to Kellian.

They piled into the small raft and Grim and Kellian paddled them toward the small ship. The dark banner of the black tide fleet flew in the wind. A raven drawn in the middle. Lucius flew off ahead and sat on the edge of the ship. Few crewmen wandered the boat pulling a string and odd ends Kellian had no interest in. But what stood out instead was a woman. Kellian knew Grim did not employ many women, only those he trusted entirely. Whichever few and far between. She was wearing a loose flowing white shirt and brown trousers, high boots, and a long sword was strapped to her back, her dark hair blew in the wind and she sat on the edge of the ship where Lucius had landed. But it wasn't until Kellian watched her reach out and *pet* Lucius that Kellian was in utter and complete disbelief.

"Who the hel is that?" Kellian asked and Grim groaned.

"Only another favor-owed freeloader." He cursed under his breath and pushed the paddles harder into the water. Kyeria sat with her head tilted up and out looking over the water, the wind sweeping her hair back. Her red hair was even brighter surrounded by the grey sea. He was in awe of her. Her beauty and grace.

"*You look beautiful.*" He pushed the thought out to her. She turned suddenly and smiled back.

"*You're not so bad yourself, Prince.*" She smirked. He loved and hated her calling him by royal names.

"*So brother, huh?*" Her eyebrow was raised.

"*My mother's son. He's very different,*" he warned. Kyeria nodded, giving him a look that said *tell me later.*

Grim let out a grunt. "Please tell me he's not using that weird head-talking method of communication." He looked to Kyeria. A blush creeped up her cheeks and she shook her head.

"Gods, help me." Grim glared at the water ahead. They boarded quickly after that, the woman helped tie up the raft to the side of the ship before her hips swung towards Grim and she muttered something to him before he glared back.

"This is Inaya," he said simply. No last name indicated. *Interesting.*

"Pleased to meet you." Kellian nodded his head in greeting. "I am Kellian and this is Kyeria."

"An honor to meet the dragon prince." Inaya curtsied then turned to Kyeria. "Hello," she said brightly.

Kyeria smiled gently in turn, ever unsure of new people. Grim made an announcement to his crew and then dismissed himself. Inaya and Kyeria wandered to another part of the ship, leaving Kellian standing alone looking out back to his homeland. He let his mind wander for a bit, sending a prayer to the goddess to watch over his sister. A squawk interrupted his thoughts next to him—Lucius.

"What?" He glared.

"You've grown rather testy in your old age," Lucius said.

"I am not old," Kellian retorted.

"Older than the captain. So old."

"Fuck off bird." He seethed.

"Suit yourself, princeling." The bird let out another screech before flying away.

Kyeria stood on the deck of a small but decadent ship next to a dark haired woman who was deeply intimidating. Near the steer stood Grim, deeply glowering in Inaya's direction. The ship's crew moved swiftly around them and Kyeria felt the lurch of the ship pushing into action.

Inaya glanced to Kyeria, "You'll get used to it." She said it gently, a vivid stark difference from her dark eyes and intimidating glower that matched Grim's. Inaya's features softened looking to Kyeria.

"Have you been on a ship before? Shadow boy over there mentioned most people from where you're from do not leave the land." The light was cresting the mountains and the morning glow was illuminating. Kyeria could feel the warmth on her back, the light catching Inaya's eyes, making her darkened eyes show their true color, rich golden specks surrounded by a brown as deep as chocolate.

"I have." Kyeria nodded, playing with the strands of her copper hair. "But not since I was a child." She looked past Inaya to the sea. "I am from an island in the far west."

"I gathered, shadow boy has been rather cagey about sharing information, but the ears gave it away." Kyeria laughed at Inaya's perpetual dismissal of the pirate lord.

"I take it you two do not get along." Kyeria smirked. Inaya met her with a loud roll of her eyes and a wave of her hand.

"I despise him." She glared up the deck of the ship, Kyeria peered over and Grim still had his eyes trained on the horizon, but she swore she felt them baring into her back only a moment before.

"He despises me as well, and all is right in the world. He's simply my ride." She began walking the deck, Kyeria following by her side.

"I'll show you your room if you need to rest." She sent Kyeria another soft smile.

"I hear you are searching for a Merstone?" Inaya questioned. Kyeria paused, unsure about why she was asking such a specific question.

"We are," Kyeria simply said, but fixed her gaze forward. The energy shifted and Inaya remained silent, guiding them below deck.

"Grim has very few quarters so this one will be for you and Kellian." She nodded forward, the door was ajar and light streamed through it. A large banister bed sat in the middle of it, a table to the right under a window that looked out beyond. She could see the waves crashing and splashing against the window. And Kyeria's gaze fixed back on the *one* large bed. She nodded her thanks and Inaya left her to her thoughts. She glided away, her footsteps near silent. She seemed to find the shadows wherever she went, easily slipping from sight down the walk. Kyeria watched her curiously until she shut the door.

She let herself collapse on the bed. Her body was exhausted from the trek through the woods and northern gate. She had never been to the isles and excitement pumped through her veins, magic under her skin buzzed. She didn't like being on the ocean surrounded by water and not land. But the ocean itself had a magic. She could sense the vast abyss under them and on all sides. She could feel life here, the ocean harboring so much of it.

Her thoughts were interrupted by the door creaking open. A mass of white hair tangled from the sea breeze and the large frame of Kellian came into view. His body took up the doorway, and she smiled. He looked too large to be in a small underdeck chamber room.

"Why hello." She bit her lip.

"Hello." His voice was gravel filled, golden eyes sharp.

"This is our room," he stated rather than ask.

"This is our room," she repeated. Slowly she untied her cloak. He walked to her, taking it and hanging it on a hood on the back of the door. He reached out, his hands trailing along her collar bone and pushing aside the fabric of her shirt. There was no mistaking the hunger in Kellian's eyes. She reached down and began to unlace her boots but a hand stopped her, clasping gently and yet firm on her wrist. He knelt to the ground below her, thrill shot through her very limbs. Kellian slowly undid her laced boots, taking one boot off gently then moving to the next. Then his hand trailed on her skin, pushing up her skirts. Golden eyes met hers, his touch was burning and her magic hummed in response.

A storm raged outside, its sudden ferocity reflected in the creaking timbers of the ship. The cabin was dimly lit by a single flickering lantern, its light casting trembling shadows that danced on the walls. The confined space felt even smaller with the tempest's howling wind seeping through the cracks, adding a sense of urgency to the charged atmosphere inside.

Kellian stood up and paced anxiously, his regal attire in disarray from the tumultuous journey.

His face was a mask of frustration and desire, each step echoing the turmoil within him. He paused by the edge of the bed, a large, imposing piece of furniture that took up most of the room, its simple wooden frame a stark contrast to the opulence of the prince's usual surroundings. Kyeria was seated on the edge of the bed, untying her copper braids and letting her hair pool around her shoulder. Her eyes seemed to shimmer with an anxious light, mirroring the turbulence of the storm outside.

"You can't keep doing this, Kel," Kyeria said, her voice strained but resolute. "Blaming yourself for that night"

Kellian's frustration boiled over as he whirled to face her, his gaze intense. "I know," he said, his voice a low growl. "But every time I look at you, I feel like I'm losing control. This—" he gestured between them, "—this is unbearable."

Kyeria's eyes flashed with a mix of anger and desperation. "Do you think I don't feel it too? Every glance, every touch... it's driving me mad. We're on the brink of this huge thing, of finally ridding the land of this beast, I wanted to help your kingdom, to pay my dues to you and your people. I should be focused on that, the mission. But I can't sleep, I can't think of anything but how all I want is to be close to you. But you're so far away Kel, you have been so detached."

The ship lurched suddenly, a jolt that sent both of them stumbling.

Kyeria's hand shot out to steady herself, landing on Kellian's chest, her touch sending a shiver through both of them. Their faces were mere inches apart now, the heat from their bodies mingling in the small space.

Kellian's breath quickened as he looked down at her, his hand coming up to cup her cheek. "I can't keep pretending this isn't happening," he said, his voice thick with emotion. "I want you, Ky. But I didn't want to push, after everything I just—I need you to know, you are the sun, guiding me always, my light that keeps me grounded."

Her breath caught in her throat, her eyes searching his face for any sign of doubt. Finding none, she closed the distance between them, her lips meeting his in a kiss that was both fierce and tender. The storm outside seemed to echo their emotions, the wind howling as if it too were caught up in their turmoil. As their kiss deepened, they stumbled back toward the bed. Kellian's hands roamed over her back, his touch sending waves of heat through her. Kyeria's fingers tangled in his hair, pulling him closer as their bodies pressed together. The bed felt like a haven amid the chaos of the storm. With a shared, breathless laugh, they fell onto the mattress, their movements a blend of urgency and unrestrained passion. Kellian's weight settled beside her, his hands exploring with a reverent touch. Kyeria's body arched into him, her body responding to every caress and kiss.

The confined space of the bed only seemed to heighten their connection, each touch and whisper amplified by their proximity. Kellian's lips traveled along her neck, his kisses leaving a trail of fire that made her gasp. Kyeria's fingers traced the lines of his jaw, her touch both delicate and demanding.

Outside, the storm continued to rage, a fierce reminder of the world they were leaving behind, their hidden kingdom that even Kyeria called home now. But below the deck of a ship, in their own chambers, they were lost in their own tempest, a whirlwind of emotion and desire that consumed them entirely. The only sound in the room was their shared breaths and the occasional creak of the ship as it battled the storm.

In that small, storm-battered cabin, with only one bed and the world outside in chaos, Kellian and Kyeria surrendered to the moment. They were bound together by more than just the confines of the bed; they were united by a powerful, undeniable connection that neither could deny any longer.

"Mine, you are mine, my love. Beyond our last breaths, beyond the farthest seas. I am yours, you are mine." Kellian whispered into her neck. She let her hand slide up his neck, pulling her lips to hers, and at that simple guidance, Kellian gave in. He slammed into her, like the waves against the ship, his arms wrapped around her, almost crushing her. But she didn't mind, she only wanted him closer. Her legs wrapped around him, and his hands drifted up so slowly to hold her face.

"Say it." His voice was almost raw, sending a shiver through Kyeria's very being.

"I'm yours," she gasped out as one hand traveled to her hair, wrapping around the copper strands. He tugged lightly, lighting chilled through her body as the storm crescendoed beyond their chambers. He groaned into her mouth. His teeth nipping her, and running down her jaw. His breath was hot on her skin, she wanted to dig in, stay in this moment forever. She slid her hands to his hair, his hips snapped forward. And he pulled her to him, their moans drowning out among the storm. Her hands pushed him down, their mouths parting in panting breaths. She let a contented smirk settle on her features, and gave his chest a small shove until he leaned back on the bed with a chuckle.

"Much better." Kyeria's voice was almost unfamiliar to herself. So sultry and unlike herself. But in this moment, in this space, she felt safe and cherished. She liked being in control, liked being devoured by his eyes alone. She pulled one leg over, straddling the white haired prince.

"Fuck." He groaned as her hands worked quickly. Clothes were thrown to the wayside, limbs intertwined. Kellian whispered praises in her ear as she took control.

"That's it." His voice pushed her on as she dragged her body down. "That's my girl."

Kyeria woke later to the sun high in the sky. They had fallen asleep easily. Kellian's fingers were tracing mindlessly on her back. Maybe she had been the only one to get rest.

"What is filling your mind?" she asked, tipping her chin up to him. He let out a deep long held sigh.

"How long has it been since you saw your brother?" she asked instead. He grunted in response. She knew he was more of a listener than the one who filled the silence. And while she was usually happy to fill that with her own thoughts, she worried. The permanent crease at his brow had persisted over the last two days.

"Years," Kellian replied, a frown deepening into the lines of his face, etching itself there in a seemingly permanent way.

"Kel–" her voice made her expression soften, he met her eyes, and leaned to kiss her forehead.

"Worry not, love," he assured her. "Grim and I can be cordial when needed. We just disagree on the morals and the thought that he can be in the wrong."

Kyeria only nodded in response, keeping her head on his chest and their legs intertwined. She wished they could stay like this forever. In that feeling of what she knew now was the soul bound, being content and happy. Breathing him in, she let her eyes close again. The feeling of his fingers trailing down her arms and back drawing circles and patterns all the way down.

The next time Kyeria woke was surrounded by blankets, a pillow under her head instead of Kellian's warm skin. There was shouting and the clanging of metal coming from somewhere. Disoriented, Kyeria rose and was met with the inside of the ship's bed chamber and not her room in the palace she had grown so accustomed to. She missed her fireplace and books, and Aura and Esmeralda having zero boundaries and bounding into her room every morning.

Instead, the bitter cold bit at her naked arms. She turned to see a grey sea, angry and viciously sloshing at the port window in the room. She rose quickly, dressed in her discarded clothes, tying her wool cloak tightly around her shoulders to fight off the cold.

She walked the creaking splintered wooden floors of the below deck and closed the stairs up to the top. Immediately a gust of wind so strong and filled with anger pushed her back, making her hand clap down on the railing with an iron grip.

"Careful Lass!" a crew man shouted out to her and leaned down, offering her a hand. She thanked the man and rose onto the ship's deck.

"We've hit a rather large storm," the man shouted over the wind. The ship rocking in the waves had her working to stabilize her feet.

"The captain is in that room there, better hurry before the next big set of waves comes crashing." The man pointed. A dim lantern glowed behind a fogged glass door. It must be the captain's quarter, she thought. She sent her magic into the air, asking for peace, it calmed only a fraction as she walked towards the dim light.

Then the ship rocked, pushing her into a wooden pillar nearby and knocking the air right out of her chest.

"Goddess above, what has angered you," she whispered to herself and pushed off the pillar. Two more wide steps and her hand wrapped around the cool metal doorknob, she thrust it open.

Entering with the gust of winds behind her she crashed into the quiet candle lit room. Grim and Inaya stood around a table with a map. Lucius was sitting by a grand fireplace and Kellian was sitting in a chair swatting away the bird. Kellian turned as she entered.

"Close the door before we all blow away in that god's forsaken wind," Grim commanded, still focusing on the map in front of him. She huffed and pushed the door shut with all her might, the lock snapping into place, and the room was again calm.

"Good morning, sunshine." Inaya sent a knowing look toward her.

"It's half past high sun." Grim's voice was dripping with irritation which was quickly followed by a wince and a sharp flare sent to Inaya who was next to him. "Watch it," he seethed through his teeth.

Inaya sent him a sickly smile. "My foot slipped."

"How did you sleep, love?" Kellian asked, walking over to her, his arm slipping around her waist and kissing the side of her forehead. Kyeria blushed and nodded. She was unused to this outward show of affection from Kellian. He was so reserved at the castle. She had an inkling of a feeling it had to do with Grim and Kellian's overly male need to assert what was his.

His.

Chills erupted on her arms despite the warm wool cloak. Remembering Kellian's heated words, "*Mine, you are mine, my love.*

Beyond our last breaths, beyond the farthest seas. I am yours, you are mine. "Kellian's gaze heated and he squeezed her hip,

"What are you thinking of?" he growled down her mind. Kyeria shivered, without sparing him a glance.

"That I am yours."

He squeezed harder on her hip and Kyeria fought to keep a straight face and not react. Inaya and Grim were too enraptured, annoying the other, to notice her or Kellian silently communicating.

"Well." Kellian cleared his throat. "Grim was showing us on the map where we are headed. Kellian pushed her forward towards the table gently, his hand sliding to her back. She noted how he kept himself touching her throughout the conversation. Grim pointed to spots on the brown stained map on the desk. Explained the isles, and how the Mermaid queen ruled under the Isles, and on the Golden Isle was were they could find one of the Merprincesses who knew Grim.

"And how do you know a Mer, let alone a princess?" Inaya pressed.

"I have connections across all the isles and kingdoms," he scoffed. Kyeria bit back a smile looking between the two of them.

"Of course you do, so well-connected, Captain." Her tone was dripping with sarcasm and Kyeria decided she liked Inaya then. She was strong and fierce and loved to annoy Grim, she reminded her of Aura. The refusal to listen to authority and annoyance to the man she was obviously infatuated with.

"Here," Grim pointed, "is where we will enter, the ocean is narrow between these rocks; this is why we will be using this ship, the Golden Maiden. She was built for the isles."

"Golden Maiden?" Inaya scoffed. "You did not name a ship that."

"I'll be sure to consult you next time I add to my fleet."

"Best you do, or else they'll all be shiny ladies," Kyeria quibbed. Kyeria couldn't hold back the laugh, it was throaty and deep. Inaya looked at her, eyes meeting her and a smile growing on her face.

"See?" Inaya pushed. "The two actual women here agree." She poked Grim in the chest. It was rather a comical scene. Inaya was half a head shorter than Kyeria and Grim was even taller than Kellian. At almost half his height, Inaya stood her ground, eyes fierce as her small finger poked Grim's large chest.

"Your boat's name is stupid," Inaya finished, with a devilish grin.

"It is a ship, Inaya." Grim sounded annoyed now, his words sighing out.

"Mmhmm, of course." She nodded.

The four of them ate dinner together in the captain's quarters. It was warm and fresh, much to Kyeria's surprise. The storm was settling outside, the ship no longer rocking back and forth under violent waves. But she could still hear the rain pattering on the glass door and deck above. By the time she and Kellian left, the rain picked up,

"Oh!" Kyeria shrieked as they were soaked. Kellian cursed and raised a hand over her head, blocking the rain from her face. She looked up, a blooming smile and stopped walking.

"Come on!" Kellian shouted over the rain and wind.

"Kiss me," Kyeria said, the rain running over her, hair drenched, clothes soaking through. He stood there, golden eyes bright. She repeated herself, "Kiss me, your highness."

That was enough to make Kellian move, one long stride and he was back at her side, hand running up her cheek into her hair.

"As you wish," he muttered before taking her breath away with a harsh kiss. Kellian kissed like it was a punishment. Harsh and hard and filled with so much emotion. Mornings were reserved for long and soft kisses. But nights, nights were theirs. He was holding himself back here in the open air of the deck. But no one was around and Kyeria pressed her body to his, Reaching for him and holding him to her, she kissed him back just as fiercely.

"Goddess above." Kellian pulled away, forehead pressing to hers. Rain falling on them. "What am I to do with you?"

Kyeria smirked, meeting his eyes lifting her chin. "Everything," she whispered.

"Fuck." His voice was deep and dark pulling her to him. They stumbled below deck. Their quarters were on the other side of the ship than the crews. Kellian threw their door open, pulling Kyeria through with him. Slamming it shut, his hand skated down her thighs and he lifted her, spinning them and pinning her against the closed door while her legs wrapped around his middle.

"Mine," he growled.

"Yours," Kyeria responded. It came out breathy and airy between the kisses, when his lips left her they trailed down her neck. He pulled them away from the door and turned, tossing her onto the bed.

"Take those wet clothes off," he commanded. She shivered, pulling off each article of clothing.

CHAPTER 16

Kellian

Kellian was a man possessed. Kyeria sat on the bed, devoid of clothing, looking as sweet as the honey of the southern edges of The Hollow. He was stunned by her beauty, her copper hair was falling loosely around her shoulders, long enough to waterfall over her curves.

"You are so beautiful." His voice came out raw. A blush creeped up her neck and cheeks and she began to shy away, to cover her stunning body. He felt a smirk growing, and shook his head.

"Don't you dare cover yourself." Her eyes were bridging on stubbornness, her emotions so plainly on her face. He loved that about her, wearing her emotions clearly, feeling everything so deeply. He had spent so much of his life learning how to even his emotions, to be calm. To use his face as a mask. But Kyeria, his Kyeria, sat on the bed, her cheeks red, eyes hungry.

"Lay back," he said. She listened immediately. "Give me your hands," he said softly, leaning over her, taking them and pinning them above her head. He held her by her wrists with one hand, the other drifted down her side, slowly, so slowly.

"Every piece of you must have been made by the goddess herself, you are utter perfection." His hand glided over the curve of her hips and he raised himself back up, dropping to his knees and taking what was his.

It took two nights to enter into the isles, another till the sun was half high when they arrived at the Golden Isle. Grim instructed them to stay below deck first, wanting to survey and enter the isles as only him and his crew, so as not to raise suspicion. The waters were calm as the ship navigated the narrow seaways between high rocks and the cliff sides of the isle. Kellian had read about the Golden Isle, flown over it even. But this close to it, it was mesmerizing. The cliff sides glimmered golden in the sun, covered in a golden gem that reflected the light between each rock and cliffside, illuminating the entire valley of sea in gold.

Kyeria and Inaya peered out a window. They had spent many of the hours Kellian and Kyeria were not holed up in their room together. Kyeria was quick to give her love to those who wandered. Inaya was a floating soul, like Kyeria had been. They both fostered such a great purpose for doing more than only the life that the gods and goddess had dealt to them.

Kellian stood, arms crossed leaning against the opposite wall, watching through a porthole below deck. His skin itched to fly through these lands. To shift and be fully free. Kyeria peered back at Kellian as if sensing his mood shift. He sent her a reassuring nod, notioning he was fine and she went back to whispering to Inaya and giggling together by the window.

"I've never seen anything like this." Kyeria motioned to the golden stones glowing on the cliff sides.

"I guess they named it the Golden Isle for a reason." Inaya shrugged. "I would love to take a few of those home with me though." She smirked.

"That would be a very bad idea," Kellian spoke up. "They are protected by the Goddess Lux, who watches over and blesses the isles, but it is told she had a special affinity for this Isle in particular and the Mer below them. Best not to anger her."

Inaya's eyes widened. "And rightly so. I did not know these were the Goddess Lux's lands." Inaya looked fearful, which was unlike the woman he had observed the last few days. While Kellian knew some history of Lux, he did not know it all. A sudden dread passed over him as they passed through this land. Coppery hair shone under the golden light and Kyeria smiled, holding up her hand to the light, it danced through her fingers. Sparkling as it went.

"Lux is Luna's sister," Kyeria said smiling. "We are welcome here." She nodded at Kellian. He wondered if her magic was what made her feel safe here, if she could sense the safety or if it simply relied on the Goddess Lux being the sister to Kyeria's own mother Goddess Luna.

After some time the ship pulled to a stop, and an old man shouted down to them, "All clear."

They walked up above deck. Kyeria's entire body shifted, her shoulders loosened, and as if wholly possessed began walking past Kellian to the edge of the ship, where the plank was pulled out and resting on rock that was the perfect height to walk across onto the hillside of the golden isle.

"Kyeria," Kellian shouted out in warning of the unknown. But she took another step then another until her bare feet hit the soil. Small flowers erupted around her, and he swore the sky above them opened up, shining light directly onto her. A silent hum fell around them and Inaya gasped next to Kellian.

"Who is she?" she asked.

"Our salvation," Kellian replied.

The three followed Kyeria onto land. Kellian pushed a pair of boots into her arms.

"We have to trek across," he said, looking sorry for the need for her to not be touching the soil. She nodded and slipped on her boots.

And they began their trek. It was a short but steep walk before the path twisted and headed down and down, and meeting them quickly they passed an area where vines grew so thickly they couldn't walk through. The thick forest surrounded them. Kyeria reached out, and the vines pulled open like a curtain. Kellian would never not be in awe of her. They continued and rounded a large open faced cliffside with golden stones exposed. Inaya reached out and let her fingers hover over them.

"Hmm," she muttered to herself. Grim glared.

"Do not get us killed," he seethed through his teeth. Inaya simply rolled her eyes.

"Through here." Grimm guided them and a lagoon was revealed. Rocks jutted out in the middle of the water and glimmering tails and endlessly long wet hair tangled around bodies. The Mer.

"Isla," Grim greeted and dropped a knee bowing low. The rest followed suit. The one with the golden scaled tail and golden hair waved, her smile bright.

"Grim, darling," she said after swimming to them in a second and emerging from the water onto the rock nearest them. As she sat on it, the light and glow of the golden rocks illuminated every single one of her matching golden scales.

"Your Highness," he replied. Her eyes snapped to Kellian next, purple eyes meeting his.

"An honor to meet a Guardian. I did not think it possible, even in my long life." She bowed her head every so slightly in a sign of respect. Kellian had heard of the Mer, but never met any of them. The Isles were ruled on their own, answered to none of the main kingdoms. Similar in a way to The Hollow, they functioned on their own, removed from the rest of the world, only fabled lands to most.

"I am Kellian, Guardian to The Hollow and heir," he greeted. "We have ventured here to ask your favor to help save our kingdom, to keep our borders safe from those who mean us harm." Kellian squared his shoulders and he bowed.

"If you would be so inclined, we, the Hollow, would in return owe a favor to the MerKingdom or a personal favor for you, Your Highness."

"Enticing offer, I must say." Isla's voice was like silk, sliding over him. He knew the Mer, like the Sirens, possessed a melodic magic. Known to sing sailors to their deaths in long ago lore. But Grim had made a deal long ago, his ships safe from the long nailed grip of the mer, in return for trade.

"Why is your kingdom in danger, young prince?" Isla asked, her purple eyes narrowing. While Isla looked young, he doubted she was younger than a century old. Mer did not age, and they outlived most beings on this continent.

"There is a beast, made of shadow and nightmares that is consuming the magic that fuels our borders," he explained. Grim stirred next to them.

"And the Captain could not help you? He is rather adept with the shadow world," she sneered. Grim crossed his arms, shadows twirling around them.

"It is not the same," Grim said sternly, "as you well know, Your Highness."

Isla ran a long finger nail down her cheek. "I suppose."

They all stayed silent and unmoving, awaiting her words. Kellian knew the Mer to be fickle in agreeing to help if it did not also benefit them. But offering a Mer princess a personal favor from another to be king, Kellian hoped it was enough.

"And you, young prince, will you fulfill the favor?" she asked, her gaze calculating.

"As long as I breathe." He nodded.

"And if you do not, it goes to the next in line. The favor is not fulfilled till it is fulfilled, no matter the time it takes," she said sternly. "Your lives are so fragile and short," she laughed. "Be it you or your great grandchildren, the Galanis line shall owe me a personal favor. And I shall bring you what you ask."

"We need a Merstone. For a potion that will help us rid the land of the Beast." Kyeria stepped forward. Kellian held himself back from wanting to step in front of her or shuffle her behind him. This innate, extreme feeling of needing to protect her invaded every cell of his body.

"Then, one Merstone you will have." Isla nodded, facing Kyeria. "You are a child of the trees, are you not?" Isla asked, her full attention now on Kyeria.

Kyeria nodded. "I am. From the northern lines. My mother was from NorHaven." The Mer's eyes went wide, her mouth opening,

"Yes." Isla's voice was only a whisper. "I can see that clearly."

Kellian peered at Kyeria, his Kyeria, in awe of her grace and power she carried with her.

"I, then, Isla, Princess of the Golden Sea, freely give you, child of the trees, a Merstone." A gleaming green stone appeared in her hand. She held it out looking to Kyeria. It was out of reach, but Kyeria smiled and reached out her own hand, magic bursting from it, and the wind carried the stone to her, gently landing in her palm.

Isla's eyes shifted to the others. "Be safe on your way. My sisters will not harm you or your ship on the journey out. You have my word." She nodded before one last lingering glance to Kyeria and slithered back into the sea.

"Well, I can cross off meeting a royal Mer off my list of things to do in my free time," Inaya announced after a minute of silence.

"Can I see the stone?" she asked Kyeria, who held it out.

"Do not touch it." Grim's hand gripped Inaya's arm. "Only the one to whom it was given freely may touch it, no one else." His voice was stern and dark. Kellian knew the lore well. Mer were slippery creatures, and a Merstone could only be given freely. There were particulars to the rule of magic surrounding them. It could not be touched by anyone but the one it was given to, lest be cursed as if you stole it from a Mer yourself. Bound to lose all sanity.

"I have to be back to my ship in three days, and deliver this one where she needs to go or face a bigger headache," Grim announced, jutting a thumb at Inaya who glared. The shadows had slithered back into his brother's arms. Kellian tried to not focus on the glaring fact that both his siblings possessed manipulated magic. They began walking, Inaya falling in step with Kyeria and walking ahead. A fierce grip clasped on Kellian's arm.

"Kel," Grim said lowly. "I have—" He paused. "I have never seen a Mer bow to anyone, even in words, and Isla just made her intention clear. Kyeria possesses a great magic, more than maybe you know. Be careful," he insisted. "I wouldn't want anything to befall you, brother, even after all the moons that have passed. I will never wish you ill."

Kellian looked at his brother, really looked. His eyes were so similar to their mothers, his shadows a direct reaction to his emotions, and they were swirling around his arms. Kellian nodded.

"She is of an ancient magic, one tied to the Hollow, as myself and Aura are."

"What do you mean?" Grim asked.

"She is dragon bound." Kellian's brows creased. "The dragon claimed her, nearly killed her, but she is to be the first rider the Hollow has seen in a century."

Grim silently took in the information, his shadows slowing. "That is —" He paused. "Interesting," he finished. Kellian smirked.

"And she is mine."

"Yes, brother, you have made that fact abundantly clear." Grim rolled his eyes and patted Kellian's back. "I have my hands full as is. Not to worry." He smiled, a rare smile, even Kellian had not seen often. Grim did not have a happy childhood, of this Kellian knew, but his father forbid any bastard children to reside in the castle. So Grim was raised by his respective father. Kellian and Grim would sneak out to run through the village or when Kellian taught him how to fist fight, taking back lessons he had learned and bringing them to Grim to teach him by the next day.

But that was a world away, and in front of Kellian stood a man, as dark and moody as the sea. One who had made many decisions to get him where he was today, the pirate lord, the privateer who had kings wrapped around his finger. The dark shadow that no one would dare cross.

CHAPTER 17

Kyeria

Kyeria could feel the magic of the Merstone thrumming in the inside pocket of her cloak. It radiated power she had never felt before. When her feet first touched the ground on the Golden Isle, the skies had opened and she had hear Lux herself:

"Hello, my sister's child. I welcome you to my land. You are destined to fulfill your destiny. To fulfill your fate. Go with grace dear Guardian, Luna's child of the trees."

The goddess had felt like the exact inverse of the goddess Luna. It was rare but not unheard of for a goddess or god to speak to their respective magic wielders. Kyeria was goddess blessed by Luna, an extremely rare honor among the fae. She had never told a soul. Only eight years of age when Luna appeared to her in a dream, whispered of her fate on the wind. When she woke she could remember not the prophecy of her fate, only the blessing. Maybe this was what drove her running from certain death right into the Hollow and their lands. To meeting Kellian, and Aura and Esmie. She sent up a prayer of thanks to Luna, for protecting her in her journey's. Kyeria felt so at peace in the Hollow. Like this was her destiny all along. Deep in her soul, she knew Kellian was wrapped up in that fate, the soulbond being a clear depiction of that.

"The magic bothers you?" Inaya asked as they walked back to the ship.

"It is an odd magic," Kyeria replied, "but magic of other gods and goddesses have always felt odd to me. I can recognise it quickly, as I did with Captain Grim."

Inaya's eyes snapped to hers. "You know the god he serves?" she asked in a whisper.

Kyeria shook her head. "He does not serve any god."

"Don't I know it," Inaya scoffed. "But you do? Luna?"

"I honor Luna, she is the source of my magic, but those blessed do not serve their gods or goddesses. They have a small fraction of said god's magic, and they may do as they wish with it, as fate deemed them worthy of the magic from the beginning."

"Do you think people are inherently good?" Inaya asked, eyes flashing back to Grim and Kellian who were walking many paces behind them.

"I do," Kyeria said firmly. "I very much do. But life is harsh, the world is all sharp corners and we lose our way sometimes. But I always hope for the good." Inaya reached for Kyeria's hand and gently squeezed before walking ahead onto the ship and disappearing into a lower room.

Kellian was rather silent during the next hour of sailing. Kyeria had tied together some rope, braiding it and making it large enough to tie off between two sail posts. She secured it tightly then climbed up, laying in the bed of rope she had braided, staring up at the sky. Pink and orange painted the sky as the clouds danced among the colors. She had her arms behind her head and the bed of rope was gently swinging with the rock of the ship.

"You look comfortable, love." Kellian's voice drifted to her when he appeared on deck.

"I would say I rather am." Amusement held her voice. "Care to join me?" Kellian let out a rare laugh, and climbed up.

"Come here," he muttered holding an arm out, and she happily folded into his arms.

"What's next, prince?" she asked, gazing to the sky.

"You save a kingdom you only accidentally stumbled into," Kellian replied. Kyeria let that sink in. Let the idea of fates wash over her.

"I can feel all your emotions through the soulbound." Kellian broke the silence nudging her. She looked up to him.

"I was thinking about fate," she replied. "When I was running from those guards, I had to make the choice, to run into the Ash Mountains, I knew the stories, the long twisted tales, how those who entered were

150

bound to a fate of insanity, or certain death. That no one could cross. But something deep inside me pulled me toward it, toward you." She sighed. Fate had a way of wrapping through life, finding a way no matter the obstacles.

"I have been on the run most of my life," she continued. "I hardly remember the Fae Lands now, my mother or father. The memories have faded with time and I never thought it possible to ever feel at peace again. That I was destined, fated to run. Always." A tear rolled down her cheek and she felt the weight of it all bury her. "But finding Ameline, she called out to me. Fate was there, then you and the Hollow. Aura and Esmeralda. I can't possibly imagine my life any other way. I feel as though I've been with you, in The Hollow, for *years*, not just the months."

Kellian let her thoughts simmer and sink; he kissed her forehead, wiped her tears and held her tighter.

"If fate brought you to me, then who am I to ever let that go?" he said, voice confident and final.

The two of them stayed like that under the stars for most of the night. Kellian pointed out the constellations he knew and noted new ones he saw to chart later in his notes in the observatory. It wasn't until the moon was high in the sky that they retired to their rooms, where Kellian worshiped Kyeria in every sense of the word.

Kyeria was sorrowful to say goodbye to her new friend in Inaya. Inaya promised if she ever needed anything, she could reach out to her, leaving her with an Evanthian address. Lucius squealed goodbye and Kyeria even reached out, patting its head before it flew back to Grim's shoulder. The shadow raven was growing on her. As cold and dead as he was.

"If you need anything," Inaya insisted, "you find me." Inaya had spent hours talking to Kyeria. Kyeria had a gentle way about her, one where people easily trusted her and found solace in talking with her. Inaya had explained how she was working off a servitude contract with the mad king, one her father had not been able to fulfill with his early death. Inaya, as strong and brave and bright as she was, was under the thumb of the king, a slave to a cruel kingdom. She boarded ships to get around the continent easily, as the mad king had a deal with the pirate lord for safe passage between missions.

"Brother." Grim nodded to Kellian. They stood across from one another for a minute, stark opposites, one bright and one dark, before Kellian pulled his brother in for a hug.

"Be safe," Kellian instructed. Inaya responded with something witty, and they left them on the beach, beginning their trek back up the small cliffside. With the horses gone and only two rather light bags, Kellian turned to Kyeria.

"Fly home?" he asked. She nodded quickly, before digging into her pack. Kellian watched her, confused, until she pulled out a black and purple glimmering corset. It was exactly how she imagined it when Ameline had instructed her to have armor made of her scales. Anwar was able to craft only a corset in the time available but the glimmering purple turned black depending on how the light hit the scales, creating the most amazing reflections Kyeria had ever seen. It also provided a layer of protection while riding a dragon, the scales providing a strong barrier between her skin and the scales of the dragon she was riding.

"Anwar made it for me," Kyeria beamed. Kellian was in shock. The old texts were filled with tales of dragon riders but it had been so long since one existed that he had never seen any artifacts of riders.

"It's perfect," Kellian finally said. He pulled his pack off of his shoulder and set it at her feet before taking several steps away from her in the clearing and shifting. The gorgeous white shimmering scales never failed to stun Kyeria into silence. She swung both packs over her shoulders after securing the corset fully over her tunic and pants.

It took them a quarter of the time to fly home rather than ride horses. The views were stunning. Kyeria was thankful for the short fight, since holding on to Kellian without a rider's seat was rather difficult. But he flew low and slowly to accommodate her.

When Kellian and Kyeria arrived back on the castle grounds there was a commotion. A guard Kyeria did not recognise was running towards them as soon her feet hit the ground.

"Your highness! You must come quick!"

"What is it?" Kellian said sternly, watching the frantic eyes and stature of the guard, he was out of breath from running to them from across the grounds.

"The princess, your majesty, it's the princess," he gasped out. Kellian took off running in the direction the guard had come from. Kyeria followed quickly, her own heart rate spiking. She heard Esmeralda's cries before she saw her.

Nox was on the ground just past the castle's iron gates.

He wasn't moving.

"Get up!" Esmeralda screamed, setting Kyeria's nerves further on edge. Esmeralda was the calm one, she never raised her voice.

She was pulling at Aura, who was in Nox's arms. A smell of iron and bitterness filled the air. Her magic hummed and the wind whispered:

It is coming.

It is coming.

Kyeria's skin bristled, and she looked to Kellian. *"Something is coming,"* she told him down the bond.

"Soldiers, places!" Kellian screamed. "Close the gates!"

"Close the gates!" the soldiers repeated, and many began pulling on the ropes to drop the iron gate. Someone ran up to Kellian, appearing with his long sword, intricately engraved with a swirling design down the hilt, and a golden gem at the top surrounded by silver, twin to Aura's that was bloody on the ground next to her.

"Get up!" Esmeralda shouted again, pulling at Aura, but Aura did not budge. Her grip was on Nox, her face buried into his side. His eyes were closed.

"Aura." Kellian's voice boomed over the havoc. She lifted her head, eyes rimmed red, a slash down her cheek and neck, angry and protruding.

"Aura," Kellian said again, devastatingly soft.

"I won't leave him," she gasped out. "I will not leave him." She screamed when guards tried to get close to them. Nox was not moving. His dark skin was void of color, his dark hair was laying limply, his once tan shirt soaked through with blood and dirt turning it an awful muddy color. Kyeria took a stilling breath. Focused her magic on him. Faintly she could feel his life source, it was there but weak.

"Aura." Kyeria knelt down to her, placing her hand on her arm so softly. "Aura," she repeated. Her golden eyes cleared only slightly.

"Kyeria, please. Please save him." She was gasping between sobs, tears streaming down her dirt stained cheeks. Kellian stood in front of them, sword drawn and gazed beyond the gate. Soldiers were stationed around him, above the gate on the walls, arrows positioned.

"Kyeria, what is coming?" Kellian said down the bond. Kyeria shook her head, so many things unraveling at once.

"I—I don't know," She whispered.

"Kyeria!" Kellian shouted, turning to her, "what is coming?" His eyes begged her to focus her magic. She closed her eyes, and threw her palms to the dirt below them, letting her magic cast out like a web searching for any living thing. The earth shuttered, the magic of the land retreating. It was the shadow beast.

"It's on the outer rim," Kyeria said. "The village on the river." She gasped, the map forming behind her closed eyes. "Kellian, it turned around, it is heading towards the village."

Shouting insured around them, Kellian shouting orders. The royal guard formed around them and Kellian was having his silver armor put on, the deep red capes hanging from them. The high guard. The high guard were a small part of the Hollow's army, the highest ranked soldiers, most skilled, most lethal. Nox was the second in command to Kellian. But he was bleeding out on the ground.

Kellian looked back before they raised the gates and the high guard began moving.

"Stay here, help my sister and Nox. Please." Kyeria could not ignore the plea, the desperation in his voice, seeing his sister hurt and hurting. She nodded firmly.

"I love you," she whispered down the bond. She wasn't sure how far it reached and he was out of view when she said it. She hoped he heard nonetheless, because he walked away to help his kingdom and his people, and he took her heart with him.

After Aura finally let go of Nox, Esmeralda and Kyeria rushed in. Esmeralda quickly began heeling the shallow wounds, grabbing potions from her bag and using them when needed. Kyeria got to work on the deepest wound on his side, taking the time to piece the skin back together, closing the gash. But the wound was deep and the dark magic

154

of the shadow beast had left its mark. A dark marring black scar that looked like lightning was forming over his skin as Kyeria healed the wound. Like a signature from the beast's magic. Her magic shivered when it touched it, it felt like pure chaos, dark and twisted.

"Is it spreading?" Esmeralda asked, peering over.

"Not anymore," Kyeria responded by pushing her magic into Nox. She felt her body exhaust itself. Healing deep wounds was not an easy task, and her magic was reacting in turn.

"He is stable enough to move." Kyeria let out a tired sigh. Aura was next to her still.

"Can you still sense his lifebond?" she asked desperately. Her voice was raw and cracked.

"It is faint. But it is there." Kyeria sounded hopeful but sad. It was a big hit, one that would take out any normal person and she did not like the lingering darkness of the magic from the shadow beast. That kind of chaos magic was not meant to be trapped in a body. "Let's get him into the castle." Kyeria instructed some guards standing watch to help them. The gates were closed and guards were posted at every entrance. Kyeria was almost surprised at the quantity. Has she ever seen this many guards in the castle? Once Nox was stable and in the infirmary inside the castle, the attendants kept him comfortable, although he had not woken yet. Kyeria assured Aura he would be okay in time and then met Esmeralda in her potions room.

"I have the stone. But I have to be the one to use it, which I think means I should make the potion to channel the stone as well," Kyeria informed her by showing her the glowing green stone.

"According to the last text I read on ancient Mer curses, I will not be touching that thing," Esmeralda informed her. "Even if it is very pretty." She leaned in, admiring the colors and inscriptions on the front. Kyeria tried to not let her mind wander to Kellian but she couldn't help but worry. She wanted to be there with him, by his side fighting. But he needed her here, to watch over Aura and make sure she would be okay.

Kyeria took a break later that day, walking to the caves to see Ameline. The dragon had doubled in size over the last week while they had been gone. Her scales were darker, but still shone purple in the light. She could take off and fly for a short amount of time, but her wings were not at full strength yet, still growing. Ameline was all too happy to show Kyeria how shiny her scales were and that she had shed more of the smaller scales and saved them for Kyeria. Kyeria did not know it was possible for a dragon to be gleeful but when Kyeria entered the caves wearing her dragon scale corset, Amelie was beaming. If a dragon could beam.

"You look lovely," Ameline mused. Kyeria did a little spin,

"You like?" she asked, receiving a nod from the dragon. Her eyes were rose colored today, changing in the light. Kyeria wondered what that meant. Ameline gossiped about the inner workings of the priests, how one of the Dragons who lived in the northern ice covered lands had visited while they were gone with Fendiah. His name was Amadeus and he was the last living relative of Ameline's. Kyeria had a million questions, but Ember fluttered to them while they were in the meadows.

"Lady Esmeralda is requesting your presence, Miss Kyeria." She smiled. Kyeria said goodbye to Ameline and walked with Ember through the grounds back to the castle. She told her about meeting a Mer and riding on a ship. Ember glowed with the information. They parted ways when Kyeria reached the large glass doors; she made her way into the castle to see Aura passing the hallway.

"Aura." She stopped mid-step.

"Something is wrong." Aura began pacing again.

"Nox will be okay, healing takes time," Kyeria started but was quickly cut off by Aura.

"No. Kellian. Something is wrong with Kellian. I can feel it." She tapped her chest. Her red rimmed sleepless eyes met Kyeria's.

"Why can't you feel it?" Aura panicked. "Something is wrong." Her eyes were frantic, her hands shaking. Kyeria walked towards her like walking towards a barn cat, slow and steady not to spook her.

"Aura," she said gently, "I need you to take a breath." Aura did as she asked

"Focus on that feeling, try to harness that magic," Kyeria instructed. Aura calmed only a fraction but she shut her eyes. Light was glowing on her fingertips.

"Now what do you feel?" Kyeria asked. She tried to focus on her own soulbond but her magic was exhausted. She felt no disturbance, though she ventured she would only feel it through the bond if it was a mortal wound, the way Kellian had felt it when she was burned. She fixed her weary gaze to the windows and threw out her thoughts down the bond, like blindly throwing a net, no idea if it would reach him.

"Please be okay."
"Come back to me."

"It–" Aura said out loud, startling Kyeria back to reality.

"I think he's okay, it feels... scared, the emotion I can pick up, it's fear," Aura said.

"Okay..." Kyeria said slowly. "Let's go find Esmeralda, she'll have a calming potion, I think we both need one." She linked her arm with Aura and led them to Esmie. Esmie was buried behind a stack of books.

"Oh! You're back!" She lit up, her expression sombering when she saw a shaken Aura.

"What happened?"

Kyeria ushered Aura forward, sitting her in a deep maroon chair surrounded by stacks of books with candles on them. Emeralda's potion room was a direct reflection of her and who she was. Warm and inviting, filtered red hues lit by candle light making the space one someone would want to sit in for hours.

Once Aura was sitting, Esmeralda poured tea into a cup, stirring in a light purple potion with an engraved miniature spoon. She carried it over to Aura, and handed it to her, then went to the other corner pulling a soft blanket from an array of colorful knitted ones. Kyeria couldn't help her smile growing at the site, the handmade blankets and a warm cup of tea. Esmeralda whispering to Aura and assuring her everything would be okay, that Kellian was one of the most skilled fighters in the kingdom. But Kyeria noticed her words were cut off. Because it was Aura and Nox who were the next strongest fighters behind Kellian, and they knew Aura was thinking the same. That Aura should be with them, that Nox was laying in an infirmary bed healing from wounds caused by the very beast Kellian was going after. Kyeria took a calming breath, walked to the other two women and sat on the low cushioned stool next to Aura, Esmeralda crossing her legs on one of the floor mats that was embroidered with flowers, also likely another project.

They spent the next hour like that, Aura settling herself. Then coming back to them and beginning to plan out her next trek.

"You have the Merstone?" Aura asked, eyes clearing. Kyeria nodded and pulled out the stone. It was cool in her palm. Magic humming from it making her own magic stir in response. As she flattened her palm revealing it to the girls, Kyeria gasped. Like a sword had been plunged into her stomach, she fell to her knees, unable to breathe. Pain laced through her, consuming her every sense. Her magic jumped around trying to find the wound, trying to heal her. Faintly, she could hear Aura and Esmeralda shouting, hands on her shoulders. She was shaking. No, someone was shaking her.

"Ky!" Aura shouted. "What happened, what is it?" Her face was horror stricken, like something in her soul knew it before Kyeria could utter the words.

"Kellian," Kyeria gasped out, holding onto her side where the wound did not exist.

Esmeralda jumped up. "We must go!" she shouted, running around her room, attaching a few potion bottles to her belt, daggers slipped into place. Aura rose from the ground as well.

"Let's go." Her voice was even and sure. She walked to the door, her sword with the golden gem in the hilt to match her striking eyes was in her hands, and she was walking with a vengeance through the castle halls. Kyeria shot to her feet, trying to shake off the phantom pain, and chased after Aura, Esmeralda next to her. A door slammed open, echoing in the hall. All three of the women halted.

"What's happening?" a deep and angry voice grunted out. Nox stood, hair long and grown out, his side bandaged.

"Nothing, you stay here," Aura instructed, words clipped.

"Where you go, I go," he said, voice low and raw from a day of what Kyeria presumed was not speaking. An invisible conversation passed between them and Kyeria stood analyzing them.

"Fine," Aura conceded. An audible gasp shot from Esmeralda. Aura never conceded, let alone to a man, let alone to Nox. *Something had changed.*

"Give me a minute."

"Meet us at the stables." Aura turned on her heels and marched away. Esmeralda shot Nox a sympathetic look then ran after Aura.

Kyeria stood, feet planted to the wooden floors.

"Are you well enough to fight?" she asked Nox. "I can't heal you, I won't have enough for the both of you."

"I am well enough," Nox grunted, pulling on a chest plate. Kyeria sighed, stepped forward, and helped him with his armor. The red cape signifying him as the high guard was covered in dirt. But it would do for now. She nodded him ahead.

"Let's go," she ordered, arms crossed against her chest. She was already wearing her dragon scale corset, her daggers strapped to her side and thighs. Magic was humming, springing from her fingertips, wanting to be used, needing to be used.

Everyone mounted a horse. Aura and Nox to one so he wouldn't fall right off the horse despite saying he was fine. The four rode west hard, following the bitter painful beacon in Kyeria's mind.

Be okay.
Please be okay.

The noise hit them before they could say anything. Shouting and screaming. They were well into the village now. The houses on the ends were demolished. Collapsed into the ground and villagers were huddled in fear behind a failed wooden frame. A few of the villagers pointed east when they saw the dragon princess and her people. Whispering words of thanks as they passed.

A large shadow loomed over the houses across the way. Aura shot off her horse, leaving them all behind. Kyeria was on her tail, then passing her with her magic and the wind pushing her forward.

It steals our magic, child of the trees, do not let it take yours, the wind howled to her. Chills erupted on her arms. Soldiers were swinging blindly, two were on the ground unconscious. Kyeria's eyes swept the field, her bond calling out for Kellian.

Aura charged full speed at the beast. Esmeralda followed suit with Nox by her side. Fury fueled Aura, a battling cry as she was consumed by the shadows. Her light burst through it like a flame. The creature screamed. But Kyeria couldn't focus on it, she was running through the chaos trying to find Kellian.

Please, Goddess protect him. She sent up a prayer and the sun streamed down showing her a path, the wind whispered:

Quickly.
Quickly.

Then beyond the trees was Kellian, hunched over, bleeding from his side and hunched over another soldier. "You'll be okay," he insisted to the soldier.

"Kellian!" she shouted, and she ran, the trees beside her blurring, even the image of him blurring. She was crying, tears streaming down her cheeks, gasping for air. Gasping at seeing him alive, seeing he was okay.

"Kyeria." He lunged for her, sweeping her up into his arms. His armor pinched against her, the steel was cold and biting against her arms, but she didn't care, nothing mattered other than seeing him with her own eyes, him here, him okay, him breathing.

"My love, why are you here?"

"I felt it, I felt you being struck and it felt like I was dying, like *you were dying, Kel.*"

"Shh," he soothed, hand stroking her hair. "I am fine, just a flesh wound. The dragon blood runs deep, takes more than a little wound to take me out," he assured, kissing her forehead. His hands held her cheeks as he looked at her. She peered down at the blood running down his side, armor burnt and disintegrated. She made a note to study that later, *how had the shadow beast been able to melt metal?*

"Who did you bring? I'm assuming the fiery light is my stubborn sister?" He asked with a smile growing. Kyeria let out a sigh, tilted her chin up to look at him and nodded. Aside from the easy smile, Kellian

160

was covered in dirt and grime, blood smeared across his forehead, a small gash on his cheek. Kyeria brushed a thumb over it, letting her magic seep through and close the wound.

"She can't really be argued with," Kyeria said while healing the small wounds on his face and neck, then pressing a hand on his side; the gash was large but she could stop the bleeding for now. Her magic swelled, moving toward him without any effort. Her body, her magic, was so intune with Kellian, it knew every part of him and ached to heal him. A shiver ran through Kellian, his eyes were stormy as he watched her. Shouting from the soldiers and the chaos beyond broke them out of their trance. "Fuck, is that Nox?" he asked moving forward.

"Nox!" Kellian shouted, and dark brown hair swayed and the dark permanent angry eyes turned to meet Kellian.

"Hello friend, think you could keep me from the action?" Nox smirked. Kellian laid a hand on his shoulder with a determined smile.

"Never," Kellian said firmly.

"Now let's go get my sister out of trouble," Kellian grumbled. Light was going off like little explosions inside the clouds of shadow. The darkest parts being where the beast was solidifying. Then, suddenly a purple flash of light and a large explosion boomed. The shadows withered back into the trees away from the village. Another roaring battle cry, but this time it was Esmeralda. Fury on her face and a potion bottle in one hand, the other flowing with magic. Kyeria began pushing her magic into the ground, reinforcing the wall of the village with deep roots and branches, leaves intertwining. Aura was jumping, hurling through the air, throwing light. Kyeria pushed the air toward her friend to cushion the fall. When Aura landed one knee down, she glanced back, a wicked smile on her face.

"*Thanks*," she mouthed and took off towards the beast again as it retreated. Nox let out a deep sigh and took off after her. Kellian shook his head and turned to the villagers.

"Let's gather the people." He instructed the soldiers, "Clean up what we can and find housing for those who have lost theirs."

Quickly the soldiers all moved into action. Helping people stand, guiding them to safety. The aftermath of the shadow beast was grim but not too extensive. Mostly, the people sat shaken and Kyeria watched as Kellian jumped into action. She saw him shine here, the dragon prince, the heir to the kingdom, the Guardian of The Hollow.

The clouds were moving in above, and a cold breeze pushed through the village. Two buildings had been demolished, only piled of stone, and small pieces of a once home lay there now. A small child was pushing a little stone aside. Kyeria used her magic to push the large stone away, smiling at the child. She helped clear the rubble and mess. The little girl who had red hair similar to her own was looking for something. A few sprites flew by, helping guide the people and lift spirits. Kyeria watched it all, eyes glassy. She hated destruction. This village held many children and she couldn't imagine the toll something like this beast would take on them. She never wished that type of fear on anyone. The fear she had known so well.

Kyeria bent down to her knees and looked at the little girl.

"I am Kyeria, what is your name?" she asked.

"Percy." She gave a shy smile and her hands clasped in front of her, fidgeting.

"What are you looking for?" Kyeria asked gently. She knew that look. Something lost, something that meant the world to this child.

"My doll," Percy whispered, eyes glassy with tears. "My mother made it for me."

"Okay, let's keep looking." Kyeria smiled and began moving more stones aside from what she assumed was the center of the home.

Kellian was talking softly to some of the older village women, helping them to areas that some soldiers had set up to treat wounds. He looked over to Kyeria smiling at her.

"*Thank you,*" he sent down the bond. Kyeria turned her head in question. "*For helping my people.*" He smiled then went back to tending to a wounded woman. Kyeria and Percy looked for a while before finding the small doll tucked in the furthest corner, dusty and dirty but whole. Percy hugged her so tightly, Kyeria almost fell back, letting out a smile and a laugh.

"Thank you, Princess!" Percy exclaimed.

"Oh—" Kyeria started but Percy ran off to a few other children showing off her doll.

"*Princess has a nice ring to it.*" Kellian's voice down the bond was playful but sincere.

"I am not a princess." She shook her head and busied herself helping some other villagers across the way.

"*No, but a queen,*" Kellian's voice down the bond was as low as a whisper. It startled Kyeria, as if it was a thought he didn't mean to send down the bond. When she looked back to him, he was busy moving things aside and working. She shook her head, a smile playing on her lips despite trying to rebuke it.

Kyeria looked off into the forest. It was getting dark and Aura and Nox were still out there. She spotted Esmeralda doing simple healing spells on artificial wounds and walked over to help her with the bigger ones. She sent a prayer to Luna to watch over Aura and Nox and focused on the people here, alongside Kellian and Esmeralda.

CHAPTER 18

Aura

"You go east, I'll circle from the west end." Nox's voice was low and commanding. His dark hair was wet with sweat and stuck to his forehead, dirt and blood scattered on his skin. Aura could see him wincing every few steps, and would bet he was bleeding under his armor.

Aura shook her head. "Let's just run it out of the village line. We are not ending the beast today, not in this state."

Nox's head snapped, his disapproving leer evident on his features, eyebrows creased.

"Is that an order, princess?" he ground out with sarcasm and a hint of bite. Aura straightened, standing tall, the cool metal of her sword in her palm

"That's an order," she commanded. Nox was twice her size, with menacing dark features. His onyx hair gleaned under the light and his ocean blue eyes were nearly black now. His strong jaw was brushed with the beginnings of a beard from the days in the infirmary away from his own rooms. It did not deter from how painfully beautiful he was. No one could ignore his sharp features, and toned muscles. Even through his armor he was a sight to behold, determination hard on his brow. His eyes were sharp still as he bowed his head. His own hand tightened on the hilt of his gleaming silver sword. It was twice the size of her own. The metal was thick and heavy unlike her own, which was thin and light. Nox had made them both, of course. Hers was adorned with a gleaming golden dragon stone in the hilt, signifying hers as an heir's sword. The Guardians all had swords perfectly crafted for them with a dragon stone. Nox's father had been the one to craft her first sword, but as she grew and began training more seriously she wanted changes, so Nox had melted it down and shaped her a new one.

"On your call, Princess," Nox grumbled.

"Goddess, stop calling me that."

"You outrank me." He shrugged. "Technically," he muttered.

"If it doesn't bruise your ego too much, *guard*. Then flank west and we push the beast past to the farthest forest line."

"Aye aye, captain." Nox saluted her, eyes dark and movement stiff.

"Goddess above, give me patience," she mumbled under her breath to the sky. Then they moved, pushing in from either side. Aura let out a burst of light from one hand as they ran after the beast. The shadow creature shrunk away from the light, screeching as it went.

By the time they pushed the shadow beast back and it ran back deep into the forest, the sun was casting low signifying it was later in the afternoon. Aura was dripping in sweat under her light armor she had rushed to dress in. She pushed her white locks away from her face and let herself sit under a tree, basking in the shade and the light breeze. The trees bristled and she wondered what they were saying. Kyeria bloomed in her mind. What a gift to be able to sense and communicate with nature like her. She wished she had a sliver of magic so intuned with the earth but all she had was pesky light. Seemingly all it did was gleam brightly and ward off beasts made of shadow.

"All clear." Nox jogged up to her, breath hard and heavy.

"Took you long enough."

"Sorry to keep you waiting, Your Highness."

"Fuck off," she said standing, her back still facing the thick tree trunk. Shade enveloped them, only pieces of light scattering through the leaves of the late afternoon now.

"I've some other ideas," Nox growled and pushed her back into the tree. The bark pushed into her armor and bit into the sides of her linen shirt where armor didn't reach. Aura let out a gasp despite herself.

"We need to get back," Aura insisted, hand on his shoulders. She was thinking of shoving him off but while her mind dreaded the possibility, her hands were gripping his red cloak that hung off his armor and was pinned around his neck. She hands pulled him to her and within a blink, his lips crashed into hers. Everything in her stilled. The magic in her veins went quiet, her body immediately listening to his. His large hand gripped her waist, pushing her back. She felt the world go quiet. The only awareness was of him.

His lips.
His touch.
Him.

A roar from above the trees made reality crash back into their little world. Aura's hand quickly shoved Nox off her. He stepped back with a grunt, scratching his neck with an eyebrow raised.

"You seriously didn't hear the gods-damned dragon?" she sneered. Brushing dirt from her pants, she huffed. As she readjusted her sword in the hilt, she let the control she was so familiar with, so comfortable with, snap back into place.

She stepped out from under the trees and looked to the sky. A dark dragon whose scales were gleaming purple in the small sunlight flew overhead.

Ameline.

Aura strained her eyes to look closer. She did not hold far sight like Kyeria, but Kyeria's red hair was loose and flowing and she was evidently on the back of the smaller dragon, a leather riding seat in place and golden embroidery lining every stitch. The wind picked up as the dragon flew down and landed in the field.

A bundle of red hair, wearing borrowed dark training leathers climbed down a wing. Ameline was a quarter of the size of Fendiah but she was still massive even for her young age. Aura wondered how large Venille Dragons grew. She mentally made a note to ask Esmeralda for some dragon history notes. Aura should of course know this, as the heir to the kingdom and mostly a Guardian. But since the blessing of a dragon form from the goddess had passed her and gone to Kellian due to a childhood illness, she hadn't found herself interested in anything dragon related. Until Ameline.

"Hello lightbringer," Ameline greeted Aura, tilting her large scaled head in greeting.

"Ameline!" Aura greeted, a smile breaking through her annoyed facade she had thrown Nox. She walked past him and broke into a jog to get to Ameline and Kyeria.

"Ky!" she shouted, hugging her friend. Her golden copper curls were flowing around her face, loose and free, her dress stained and dirt covered.

"Is the village okay?" Aura asked sullenly.

"It will be. A few houses are damaged but we have everyone in a bed for the night and will begin rebuilding tomorrow." Kyeria nodded. Aura took in Kyeria. Her eyes looked tired, sunken dark circles lay under them. But her smile was bright as always.

"We need to harness the Merstone," Aura said lowly. "This damned beast needs to go back to Hel itself."

Kyeria nodded her agreement and reached into her shirt pulling a lightly glowing green stone from around a wax string, wire wrapping around the stone elegantly in the way only Esmeralda knew how to set stones into jewelry. Aura reached out but Kyeria pulled back.

"It has an odd magic. Only freely given. Esmeralda is working on the potions, and when it is ready, I will cast my magic into the stone to you, your light should, in theory, then be amplified enough to shatter the form the beast has taken, banishing the pieces back into the cracks of this land and down into Hel. I will cast a net of magic to push it down through the earth and soil, trapping it with only one way down back to Hel.

Nox walked up to them. Aura could feel the air change and the low growl from Ameline shook the ground. Kyeria reached out, placing a hand on her neck.

"It's alright. We like him," Kyeria assured. Ameline bristled.

"I do not trust any human man I do not know," Ameline growled through gritted teeth.

Nox took a slow step forward, and shocked Aura by bowing to the dragon.

"It is an honor," he spoke loud and clear. Not one waver in his voice. Aura felt a bloom of pride.

"And why should I trust you, boy?" Ameline's scratchy voice was low and menacing as it came out.

"I serve the crown. My life is to protect the Guardians as the guardians is to protect your own. I am your sword to command. I would lay down my life to protect both the Prince," he sent a glance at Aura, "and the Princess."

Aura felt the chill erupt over her skin, climbing up her legs and arms. She shook it off, pushing down the reaction. *It meant nothing. It was simply his job.*

"*You are of what name, boy?*" Ameline asked

"Nox Greenwood." He stayed bowed, head low.

"*Ah, I know of you,*" Ameline said, her voice lighter.

"*You must make my rider a sword for her seat, a place to store it. A traditional dragon rider's sword,*" Ameline commanded. Nox nodded.

"It would be an honor."

"*Rise, boy.*" Ameline shook her wings, a gust of wind blowing towards them making Kyeria hold in a giggle, biting down on her lip to hold it in. Aura saw the flint in her eyes and wondered what her dragon and the wind were saying to her.

"Now that introductions are over," Kyeria waved, "let's get back to the castle. We have preparation to undo this beast forever. See you there." She smiled coyly looking between the two of them and then turned on her heel, climbing Ameline and remounting herself into the riders seat. It was the deepest of brown leather and the golden embroidery sparkled in the small light left. Nox huffed next to Aura.

"Wishing you could fly?" Aura poked him.

"At this moment?" he said touching his side she knew was deeply wounded from the raider attack. "Yes."

"Come on, you big baby," Aura teased. She saw his eyes react to jest, light and playful matching her own. But his body didn't share the same sentiment. It was slow and worn down. Aura sighed and they began the slow trek back to the castle. She wished she could simply shift into a dragon and take them both home. But fate had other plans.

CHAPTER 19

Kellian

Kellian looked around his tower. The observatory was covered in painted constellations where stone stood out, but the walls were mostly made of glass windows. At this exact moment, all of the windows were open. He had taken flight after the attack, needed to clear his mind in a way that only flying could solve. When he landed on the roof of his tower he shifted back, climbing down the protruding steps he had attached to one of the stone pillars holding the glass ceiling open. The large ceiling was made of glass that could be opened so he could take flight from his tower and come back to his own space. It was his small solace in the world. His place of peace. No politics, or royal duties or looming issues, just the open sky and the stars and his own slice of Haven.

It had been hours since he had dropped Kyeria down by the caves to see Ameline and he had returned, when the wooden door to his tower creaked open. A familiar blur of red curls as Kyeria ran in. Her smile bright, the light emanating from her like light gleaming off of water.

"Hello, love," Kellian greeted as she walked into his open arms. He held her close, pushing into her neck and inhaling. He loved the scent of her, of his soulbound. It was like the morning after rain in the forest, fresh and light and brimming with possibilities.

"It has been quite the day," Kyeria mumbled against him. He grunted in response, the vibration of it jolting her and making her giggle.

"You smell." She shook out of his grasp. She was met with another grunt.

"All talked out for the day?" she asked playfully. The crease between his brows softened, his eyes followed suit. But he knew that she understood him. She understood him more than anyone ever had. How he would retreat after conflict, do what was needed but then prefer to be alone. However, alone now did not seem to be what he craved, he only wanted to be with her.

"Come on." She tugged his arm and pulled him towards the door. They walked down the tower steps, through the small labyrinth of halls to their own wing of the castle. Their wooden doors still stood tall facing the other. The only rooms on this floor.

"Yours or mine?" she asked, squeezing his hand and bringing him back to reality as his mind had wandered and they had walked silently.

"Mine." He could feel the growl come up from his chest. The innate need to have her with him, touching him.

"You certainly have quite the grand tub," she mused aloud, her words tinged with playful challenge. She hadn't shielded her thoughts from him as he had taught her, so he felt her excitement and daring pulse down their bond. He responded with a low grunt, a sound that might have been mistaken for a farm animal's lament, though his energy was all but drained. Her mesmerizing green eyes bore into him with an intensity that made him yearn to kneel before her, to offer her a devotion as profound as her wildest dreams.

Kyeria guided them inside, her demeanor as assured as if she were in her own space. His room, though similar to hers, held its own distinct touches: a grand bed against the far wall, a spacious hearth flanked by a solitary leather chair, and a table cluttered with books. A large desk, its surface buried under a chaotic scatter of papers, overlooked the windows, while the tall, windowed doors led out to his mother's lush gardens. The washroom, however, was a marvel of opulence, twice the size of hers, with a magnificent copper tub taking center stage. As she moved about with ease, Kellian watched, his irritation barely masked by the flicker of admiration he felt for her bold confidence.

Clothes lay scattered like fallen petals along her path, and when he finally reached the door frame, only her long tunic remained—an ephemeral veil against the exposed allure of her bare legs. Each glimpse of her unadorned skin teased him, weaving a tapestry of longing and restraint.

She waved him forward as if to say *get in*. And he cracked a smile at her, stripping his clothes off and lowering into the tub. She herself stayed outside the tub, leaned over and palmed the water into his skin. His tight muscles relaxed under the mixture of her touch and the hot water. She lathered soap in her hands and washed away the dirt before moving to his hair and he swore to all the gods and goddess that this, here, was Haven. This was the afterlife where all good and kindness lie and souls are given rest. The ultimate paradise and gift of one's life.

By the time she had finished, he reached over to her, tugging her shirt over her shoulders and dragging her in. They stayed like that until Kellian did the same for her as she had done for him. He lathered the soap and cleaned her tired muscles. She couldn't help the moan escape from her lips as he pressed into her neck and washed her hair. Only a chuckle from him made her shake under his movements.

They emerged from the bath when the water had grown cold. Kellian wrapped Kyeria in a towel, his movements deliberate as he dried her with tender care, ensuring every inch of her was warm before turning to tend to himself. He slipped into a tunic and ventured out to find her warm clothes, returning with a luxurious silk robe. Leaning against the doorframe, he took in the sight of her, absorbing the reality of her presence in his meticulously ordered life.

The chill in the air was sharp, but it was nothing compared to the intensity of his emotions. He was utterly captivated by her—by the way she filled his space, his world. The realization struck him with a force that seemed to pierce through his very core.

He loved her.

The thought surged through him, raw and undeniable, as if it had been waiting in the shadows of his heart, now bursting forth in its full intensity.

He loved her.

Silken robe draped on her shoulders, she pulled at the long strings, wrapping them around her waist when her hand stopped abruptly.

Her breath caught and he could feel her shock through the bond. Green eyes met his, they were dark green now, only sparkling bright in the corners. The large window let in the streaming moonlight. And in that light he could see tears welling in her eyes. He pushed himself off the doorframe and strode to her in three long steps, his hand immediately going to her, sweeping over her cheek.

"What is it?" he asked softly.

She breathed. In and out. In and out.

"You—" she began, and then paused, her eyes getting larger. His eyes were frantically searching hers. What had happened in her mind in the last few seconds? What was causing her pain? But he silenced his thoughts and listened to the bond, in the way she had taught him, to still his mind and take in his surroundings. There was no pain or fear or anger there. All causes of crying he knew could be traced back to those emotions. But they were devoid of existence. Here in this space, she was emitting joy. Pure unadulterated joy. But tears were in her eyes.

"You love me," she said clearly after clearing her throat. Kellian felt his body relax. Felt the muscles release, the tension erased. And a smile erupted.

"Why are you crying, my love?" he asked again.

"You—" She paused and let her hand rest on his chest and the other on his own cheek. Her expression so soft, her skin so golden under his touch. "Love me," she finished.

"Of course I do," he replied with a sigh. His breath escaping him and his forehead resting on hers.

"You are my everything," he whispered into her lips. Kissing her once. Deeply and slowly, only a hint of need at the end of it. "Kyeria. You are my guiding light, why I want to do more and be more. For you, for my kingdom. You bound into my world, and I don't ever wish to be parted from you." He smiled looking at her, his hands holding her face. He reached out gently, tipping her head back and kissing her neck.

"You are everything," he whispered into her skin. Goosebumps erupted where he kissed. And he loved the physical reaction he had over her body.

"Kel." She stopped his wandering hands and pulled him back, his eyes to meet hers. Golden and green. "I love you," she whispered back then leaned in, catching his lips in hers.

He lost himself to her, as he knew he would every night, if she'd have him. Her legs instinctively wrapped around his waist as he carried her to the bed. His movements were deliberate and tender, each kiss a whisper of devotion. The satin robe was soon discarded, and his tunic was torn

172

from his body by her eager hands. She was a wild, untamed force of nature, and he was utterly captivated by her.

A day later, Kellian sat in Esmeralda's potions room with Kyeria, Aura, and Esmeralda. The sun was high in the sky and Esmie was huddled over her potions, explaining how close she was to getting it just right but the recipe in her Gran's book had been slightly smudged and she couldn't quite read one of the measurements.

"I think this is right," she mumbled, sprinkling in a handful of something dark mixed with crimson red leaves.

"How do we know exactly..." Aura trailed off, biting at her fingers and looking quickly between the potion and Kellian.

"I'm sure it's fine!" Kyeria cut in, walking over to Esmeralda with a smile. Aura was perched on the arm of a chair Kellian was sitting in. He could feel the anxiety rolling off of her, her shoulders were tense, and she only bit her nails like that when she was a child.

He leaned in next to her. "Worry less sister, you're going to make yourself sick," he whispered. She spun on him and a glaring, piercing stare told him he should have just stayed silent. She pushed off the chair and walked over to the other two women. She crossed her arms and waited, as Esmeralda began re-reading the recipe and directions in the old and torn notebook from the elder winter witch who had long since passed.

"Maybe we should test it?" Kyeria offered.

Aura looked to her with uneasy eyes. "Explain again how this works?" Aura asked.

"The potion will be poured on the Merstone, and then Kyeria can give it to you freely, accepting to transfer the power to you temporarily with this spell here," she pointed towards her book, "and then you push your light through it in your hand I would assume, and amplify it." Esmeralda motioned with her own hands, using a crystal on her desk.

"And no creepy Mer magic will curse me forever if I touch that thing?" Aura's voice was thick with hesitation.

"No, this spell will give you access to it temporarily, it's a loophole essentially. Since Merstones can only be gifted freely from a Mer to one being and it is theirs until they die, only passed on to their own offspring. Anyone who tries to take it or steal it or wear it otherwise faces the," Esmeralda threw her hands in the air-quotations, "creepy Mer magic."

Kyeria bit her lip to hold back a laugh. None of them had realized how superstitious Aura was about the Mer until the existence of the Merstone in the castle. She looked like a ghost, skin extra pale even thinking about touching the gods damned stone. Kellian pushed himself up with a grumble.

"Come on Aura, you will be fine," he assured her.

"Can't you just amplify his dragon or whatever," Aura's brow creased even further.

"Fire, even dragon fire, doesn't do much to this beast, you know this, we have tried," Kellian argued. "It's you, Aura, your light, your magic that can settle this for good and keep the kingdom safe."

Aura let her crossed arms fall and go slack at her sides, her brow relaxing and a serious look befalling her features, she only let out one word, "Oh," and then turned on her heel and walked out the door. The three that were left, Kellian included, all gaped at the door, shocked she just turned and left without a word.

"Um-I-" Esmeralda stuttered, the potion in her hand and the stone in Kyeria's outstretched one.

Then the familiar sound of boots stomped back down the stone floor.

"Are you coming or what?" Aura shouted down the hall.

"Oh!" Esmeralda exclaimed and grabbed her things. "No time like the present!"

Kyeria shot Kellian a look before saying down the bond, *"Are you sure you are okay with this?"*

"Yes," he replied in a clipped tone.

"I know how protective you are over her, and I just–"

"I would take her place in a second, but I have tried over and over again with Dragonfire and it does nothing to this beast. It is from the fireland of Hel, it is immune to it, but light, light it seems to be terrified of, so if we can hit it, hard, then maybe we can finally get rid of this beast for good. We can stop the borders from shrinking and then work to get them back to where they should stand. It is my life's burden to protect

174

this land and guard these dragon grounds. And while I wish it could be me, Aura is strong, she is an heir just as I. If she is the one to be able to defeat this leech once and for all then I will be by her side, and protect her with my life. But that is all I can do." Kyeria's gaze was soft as it always was for him; she took in the information and nodded. Then held out her hand for him, and they walked together out of the castle, to the open fields where Aura and Esmeralda waited.

"Who wants to be target practice?" Aura asked as a dagger flipped through her fingers lazily.

"What are you all doing?" Nox asked, walking out to them. They all turned, and Aura couldn't help but smirk.

"Just in time," she sang.

"No," Kellian and Kyeria said at the same time.

"You will use that." He pointed at a target left behind from the archers in the field. It was about two dragon lengths away and a large circular piece of wood.

"Fine," Aura grumbled and let out a large sigh then turned to face Kyeria.

"Give me the evil stone." Her hand was held out in false annoyance, and Kellian knew she was using her bravado to mask her fear but he smirked all the same at his sister. What a little monster she had become. His favorite one. Filled with the fire of their father and the wit and cunning smartness of their mother. Sure, Aura was kind and graceful and could handle royal life well, exceptionally well at that. But she was meant to be here, on the ground, fighting, training and forging herself into a weapon that no one could use against her. Pride filled him. While he had his dragon from, she had this. She might not see it yet, but her burning light was a force to be reckoned with.

Kellian's eyes flashed to Kyeria. She was sure footed and focused. She let out a steady breath and began chanting the old language, reading off from the book Esmeralda had handed her, while the Merstone glowed, bright and eerie. He could hear the stone, a piercing melody coming from it. He recognized it of course, it was the tune of a Mersong. The ones that can enchant people to their deaths, to follow a Mer where they go, to the blackest parts of the sea.

"To upon you I do part the gift for only a moment," Kyeria spoke in the old language. Her accent rusty and clipped, unused to forming such words and sounds. Kyeria looked to Aura and then held out her hand, palm facing the sky. Kellian looked up and saw Ameline circling high above. She must be speaking with Kyeria, he realized, as her eyes looked glazed and tilted up to the sky as well. When Kellian looked back to his sister, the Merstone was in her hand. She flinched at it as if it was burning her, but held tight, took in a steadying breath and wrapped only her fingers around it, pushing her palm out to face the target across the field, with both hands. Light erupted from her, while a soft light surrounded her, the stone focused it, creating beams of concentrated light that flashed out, hitting the target and completely disintegrating it.

"Holy shit," she cursed, pulling her hands down. Her hand that held the stone was shaking slightly, and Kellian felt a tug of worry in his chest. He didn't like that it was hurting her. That shouldn't be happening after the ritual. Aura looked at the stone, it glowed clear now instead of green, as if her magic was pushing through it, filling the stone itself. A chill ran through her and she tossed the stone towards Kyeria, who caught it with a start.

"Well, I guess it works." Kyeria laughed, in awe of the power.

"*Her hand is shaking.*" He could feel his eyebrows creased and the anger settling. He did not like a plan that hurt Aura.

"Adrenaline?" Kyeria asked

"*I don't like it.*" His tone even down the bond was gruff. Kyeria nodded all the same, sensing his shift. She moved to Esmeralda and whispered a few things. Nox was at Aura's side; they were arguing about something quietly then Nox grabbed Aura's hand and pulled it to him, twisting it palm up. Kellian took three long strides and was by her side ready to throw Nox down. But when he looked at Aura's hand, it was burned, red and splotchy in the exact size and shape of the Merstone.

"Think I'm cursed?" Aura asked, teasing in her tone but shoulders tense and eyes serious.

"Nah," Nox countered and dropped her hand, but he sent a glance to Kellian who nodded ever so slightly. Nox wanted to talk, and Kellian had some damned questions about why Nox felt comfortable enough to grab Aura's hand and forcefully look at it.

"Let me see." Kyeria nudged Aura. She held out her hand reluctantly and Kyeria closed her eyes and let her fingers drag over Aura's palm. Slowly as her own fingers passed the burn the redness dimmed and the damage was healed.

"It's only a surface burn," Kyeria confirmed, turning Aura's hand back and forth slowly in her own, eyes honed in on it. "I think you made the actual stone heat up and burnt yourself," Kyeria concluded. Esmeralda was then also hovering over them.

"That is interesting," Esmeralda murmured.

"It worked," Kellian said, voice low and nodding at the burnt ash wooden target that was still smoking.

"Looks like we have ourselves a weapon." Aura smirked. Her mask fell into place sharply. The small uneasiness that Kellian recognized on her brow had smoothed. Her tone lifted to her normal care free cantor but he knew the mask well. He often wore it himself as they were raised to be. Calm, collected, and immune to pain.

Aura caught him staring and gave the smallest tilt of her head as if to say *let it go*. So he did. He would not be the one to tell his stubborn sister what to do unless necessary. They needed a weapon to defeat the beast, and now they had it.

CHAPTER 20

Moonlight draped through the grand windows of Kellian's chambers, painting the room in silvery hues. Deep into the night, she awoke, her skin alight with a whisper of magic and a heightened sense of awareness. Reaching out with her mind, she sought any anomaly in the shadows. A soft, familiar laugh rippled through her thoughts, a gentle reminder of her dragon, Ameline. She felt her essence drifting, like a spectral presence, soaring just beyond their castle's embrace.

"*You should be asleep,*" Ameline spoke in her mind lightly.

"*So should you,*" Kyeria responded.

"*I am a dragon, I do as I will.*" Ameline's tone, while light, held a small annoyance like she was reaching the attitude a human might have when they were thirteen years of age. Kyeria smiled to herself. Soft blankets covered her and a weight around her waist alerted her to Kellian. He was stretched out on the bed, one arm slung lazily over her waist, keeping her in arms reach.

"*What is bothering you?*" Kyeria asked Ameline. She could feel the unease of the dragon through the wind and the clouds and the bristling of the trees. The land felt uneasy.

"*The ground is awake. I do not like it,*" Ameline replied low and a growl shot through her mind. Kyeria slipped out of Kellian's arm, doing her best to not wake him. She looked back at his sleeping form, so handsome and at peace, as she regretfully turned left the bed. Slipping on her riding pants and boots and tucking in her tunic to bare off the chill. She spotted her wool cloak along on the back of Kellian's desk chair and swooped it up before slipping through the open windowed door and down the steps into the gardens. The stone faced guard only nodded at her in acknowledgment. She smiled all the same to the unknown soldier and went on her way.

"Fancy a flight?" Kyeria asked. It took a few moments for Ameline to answer this time. But she heard the loud flap of her wings in the wind before she heard Ameline's reply in her mind.

"Why do you think I am here?" Kyeria could feel the attitude through her tone. She assumed the dragon was rolling her eyes in an annoyed manner.

"So sorry to keep you waiting," Kyeria teased back.,

"It's too early for sarcasm." The dragon's tone was thick with annoyance now.

"I agree." Kyeria fixed her with a look as she landed. Her brows raised, and arms crossed, leaning against a boulder in the clearing.

"Tell me what happened." Kyeria stood tall, her voice firm. She knew Ameline, despite her attitude, respected her and would go into every event sharing her full knowledge with Kyeria to help them be prepared. They had only been able to fly together recently. Ameline's growth had seemingly doubled over the last week. She was much larger than Kyeria, and climbing up her wing or leg to get to the rider's seat was more of a daunting task at present. Ameline's scales had turned darker, only in the direct light could one see flecks of purple and red. In the darkness of night she appeared rather menacing and as dark as a shadow itself.

"The Hel beast is too close. I can sense it and it's awful death filled reek. I cannot sleep because of the wretched thing," Ameline snarled. Her claws dug into the earth making it shutter and her teeth bared in the direction of the trees to the east.

"We plan to use the Merstone as early as tomorrow," Kyeria informed her dragon. "The testing went well."

"Yes, Aura visited me in the caves."

"She did?" Kyeria was filled with slight shock rocking through her. While Aura seemed curious, she usually stayed at a bit of a distance from the dragons. An inner battle lay thick in her, as the one passed by the dragon blessing.

"I asked to see her light. She is unlike any I have known or heard of. A light bringer who was fated to be dragon blessed but is not." Ameline

shook her head, scales gleaming in the catching moonlight ever so slightly.

"Her light power, do you recognize which god it comes from?" Kyeria asked.

"Long ago there was a god of the sky, that loved the goddess Luna, he granted magic on those in the good graces of Luna who were not chosen as a show of favor. The god of the sky was also the god of light. His name was Ari. Few were blessed with so much light they were called light bringers. They are rare, I do not know of a time this land last saw a light bringer," Ameline explained to Kyeria and as she stood next to her, Ameline reached out her head nudging Kyeria.

"She is unsure of her own power and her place here. She may not say it out in the open but I can sense it as might you," Ameline added. Kyeria tilted her head at Ameline. She was rather observant, almost as observant as she was herself. Though, that ought to make sense as they were bound to each other and alike in many ways.

"I am glad she came to you." She meant it deeply, she hoped Aura came to see her worth as they all saw her. Kyeria's thoughts were cut deep as the forest rumbled out a nightmarish scream.

Ameline perked up, standing tall, triple the height of Kyeria when standing. Kyeria cast out her magic like a net, gathering herself into the earth and seeping into the soil along a path towards the trees' cry. She found death. Dark and looming, sucking the life from the very earth itself. The shadow beast had found a crack in the earth, and a small sliver of Hel itself was peeking through and trying to gain strength from these lands. Kyeria turned to send out a message through the bond to Kellian but she could see him, linen tunic flowing in the wind, dressed with a sword strapped across his back and a steeled gaze past her to the trees. While he may not possess the powers Kyeria did, connecting her to the earth, this was his land, his home. And nothing happened without his knowledge. His gaze reached her, through the mist gardens to the field where she stood.

"I have sent for Aura." His voice was drenched in sleep, low and gravel toned. She felt her body reach to him, felt the chill run down her spine.

"There is a crack. Past the forest edge to the east, we can banish him back to Hel with Aura's light and the stone," Kyeria replied back. She felt

the grunt Kellian sent down the bond instead of a worded reply and Kyeria couldn't help the smile tug at her lips at him.

"*Let's go.*" Ameline cut through the cold air, her voice deep, breaking through the silent night. Kyeria bristled at her speaking aloud, so unlike her to do so. She eyed the Dragon, taking in her unease as she stretched out her front leg for Kyeria to climb. She held onto the leather hand holds of the riders seat and tapped her foot to alert Ameline she was ready. Ameline muttered a "Hold on," in Kyeria's mind before taking off into the sky. The feeling was new but still exhilarating. They burst past the misty clouds that hung low and into the night sky. The stars were blinding above the clouds. Soon the clouds parted again and a glimmering white dragon broke through them. The cloud shifted apart, as if bowing to him. She felt the wind on his tail, pushing him along.

"*Hello, love,*" his voice down the bond was sickly sweet, like honey. She smirked at his dragon form, the same glowing golden eyes staring back at her she knew so well.

"Let's go catch us a Helian Beast," Kyeria said, voice laden with determination. She peered down, the castle was small but she saw the two horses, bounding at full speed out of the castle walls and down the eastern path. Cloaked in the night their forms were dark but the long white hair of Aura was a tell tale sign, with her ever following shadow of a man on her heels.

It was time.

Kyeria, Kellian, and Ameline arrived first landing on the far edge out of sight from where Kyeria could feel the beast. Kyeria turned to Ameline.

"*Go home,*" she said sternly, not wanting the young dragon to get hurt and knowing Dragonfire was of no use for them.

"*No,*" Ameline countered, her voice firm and unmoving. She clawed her feet, barred into the soil.

Kyeria shook her head. "*I cannot look out for you. Take to the skies if you need, your wings are still fragile and not fully developed.*" Kyeria tried to keep her voice firm but soft, not wanting to offend the Dragon but also needed her to stay safe; she was too young and too important.

"*A dragon, let alone a Venille, as I am, can not be taken down by a mere Helian beast of shadow,*" she snarled back. "*Do not insult me so.*"

Kyeria dismounted, pulling her dragon-scaled corset tightly around her and adjusting her armor.

"Do not get hurt." Kyeria stood her ground, then her eyes softened as she looked back at the dragon. *"I could not bare it." The* last part was barely a whisper even in her mind. Ameline's head tilted at Kyeria, taking her in. Kyeria could sense her mind churning but was interrupted by the sound of pounding hooves. As she turned, Kellian shifted into his human form again and Aura was dismounting, shoving a sword into her brother's hands and stomping towards Kyeria.

"Do you have it?" she asked. Aura was poised and ready, her white hair pulled back half-braided away from her face. She was wearing form-fitted silver metal armor, her own Guardiansword clasped in her hand. She looked as though she was not woken in the middle of the night to fight a beast but like she had been waiting and ready. Nox dismounted his own horse, tying the two to a nearby tree before joining them. He nodded at Kellian who responded with a low grunt.

"What's the plan?" Nox asked the group.

"From what I can tell, the shadow beast is against a cliff side within the dense forest edge just beyond this break here." Kyeria took her finger in the dirt and began drawing a map, raising her hand to point at the break in trees just beyond them.

"Nox and I can flank in on the west, distracting the beast, then you and Aura use the stone, direct it at the beast near the crack into Hel," Kellian continued before looking to Kyeria, "Can you close the crack in the earth?"

"That's unheard of, Kel," Aura cut him off, shaking her head. But Kyeria closed her eyes, felt her magic—it was overflowing in the well. She had been gaining strength after much training, but most of all being in this land, her magic swelled at the freeness here. She had been Goddess-blessed, she could feel the magic tickling her fingertips as she faced Kellian with a firm glance.

"I can do it," Kyeria said. Ameline bristled behind her in assurance or maybe pride, and they all nodded to each other. Kellian and Nox confirmed their plan on how to position the beast and back him into where the earth fell into the depths of Hel. Kyeria confirmed it, the trees whispering to her in assurance as well.

Quickly.

Quickly.

The wind howled. Kyeria and Aura moved into position glancing at the men as they moved in the opposite direction. Nox was dressed in dark training gear, his royal armor in place, so dark next to Kellian's shining armor. Kyeria saw Nox watching Aura as she looked on to the forest. She noticed his eyes clouded over and sent him a reassuring smile, before shifting to see Kellian's eyes already on her.

"*Be safe,*" she whispered down the bond.

"*For you?*" A smirk tilted his lips. "*Always.*"

Aura and Kyeria walked quickly, Kyeria did her best to soften the soil under their footsteps, making them nearly silent. They slid from tree to tree until the overwhelming sense of death and decay filled the air. Aura held the disgust clearly on her face.

Kyeria focused her mind on that of their surroundings instead. Taking in the wind, the trees and the land, she could feel the earth shutter under his feet, leaving decay there. It was then she saw a gleam of the crack in the earth. Like a black hole was under it, smoke and shadow gathered above it, tendrils slithering out and meeting with the beast, his shadowy form growing larger by the minute, leaving a stuttering eerie feeling in the air, like the rotten core of the beast was leaking into the air itself.

"*We need to move quickly, it's getting bigger somehow, pulling from Hel,*" Kyeria rushed down the bond to Kellian. Within a blink, a stir from across the way, followed by a battle cry and Nox, like a soldier of the night flew forward, charging at the beast. Kyeria eyes caught on the sword. It was glowing, gleaming, shining even in the night. She gasped silently and looked at Aura who glowed with pride.

"What?" Aura whispered with a smirk. "I just enchanted the sword with my light with Esmeralda's help of course." She shrugged and Kyeria bit down on her lip to hold in a laugh. Goddess above, Aura was something else.

"Ready?" Kyeria asked her snow-haired friend. Aura nodded, eyes glowing on the corners and light began seeping from her skin and twisting around her hands.

"Ready," she confirmed. Kyeria pulled the stone from around her neck, muttered the spell, and pushed it into Aura's open hand. Kyeria pulled deep into herself, dragging the magic up. It was waiting for her, eager and ready to be used. Kyeria let the vines wrap around her own arms, cutting them off from the earth and controlling them with the water inside of them alone. Ready to use them like spears, she held her ground, ready to fight as she flanked Aura. She charged forward, held out her palm, then grasped her other hand around the wrist holding the Merstone and she let out a scream.

White light burst from her, all the slithering tendrils collecting into spears of light that shot through the beast, who let out a blood curdling scream. It began to shrink away and Kyeria turned, pulling up roots and vines to trap the beast where they needed to, Aura sending bolts of light, stinging it when it tried to move out of the space they needed him, caging it entirely.

"Push it down!" Kellian shouted over the chaos. The beast turned at the sound and a shadowy hand lashed out at Kellian. His Guardiansword swung trying to block the hit. And while the slice of the metal through the smoke made the beast pull back, the hit landed.

Kellian went down.

Kyeria felt the air knocked out of her as it did to him, and she staggered. The beast whirled on Kyeria and broke apart the vines, the leaves withering into black, then nothing. Kyeria cringed at the feeling, the overwhelming death and decay that swept over her as he killed the living things she brought up from the earth.

"Goddess protect us," she muttered, sending a prayer up out into the world, hoping it reached Luna. If she was Goddess-blessed, then now was the time to call in her favor, to use her magic in all its power. She held out her hands and magic burst from her. The well was draining too fast, and she pulled back, trying to harness her restraint. Magic was such a fickle thing to call on, especially since she had essentially taught herself as her magic matured, without the guidance of a council or her people after the war.

Kyeria felt the magic crashing like a tidal wave out of her fingers, as if directly defying her command to slow. At the same time, Aura positioned her light. It was dimmer than it had been before but she screamed into the night, her battle cry echoing through the empty forest edge, bouncing off the rocks and around them. The beast let out a bone-chilling screech. Aura and Kyeria moved into position, flanking the right side, Nox on the left next to Kellian. The boys had their swords at the ready, slashing at the beast pushing it just enough back, towards the deep menacing crack in the soil and up into the rock. Aura was charging, Kyeria at her side throwing out her magic, calling on the wind and the blessing of Goddess Luna. The shadowy tendrils on the beast whipped out, slashing at Aura, she staggered back but held her ground. They pushed on towards the edge of the rock, towards the gate into the underworld; a sliver of Hel.

The shadow beast was shrinking back and back and with one final push of magic, a seemingly unphased flow of light from Aura, the beast fell back. Shadows detaching and disintegrating into the air with the Guardian Swords now both glowing with the same light that burst from Aura. Her hands were split, one powering up Kellian's sword and the other on the beast. Kyeria pushed further and further, tumbling, barreling towards the end of her well; the earth was sucking the beast into it, banishing it to the underworld.

The trees chanted; the wind howled. The earth itself, every living being on this side, pushed and pushed and the crack in the earth began to heal itself. The rock cracked back into place, the soil filled. Kyeria pushed her magic deeper, closing off the earth as far as she could until there was no decay, no hint of death the creature had possessed and any bit of Hel that was leaking into their world was banished.

The Beast was gone.

With a huff, Kyeria sulked back, her legs weak under her, her breath ragged. But a *thump* pulled her out of her exhaustion. She looked to her left and Aura had collapsed. Then the wind whirled past them and she could sense Ameline flying closer, landing in the opening between the trees—her smaller size letting her fit—and she walked, clawed feet thumping into the ground past them all to Aura who lay unmoving on the ground. Nox was running, Kellian was running, and Kyeria was on her knees already, next to her. Hands already reaching out for her friend.

"*Stop,*" Ameline commanded. They all paused at the Dragons' command. They surround Aura's petite form that lay crumbled on the forest floor.

"*Give her a moment,*" Ameline insisted.

The wind stilled, the trees went silent and they waited, not a breath was taken until Aura's eyes fluttered open and clouded golden eyes stared back at them.

"Goddess above, why are you all hovering?" Her voice was weak and cracking but a smirk was still playing at her lips, and Kyeria let out a heavy sigh of relief. Nox's eyes were so clouded and dark, Kyeria couldn't make out the emotions there, but Kellian was painted with relief. He helped her stand and they all took in the surroundings. The land looked haggard but Kyeria's magic had seeped so deep into the soul that grass was sprouting up around them, flowers blooming, and broken branches fixing themselves. The golden light of morning broke through the tree line, low and welcoming. As if signaling the end and the beginning.

They had rid the land of the shadow beast who had plagued it, who had been eating away at the magical borders that kept this hidden kingdom safe, the land filled with magic, and a safe haven for the Dragons and the people of the hollow alike.

Kyeria felt a sense of calm wash over her. While exhaustion gnawed, it could not negate the feeling of calm. They had done it, they had finally done it. Aura was limp on the ground as Nox lifted her into his arms, but a proud smile was evident on her. The mask was off, and her real true emotion shone through. Kellian reached for Kyeria, his hand sweeping over her lower back and pulling her to him.

"Everytime I see you fight it is like watching art," he whispered into her hair. She couldn't help but smile up at him, burying her face into him. He kissed her hair and squeezed a hand around her waist before letting her go.

Aura was fussing, arguing with Nox to put her down while he insisted she could not ride back to the castle on a horse let alone stand. It was Ameline that spoke up.

"I will take her back. Kyeria go with your soulbound." Her voice was sure and certain in their minds. They nodded and Aura shockingly did not fight the idea. Nox helped her up into the riders seat and Aura shoved him off showing her strength was back enough to hold onto the dragon for a short ride home. Nox took the horses back alone and Kyeria rode Kellian's dragon.

. . .

Kellian, in his true dragon form, chose the longer path, guiding them through the clouds as dawn broke over the horizon. They soared amidst the swirling hues of pink and orange, where the night surrendered to the light of day. The stars had vanished, yet the moon remained—a rare celestial witness to the morning sky.

Kyeria released her grip from the scaled horns on Kellian's back, her fingers tracing the curve of his powerful form. She tightened her hold around his torso with her legs, then slowly extended her arms, tilting her head back to embrace the rush of the cool morning air.

"Don't fall off," Kellian's voice rumbled through their bond, a playful warning. She responded with a radiant smile, her joy mingling with the wind, and after a heartbeat, she sent a single thought through their connection:

"You'll catch me."

GILDED FOREST

part three

CHAPTER 1

Aura

T HE TWELFTH MOON OF SPRING
two weeks before the defeat of the shadow beast

Aura gazed at the sky, the wind completely knocked out of her. She shut her eyes, reaching out with her senses until she felt his presence, unmistakable and immediate. When she opened her eyes, she was greeted by the sight of an infuriatingly confident smirk. His face, streaked with dirt, framed by dark brown hair that fell across eyes of the richest, warmest blue she had ever seen.

"You'll get 'em next time Ror." Nox Greenwood reached out a hand for her.

Hitting it aside she spat, "I don't need your help." Rising to her feet and thrusting her dagger towards his throat, she threatened, "Call me Ror again, I dare you." The blade's tip pressed against his sun-darkened skin, drawing a thin line of menace. His lips curved into that infuriating smirk once more.

"Ah how my dreams always begin," he replied. She huffed, threw her arm down, and stomped past him.

Nox Greenwood was the very embodiment of vexation. Captain of the royal army, master blacksmith, and owner of the most magnificent black steed in the infantry. Of course, he had the mare Aura had coveted for herself. It wasn't often that Aura faced defeat—especially not in matters of desire. From a young age, she had walked boldly into her father's quarters, declaring her intent to train as a warrior. Her father's approving nod had been the only acknowledgment before he sent her on her way. Her mother, on the other hand, had fretted endlessly, lamenting the prospect of a princess appearing bloodied and bruised. She had urged her towards needlework, writing, and the genteel royal duties. Aura had embraced these pursuits with equal fervor. Her needlework was impeccable, she could change and clean in a very short amount of time to adhere to her mothers schedule, and never missed a single meeting or gathering where the dragon princess was expected. Her mother's complaints had faded, satisfied with Aura's grace and diligence.

Even now, long after her parents' passing, Aura remained a paragon of skill in all her undertakings. Yet despite her prowess, the title of the finest fighter was still claimed by Nox Greenwood. The thought was a constant thorn in her side.

Nox followed her as she walked to one of the armory rooms. She pulled off her armor, the chest piece and the arms, slamming them on the table. She spun around but Nox was there, crowding her, pushing her against the table.

"I hate you." She spat, heart racing. He slammed his lips into hers, his hand weaving into her hair and pressing into her. She gasped letting him in and he consumed her.

"I know," he growled back. Her nails drug down his back and he smiled wickedly.

"Fuck you," she replied, slamming her hands into his chest and moving him back against the wall.

"Would be an honor, princess," he replied. She slammed her mouth into his in response. Her hands crawling up his chest, his hands tangled in her white hair, the braid coming loose. She let out a groan before hearing the wind rustle the trees violently outside. She let out a curse under her breath and pulled away, keeping her hands on Nox's chest to keep him at arm's reach.

"I have to go." She knew she looked annoyed, she was annoyed. Deeply. Nothing like having a morning interrupted by her grandfather.

"I am not done with you," Nox said lowly, one hand on her waist squeezing. She met his eyes, something burned deep in her, the dare was clear.

"I know," she replied and spun on her heel. She wrapped her hand around her disheveled braid and pulled the string loose, letting her hair unravel completely as she walked out of the armory. Her shirt was loosely hanging on her as it did without the armor atop it. Her boots hit the muddy ground outside. She knew she herself had mud on her as Nox did, but one could not keep the Dragon King waiting. She took off jogging towards the steps to the castle, through the gardens and in through the main hall.

"Nice of you to join us." Kellian muttered as she fell into step with him. He looked presentable and clean in his royal clothing. Aura was the opposite.

"Aura." The Dragon King's voice was warm from age.

"Grandfather," she greeted. Fendiah spent most of his weeks in dragon form in his older days. He held the throne after Kellian and Kyeria's parents had passed, leaving an empty throne and two young heirs behind. Fendiah was a good leader, fair and stern but kind and he loved his people. He had instilled that so deeply in Kellian. Raising him to be the next king. Aura was the spare, the extra, the thoughts dug at her, haunting her mind. She trained hard from a young age. Determined to show her worth to the kingdom. If she wasn't meant to lead like Kellian then she would fight, she would be the best gods damned fighter in all of The Hollow. And train she did. Aura was one of the best warriors, she led missions across all the land of The Hollow, the Ash Mountains and the Dragonier Forest. But it was Nox who held the title of high guard. Aura held that of the Dragon Princess. The name—like a mocking chant in her own head.

"How was the mission to the far east villages?" Fendiah asked her as they walked. The great halls of the castle were light stone piled on top of each other, large mirrors donned the walls, art framed in intricate golden frames.

"It went well, Grandfather," she confirmed and began her report, "the east village is secure despite the receding borders. We are hoping to keep a small group of soldiers there to ensure their safety from any raiders or the shadow beast itself." The shadow beast was continuing to plague the land. Kyeria and Esmeralda had been great help in researching. While Esmeralda would stay back and work on finding more information or making experimental potions to use over the last few weeks, Kyeria had begun accompanying her on tracking missions. Aura adored Kyeria. Kyeria, a fae woman who stumbled into their lands, fell in love with her brother and bonded to a young dragon. Ameline was the first hatchling to emerge in many years. The kingdom was ecstatic with the new addition. Dragons from the Isles were bound to begin visiting to meet Ameline, the last of the Venille line of dragons. A true marvel.

Kellian cleared his throat and reported on the latest from the royal court hearings, the main villages in The Hollows center. He talked for sometime, Aura knew she should be listening but her mind wandered instead. She felt an elbow dig into her ribs. She and Kellian were walking a pace behind the king. Kellian did not look at her but his message was clear, *pay attention*. Aura rolled her eyes and cleared her throat.

"I have a training session with the children," she announced. Fendiah nodded and sent her a warm smile.

"Yes yes, go," he commanded, a hand gently patted her shoulder in approval. She bowed her head and sent Kellian a smirk, disappearing past the arches and down the steps. Walking into the gardens Aura let her shoulders fall, a light sprite flying up to her catching her attention.

"Princess!" Ember greeted.

"Hello Ember." She smiled at the familiar royal messenger.

"Kyeria is asking for you in the libraries, they have found something about that wretched beast." Ember's voice was soft and high, she let herself be fully visible at this moment but light sprites could manipulate the light in a way to appear as only a burst of light, invisible to the human eyes of full apparent as she was now.

Aura reached into her pocket pulling a small folded note. "Could you get this to Nox for me?"

Ember nodded, taking the note from her, the size comically large comparatively. But light sprites had something of an immense strength for their size. She fluttered off, note in hand, back towards the training grounds where Nox would be. The note was asking him to start the classes for her and that she would be there shortly. She took off. Walking around the side of the castle and following the familiar halls towards the large wooden doors that held the first floor of the library. She pushed one open, and was immediately met with the sweet smells of candles, old books, dust, and lavender. Fresh lavender bundles were in vases throughout the first floor, an homage to her mother that the servants began after she died. Aura's mother had a field of lavender in the gardens, and would keep fresh bushels in the library to ward off the smells of dust and cold. The servants continued it long after she was gone. And walking into the library always meant thinking of her mother, the nostalgia flushing over her.

"Aura!" Esmeralda greeted walking up the stairs from a lower level, a stack of books in her hand. Behind her was a huffing Kyeria, an even higher stack in her arms.

"Oh thank the goddess, help me with this." Kyeria groaned. The library had many levels, the lower they got the more ancient the texts, but the light was on the first floor, so they would trudge up the editions they needed here to study them instead of reading them in dim candlelight below.

"Be careful, those texts are hundreds of years old!" Esmeralda scowled, " and the only copies, so mind yourself." Kyeria made a face, glancing at Aura who bit her lip to hold in her own laughter.

"Hey, I was meaning to ask you," Kyeria asked after dropping the books on a nearby table with a huff, earning another glare from Esmeralda who pushed her curls out of her face roughly.

"The night of the ball," Kyeria started. The air stilled. They hadn't talked about it much, and Esmeralda glanced over, Aura stayed particularly still on the opposite side of the table from Kyeria.

"Where did you go? When the hymns were going, Kel explained they have magic weaved in and put people into somewhat of a trance, except the heirs of course." She motioned her hand in the air. "Okay relax you two," Kyeria added, letting out a smile. "I'm all healed now, and I am not a glass doll." Aura nodded sternly, she herself hated being treated as such, and from a young age worked to show how she was just as tough, worthy, and strong as her brother. She steeled her emotions and met Kyeria's eyes.

"You're correct, I am not affected by them," Aura responded.

Esmeralda peered over, eying Aura with a look. Esmeralda had caught Aura sneaking out of some dark corners weeks ago, and when Nox slithered out mere moments later, it didn't take long for her to corner Aura and demand to be told.

"I left you, and the guilt has been eating me alive," Aura sighed, reached out her hand and gently squeezed her upper arm. "I should have never left you, Kellian told me not to leave your side, and I did.." She sighed. Kyeria waited, her eyes soft, no anger evident in her.

"I—" Aura started. Esmie shifted her weight from foot to foot, the nervous energy was filtering through.

"Nox was stationed at the gates that night, and I went to find him."

Kyeria's eyebrow raised. "When I heard the commotion, the

screaming... goddess I ran so fast Ky, please believe me." Her eyes dropped, guilt washing over her. Leaving Kyeria that night was a huge mistake, to steal some time with Nox cost Kyeria weeks of learning to walk again, gain strength, and she was trapped in her room for so long. Even when Esmie and Aura tried to cheer her up, she needed to be outside, in the open air. It was slowly eating away at her. And that was all Aura's doing, if she would have just stayed, she could've blocked the fire faster than Kellian did, and used her light to stun the young dragon.

"Sooo." Kyeria nudged Aura, her copper hair was loosely braided today over her shoulder, front pieces twisted back and out of her face.

"So, I am the worst, and I am eternally sorry I left," Aura said, squaring her shoulders, sincerity filling her words. Kyeria rolled her eyes and waved her hand.

"Aura, please. It is in the past, and like you know now, Ameline was dousing me in dragon fire to confirm the bond. She didn't know it would hurt me. And while it did, and while the recovery was hard, I have a bonded dragon, I am to be a rider. Fate had other plans. You were meant to be where you were, as was I."

Esmeralda walked over to them then, sitting on a cushion.

"But tell us about Nox," Kyeria probed.

"Yes, do tell!" Esmeralda joined in, a mischievous smile on her lips, head resting in her hands.

"Nothing to tell," Aura dismissed it and began organizing the books in no particular order, earning another groan, glare, and her hands being swatted away by Esmie.

"Please, you wake up before the sun every morning, voluntarily to see him." Kyeria jabbed a finger at her accusingly.

"He is my trainer," Aura rolled her eyes, "and my training starts before sunrise, every morning."

"Mmhm," Esmeralda added, "because that's before the barracks wakes up, and the soldiers are in their homes."

"It is not because of that," Aura shot back.

"Goddess above," Kyeria cursed. "How long have you been sleeping with him?"

Esmeralda began giggling.

"Why are you both ganging up on me here?" Aura shot back.

"Stop avoiding the question," Esmeralda sang, Kyeria nodding along.

"I don't like Nox." She crossed her arms and sat down roughly. Kyeria burst into a smile and sat next to Esmeralda, as if settling in for a long talk.

"He's insufferable," Aura added, arms firmly crossed, crease in her brow forming.

"He's rude, and crass, and sweaty, and irritating." She continued for good measure. Kyeria's grin was infuriating, she just nodded along, grinning like a fool. "Okay," Aura sighed, "it makes for good sex."

Esmeralda smirked.

"Goddess above, cover your ears or something." Aura threw a pillow at Esmeralda.

"I am sixteen, not a child, Aura." She glared back.

"You are practically a child," Aura snided. "And I don't want to talk about this. I am late for a training class with some of the barracks children. I made Nox begin the class to come here, when Ember found me. So let's discuss the important things please." She exaggerated the last word for extra emphasis.

Aura walked back to the training grounds with heavy feet. With the weight of the knowledge that she would have to use the Merstone, and she would have to use her power to banish the beast back to Hel. But a small thrill was buzzing in her veins, pouring through her, that her light was important, and that there was a way to harness it in such a powerful way. Esmeralda had spent time looking for others with the power of light as she had, but hers was so different, gifted from a God who rarely gifted anything to humans. Though it was perhaps because the Galanis line was not quite human, closer to Fae than humankind, but drifting between the two in an unidentifiable space.

The sun was beaming down on her now, high in the sky. She pondered the mistress of fate, and where her own fate lay. Maybe it was this, this beast she had been determined to figure out and rid the land of for so long now. Spending the better part of the year pushing it away from villages, monitoring the borders where the magic retracted, making sure raiders were not finding usually protected dragon caves.

This last year had been heavy, but she liked being needed. Craved it even.

As she rounded the final corner towards the training grounds, Nox immediately came into view, a towering figure amidst a sea of young trainees. With his real sword slicing through the air with effortless precision while they flailed about with wooden mock-ups, he was an impressive sight. Aura seized the rare opportunity to watch him unabashedly. Of course, he was breathtakingly handsome, which only made it all the more infuriating that such a stunning face belonged to someone so exasperatingly obnoxious. She rolled her eyes at the thought. Goddess above, she needed to break free from this cycle of mixing pleasure with disdain and stick to simply loathing him. But she had to concede—there was something undeniably alluring about that heated, hate-fueled passion.

"Raelyn, raise your arm more. Matthias, lower yours." Nox directed the children through the movements. Most were the sons and daughters of the some high ranking members of the court, or the children in the barracks themselves. To Aura's dismay, it was still heavily male, but the few young females she always paid special attention to. Seeing herself in them. They worked harder, with more precision than most of the boys other than the top few. They had more to prove, more to fight for. It was only a few years ago now that the female children on the court members were allowed to train like the males. The barracks children were of course different, they had always been more equal, plenty of female warriors were among the royal army and guard. Aura smiled at Raelyn as she passed. She was the daughter of Lord and Lady Rivington. Few equivalents to nobles were here in The Hollow, but their families had served the Guardian's and the Galanis Line for hundreds of years faithfully, so they were awarded bigger plots of land and held many businesses within the land of The Hollow.

When Aura fully rounded the corner, a quiet murmur settled over the younglings. Wooden swords lowers and heads bowed.

"Your highness." Nox bowed his head to her, a glint in his eyes knowing she hated it when he called her by any royal names. The children all followed, clumsily bowing and curtseying to her. Aura put on her most royal mask. She smiled demurely and nodded to them in acknowledgement.

"Hello children." She smiled. "How has the Captain been treating you this morning?" All the children nervously shifted, some smiled, some nodded, some mumbled 'good'. But Raelyn had a scowl resting along her brow.

"Lady Raelyn." Aura noted, "something to share?"

"We have been practicing the same positions for nearly an hour," she chidded, then crossed her arms. "Your highness," she added at the end. Aura bit back a smile. Goddess, the attitude that this little being held in her body was bursting. She was so much like Aura at that age. Eager and despite to do more, learn more and be faster and stronger.

"And what would you like to practice?" Aura asked, encouraging the little spit fire of a girl.

"Sparing," Raelyn immediately responded. Some of the others looked around, seeming nervous.

"Mr. Nox said that we need to perfect our stances and technique before sparring," one of the boys spoke up.

"Stances are very important," Aura agreed. "May I borrow your sword Lady Raelyn?" She asked. The child looked stunned, orbed eyes looking up at Aura and handed over the wooden play sword without a word. Aura took it, and walked further into the circle, facing Nox.

"If one's stance is off, then he or she can easily lose the upper hand." She struck the sword out fast, faking a blow to Nox's side before jabbing behind a knee. His uneven stance made him fall to a knee with a grunt. The children laughed and cheered.

Nox tried to contain the smirk twitching at his lips. His head tilted down and he raised a brow at her, turning his chin up towards Aura and blocking his expression from the children.

"You'll pay for that," he mouthed, which only made her smirk more.

"Technique is also vital." Aura paused as Nox pushed off his knee and stood again, he was so much taller than Aura, but Aura was faster. She knew this and had learned to use her petite size to her advantage.

"As you see, this sword is wooden, and that one is steel." She nodded to Nox's sword. It was stunning of course, the Greenwoods made and crafted perfection. It was etched with a pattern down the center of the blade.

"If your weapon is at a disadvantage, then technique is what will keep you alive." She nodded to Raelyn who was watching closely.

"If I swing to my right," She does so slowly, and Nox moves to block her, matching her slowed down speed, "He blocks right."

"But." She paused, hit left, right again, he blocked twice then slashed out at her, she ducked and rolled out of the way.

"When you understand the techniques of sword fighting, you can anticipate the move of your opponent," Aura continues standing again and facing the class, "and react accordingly."

"The princess is much shorter than I am, would you see that as a disadvantage?" Nox asked them. They all nod in agreement.

"The biggest man wins," Matthias spoke up, "Always." His little face was sure and certain, and for his life, growing up in the barracks with other large and tough men, guards and workmen from the castle, it was probably true. In the weekend brawls the barracks would put on at the end of each month, it was almost always the biggest man who won. In this case specifically, Matthias' father. A frequenter to the fights, who won quite some gold in the process. Aura had loved sneaking out to watch them when she was younger, much to Fendiah's disapproval.

"Not always," Raelyn argued. "Princess Aura is smaller, so she can move faster."

"Correct." Nox's voice rang through the group, the small amount of praise made Aura's insides sputter and stall, as if unsure what to do with the compliment. She could feel Nox's eyes on the side of her head.

CHAPTER 2

Aura

Training went on for a while after Nox left. Aura loved training classes. She had fought to teach them, wanting to be involved in this aspect of the castle life. She herself loved training, and as a child it helped her through the death of her own parents. Gave her an outlet to pour her energy into; whether good or bad feelings fueled it. When her light powers developed, she found ways to weave it into her battle stances, her hits and blocks. Her light was strong, but not having the guidance from an elder as others did in their own trades was a difficulty she faced.

Ever since Kyeria arrived on the rocky mountain side of the border into The Hollow, her magic had fascinated Aura. She knew of fae magic, had heard the stories, and read the texts on their people and how magic was gifted down generations, each one having a strong elemental magic. Kyeria in turn was fascinated with Aura's ability to manipulate light. She had been such a wonderful addition to The Hollow. Aura had never seen her brother, Kellian, outwardly adore someone in such a way. He was rather reserved with his feelings, would stay holed up in his tower, or on long flights over the far isles or trips to Dragon council meetings that moved frequently. But when Kyeria arrived, even when they met on the mountain, something in her brother had changed. As if in a moment.

They called it a *soulbond*. A person ones soul was tied to, across all time and all versions of life. Finding each other in each and every life, cycle after cycle. It was rare. So rare that it was more myth and folklore. Kyeria had once explained the snap in her chest she felt when she saw

Kellian. That it was as if the whole world shifted, and everything barreled towards her at once, like being woken up from a dream. The description had stuck with Aura, constantly on the edge of her mind.

After training, Aura found herself irresistibly drawn to Nox's workshop. The wooden building, draped in vines with long purple flowers and deep green leaves cascading from its beams, had a certain rustic charm. She peered inside to see Nox's back, stripped of armor, his linen shirt clinging to him with sweat. His disheveled hair and the same brown trousers and dirtied boots only added to the picture of rugged intensity. The sleeves of his shirt were rolled up above his elbows, revealing arms that stretched the fabric with every movement, captivating her gaze. He was engrossed in sharpening a new sword, its delicate handle still unpolished, as he worked the wheel with a rhythmic push and pull. Nox paused, lifting his foot off the pedal and turning toward her. His shirt hung open in a careless manner, exposing his chest, and Aura couldn't help but admire the sight.

"Princess." His voice was pure gravel and stone. She swallowed suddenly, as if forgetting the words on her tongue. She *hated* being called princess by him. Something about it made her skin buzz, her blood boil.

"Don't call me that." She glared.

"What shall I call you then." He smirked. They did this time and time again. He called her names she despised, and on and on it went. He rarely called her by her name. Something about it made Aura maddened by it.

She shook her head, refusing to play his game today. Too distracted by the gorgeous steel in his hands, the small mysterious short sword.

"What is that?" Aura asked.

"That is not the question you wanted to ask." Nox smirked. Aura groaned and crossed her arms.

"If you want to know *who* it is for," Nox began, "it is for Esmeralda. Kyeria commissioned one special for her, a smaller short sword than I've never made, but perfect for her nonetheless." He smiled at his creation. Aura stepped towards him, she couldn't help her hand reaching out, her fingers dragging across the metal. Nox always used the best metals, the strongest steel in his royal swords. His father had been a blacksmith, his grandfather and so on. Nox however, after learning the craft, had decided to join the royal guard. His brother took up the shop in town,

202

holding on to the family legacy. But Nox had slowly built out his own small workshop in the barracks after gaining his ranking as captain and high guard of the royal army. It was small, the kingdom was not under attack or war, it was hidden to the rest of the realm and continent. But the last few years, flighting off the damned shadow beast, trying to keep it away from villages in The Hollow and protecting the borders from Raiders as the magical border shrunk from the beast eating away at the magic, had been not a small fleet.

"So what do you need?" Nox asked, blue eyes searching.

"Next shift?" She asked casually, as if she didn't really care. But she did. Because she wanted him to be done for the day. She wanted him all to herself.

"Not untill high night," He replied.

"Any plans on sleeping before then?" She smirked. His heated gaze matched her own.

"None," He said after a long silence, his voice thick.

"Hmm," Aura said and walked out, her hips swinging as she left his workshop, heading confidently towards his side of the barracks. She heard his soft chuckle behind her when she left. Knew he would follow not long after, as to avoid suspicion from others out at this time. She walked in the direction of his house, towards the path just south of it that lead into the gardens and back to the castle, then she snuck down a hidden path, covered with a thick screen of trees, weaving between them and towards the back of Nox's house, the backdoor was unlocked, as it usually was. She closed it quietly and walked up the stairs.

She picked up a book on his nightstand and began reading, waiting for him to arrive. On the hour, he appeared. She heard the front door creak open and lock, his boots on the wooden floors, then the stairs, then in the doorway. Aura felt his gaze on her, burning through her before she lowered the book. Her eyes peeked over, Nox held her gaze with obsidian eyes. The light blue was stormy and dark now, as it always was when he was thinking certain thoughts.

"Took you long enough." Aura's impatience leaked through her words, but she was smirking her usual way, all for him.

"I'll make up for it," He said, strolling towards her, his strong hands were black with grease and dirt, as if he finished his work and came straight over, forgoing cleaning up beforehand, he pulled at his shirt, stretched his hands above his head and yanked it off. It unceremoniously floated to the ground. His boots were kicked off in a hurry, then he was there, above her, plucking the book out of her hands and bending the corner of the page down to mark her spot and placing it back on his nightstand. Then his hand went to her face, slid down her neck slowly, leaving a trail of grease and dirt much to her annoyance.

"You did that on purpose," she seethed.

"What are you going to do about it?" He threw back, she reached up, her hands tangled in his dark locks and pulled hard. Crashing his lips to hers. His hand pressed down on her in response, and his large form straddled her.

"At a loss for words, *Princess*?" Goddess his voice, it was like pure venom, honey and poison to her ears.

"Still making up my mind, *Captain*." She spit back and was rewarded with a smirk. Goddess above, she loved that stupid smirk. It creased along his strong jawline, his beard was short, as if he forgot to shave it off as he usually did, it was rough along her skin. He dragged his lips, his shadow of a beard scraping along the way.

"Don't call me that," he growled.

"Then stop calling me princess."

"No."

They collided again, a mess of limbs, breathy kisses and grasping each other. As if their time was ticking away faster and faster, as if it was the last time they would feel each other in this way. Aura tried to convince herself it was. This was the last time. No more fucking the Captian of the Guard. Goddess, her brother would kill her. She owed it to her family, to her kingdom, to focus on them, not this.

But the rough hands around her softened, and began worshiping her. Nox pulled himself off of her, he stood, then reached for her again, each hand grasping a thigh, his muscles flexed and he pulled her towards the edge of his bed, then sank onto his knees.

"I am starved." He growled out before she was overtaken but pure lust. They indulged in every piece of themselves, Nox especially. His eyes met hers, both fire burning so deeply around them. She felt herself glowing. Like magic was tingling all around her. Then she felt him pull away, she opened her eyes again and looked at him. He stared in awe.

"You're—" he started. She was in fact, actually glowing. "Fuck, are you okay?" He asked, suddenly worried.

"Perfect." She smiled. Really and truly, she felt like the sun, beaming bright. Basking in pleasure.

"Fuck," he muttered before grabbing the back of her neck and pulling her to him. Their lips collided again, they fought in dominance, danced around each other before Nox won out, her lips parted in a groan and he took the moment, his tongue taking over her mouth. Her hands wandered to his hardened length. She teased him, earning deep groans from him as she did. But only for a moment before he ripped her hand away and pinned both above her head. Nox shook his head.

"Not yet." His voice was a command, a promise of more to come. Aura, utterly surrendered, felt like melted butter beneath his touch. What could she possibly do to deny this man who had so completely unraveled her? How could she resist when every fiber of her being craved him? It was a battle she knew she would lose each time; her body had already surrendered to his touch, his lips, his ability to please her in ways she could scarcely explain.

Nox's hands roamed with a practiced grace, exploring the contours of her body with an almost reverent touch. His fingers traced delicate patterns along her skin, igniting a cascade of sensations that made her gasp and writhe in response. He leaned in, his breath warm and tantalizing against her ear as he whispered, "You're so beautiful when you surrender like this."

Aura's heart pounded as she felt his lips brush against her collarbone, each touch sending electrifying shivers through her. His gaze was unwavering, dark eyes locked onto hers with an intensity that made her feel as if they were the only two people in the world. The air around them seemed to thrum with a palpable energy, their shared desire a living, breathing entity.

He shifted, positioning himself above her with a deliberate, slow movement that heightened the anticipation. His touch was firm yet tender, a paradox that drove her wild. The space between them seemed to pulse with an unspoken promise, each moment stretching out with delicious tension.

Aura's hands, freed from their earlier constraint, sought out his body, her fingers tracing the lines of his powerful form. Her touch was both a plea and a caress, an expression of the raw need she felt.

Nox's lips found hers again, his kiss deep and hungry, a melding of passion and possession. His tongue danced with hers in a rhythm as old as time, their bodies moving in a synchronized harmony that spoke of both longing and fulfillment.

As the intensity of their connection reached its peak, the world outside ceased to matter. All that existed was the profound pleasure they shared, the way their bodies intertwined in a dance of pure ecstasy. In this moment, any thoughts of resistance or inner conflict were swallowed by the overwhelming tide of their passion, leaving only the sensation of being fully, exquisitely alive.

Aura cracked her eyes open to find herself surrounded by unfamiliar dark green curtains and the heavy weight of a bare arm draped across her shoulders. Realization hit her with a jolt: hours had slipped by and she had fallen asleep.

"Fuck," she muttered, her voice edged with panic as she shoved Nox's sleeping form away. "Fuck, fuck, fuck." She scrambled around the room, desperately searching for her clothes. Nox groaned, burying his face in a pillow, completely naked. His muscular frame was on full display, but Aura barely registered it; her focus was solely on escaping his room, his house, and returning to her own quarters before the servants noticed her sneaking in at nearly midnight.

In a fit of frustration, she grabbed one of Nox's boots and hurled it at him with all her might. It struck him squarely in the shoulder. He swore and rolled over, grumbling, "What the Hel was that for?"

"We fell asleep," she snapped, not waiting to see his reaction, nor how his bright blue eyes might catch the moonlight.

"Fuck," he groaned in response, and she nodded, as if to agree, *Yeah, that's exactly what I just said.*

Aura tugged back on her training clothes as quickly as she could. Then lightly ran down the stairs and out the back door, leaving a slightly dazed and half awake Nox behind her.

She weaved through the familiar trees and walked through the back garden when she heard a noise. She paused, it was coming from the path that led out to the meadows and the dragon caves outside the entrance.

"Aura?" a familiar female voice whispered through the night.

"Goddess above, what are you doing out here?" Aura asked, rushing towards her friend's voice. Kyeria moved from behind the trees blocking her, a wide smile sitting comfortably on her lips, she was also in training clothes which made Aura cock her head.

"What were you doing?" she asked, raising an eyebrow.

"What were *you* doing?" Kyeria bounced back at her. They both eyed each other before bursting out into a fit of giggles.

"Why are you wearing training clothes?" Aura asked, knowing Kyeria did not do any sword or hand to hand training today. Not that she needed it since she was the most advanced female fighter she had ever met, even compared to the female guards in the royal army. Kyeria was shockingly fast, and even more shockingly deadly.

"I—" Kyeria cleared her throat trying to school her facial features into a serious look. But she failed as she always did, Kyeria was just a little beam of sunshine. Aura admired that, Kyeria had an uncanny ability to see the best in everyone and everything.

"You'll never guess." Kyeria bit her lip as if begging Aura to guess.

"Dragon caves?" Aura asked, assuming from the direction Kyeria had been walking from. She nodded.

"Ameline?" Aura asked again, receiving another nod and a growing smile from the copper haired fae.

"Ky," Aura gasped, "holy shit." She noticed then, her hair was disarrayed, her clothes slightly ripped, and she was wearing a dragon scale corset, one that was made from Ameline's very scales, one made for a dragon rider. Aura knew Kyeria had been waiting for Ameline to get strong enough to fly. And they had this communication with each other, able to sense every mood and shift, so if Ameline was ready, Kyeria must have known and come out here. Even in the dead of night, not wanting to wait.

"It was amazing." Kyeria beamed. "Unlike anything I expected," she whispered into the night. Aura smiled back at her friend and linked their arms as they began to walk back to the castle.

"How did you know it was time?"

"I couldn't sleep, which oddly enough, usually Ameline is also restless when that happens, something was tugging me down here so I walked to the caves, and she was just waiting for me, so impatiently." She rolled her eyes. "So we tried again, after days of falling off, or her not being able to stay in the air for more than a few seconds. And it worked, her wings were strong enough. We took a short flight but goddess, it was amazing."

"Was it different than flying with Kel?" Aura asked.

"Very, while Kellian and I can communicate through the bond, Ameline and I are connected differently, she's in my head and I'm in hers but I can sense her emotions more. Probably why it wakes me up when she is also up. But flying with her, being able to read each other that way and communicate when to dip and raise and land—" Kyeria paused, a far off look in her eyes. "Unlike anything," she finished.

They reached the familiar castle stone walls, arms linked and strolled past the stone faced guards on watch outside the doors. Once inside they walked down the great hall and down towards the bed chambers. Aura paused at her hall and hugged Kyeria goodnight. Happy to have shared that moment with her. She rounded the corner and froze, her breath catching in her throat. There, standing resolute outside her door, was a figure all too familiar: Nox.

"Leave," Aura snapped, her voice sharp as a blade as she tried to push past him.

"I'm stationed here," Nox replied with a simple, almost indifferent tone. His armor gleamed with an unyielding shine, the crimson cape cascading down his back like a warrior's banner.

"No," she retorted, her eyes blazing with indignation. "You are never stationed here."

"I am tonight." His voice was clipped, barely concealing a thread of command beneath the surface.

"No." The word was a fierce command, her gaze locking onto his with fiery intensity. "I command you to stand down." Her voice was a seething hiss, a declaration of her authority.

Nox's eyes widened imperceptibly, a fleeting crack in his stoic facade before it reasserted itself, concealing any flicker of emotion. "Go to bed, princess," he said, turning his gaze forward with the cold detachment of a sentry.

Aura's anger flared, a tempest within her. She shoved her door open with a force that reverberated through the hall, slamming it shut with a decisive bang. She didn't care if the entire castle awoke to her fury; the door's crash was a small release for the volcanic rage boiling within her.

She stormed to her bed, ripping at her clothes as if shedding the remnants of her frustration. The familiar scent of Nox lingered on her, a reminder of the evening's unsettling end. With a frustrated flick, she tossed her garments across the room, then poured the tepid water from the buckets into her tub with a splash.

The soap was an unforgiving bar in her hands as she scrubbed furiously at her skin, her motions harsh and relentless. The friction turned her skin raw, but the sting was a bittersweet balm to her frustration. She rinsed off in the frigid water, its chill cutting through her heated rage.

When she finally returned to her room, she donned a blue silk nightgown that whispered softly against her skin. She collapsed into the sea of pillows, pulling a soft fur blanket over herself with a sigh of weary resignation. Her mind was made up: this was the end.

She vowed, in the quiet of her room, that she would be done with him. Tonight was the last time.

The next morning, her promise to herself was shattered apart with a soft knock at the door. The sun had not even crossed over the mountains yet, only a soft faint glow of morning was dusting the sky. Aura rubbed her sleep ridden eyes. Her muscles stretched with a raise of her arms above her head and she couldn't stop the groan from slipping past her lips at the stretch. The knock came again. She shuffled to her feet, throwing the soft blankets off her. Her bare feet hit the ground and padded along her wooden floors as she walked to the door. She heaved the heavy door open only a sliver.

"What?" she snapped out, not knowing who was there. She was met with the familiar pine smell of Nox. She inhaled deeply, letting it waft over her and settling into the calm familiar feeling. Then she froze, *no. She would not let herself fall deeper into this.*

"What do you want?" She whispered out impatiently, meeting his eyes. His brown eyes were darkened and clouded, his gaze not meeting her, instead it was lower, wholly focused on her body instead. *That was rather rude.* Then she remembered what she was wearing. A thin blue satin sleeping gown. The lace of the neckline came down rather low and did nothing to cover her pebbled nipples from sight. *Oh.*

Heat ran through her at the thought of him being so acutely aware of her, of how much she wanted him. Not her, but her stupid godsdamned body that just reacted to him in this manner. He pushed the door open easily, just wide enough to walk past her stunned form, and closed it behind him.

"I've got a few minutes," he said pulling his armor off his body already,

"Excuse me?" She glared. "You just come in here, and start stripping. Just assuming that at this goddess forsaken hour you just get to barge into *my chambers*."

His hands paused, and he looked at her.

"Then tell me to stop," he said, voice low. Then he stalked towards her, his hand hovering over her cheek, leaning down his lips only an inch away from her skin, he breathed, "tell me to stop."

Aura's heart stuttered, the breath in her lungs pausing. The anticipation of his lips on her neck, of his hand on her cheek that would inevitably slip down to her neck, made her skin feel alive, her heart beating rapidly in her chest. He was a drug, and she couldn't stop herself from leaning into his open palm. It was warm on her check, his thumb brushed her soft skin and he whispered again, his lips still still hovered over her neck.

"Last chance," he mumbled. She let her eyes close and her head fall back, opening her neck to him more.

"What do you want, *princess?*" he whispered again. Her eyes snapped open, focusing on him, and without a single pause or stutter she said the word before her own mind could stop her,

"You."

CHAPTER 3

Aura

P RESENT DAY
The clouds were flying by Aura, her white hair streamed behind her like a silver banner. Despite the blood and bruises from the recent battle, she felt a profound joy and freedom she had never known before. Flying was everything she had ever dreamed it would be, a liberation beyond her wildest imaginings. Yet, even in this euphoric moment, a shadow lingered at the edge of her thoughts. The ache of her past reality—what might have been if she hadn't fallen ill as a child—gnawed at her. She longed for the ability to shift as Kellian did, a gift she had been denied. The dragon under her bristled.

"Your thoughts are so loud, do not waste your days wondering about what could have been, lightbringer." Ameline's voice skated down the back of Aura's mind like ice. She didn't reply to the young dragon, she cleared her mind, letting the wind wash away her thoughts high above the ground. She closed her eyes, took in a steading breath in, and one long breath out, then straightened her back, and pulled her arms off the hand holds on the leather rider's seat. She pushed them to her sides, and held them out, spreading them out like a bird, tipping her head back, she laughed, pure and true. She was flying. Finally.

"You were meant to be in the skies, Aura." Ameline says gently, as they land in the meadow outside of the main dragon cave entrance near the castle. Aura slipped down from Ameline's scaled back with a wince, pain shooting through her, she couldn't even pin where it was coming from, her whole body was just aching.

"Thank you for bringing me back. For—" Aura faltered, her gaze locking with the dragon's eyes. "Goddess above, flying was—" She shook her head, a radiant smile breaking through her pain, despite her tattered clothing, bloodied knuckles, and the deep exhaustion that left her magic drained.

Ameline, now a majestic and formidable presence, gazed down at Aura with a steady, contemplative look. The young dragon had grown impressively over the past few moons, her once-immature form now powerful and graceful. She was more than capable of carrying a rider, a fact that delighted Kyeria immensely. With her scaled wings spread wide and her eyes shimmering with an ancient wisdom, Ameline exuded an aura of both strength and gentle reassurance.

"Your guard is waiting for you." Ameline nodded towards the castle, a shadow of a man was walking towards them, the light obscuring him.

Nox.

"He's not *my* guard, he is just a guard." Aura shook her head. The Dragon simply turned and left walking towards the caves, a monk waiting at the entrance to remove the rider's seat from her back. Aura smiled after the dragon. Ameline was still such a mystery, but she was warming to the people here, and she was a fierce protector of Kyeria, so in Aura's book that was a great show of character. Nox was past the gates now, stomping into the meadow, his dark and gloomy form was completed by the angry scowl on his brow.

"Took you long enough." Aura rolled her eyes, crossed her arms and planted her feet firmly, refusing to move an inch towards him. After all, she had just banished a shadow beast to Hel—he could certainly come to her.

In two swift strides, he was upon her. His arms enveloped her with a fierce urgency, a desperate need that sent shivers through her battered frame. "Shut up," he growled, his lips crashing onto hers with a hunger that belied the gentleness with which he tried to touch her. His kiss was a conflagration of raw emotion, searing and intense yet tender, as if he feared that any roughness might further bruise her already aching body.

Aura let herself surrender to the kiss, her resistance melting away as she pressed into him. Hidden away in the sanctuary of the meadow, surrounded by the shielding embrace of trees, she allowed herself to be engulfed by his presence.

When he finally pulled back, his breath ragged, his gaze held a raw edge of desperation. "Do not," he said between breaths, his voice a rough whisper, "do that again." The words were both a plea and a command, his eyes pleading with her as though the very thought of losing her again might tear him apart.

Aura, still reeling from the intensity of their reunion, pushed weakly at his chest, a feeble attempt to create space. But his grip tightened, pulling her back to him, as if he could not bear to let her go. The moment hung between them, fraught with the unspoken fear of what might have been, and what still lay ahead.

"Everything hurts," she confessed, her usual veneer of strength slipping as it so often did around Nox. He had a rare gift for penetrating her defenses, seeing through her carefully constructed shields and masks to the core of who she was.

"I can fix that," he replied, his voice a rough whisper, like gravel shifting underfoot. Though she felt an impulse to roll her eyes at his predictability, she was instead warmed by his words. Her heart fluttered, and she managed only a dismissive "pfft" in response.

Nox studied her for a moment, his stormy sea-colored eyes softening with a tenderness she seldom saw. "Come on," he said gently, his voice imbued with a soothing calm as he reached out and took her hand in his. With a reassuring grip, he guided her back towards the palace, his presence a comforting anchor amidst her pain.

The walk back was slow, but Nox didn't comment. For once, their normal spitted words and sharp jabs were not to be found. Aura refused his arm to help her walk, she limped back on her own, her head held high, her shoulder squared. She was a damn princess after all.

"Should I call for someone?" Nox asked as they walked into the barracks nearest the gardens. She knew his own quarters were nearby, she knew the building well. She couldn't sneak him into her own these last few weeks, that would be ridiculous.

Aura fought her own mind for the hundredth time of the day, she hated asking for help. She hated needing it. Nox could see through her neutral expression, through her warring thoughts. His hand tapped her upper arm and gently directed her towards his own room.

The barracks were usually packed in tightly, the soldiers sharing a hall of dorms, larger suites for those with families or separate small apartments. But the Captain of the Guard had his own building, his own home to call his own. Separate from the rest of the barracks and closest to the castle itself. They walked around the back, down a gravel path with flowering bushes kissing each side. They walked in silence, he held out his arm for her on the stairs, which she begrudgingly used. But again, no sparring words came from his lips. It was almost disconcerting. Unnatural.

"Goddess above, stop being so nice to me." Aura finally broke the silence after Nox held the door open for her and she walked past him into his room. She had been here before of course, but in a more rushed way, and she never really looked around, let alone stayed long after. But in the early morning light the room was bright. Warmth covered the space. It was calm and lived in, pieces of Nox were throughout the room, small trinkets lined a shelf, worn and cracked spines of books stacked near his bedside. Dark olive curtains donned the windows. He walked over, pulling them closed and pointed at the bed.

"Sit," he grunted. She crossed her arms instead.

"Don't tell me what to do," she bit back.

"Take off your armor, princess." He turned on her, a smirk and a sickly sweet tone. Aura shivered at it and made a face, hating the name even when her body reacted to it.

"Off. now," he commanded. And while Aura hated being told what to do. Nox's tone made her move her sore arms nonetheless, pulling the armor from her shoulders. The metal on the side of her arms had decayed from the shadow tendril that had slashed out at her before they banished the beast, she pulled the armor from her skin with a hiss of pain. Nox placed a hand on her own, stopping her.

"Let me." He kneeled before her, making her heart stutter at the sight. Nox reached across her for a salve on his bedside table and pulled the lid off. His touch was so soft, she wasn't sure if she was imagining it entirely, but she felt the relief of the healing salve immediately. He gently applied it to the open skin before continuing to slowly peel the armor off. He dropped it to the floor with a clank and Aura followed it, watched it tumble and rest on the ground, all broken and cracked. She loved that armor. It was custom made and gifted to her from the King, for her last birthday. She let out a heavy sigh as Nox rolled up the side of her tattered shirt, she raised her arms with another wince slipping out despite trying to mask it. The linen shirt slipped over her skin, leaving her bare but a binding on her chest. Another wave of relief as Nox gently covered any wound or bruise with the salve.

She waited as he finished covering any and all bruised or broken skin with the healing salve. She wore only a binding over her chest that was normal for under armor. It pushed her breasts down rather thoroughly. Although she had not wrapped the binding tightly when she originally dressed, it felt so restricting now, pressing down on her chest and making her feel trapped. She pushed away Nox's arm and stood suddenly.

"Just—" She rushed out, putting distance between them, "stop."

The world was crashing down on her, wave after wave of harsh waves of panic hit her again and again. She couldnt breath, she couldn't speak, she felt like someone was sitting on her chest. Her eyes shifted around the room before spotting the small light from the washroom. She vaguely recognized that Nox had a look of confusion and maybe a twinge of hurt on him. That he had stepped closer, hands held out, how one might approach a frightened horse.

"Stop." She nearly shouted before turning on her feet and to the washroom, slamming the door behind her shut. She felt her body slide down the closed door, her body crumble onto the ground. *What the fuck was happening. Why couldn't she breathe?*

"Ror—" a soft and maybe even desperate voice floated to her through the haze. "Princess, are you alright?"

He was concerned for her, and it was fucking wrong. All of it was wrong. He shouldn't care. *They didn't do that.*

They trained, they fought and they let off steam together.

That was it, that was all.

No emotions.

But this last week everything had changed. Aura fought off her own feelings, Nox laying lifeless in her arms flashed in front of her eyes. And she let out a strangled sob. Felt her body curl into itself. *Breathe Aura, you need to breathe.*

Again, her nightmares resurfaced before her eyes. It was Nox, bloodied and barely breathing in her arms, Kyeria hurt and being pulled into the gap in the earth, into Hel itself. It was Kellian falling from the sky in dragon form, shot down. It was all impossible, it hadn't happened. But her nightmares felt so real, they haunted her, they made her heart sputter and stall. She was useless like this. Completely and utterly useless. How had she ended up like this, she was a princess for fucks sake. *Get it together.* She fought herself, tapped in her own mind. Silently screaming behind the bars of her own body.

"Aura," a strong familiar voice broke through her living nightmares.

Aura.

He had said her name.

The lock on the door creaked, being unlatched from the outside. Maybe even broken. Then the door pushed gently on her back. She pulled her body forward and out of the way, but stayed on the ground. Her arms were wrapped around herself, holding her knees to her chest. She was gasping for air, for any semblance of normalcy in the realm of breathing. But she could not get her heart to settle, it beat so fast she was sure it would just give out at any moment. *What a pathetic way to die.*

A gentle hand was on her cheek, then the same on the other. Nox's blue eyes stared at her blank expression. Tears were streaming down her cheeks and he brushed each one away as they came.

"Tell me something you see," ,e whispered to her, gently pressing his thumb under her chin.

"You," she gasped out through uneven breaths.

"Something you can hear?" he asked. She focused on him, his eyes became brighter to her, his features clearer. Maybe her tears were stopping. *Pathetic stupid tears.*

"Your annoying voice," she spat out, still breathing hard but no longer gasping.

"Something you can taste.," he whispered again. He was closer, the breath of his words brushed her lips. She opened her mouth to ask what the hel he was talking about. Her eyebrows were creased and glare in place. But instead of responding, she was cut off. His lips met hers, gentler than usual but still with force. He used the gasp of surprise to take control of the kiss. *Goddess above, if Nox knew anything, it was how to kiss a woman.*

She melted into him, into his touch, gently holding her face, one hand slipped back and tangled into her hair. Aura couldn't stop the reaction her body had to her. He kissed her like he needed her to breathe, like the world would slip away if he stopped. Maybe even, like she would. Her mind was whirling with empty bliss. It always did with Nox. His touch, his lips, were the only thing that could silence her mind.

A noise from outside brought her back to reality, and she shoved at his chest. His touch disappeared immediately, he pulled back and put space between them.

"What the fuck was that for?" she snapped at him. Nox again looked stunned. Seemingly they were both wearing their emotions today. An unsettling and abnormal event for the pair of them. Because, that was not just a kiss, not a heated before action to ripping each other's clothes off. That kiss was slow, and warm and comforting.

They did not do that. Aura peered up at him, a million thoughts racing in her mind, but this inability to make any of them come out of her mouth, so she was a statue, silent and wide eyed. Nox slammed down a blank expression, but his eyes betrayed him. As they always did. Aura could tell everything about how he was and what he was feeling by his eyes alone. They were clear now. Like the great lake in the Ash Mountains she loved so much, bright and clear.

"Sorry," he mumbled and pushed his hair back, sliding his fingers through the brown locks with a sigh. She let her head fall back against the wall she was leaning on.

"You called me by my name," Aura said, staring at the ceiling instead of the giant form of the man sitting on the washroom floor with her. He took up the whole walkway, it wasn't a small washroom either. She noticed the copper tub in the middle, the mirrors that adorned the wall across and the cabinets, she was sure were meticulously organized.

"Slipped out." His voice was casual, relaxed. But he never called her by her name. She could count the amount of times on one hand. It was rare. It was unsettling.

"Sorry," He mumbled again.

"Stop saying sorry," she groaned, lifting her head to meet his gaze. "Seriously, stop being so nice to me." Her eyes narrowed, reflecting the irritation she felt.

He faltered, his gaze dropping to the floor, and his eyelids squeezed shut as if to block out her piercing stare. "You were crying. I've never seen you cry," he finished gently.

If the crying wasn't embarrassing enough, the gentle manner he was handling her in was worse. Additionally she had cried in front of him. That was almost worse. He was just knocked out cold at the time. The memory of her vulnerability—the tears she shed while he was unconscious, the world crumbling around her—haunted her. It was a nightmare she relived in fragments: the raid, the battle, and Nox's blood staining the forest floor. They had gone to the border to handle the raiders, expecting to find trouble but not the devastation that awaited them. The shadow beast's magic had dissipated prematurely, leaving them exposed, a beacon to their enemies. Nox had been struck by a blade, a cruel wound that sliced through his side. Despite the injury, he fought on, while she, overwhelmed and desperate, faced off against two raiders. She had thought him fine—until he wasn't.

The journey back to the castle was a hazy blur of fear and panic. The soldiers dispatched the raiders, but Aura's focus was solely on Nox. When he collapsed, her world narrowed to the sight of his blood-soaked side, the deep gash that seemed to expose bone. Desperation drove her to tear away his armor, revealing the extent of his injury. Soldiers rushed to help, but she screamed at them to return to the border, her only concern was his survival. Kyeria and Kellian arrived as Esmeralda dashed down the stairs toward her. Everything was a chaotic whirl, her cries of distress mingling with the urgency of the moment. It felt as though she was drowning in the crushing weight of it all, the realization of her fear and helplessness surging over her like an unforgiving tide.

She knew she was crying, she felt like she couldn't breathe like it had just happened. Like the waves had finally pulled her under.

"I—" she started and stopped, pushed her hair out of her face, and took a deep breath. "I felt like I couldn't breathe," she explained quietly, as if not wanting to fully admit to the weakness. But Nox didn't make fun of her or have a witty comment. Instead his eyes turned stormy.

"I've had that too."

Aura's head snaps up, taking in the man across from her. "You have?" she asked.

"Yeah," he replied simply. "That's why I asked you those things, distraction helps."

"Oh." Her thoughts were knotted, messy and unreadable, even to herself. The best she could muster was the one word.

They sat like that for a while. Silently on the floor of his washroom before Nox was the first to break. "You should clean up. I'll give you the space," he said, standing and leaving without a glance back towards her. Aura let her limbs feel heavy as she sat there for a few moments. But that was all the self pity she allowed herself.

Pulling her sore body up, she walked to the massive copper tub in the middle of the room. It must have been made larger for Nox's massive body but she was sure it would wholly swallow her. Though soaking in a giant bath sounded like just the thing to bury her demons.

There was a knock at the door, too gentle and soft to be Nox. When Aura padded over to the door she opened it to reveal a young servant girl. Her face looked fairly familiar, she worked in the castles.

"Hello your highness, I have hot water and some soaking salts for you here." She leaned down to hold up the large buckets. She saw two more by the front door behind the girl. Aura nodded to her and held open the door wider. The girl made quick work of carrying the large buckets of hot water and pouring them into the tub. Bath salts in a jar left on the ground next to the tub, then the girl disappeared, returning a moment later with fresh clothes and a towel for her. She curtsied and turned to leave.

"Excuse me—" Aura spoke up. "Please keep this to yourself."

The girl looked stricken, bewildered by the comment. "Of course, ma'am. I wouldn't dream of it. It's an honor to be of assistance." She bowed her head low and curtsied.

"What is your name?" Aura asked.

"Mae, your highness." She stayed in a low bow.

"Thank you, Mae." Aura nodded to the girl. Her hair was the darkest of blacks, her skin paler than the moon as if the sun had never touched her. Her eyes were dark brown as well. She was small, the same height as Aura, wearing a brown cotton dress and a white apron. She smiled sweetly to the princess and bowed her head again before turning to leave.

Once alone, Aura sank into the embrace of the massive tub, letting the day's exhaustion melt away with each ripple of the water. The steam curled around her like a comforting shroud as she allowed her mind to drift and her muscles to relax. The soothing warmth lulled her into a gentle slumber, her eyes drifting shut as she succumbed to a dream.

Suddenly, the door creaked open, and a light shake roused her from her dream. "Ror—Goddess, wake up, do you want to drown?" The insistent voice was unmistakably Nox's, somehow intruding upon her dreamscape. She blinked awake, her senses slowly returning. The comforting, earthy scents of home—trees, dirt, pine, and warmth—invaded her awareness. Her eyes shot open, and she became painfully aware of the water enveloping her.

"Princess?" The gruff voice came from her side. Turning her head, she saw Nox's face, etched with concern and frustration. Realization hit her like a cold splash: she had fallen asleep in the tub, a luxurious basin much larger than her own.

"Shit." She scrambled to rise, the lukewarm water cascading down her chest as she tried to regain her composure. The once frothy bubbles had long disappeared, leaving her naked and exposed. "Shit!" She yelped, hastily covering herself with her hands and drawing her legs to her chest. "Turn around!" she demanded, her voice a blend of embarrassment and urgency.

"It's not anything I haven't seen, *Princess*." She could feel the sarcasm in Nox's voice. It was dripping. He was wanting to push her, to get a reaction. To play their game.

"Hand me a towel and get out," she seethed, not in the mood for games. He simply shrugged, did not avert his gaze, and handed her a towel. He took in her dripping wet body with hungry eyes.

"Fuck off." She groaned and stood, the water dripping down her every curve. She held his gaze as she wrapped the towel around herself and went to step out of the tub. A small issue since it was huge and stepping over, while keeping the towel in place would prove to be difficult. Nox smirked, seeing the issue and stood watching.

"You're just going to stand there and watch me struggle?" she snapped. "Why is your tub so godsdamned big?" She felt her anger rising again. Nox just had this way to make her want to scream.

The good and bad way.

Currently: the bad way.

"Happy to help, all you have to do is ask, Princess." The smirk was permanently etched in his stupid face. She hated him.

"Give me a hand then you giant idiot." She caved, rolling her eyes. He looked so damn proud of himself for winning this one. Held out a hand and she took it begrudgingly. Stepped over the high edge and tried to not slip once both feet were on the cold ground. But the water slopped over with her last step and she fell forward. Arms wrapped around her waist, setting her upright, her feet back under her. The hands stayed.

"Careful, your highness." His voice was low and deep, testing her, teasing her.

Not today.

"I think I need a healer," she announced, making him snap up straight, the smirk erased and the look of a royal guard replacing it. Dutiful and serious.

"I will call for one, immediately."

"I need to change first, then I'll see one in the castle." She pushed his hand off her and took steady steps towards the pile of neatly folded clothes Mae had brought her.

"Get out." She waved a hand. He listened this time. The comment about needing a healer making him scurry out. She felt the jab of pain in her side. Soaking in a tub that long with an open wound was not the best idea. But she had done it anyway, craving the warmth and comfort. She heard the front door open and close while she dressed in the washroom alone. When she was finally dressed and opened the door, she found Kyeria sitting on a bench instead of Nox or another healer.

"Cute place." Kyeria smirked.

"Don't say it." Aura groaned and walked over to her friend,

"Not a word." Kyeria shook her head in mock seriousness. "Nox, said you need a healer, figured this was best to keep your current location discreet."

"Does Kellian know I am here?" Aura groaned again.

"No."

"Thank the gods."

"But he'll figure it out soon enough." Kyeria sighed, and motioned at Aura's side. She tugged up the shirt to reveal the wound. Kyeria went to work, lifting her hands over the wounds, her healing magic glowed warm on Aura's skin. She was used to it of course, she had been mended and healed hundreds of times in her life. As a child she was constantly falling out of trees or playing with swords too big for her that would inevitably end up with her hurt.

"Well, it's not anything anyway," Aura argued half heartedly, earning another knowing look from Kyeria. Her copper hair was swept up behind her neck into a collection of twists. She was wearing a simple cotton white dress and a green corset. Aura wasn't exactly sure how much of the day had passed, maybe the whole thing.

"He'll be mad Aura," Kyeria said gently. "Nox is one of us, one of the inner circle. He is Kellian's most trusted ally. His second in command."

"I know. I know." Aura shook her head. She had really wrapped herself up in a mess. Getting tangled up with Nox, her own trainer, the high guard and captain, was a mistake. She knew this. She knew this the first time, and the second, and the last. But the minute he touched her, it didn't matter. Nothing did. Only his touch, she needed more and more of it.

"If you care for him—" Kyeria started, eyeing Aura. She rolled her eyes,

"I can't stand him." Aura waved a hand dismissing the comment. Her friend only smiled and looked like she did not believe Aura even in the slightest.

That was a problem for another day.

Today, she needed to sneak back into her own castle.

CHAPTER 4

Nox

The training grounds were busy, as the barracks usually were mid week. Soldiers were training in different circles. Nox was in the center of the biggest; sweat was beading on his chest, on his neck and forehead. His shirt had been stripped long ago, swords were thrown to the sides. He was in the ring with a bloodied nose, most likely what would be a black eye and a split lip.

"You're off your game, Greenwood!" a soldier yelled from the side. He was leaning on a fence, others crowded around watching the fight. Lucas was grinning like a fool as he spit blood from his own mouth. No one ever got in many hits to Nox, he was bigger and stronger. He had earned his place as captain, he was essentially undefeated in the ring. But here he was, a handful of punches had made it past him and his head was spinning as a result.

"One last round, Black," Nox seethed through his teeth. Lucas Black was one of his closest friends. He was a brother really. Other than Kellian himself. While Kellian and Nox were similar in age and grew up on castle grounds, Lucas had shown up as an orphan at sixteen. One of the older soldiers took him in after his mother died of a sickness that had plagued his village. He was from the northernmost villages, just before the borders and the northern gate to the isles. He had grown strong, a good fighter, loyal to the bone. Everyone liked him and his cheery disposition. The exact opposite to Nox himself, who instead distinctly reminded others of an angry rain cloud. Dark and brooding and could potentially turn into a storm.

"Raise the stakes, old friend?" Lucas shouted over to him. Nox nodded for him to go on, shifting his weight from one foot to the other. "You lose, I cover your tab at Mayers Pub," he started making Nox scoff. He had a tab alright, aside from the generous salary of being the captain, Nox had spent almost every night at the Pub before a few weeks ago. Before Aura.

It seemed more than just a few weeks now. She consumed his every thought. She was striking and beautiful and terrifying. Aura was the only one who could keep up with his sharp tongue. The only one who refused to back down from him. She did, in fact, outrank him as she was the princess, heir and a guardian to The Hollow. That only made him want her more, of course. But his favorite thing about the white haired tiny chaos creature was her ability to gut a man without a single thought. She loved her daggers more than any other weapon. Used her size and speed to her advantage. He had taken over her training a year ago, after one of the older soldiers retired. Kellian personally asked him to oversee her training, saying he wanted her training with the best. At all times, so she was always ready. Aura did not have the ability to shift as Kellian did. While still an heir, he assumed Kellian worried about his more human sister if anything were to happen.

In the last year they had trained, and Aura had focused all her energy on hunting a shadow beast. One that had finally been locked back into Hel where it belonged last night. Aura had proved herself over and over again. But Kellian never stopped worrying for his sister and had then given Nox his last command, two weeks ago.

To be her personal guard.

Aura however, did not know of this, and it was after that things became a little more confusing, and Nox had seen her in a way he hoped no other male would ever do again.

Fuck, what was that.

No.

She was not his. He had to accept that.

"And if you win—" Lucas pulled him out of his thoughts. The same thoughts that had clouded his mind and let the damned man get in four punches. "I'll cover your night shifts for a month."

Nox paused, shifting his weight from heel to heel, a month was a long time. And nights free meant more nights with *her.*

That was enough to get his shit together.

A shout from another soldier indicated for them to fight. This time, Nox cleared his mind, slamming down his mask. All his emotions shoved behind the steel. He threw punch after punch, dogged Lucas' hits easily and landed two punches inturn. Lucas grunted in frustration. This round was about to be a lot harder for him.

A few minutes later the fight was over, Lucas sporting a matching broken lip and blood trickled down from a cut on his brow. Both men's knuckles were blotchy and red.

Nox grinned like a fool.

He had won.

It was night when Nox returned to his house. The gravel beneath his boots crunched, with the moonlight lighting his path. They had all headed to the pub after the fight. Nox was slightly wobbly on his feet, much to his own dismay. He shoved the key into the front door, unlocking it easily and made his way up the stairs, he was anything but quiet. He missed a step and banged a sore shoulder into a wall. With a groan, he pulled himself up and went up the last set of stairs. When Nox got to his bedroom, the door was askew. He assumed Aura had left to see a healer. When she said she needed one after nearly drowning in the tub, he had run to find Kyeria, knowing she would be the best. He shouldn't have left her alone in the tub after such a long and exhausting battle, but finding her there, limp in the water made his skin crawl.

It rattled him, and he *didn't do rattled.*

He pushed his way into the room, the door creaking as he entered. The bed before him was a chaotic tangle of pillows and blankets, a testament to the disarray of his mind. Without hesitation, he shed his clothes, which still carried the stench of the pub, and collapsed onto the disheveled bed. The mattress groaned under his weight, and he let out a weary sigh, only to be jolted upright by a soft mumble and a groan.

In the dim light, Nox strained his eyes to make out the figure nestled among the tangled sheets. Long, white hair fanned out across the pillows, a stark contrast against the dark fabric. Her small frame was almost swallowed by the mass of blankets, her presence so unexpected that he had nearly missed her.

Aura.

The princess who had always made it clear—never spend the night. Yet here she was, fast asleep in his bed, her form curled into the warmth of his sheets. She had waited for him, despite everything. A pang of guilt twisted in his gut. The battle, the near loss of her—it had shaken him more than he cared to admit. And now, to see her here, in his home, her presence, a quiet reminder of what he had almost lost, weighed heavily on him. She had waited for him, and the thought of it settled deeply, a bitter mixture of regret and longing.

"Princess." His voice was a gentle murmur, barely more than a breath as he poked her shoulder. She only groaned softly, her form curling deeper into the pillows, her white hair splaying across the bed like a silken halo. Nox exhaled heavily, the weight of exhaustion pulling at him. He was too drained to rouse her now, and a reluctant part of him didn't want to at all.

A stark internal conflict waged within him. He had always braced himself for the fleeting nature of their encounters—heated, passionate, and then over as quickly as they began. This was different. She was here, asleep in his bed, her warmth an unexpected balm against the chill of his loneliness. He slid under the covers with deliberate care, trying not to disturb her, but she stirred slightly, turning to face him with a sleepy murmur. His heart ached as he felt her body nestle closer, her trust in him manifesting in this rare and vulnerable moment. Nox wrapped his arms around her, pulling her snugly against him, his touch both protective and tender. It was a rare and precious intimacy he had never thought to experience—an intimacy he had only dreamt of, never daring to hope it would come to pass.

The truth clawed at him, a gnawing awareness that this closeness was something he had never been granted before. She had always made it clear: their encounters were transient, a fleeting storm of passion and then separation. This, this quiet vulnerability, was a new terrain, one that stirred a turbulent mix of fear and longing within him. The trust she placed in him, even if she was unaware of it, was a fragile thing, a trust that took more than just the nightly visits to forge.

He knew he would face the repercussions of this unanticipated closeness in the morning. For now, he would hold her, savoring the warmth and the rare comfort of her presence. As he closed his eyes, he wrestled with the tangled mess of emotions that surged within him, knowing that the consequences of this night would weigh heavily on his heart come dawn.

Nox jolted awake with a sharp punch to the arm, his eyes flying open in surprise and irritation. "That is a very rude way to wake someone up," he grumbled, rubbing the sleep from his eyes. The dim morning light filtered through the curtains, casting a soft glow over the room. Aura, perched on the edge of the bed, leaned over him with a look of exasperation, her tousled hair framing her face.

"Why didn't you wake me!" she demanded in a fierce whisper, her frustration barely contained.

"You wouldn't wake up!" he protested, raising his hands in mock defense. Despite his efforts, she delivered another sharp jab to his arm. "Fuck!" he hissed, trying to keep his voice down as the sounds of the waking barracks drifted in through the window. His shift wasn't due until noon, but he usually stayed up with the early crew, overseeing the soldiers. Today, though, he had let Lucas take over.

"Just use the back door," Nox muttered, burying his face in the pillow, hoping for a few more moments of peace.

"Nox!" She poked him again, and then again, her touch insistent. He finally dragged himself up, meeting her gaze with a mix of irritation and curiosity. "What?" he grumbled, his patience wearing thin.

"I'm sorry," she said softly, her voice almost a whisper.

His breath caught in his throat. The apology, so rare and unexpected, halted him mid-grumble. He stared at her, taken aback by the sincerity in her eyes.

"I was a little rude when you woke me in the bath, that was dangerous. I shouldn't have done that when I was that tired. Let alone with an open wound." Her head dropped. The disappointment in herself was evident. He knew she struggled with this, watched her push herself down, trying to be smaller and smaller. So he plastered on a smile, even a little smirk, and reached out a hand, tilting her chin up.

"You just love to drive me crazy, *princess*." His deep voice carried a weighty resonance. Her eyes slowly dragged up to look at him, taking in his shirtless self.

"It is rather fun." Aura smiled and bit her lip to try and stop from continuing to smile.

"What time is your next shift?" She asked, her eyes sparkling with mischief.

There she was.

His little storm cloud.

"Hours from now," he said, propping up on his elbows. She hummed her answer then pulled the blankets aside to get under them again, pulled a leg over his waist and straddled him.

"Seems like I'm stuck here till you can sneak me out," she said, trying to rationalize her excuse. He could see right through it. She wanted to be here instead. With him, with his touch. But she had a hard time admitting that to herself. He was fine with giving her the time, giving her the games and the teasing and the verbal sparring. He would be what she needed him to be.

As long as he was hers.

"Anything in mind?" He smirked.

"I have a few ideas," she said back, her golden eyes glowing dark and clouded. He always adored that about her. Aura was bright, always. She was light incarnate, aside from her literal light powers. But when she wanted him, when she was turned on, she was dark and cloudy, like a *storm*.

The hours passed quickly. Their limbs were lost to one another, tangled in the bedsheets. His rough hands had roamed her body, and thoroughly spent them both. She had washed again before pulling on a fresh dress someone had brought her. It was simple, but it was blue. Goddess above, Aura in blue, was the most dangerous combination. She was striking, and breathtakingly beautiful.

"So, we had training in the forest and then you escorted me to the gardens later?" she said, making up their cover. Nox shrugged, he would go along with whatever she chose, it wasn't hard, she had sound reasoning behind most of them. They snuck out the back door, Nox locked it this time behind them and they took the small, barely visible path through the trees to a main garden path walk. Then they began their fake walk through the gardens.

The sun was high, Nox had donned his armor, his red thick cape attached to the neck, signifying his ranking. The others had grey capes for the second highest rankings, below that were no capes and only armor. It was earned in the royal army. Nox had earned his grey cape early on, being the youngest to ever receive a grey.

Kellian had made Nox his high guard a few years back now. They had always remained close even after the separation between a barracks kid and a royal was larger than it was as kids running through the castle grounds, forests, and mountains. Kellian had been blessed with the ability to shift into a dragon form and Nox was the first he told it to. They were loyal to the other. Because of that, the whole fucking his friends sister thing sat uneasy in him. But he shook it off anyway.

Nox stayed a few steps behind Aura as she walked, escorting her in a professional capacity instead of walking with her. He was rather fond of watching her as she moved gracefully through the gardens; they looped back to her mothers gardens filled with lavender, light sprites bouncing between the gardens, butterflies flew by aura, as if they wanted to be near her and her light. She was faintly glowing at the moment, something Nox had begun to pick up on. Her hair seemed to glow in the daylight. Sometimes a dull light encircled her hands or arms, swirling up her limbs in a way that was practically invisible unless the sun hit just right. The first time Nox had noticed it, he began to pay closer attention. On their many excursions out to track the shadow beast, Nox realized just how powerful Aura's light was. Before the shadow beast, she had not used it much, not that he had seen. She seemed to be hiding it, not liking to use it at all it seemed. But in the past few weeks, something had shifted, he assumed she found purpose in tracking and ultimately banishing the beast back to Hel. He was itching to know what she would do next, what self imposed quest she would pick to take on. Aura was not one to sit still for long. He would probably catch her sneaking out in the next few nights, wandering into the mountains to sit at the lake. He had followed her there a few times now; not that she knew. Since Kellian assigned him as her personal guard, he was tasked with knowing where she was at any given time. And while Aura was rather slippery, he was in the shadows following.

Nox followed Aura around the gardens before she announced she was going to her rooms. He escorted her there, watched her close and lock the door behind her, and waited for Lucas to finish his sweep. His golden hair and tall stature made him stand out in the dark stone walkway, he peered at the paintings on the wall before eyes swept the rest of the hall, spotting Nox at the end. He nodded walking over.

"Nox," he greeted.

"Did you find anything?" Nox asked. Lucas had sent a message to Nox late the night before, one of the light sprites left it on his open window sill, a small gleaming stone atop it, an update from Lucas on a rather unsettling issue.

"Nothing, her door was unlocked, and only the desk looked rearranged," Lucas updated. It was about a week ago that Lucas had spotted the post outside of Aura's chamber empty, the door ajar, and when he entered, someone was slipping out of the window in a black cloak. He had reported it to Nox immediately. Aura had been with Nox that night in his own home. While she was safe and threat levels were normally rather low, someone sneaking into her rooms and rifling around was not something he liked. Nox wanted to gather more information before speaking with Kellian, but her rooms being rifled through twice filled him with unease.

Nox knew it was time to tell Kellian.

Which meant explaining why Aura was not in her rooms, *for multiple nights.*

Nox left Lucas at his post, and took off on the familiar path past the bed champers and to the towers, one specifically that held Kellian's Observatory. It was a glass encased tower, all of his treasures and findings filled the room. Vines wrapped around the open pillars and bloomed, no doubt an addition from Kyeria. He had been there many times, the two of them would hide in the old tower when they were younger, hiding from trouble or a prank they had played on someone else.

Nox knocked on the familiar wooden door. Some shuffling ensued inside before he heard Kellian shout, "Come in." Nox pushed open the door, and saw the disarray. Papers were strewn along the tables, and Kellian was leaning over a telescope jotting down notes, his hair a mess, and unsurprisingly looking overly tired.

"Kel," Nox sighed. "Have you even slept?" he asked his friend.

Kellian only waved a hand dismissing Nox and his worry.

That was the end of that.

"I have something I need to inform you about," Nox said, keeping his tone as even as possible. But Kellian spotted it and turned, abandoning his task at hand immediately.

"What's wrong?" The pen was dropped to the table, his golden eyes were pinned to Nox. Nox sighed.

"Last week—" Nox started, earning a glare from the prince. Kellian was a kind royal, he had always been, he would lead with that kindness, but he was fiercely protective, especially over his little sister. Nox tried to shut off his mind, quell his emotion behind a wall of stone. *This was not going to be easy.*

"Lucas was doing night rounds, on Aura's wing."

"When?" Kellian's voice was clipped.

"While you were gone with Kyeria to the Isles," Nox reported smoothly.

"Where were you?" Kellian glared. Nox swallowed and continued.

"Lucas had the shift. He does rounds every two hours, otherwise is posted by the door," Nox explained. "When he got back from a round, Aura's door was ajar. He knocked and called her name, sometimes she's off with Esmeralda or Kyeria into the night." Kellian's eyes glared further, "but with you both gone, Lucas entered and someone much larger than Aura was sneaking out a window, wearing a dark cloak. He did not catch their face, and they disappeared into the night," Nox finished.

"Did anyone hunt them down?" Kellian asked, voice struggling to stay even.

"Yes, Lucas followed on foot, and sent a sprite to alert the guard on watch that night, and one to me." There was a pause, Nox felt his heat rate escalating, already seeing the next question from the prince,

"Where was my sister?" Kellian's voice was dangerously calm now, like he could see right through Nox's calm exterior. Nox took a steadying breath and met Kellian's eyes directly.

"With me."

In a second, Kellian had moved, slamming Nox into the stone pillar behind him.

"In the middle of the night, Nox?" he seethed. Nox swallowed and nodded trying to remain calm, despite the dragon prince who stood with fire in his eyes, and hand pushing into his shoulders, pinning him to the pillar.

"Yes." Nox nodded. Kellian shoved him again and let him go, taking multiple quick steps back from Nox, he ran a hand through his long white locks, palming his face.

"What the fuck," Kellian growled. "My sister?" he screamed. "My fucking sister, Nox."

"It wasn't my secret to tell." Nox's own disappointment in himself shown, in angering his most trusted friend, in angering the prince, the brother to the woman his heart was tangled with. "Not until now, not until she could be in danger."

Nox had never wanted to keep it from Kellian, but Aura insisted, it was just a way to relax as she said, it wasn't anything. The words still stung in the back of his mind. It had become more complicated than that now. He knew it. She knew it. But neither had uttered any verbal confirmation that the looks they shared were more heated, carried more importance and meaning than they used to. The sharp words and jabs they sent each other were once real, true words, but now, they were only a game. Just the precursor, then they were electric, if not explosive. Nox didn't want to give that up, so he had kept his mouth shut. But this was different and he had been battling himself knowing he needed to inform his commander, the prince to the kingdom. But the last few days had been chaotic, he almost died, they all fought back the beast, and finally rid it from the land. There wasn't exactly a spare moment to tell his friend, *"By the way, I am sleeping with your sister, it's not serious just letting off steam. Until we almost died and everything changed but it's no big deal!"*

"I trusted you." Kellian seethed. His stare was lethal, and Nox questioned his ability to leave this tower not bloodied. Because he knew, Kellian may not like to fight, not in human form, but he could pack a mean punch. Nox would much rather not be on the receiving end of the rage brewing on his face.

"Kel, listen—"

"Don't you fucking dare. My sister, Nox! The person you are meant to be guarding, protecting, not fucking." He spat out the last word like it made him physically ill.

"Kel—"

"You're dismissed." Kellian turned on his heel, back to his desk, sitting with a humph and picking up a pen. He began writing and ignored Nox completely.

"We need to discuss the intruder—" Nox crossed his arms, staying in place.

"Send someone else." Kellian glared. Nox sighed, walking towards the prince,

"I understand you are mad, we did not plan it, it just...happened," Nox said gently. Kellian let out a groan,

"I do not want to hear it, Greenwood."

"Fine—" Nox bit out, "but hear this, someone, and I don't know who, broke in to the princesses room, rifled through her desk and correspondence and left in the middle of the night. We have an issue Kellian, and she doesn't know yet, I came to you first."

Kellian's writing paused before looking up to Nox who was hovering over him now.

"I am fucking pissed at you," Kellian said, dropping the pen loudly and crossing his arms. He leaned back on the creaky chair and stared outside. Nox watched the shift, watched the Heir take over from the older brother.

"Why would someone break into her rooms, what could they have been looking for? We are a peaceful land."

"That's what we need to find out."

"We need to tell Aura," Kellian said sternly. "She deserves to know."

"I agree, but my command is to you first, your highness." He bowed his head. Nox could put aside the frustration of his own personal issues and be the loyal soldier. He was Kellian's second in command, his captain. His life was dedicated to keeping this family and this kingdom safe, as Kellian was to this sacred land and protecting the Dragon's home from the outside world.

Kellian reached for a small fairy whistle that sat on his desk. It was a simple small instrument, carved into a tiny piece of wood, only the length of a finger. Kellian raised it to his lips and blew into it. There was no sound to the human ears, but it was high enough of a pitch to alert the light sprites that served as royal messengers. Ember fluttered in through an open window quickly.

"Your highness." Ember bowed her small glowing form to the prince.

"Ember." He nodded. "Nox has reported someone who trespassed into Aura's room whilst she was gone. I would like two sprites stationed at her window, and one stationed at Kyeria's and Esmeralda's each." He informed her. She nodded quickly.

"Right away, highness." She turned to Nox and waved, a cheery smile evident on her glowing features, Nox nodded in acknowledgement. He had always liked Ember. She had worked her way up the ranks of the messenger sprites, from a young sprite when he and Kellian were younger to the lead messenger for the heirs themselves. Ember's form fluttered away, back out the window and through the skies. Nox saw two dragons flying, a large grey one and a small deep purple one. He knew Ameline was the smaller of the two but not the larger one. It was darker than Fendiah's dragon.

Nox nodded in the direction. "Who is here?" he asked Kellian. Kellian rolled his eyes.

"An elder from the council, he is insufferable. I hope Ameline is annoying the Hel out of him."

Nox grinned, *oh she was.*

"Is this really necessary?" Esmeralda's voice was calm and dismissive as she continued to pore over her book. Nox's presence at the doorway of the library's first floor was rather normal these days, but Esmeralda did not like having a guard nearby, which was made known by her small scowl on her brow. The room exuded a cozy ambiance, with a crackling hearth casting a warm, flickering glow against the rich, wooden shelves. Esmeralda sat comfortably on a cushioned bench beneath a large, sun-drenched window, a thick knitted blanket draped over her lap. Kellian had ordered extra guard on the whole royal family, Esmeralda included. But the young witch was not the biggest fan of having a shadow.

"Yes," Nox replied, his arms crossed in a firm stance. He opened his mouth to press his point further but was cut off by the sudden, loud meow of a cat. His gaze darted around, searching for the source of the noise amidst the sprawling shelves and soft, golden light of the library.

Esmeralda's lips curled into a mischievous smile as she pulled the blanket back slightly. Nestled amidst the folds of fabric was a tiny, fluffy black kitten, its eyes wide and curious. The kitten let out a soft, plaintive meow, and Esmeralda giggled softly at the sight of Nox's bewildered expression.

"What is that?" Nox asked hesitantly.

"My cat." She responded with twinkling eyes, seeing if he would say anything. He did not say a damn word. Because the last thing Nox was going to get involved in was a cat in the castle, when Kellian hated the creatures and had banned them from being inside the castle ever.

"I did not see this," Nox grumbled, "stay here till your guard arrives." He quickly turned out of the room and down the stone hall. He was not looking forward, lost to his own grumbling when he turned a corner and ran right into someone. A small squeak came tumbling out and he reached out his hands to catch the person before they both toppled over to the ground.

"Look where you are walking!" Aura scolded him, and shoved his arms off her. He rolled his eyes and looked down to the petite princess.

"You are not supposed to be alone," he said, looking behind her and finding no guard.

"Turns out Issac isn't great at his job," she said, crossing her arms, a stubborn look on her brow. She leaned against the wall, her hip jutting out. He noticed her clothing then, training clothes. A long linen tunic over brown trousers and high laced boots, her sword strapped to her back, a dagger at her thigh.

"Where is he?" The guard on duty was supposed to be *with* Aura.

"I slipped out." She shrugged. "I don't need a babysitter."

"Take it up with your brother, Ror."

"Stop calling me that!" She scowled.

"Sure thing, *Princess.*" He smirked and walked past her, determined to find Issac and give him a little training on how to avoid losing a princess.

CHAPTER 5

Aura

"Shut up." Aura squealed, seeing the small black ball of fur in Esmeralda's lap as she entered the library. "Kellian is going to lose it!" She laughed.

"Well, I know he had that rule, but—" She looked worried, eyebrows scrunched up, her eyes looking sad.

"Oh please, Kel would do anything for you. Just ask really nicely, maybe add a tear or two and you're golden." Aura smirked. Esmie paused, in thought,

"You think?" she smiled.

"I know." Aura nodded, then walked over, picking up the small ball of fur and cuddling it in her arms. "What is your name sweetness?" She purred to the small creature. Esmeralda was beaming again.

"Mittens! I don't know if it's a boy or a girl, I just found them outside by the barn. One of the stable hands said that they'd been wandering around the last few days, no mom or sibling in sight. It's getting cold at night so I wrapped it up and brought it inside." Esmie's eyes were filled with adoration to the small kitten and Aura knew there was no way her brother would take that away from Esmeralda. Esmie had come to them rather young, her parents dying in the war a decade after deciding to go and help the fae. Only her Gran was left to be the royal witch, and she taught Esmie as much as she could before she passed not long after. Kellian and Aura had sort of just taken her into their family after that. Moving her rooms closer to theirs, and adopting her into their own lives. Kellian knew what it was like to lose parents so young but old enough to know what was going on. Aura was so young when their parents passed that she held few memories of them. It was why Kellian was so protective of Esmeralda, he knew the pain of losing family after knowing them. She was an added sister after that. Stayed with them, ate with them, and attended royal meetings with them. She was family.

"Goddesses, tell me that is a sweet little kitten!" Kyeria said walking into the library and up to Aura, to see the cat.

"Meet Mittens!" Esmeralda announced. Kyeria fawned over the kitten, as she did all animals. There was no way Kellian could say no now. Not when all the girls were attached to this little bundle of black fur. They spent much too much time fawning over the kitten before discussing research. Kyeria said she was looking into the people who had been captured by the mad king. Talking with the light sprites and trying to gain more information on the status and if they could help. Aura nodded enthusiastically, it had been something prying on her own mind as well but Kellian had always dismissed Aura's pleas to go on a mission to get them back. Esmeralda found more information on the Greenburrow line and how it was connected to dragon riders. Kyeria had been riding Ameline rather successfully now as her dragon began to get stronger and stronger. Kyeria had mentioned that Ameline wanted to meet with the council and introduce Kyeria to them. After they discussed all their updates with one another, boots were heard stopping down the hall. Aura turned, already knowing it was her brother.

Kellian turned into the library. He was wearing a rather fancy coat, golden embroidery all up the chest and arms, with his formal trousers on. He looked rather fancy for a midweek late afternoon.

"What is *that*?" Kellian asked, glaring at the kitten.

"Um—" Esmeralda mumbled, "mittens."

"Excuse me?" Kellian scowled. Kyeria inserted herself walking up to Kellian, a hand on his arm, leaning into him.

"Esmeralda found a sweet, helpless, motherless kitten in the stables," she said sweetly. *Really had to throw in the helpless and motherless part in there, huh?* Aura thought.

Kellian melted immediately as he looked at Kyeria. It was only slightly sickening. Aura smiled nonetheless and peered over at Esmeralda who sat waiting.

"Fine." He groaned. "But this is the only exception. You can have one," he said sternly. Esmeralda nodded quickly.

"Promise!" She squealed and ran over to hug Kellian. He sighed and hugged her back. He really couldn't say no to her.

"Can we discuss the people trapped by the Mad King?" Aura asked her brother later that night. They were in what was once the 'War Room'. The Hollow had been a secret kingdom now for over a century. Hiding behind the magical border that stretched over the Dragonier Forest to the South, the Ash Mountains to the East, and to the edge of land North before the water of the Isles. It was five years ago now that a group of people from The Hollow had ventured beyond the borders, to bring back information and updates from the outside realm. Instead they had been captured by Evanthian soldiers, and brought back to their king. Lovingly called, the Mad King, as he was, in fact, mad.

The Mad King started the war a decade ago that pushed all magic wielders, and fae off the continent. Thousands were killed, the rest pushed back to their home land of the Fae Islands. The witches went into hiding, many also killed alongside the Fae. The Mad King despised magic, and wanted it gone. When he captured the group from The Hollow, he did not kill them, he enslaved them. His own personal magic. Two witches, a fae, and a villager. The light sprites had reported back that the human had been killed after the first year, the witches and fae unharmed, but locked in the dungeons. Only pulled from when the King demanded it.

"Who were they?" Aura asked. She had been too young to be included in the council meetings when it happened. Too young to even be told the whole story. But she knew now, she demanded a seat at every council meeting. Kellian and Fendiah agreed without fight, some of the council members disagreed but were outnumbered. It was a sore topic, one Kellian did not like to speak on. He did not agree with Fendiah's plan to wait, to not rescue them.

"Villagers, not of the court." Kellian sighed, knowing that was what his sister meant. Aura sat down in one of the oversized chairs, the fabric beneath her puffing out with dust. She swatted away at it,

"Of course," she mumbled. "Can you talk to him?"

"Grandfather has been gone so often now." Kellian sighed. It was true, in his old age, he was a bit of an absent king. A beloved one. But absent.

A hidden kingdom was not one that needed much from a King, and most royal duties had now fallen to Kellian himself. Fendiah handled the dragon council meetings that could take many weeks. Relayed back the information and Kellian ran the kingdom for the people. Aura held open court, hearing the villagers' concerns once a month. Aura had helped Kellian split the royal duties, a gesture that left her yearning for something more. For the past year, she had thrown herself into tracking the beast that had plagued their lands, channeling all her energy into eradicating it. And succeed they did. But with the beast vanquished, she was left with an insistent void.

"I want to go," she declared firmly, her shoulders squared in determination.

Kellian's brow furrowed in concern. "What do you mean?"

Aura took a moment to assess her brother. He appeared older, more regal, ready to assume his role as king. Fendiah, she knew, was ready for retirement. Yet, her own ambitions burned fiercely within her.

"I want to lead a rescue mission," Aura said, her voice steady with resolve. She outlined her plan to him, describing how she could assemble a small, skilled group, aided by sprites familiar with the Evanthian castle, to perfect their strategy. Kellian listened intently but was clearly reluctant to endorse her involvement.

"We could send soldiers," Kellian countered, his voice tinged with unease.

"No," Aura insisted, her voice unwavering. She locked eyes with her brother, her stubbornness echoing their mother's fiery resolve. "I need to be the one to go."

Kellian hesitated, a flicker of worry in his eyes. "You are needed here."

Aura shook her head resolutely. "Kyeria can take over my responsibilities. She will be their queen soon enough." Kellian's face softened with pride as he thought of his soulbound, the fire-haired Kyeria. The bond they shared fascinated Aura, a mystical connection she had only read about in old tales and dusty library books. She was eager to discover the depth of such bonds herself.

"She'll be a good queen," Aura said with a smile, her eyes meeting Kellian's. "And you'll be a good king."

Kellian studied her for a moment, understanding her need to engage in something meaningful, something that would allow her to contribute to The Hollow. They were two sides of the same coin, and he knew that she needed to focus on something that made sense, that fulfilled her.

"Okay," he said slowly, his voice filled with reluctant acceptance. "Give me a list of your top three choices within the week."

Aura's smile widened as she eagerly accepted. She surged forward to embrace her brother, her gratitude pouring out. "Thank you," she whispered into his chest.

Kellian held her close for a moment before releasing her. "I need a full plan, I'll be the one to approve the plan," he said, his voice steady.

Aura's face lit up with unrestrained joy. "Whatever you say!" she said, her excitement barely contained as she waved and left the room. Now, she had to assemble a team to infiltrate an enemy castle and rescue three prisoners. It was a daunting task, but one she was determined to conquer.

CHAPTER 6

Aura

"What?" Kyeria stood shocked, eyes wide and mouth hanging open after Aura announced she had a new mission. The library's fire was lit and burning dimly, providing a cozy light in the room where Kyeria and Esmeralda were when Aura entered.

"I know it's a lot, but I need to keep myself busy." Aura sighed.

"I understand that," Kyeria said gently, her eyes soft, "and I am glad it is happening. They've been trapped there too long, but how are you even going to get them out?"

"I don't exactly have the whole thing figured out, I'll run it by Nox." Aura shrugged. Esmeralda looked between the two.

"So—" Esmeralda dragged on the word and barely concealed her giggle. Aura shot her a glare in response.

"Come on—tell us!" Kyeria poked. Aura crossed her arms, a frown embedded into her expression.

"It's nothing—like I said, it's just letting off steam." She rolled her eyes and busied her hands. "I still hate him." Aura concluded, nodding as if convincing herself instead of the others.

Wasn't that what she was doing? She thought to herself.

"We just thought—" Emeralda spoke up.

"Listen, I know you—" Aura points towards Kyeria, "are madly in love or whatever, and you—" she points to Esmeralda, "are a baby."

"Am not!" Esmeralda chided, Mittens curled up in her lap. She swore the little cat glared at her.

"Forget it." Aura threw her arms down with a huff and turned on her heel. She heard Kyeria and Esmerlda calling after her, but she didn't want to be questioned about something that she herself was so tangled up about. It was supposed to be nothing.

But her recurring nightmares of Nox dying, and her screaming into the nothingness, were steering her towards the fact that there might be feelings there. Aura, however, did not have time for that. So she shoved down the thoughts, deep into a little box in the back of her mind. Locked it shut and forced her mind to focus on her new task.

Rescuing the magic wielders who were currently intrapped by the Mad King.

By the time Aura was walking into the barracks training grounds, she was armored in her favorite training clothes, a sword strapped to her back, and four daggers hidden in her clothes or strapped to her thigh. She was ready to fight off some of these tremulous feelings.

"Your Highness!" Someone greeted her from behind. She threw a quick glance, recognizing the guard, Lucas. He was friends with Nox, she recalled.

He would do.

"Pick a weapon, we're sparring." There was no question in her words, only a command. And while Lucas looked slightly bewildered at the announcement, he picked up a sword and followed her into an empty ring.

"First blood," she announced. Lucas' eyes went wide,

"Your highness—" His brows creased.

"I said—first blood, or we can change that to who passes out first, and it won't be me." She seethed. Her emotions were wafting off of her. Rolling through waves of rage, which tended to be where her emotions spiraled into. She knew it well, was comfortable here, with her rage.

"Sword up, soldier."

Lucas did as he was told, she watched the emotions drain from him, watched him transform into just that—a soldier.

She did the same, and let her body be a weapon.

He attacked first, and that was when she decided she rather

respected Lucas. She blocked his attack, let him make a few more to wear him down before striking out herself. He was faster than she expected. He was leaner than Nox, but just as tall. He slightly resembled a green bean, now that she thought of it.

"You can do better than that!" Aura shouted, wiping the sweat from her forehead. A small crowd had formed, gathering around the edges of the rings that was encircled with a wooden fence.

"Come on Lucas!" Someone shouted in the crowd. Aura smiled, wickedly. She threw out a fake attack and he blocked exactly how she expected him to. As she always did, she used her small size to her advantage, and ducked under his swing, rolled behind him and held her sword out, just barely dusting his shoulder. Crimson red bloomed at the shallow cut.

"I win." She smirked. Lucas whirled around, and swiped at his shoulder, revealing small trickles of blood on his fingers. He cursed and kicked at the dirt.

"Who's next?" She called out to the small crowd. Another man laughed and pushed out a smaller soldier. One she did not recognize. When the soldier lifted their head, the short black docked hair belonged to a woman. Young, maybe the same age as Esmeralda. Aura assumed she must be a first year recruit. She smiled.

"I'll go easy on you!" Aura shouted out to the woman. "What's your name, soldier?"

"Lia," she replied, walking forward, no sword in hand, no weapons to be seen at all. But she strode into the ring after ducking under the fence.

"Alright Lia, you pick the weapon." Aura nodded to her.

"Daggers," Lia replied quickly. Aura smirked and held out her sword to Lucas who stood just behind the fence to her right. Lucas took it and leaned against the fence, ready to watch.

"Do you need to get any?" Aura asked.

"I have them," Lia replied. Her face was stone. No obvious emotions lay there. Aura simply nodded, it would be nice to spare with someone new, she was getting tired of beating all the boys.

"Ready?" Aura called out.

Lia nodded and an onlooking soldier shouted, "Begin!"

Lia was shockingly fast, almost as fast as Aura herself. It was exhilarating. They danced around each other, Lia pulling daggers from hidden compartments on her person. It had been some time since Aura had fought in closer combat. Usually leaning on her sword instead of her daggers. Lia's daggers were silver, engraved at the hilt, with what looked like runes. Aura's daggers all held a golden stone at the hilt, specific to the heir's royal weapons. The blade was made of the strongest metal, forged from these very lands. Each of her daggers had different hilts, some golden, some bronze, some silver. She adored each and every one of them. They had all been specially crafted for her, as was her sword and armor. A perk of being the unimportant heir, she thought.

"Lia!" a familiar voice boomed. Lia froze and Aura had to pivot so her attack did not slice through Lia's stomach. Aura cursed and regained her footing.

"You're ruining my fun, Captain." Aura glared at Nox. She focused all her energy on that glare because he was standing right in front of a beam of sunlight. His dark hair was not tied back but loose, his blue eyes bright. Nox was not wearing armor, no, he was wearing a simple linen shirt and trousers. And Aura swore to all the gods and goddesses, he had never been more painfully attractive.

"Lia, you are on the west gate as of two minutes ago." Nox ignored Aura, giving out orders. Lia scrambled out of the fenced ring, muttering a sorry and scurrying off towards the west gate. Other soldiers chided and grumbled at Nox for ruining the fun. But silence fell over them, with Nox's scowl.

"Everyone, back to work," he commanded. All the soldiers dispersed rather quickly. Like field mice.

"That was rude." Aura glared. Nox stalked towards her, feet pounding into the dirt ground, he was angry. Her heart beat faster as he grew nearer. He leaned over the fence to her.

"We need to talk."

Just like that the excitement drained from her. He seemed mad, not the fake playing their game type, but the real kind. Nox was actually rather terrifying when mad. She nodded and sheathed her daggers, Issac walked up to them, handing Aura back her sword before walking off to busy himself far from the angry Captain of the Guard who still held her gaze.

"Come on." Nox jutted out his chin to her, and began walking towards a weapons room across the way. She followed on his heels, her curiosity winning out beyond her usual stubbornness.

"We have a problem." Nox sighed as they entered the building. It was wooden and cool, tables lined an open space, weapons hung on the walls in a chaotic but organized fashion. Daggers went with daggers and swords with swords. Bows and arrows were scattered along a table, other various odd weapons strewn along the walls. She knew they trained with every available weapon, so that anyone could pick up any weapon and be ready.

"Just let me finish first, before you jump in," Nox said, making Aura's curiosity soar and heart pound. Something was wrong, that much she could see.

"First—Kellian knows," Nox said, his eyes locking onto hers with an intensity that silenced her.

Aura's casual lean against the table snapped into a rigid posture. "What—" she began, but Nox raised a hand, effectively cutting her off. Her mouth snapped shut, and she watched him expectantly.

"He knows because I had to report to him that someone was in your rooms," Nox continued, his voice steady and unyielding.

"No one was in my room," Aura said, shaking her head in disbelief.

"There was, Issac reported your doors unlocked and open. He saw someone in a hooded cloak escape out the window, followed them but lost them past the gates."

Aura stood wide eyed, feeling an unease wash over her.

"Kellian demanded to know where you were, and where I was that night."

"And you couldn't have lied?" Aura spat, her fury bubbling up like molten lava, scorching her insides and flushing her cheeks. Her rage was a roar in her ears, the kind that made her want to hurl a scream at Nox. The last thing she had wanted was for anyone, least of all her brother, to know about them.

"No," Nox replied with a dispassionate calm. The simplicity of his answer only stoked the flames of her anger. Aura shook her head. She knew it was that straightforward—Nox was bound by duty as Kellian's Captain to report and protect the family.

They stood in the thick silence that followed, the minutes stretching out painfully. Aura's mind was a cacophony of thoughts, each tangled and indistinguishable from the next, creating a deafening noise in her head.

"Listen—" Nox said, "what if you stay with me for a few nights?" Aura opened her mouth to argue.

"Hear me out." He stepped towards her. "Issac and Lucas will be on guard in and out of your rooms, so if someone tries again, they will catch them." His hand reached out to take her shoulder. "It could be nothing but—"

Aura saw it then, the crack in the clear blue eyes. He was worried, really and truly worried. Seeing that emotion plainly on him, then his touch, it soothed any fire in her, all the rage simmered and died. She nodded, shocking both herself and Nox.

"Alright," she said so quietly it was nearly inaudible. Nox nodded as well, squeezed her shoulder and leaned back on the edge of the counter behind him. Letting his body go slack, he rubbed a hand over his face slowly, then pushed the hair out of his face.

"I also wanted to talk to you about something," Aura spoke up sitting at a table. Nox walked over in one stride and sat across from her.

"I am going on a mission," she announced.

"Gods above," Nox muttered, dropping his hands on top of his forehead.

"And I want you to come with me."

The silence was deafening. Aura felt herself grow nervous at the lack of response. She hadn't exactly prepared to approach this topic in this way, but what was done was done. So the announcement that she was going on a mission and wanted him with her floated in the air between them.

"Where?" Nox asked after what felt like forever. Aura let out a sigh and began to explain. When she was finished, Nox was again resting his forehead on his hands.

"And Kellian approved all of this?" Nox asked.

"Yes."

"He expected you to escort me," she says, snarling at the last word. She didn't need anyone to escort her, but she could admit that having Nox with her would be extremely helpful.

"I'm sure you loved that." Nox smirked. Aura let herself feel relieved for a moment, at Nox being himself again, easy smiles and flirtatious comments.

"It makes sense," she shrugged, "and two other people."

"Two other people?"

"Yup." Aura propped her own cheek on her hand. "Any ideas?"

Nox groaned again. "It's getting late, let's do this tomorrow." Aura looked around, realizing that only candles lit the space, that no light drifted in from the sun as it had long since dropped far below the mountains. They walked outside, the moons were high in the sky, lighting their way. Aura was always so fascinated with the moons. There were two main moons in the realm. One was seen all year long, and a smaller one was seen to its side only in the summer nights. The second moon was smaller, but just as bright. While Kellian studied the sky and the stars, Aura had spent her time reading about the moons. The centuries old tales about two lovers, one bound to the sky only one season out of the year, the other forced to every night. And only in the summer could they be together. It was a tragic tale actually, about how the lovers had been cursed even in death. To not enter the shadowfold, where souls go to death. That they were cursed to never find rest, and burdened to light the sky every night for an eternity.

Aura trailed behind Nox to his home, which perched above his workshop. They climbed the stairs at a leisurely pace, and Aura found herself wishing for something more comfortable as they reached his bedroom. Nox disappeared into the washroom, leaving Aura to remove her boots and place them neatly by the door, beside his own.

When he reentered the bedchamber, she was yawning, so big her eyes were glued shut. When she opened them however, she was met with a bare chest. Defined muscles carved into his stomach, and down into a deep V shape that disappeared behind a towel he had wrapped around himself. His hair was damp, and his eyes clear. He reached into a dresser finding a dark brown linen shirt and pulled one out, tossing it to her. Aura caught it easily, and nodded thanks. Shaking off the lust consuming her, she walked past him into the washroom, closing the door behind her.

Stripping off her own clothes and letting them sit in a pile, she threw cold water over her face and changed into the shirt. Nox's shirt smelled like warmth and pine trees, old wood and an open fire. She let herself indulge in it, for only a moment. The shirt fell down mid thigh on her small frame, slightly consuming her. She pulled the ties on her hair and began undoing the meticulous braids. Her hair was left wavy, falling to her hips. She always loved her hair, never cutting it, unless forced by a hovering lady's maid who insisted on 'just a trim'. Her mother's hair had been long, or so she had seen in paintings. Aura loved to share a feature with her mother, she wished so deeply to have known her more, and for longer. But keeping her hair long, and in braids, was her own way of keeping her late mother close to her.

When Aura stepped out of the washroom, she found Nox propped up in bed, his head resting on the pillow as he flipped through the pages of a book by the soft glow of a candle. The scene was striking: his bare chest gleamed in the dim light, his formidable frame sprawled across the bed, and the delicate leather-bound book seemed almost swallowed by his large hands.

"Is this all an elaborate scheme to get me to stay the nights with you?" Aura's eyebrow arched with the question, her tone light. Nox peered up from his book lazily. He smirked at the image in front of him, her in his shirt and nothing else.

"Perhaps," Nox said simply and went back to his book. Aura bristled at the lack of attention. Part of her knew he was doing it on purpose, but she didn't like to be ignored; hated it.

She strode over to him, and climbed onto the soft mattress, past the extra blankets she knew he kept for her when they mysteriously began appearing after they would sneak in late night trysts. She crawled to him, and his brows arched, peering over to her without moving his head.

"Is that interesting?" She purred, and threw a leg over his hips, straddling him.

"Painfully boring, actually." Nox snapped the book closed, blindly setting it on his nightstand, keeping his eyes on her instead.

"Aura," He began, his heated expression melted away, replaced with a serious one. His hand went to her waist, out of habit. He lazily pulled his hands up her curves, then back down, stopping at the lowest point of her hips. They rested there as she waited.

"You really want to go on this mission." His voice was unusually soft, the way it had been when she felt she couldn't breath and after the shadow beast ordeal. She felt cut wide open by it. By the gentle manner in which his hands held her, it made her heart fray, coming apart at the seams.

"I-I" she stuttered. "Don't pretend like you care," she said instead, her tone coming out harsher than she meant it. Nox looked slightly taken aback at first, but recovered quickly,

"Of course I care," he said sternly, squeezing his hands around her, "gods don't ever think I do not." He shook his head, brows creased. The room felt so dark under only two candlelights. It made his dark hair the color of onyx, his blue eyes like a night sky instead of the open sea.

Aura took a steadying breath, "I just mean, we don't do that."

"Do what?" Nox muttered, looking hurt.

"This, soft touches, caring about the other on why they are doing something." She pushed herself off of him, needed a physical space between them. His touch muddied her brain, made her too soft.

"*Princess*," he said sternly, turning to face her now that she sat next to him instead of on top of him. "I do care, as much as you want to ignore that fact, I do." He ran a hand through his hair with a sigh. "I get that you can't do more than this, I do. I am not asking for more. But I do care, if you are okay. This last week has been more than people in this land experience in a lifetime, and you want to jump into another mission. One that goes outside of The Hollow, which you have never done." Aura opened up her mouth to speak but Nox held a hand up. "Hear me out, please?" he asked gently. It was the tone that made her pause. His eyes were clear, he wanted to speak his mind. And Aura knew it would only cause more confusion for her emotions, but she didn't have it in her to stop it. "You are also a magic wielder, something that is illegal in the realm, the dangers on the road, they are untold, and while I know you are able to take on anything you put your mind to, I need you to understand that I care if you are okay. Because jumping into this—if something happens"—he paused again, looking her in the eyes, with such a severe sincerity it took the breath from Aura's lungs"I couldn't live with myself. So I will ask once, are you sure you want to do this?" He asked, reaching out a hand to take hers. She was jolted by the touch, because it made her melt. Made her hardened self, her lock on her emotions falter. But she sat upright, and nodded.

"I am sure."

Nox nodded seriously. "Then we go together."

CHAPTER 7

Nox

Nox felt his mind wandering deep into the night. Aura had been certain she wanted to take on this mission now. It was simple for him, he would follow her to the depths if she asked. Even if she didn't ask, he would still traverse the shadowfell for her, the streets of Hel if that was what it took to keep her safe.

Aura was tucked into his side, despite sleeping at the farthest opposite side of the bed when she first went to sleep. In her dreamstate, she inched closer and closer to him, before curling into his side. His mind was much too awake to sleep however, so he stared at the ceiling in his chambers and cataloged who would be best to accompany them on their mission. But the more he thought about it, the riskier it sounded. Kellian had approved her to take 3 people with her, and while he knew that was based in safety, Nox felt uneasy. More people with them traveling would draw eyes. But if Nox and Aura traveled by themselves, they could simply be a traveling pair, nothing unusual about it. While Aura had never gone far outside of the Hollow, she had been to many edges of the borders, fought off raiders and other attacks on lands where the border had shrunk back from the shadow beast. She knew some of the evil men that wandered the Evanthian land. The Mad King had harbored and fostered a type of chaotic evil in his lands. After outlawing any magic wielders, those of witch or fae descent, the king had sent out rewards for anyone who caught one roaming the lands. A high reward since it was so rare now. That was what had brought Kyeria to their lands, why after a decade of traveling in hiding, she had no choice but to run into the Ash Mountains despite the terrible tales of certain death for any who passed. Her magic, and heritage had let her through. Nox knew, logically, that Aura understood the dangers to the best of her ability, but she hadn't experienced them.

Nox had.

He tried to shake the nightmares from behind his eyes. He was so young, when his parents had traveled to The Hollow. His family had been displaced after the Great War, after helping the fae and magic wielders. They found their way back in and Fendiah himself had escorted them back across the borders. But those years outside of The Hollow would haunt him for years to come.

Nox let out a sigh, pushed his hair aside from his face, noting he desperately needed a haircut but he knew Aura had liked it long so he had kept it so. She had these tells, they were so obvious to him now. She touched things she liked, whether it was a sword or a weapon, her fingers danced along, or his hair she always touched more when it was longer below his ears than cropped short as the other soldiers in the royal army. Nox reached out to her, her body so small curled into him, and he wrapped an arm around her, pulling her even closer to his chest. Her cheek nuzzled into him more, and she hummed in her sleep state. He let himself drift off then, content by her being in his arms.

The air was being sucked out of him, all around him actually. It thinned and thinned and only smoke was left. He felt the edges of his limbs warming but not quite burning before his eyes shot open. His childhood house was before his eyes, burning brightly in the night. Villagers outside screamed, as their small hut on the outskirts of a village in The Open Lands went into flames.

"Nox, wake up son!" His father shouted, he bolted upright and frantically looked across the small room to the other bed, where his little sister slept. Instead, he saw a large burning beam. He screamed and screamed, his lungs raw with the effort of trying to get to her. But his father had caught him, before he could fling himself into the flames engulfing the room.

"Nox, stop!" His father shouted, dragging him out an open door. The smoke was so thick now, Nox could barely see in front of him, only orange and red flame, and black smoke.

The outside air was like being shoved under a thawed winter lake. The roaring of the fire was dull to his ears as they picked up another sound, so much worse. His mother, on her knees, tears streaming down her cheeks, screaming so frantically, it burned into his skin worse than the fire itself.

"Nox!"

"Nox, wake up." The voice was sweet and familiar, like the sunrise over The Hollow or the sun after a rainstorm. His eyes cracked open, and he felt himself wake up fully. He was not in the small hut his family once called home, he was in his own bed, Aura's hands on either of his face, golden eyes shining down at him, etched with such deep worry that he shot upright. Something had to be wrong.

"Shhh." Aura shushed him and curled her body around his, wrapping her arms around him. "You're okay," she said so gently that the tone felt so foreign from her lips.

"Sorry," Nox muttered to her, leaning his head down into the crook of her neck and hair. He breathed her in, her scent calming him immediately. He was in the barracks, in his own home, Aura by his side.

"It's alright." Aura squeezed him tight and let the silence of the night envelop them. After a handful of minutes Aura spoke up again quietly, as if afraid to voice her concern, "do these happen often?"

Nox leaned back on the headboard, rubbing his hands over his face. "Not for some time." He shook his head.

"Like years or weeks?" she asked again. Her voice was soft and when he met her eyes again, they glowed in the moonlight. She herself glowed, as if her magic was ready to protect him, reacting for her.

"Um—" he groaned, " a week."

"What are they about?" she asked, moving closer to him and leaning into his side. It was rare she showed such blatant affection to him, but he knew this was how she knew how to show love, how she expressed it, by being present as she had with Kyeria and Esmeralda and he was sure many others.

"Did Kel ever tell you about why my family came back to The Hollow?" he asked. She shook her head in reply.

"I remember you showing up when we were young, you and Kel were always getting into trouble." She smiled up at him. It was so blinding he had to swallow and recollect himself before beginning.

"My parents had fought in The Great War, with the fae. After the war they were far from here so they started their life, they had me and not long after my sister." He heard Aura's small gasp, he knew she didn't know, didn't know he had another family than his mother.

"We were in The Open Lands, our house went up in flames in the middle of the night, and—" he paused, trying to swallow down the emotions. Aura reached out, taking his hand as he had done early for her. She intertwined their fingers though, giving him a small burst of strength to continue, "my sister did not make it out. We came back to The Hollow, my mother was never the same, but my father, he left in the night after we were back. Left a note that he was setting out to find the bastard that lit our house a flame." Nox shook his head. "He never came back."

Aura squeezed his hand and looked up to him with watery eyes.

He pulled her close. "The nightmares, I am there again, sometimes I wake before a beam falls and I can't get to her, or after, but no matter the dream, I can't save her and I am dragged out of the house."

"That's horrible," Aura whispered.

"The lands out there, the realm...it is not a good place to be."

Aura nodded. "I know the dangers," she said quietly.

"You don't." He shook his head. "I barely do, I was so young, and the people out there are brutal and remorseless, they'll kill someone for the bag on their back."

"We will be careful," she insisted. "Go back to sleep," she whispered as he slid back down under the covers, letting his head rest on the pillow. She stayed with him that night, curled into his side, not from a movement in her sleep but because she decided to be there.

The next morning, Aura and Nox began with training before the sun rose, back to their usual schedule. Lucas reported no movement on anyone near Aura's rooms, and she agreed to stay the night again with him to be safe. Her being this agreeable was a little unsettling, but her eyes were lined with a fraction of worry every time she looked at him, but he knew it wasn't pity. She herself would hate to be looked upon with pity. No, she was seeing him differently. Nox had yet to decide if that was something he liked or not.

Aura went on her way to her training classes with the younglings and Nox went to find Lucas and Issac who were in the small armory building.

"Hey boss," Issac greeted as Nox walked into the room.

"I need to talk to you both," Nox informed them, sitting at one of the tables. They followed suit, the wooden bench creaking under them as they sat.

"I am being assigned a mission, out of The Hollow," he began. Issac and Lucas shared a look,

"Sir?" Lucas questioned.

"Lucas, you are my second. You will oversee the everyday. Issac, you will take over Aura's training classes with the younglings."

"The Princess is leaving The Hollow?" Issac's wide eyed response received a nudge from Lucas.

"Yes Sir." Lucas nodded.

"I am going to inform you on what is happening, but it does not leave this room. Understood?" he asked them. They both nodded sternly and Nox explained the group of magic wielders who were from The Hollow, trapped by the Mad King and how he and the princess were going to trek to the castle with the help of light sprites sending information ahead and sneak out the prisoners. Lucas, Issac, and Nox spent the next hour helping come up with a plan on what path to take and Nox called for Ember at the end of their meeting.

"Mr. Nox!" She beamed. "How can I help you?" Her voice was honey sweet as it always was, she glowed extra golden today, as if a small bundle of the sunset itself.

"Get as much information about the layout of the Evanthian castle and the movements of the magic wielders from the sprites stationed there, send your fastest, we only have a few days before we travel."

"I will do just that." She nodded, then paused, slowing her flutter and sitting on the lantern outside the armory where Nox was standing. "The prince has asked me to accompany you on the journey," she explained. Nox nodded, knowing it was smart to have a sprite with them, someone who could go back and forth with messages and turn invisible to the human eyes when needed. Ember continued to explain that she had sprites stationed inside the Evanthian castle that rotated out and traveled back here with information and messages from the magic wielders that were trapped. Kellian had seemed to have been plotting to get them free over the last few years. But a rescue mission could compromise the very existence of The Hollow. The Hollow were Dragon lands, sacred and protected by the Galanis Line, and in leaving and rescuing some of his fellow Hollow people, it could put at risk the knowledge of the purposefully forgotten kingdom.

"Alright, get yourself prepared, and let Aura know as well." He nodded to the sprite who smiled and waved before flying away, a small path of light following her as she went.

Nox was quite fond of the sprites. There were many small families of them throughout The Dragioner Forest. A trusted group had become the royal messengers decades ago, that specific family trusted with getting information quickly throughout The Hollow. Ember's own sisters worked in a duo to travel into Evanthia and come back with information to The Hollow. They had sent directions, drawing out a rough map of the castle and the dungeons itself, and promised to meet Nox and Aura outside the last village before the castle walls.

After Ember went on her way, Nox decided to patrol the castle, near Aura's chambers. He walked through the gardens, something Aura did often before taking the garden entrance into the stone castle, vines twisted up around the doors and up the stone facing of the castle, the lanterns on either side of the door were lit, creating a dim light. He nodded to the guard posted at the doors and walked inside. The stone kept the castle rather cold even as they got closer to the summer. He went down the familiar halls, glancing over all the dark corners, before he got to Aura's chambers, the door was ajar, and he walked through assuming Aura was inside.

"Your Highness—" he stopped, seeing the empty room, a window open and the curtain flowing in the wind. It was dawn now, the sun setting casting a pinkish hue across the room. He scanned the room, and took a few steps back, making it sound like he was leaving, he creaked the door shut behind him, falling to the shadows. A russell of noise was heard, then from the washroom, a hooded figure emerged. They were taller than Aura, immediately putting him on high alert. He leaped forward, knocking the person down.

"Thief," he growled pinning them under him, he ripped off the hooded cloak to reveal a servant. The same brown haired, and freckle-faced woman who had brought Aura clothes at Nox's house after the shadow beast had been banished and Aura was hurt.

"What did you take?" he seethed, pulling her up with him to his feet. He kept a hand on her cloak, holding her from escaping.

"I-I" she stuttered, her eyes watery with tears. She was young, he noticed, that of Esmeralda's age maybe. "I'm so sorry sir—I mean no harm!" She held up her hands.

"What did you take?" He asked again, a lethal tone. She shook with fear.

"I was only delivering Aura her elixirs! And leaving a note!" She revealed a piece of parchment that had been rolled with a red seal on it. He went to speak but Aura walked into the room at that moment.

"Nox! What are you doing, let Mae go!" She ran forward towards them. Nox unhanded the girl, and she shrunk back,

"I'm so sorry," Mae cried.

"Show me the note," he said, holding out his free hand. She dropped it there and Aura plucked it out from Nox before he could blink. She ripped it open.

"What is this?" Aura seethed, looking up with a deathly glare to match Nox's own. He tried to conceal his pride. She was terrifying, *he loved it.*

"Someone came to me, I don't know who, they were wearing a mask. They said I had to deliver this, or they would hurt my family!" Mae was sobbing now, her body racked with hiccups.

"Who?" Nox pressed.

"I don't know, I swear!"

"What did you leave other than the note?" Aura asked, crossing her arms. She pulled out a sprite whistle from her pocket, and held the thin piece of wood to her mouth. Ember appeared rather quickly.

"I was just on my way and I—" Ember stopped mid sentence, taking in the room. "What is happening?" she asked, her golden glow getting darker.

"Ember, get my brother here, quickly," Aura commanded. Ember nodded fiercely and flew out of the room.

Aura paced the room, brows creased and eyes dark while they waited for Kellian. Mae was sitting now in a chair, her crying was quieter now, but she hunched over in despair nonetheless.

Kellian stormed into the room, his presence filling the space with a palpable tension. His white hair was neatly tied back, accentuating the severity of his expression. He was dressed in formal attire, richly embroidered with golden leaves that traced down the sleeves, glinting ominously in the light. His golden eyes, usually warm, were now dark and stormy, reflecting the intensity of his anger. "What is the meaning of this?"

"Mae was the one sneaking in," Aura pointed out. Nox glared.

"Why?" Kellian seethed. Nox forgot how terrifying the heirs could be together. While Kellian was quieter than his sister, more reserved, he would tear down anything that affected his family and their safety. That was one thing he and Nox had always agreed on and put first, above all else.

Mae explained herself again, and Kellian pressed her more. She said she remembered it was a woman, and she had never looked into the potion but it looked like bath oils and she had set it down next to Aura's tub. They sent for Miss Bells to take Mae to her rooms and keep her there, sending a guard to her family to watch over them and calling for Esmeralda and Kyeria.

The group of them all sat in Aura's chambers, sitting in chairs and windows in front of her bookshelves.

"And what did the letter say?" Kyeria asked softly. Aura let out a sigh and held out the opened parchment. Nox had not seen it yet; Aura had been keeping it from crumbling in her hand, holding it so tightly that he could see the strain in her hands.

"Read it outloud," Kellian said. Kyeria looked to Aura in question as if asking permission. Aura nodded and Nox moved to herside.

"You were never meant to be. You are the princess who was cursed," Kyeria read aloud. Everyone looked at each other in worry.

"This smells like a magic suppressant." Esmeralda spoke up, walking out of the washrooms with the bottles in her hand. "Have you used it?" she asked. Aura shook her head, *no*.

Aura hadn't even been here in her chambers, she had only bathed in Nox's rooms. It was lucky in fact, that whoever sent this assumed she was here and using it, but nonetheless Nox felt rage boiling over.

"Who did this?" he asked, barely containing his anger. Kellian shot him a glance.

"When you were little, and so sick, there were rumors that you had been cursed, and the punishment was not being able to take dragon form," Kellian said quietly. Kyeria was at his side, standing with him and let out a gasp.

"Maybe it was one of the servants from that time that had the old faith?" Esmeralda said. "I'll run a tracing spell on the oils, it has to be someone with basic magic knowledge."

"What does a tracing spell tell you?" Nox asked.

"The general area the spell was originally cast in, could help narrow down a village," Esmeralda explained, her eyes worried and glancing at Aura. They were all waiting for her anger, for her determination to fix the problem or find the person, but instead she sat silently in her chair, looking out the window.

Kyeria was the one to finally clear the room, ushering everyone out and giving Aura the space she desperately needed. Nox, having reassured Kellian and the other women, remained behind, his presence a steadfast anchor in the chaos. As the last of the visitors left and silence settled over the room, Nox approached Aura. He knelt before her, his eyes filled with concern as he met her gaze. Aura looked up at him, her eyes shimmering with unshed tears.

"It is my greatest fault," she whispered, "not being able to take up my namesake, to not be blessed with dragon form like my ancestors before me."

"It is not a fault, we have no control over the gods and their hand in fate." He shook his head. He remembered the rumors circulating when he and his family came back to The Hollow, how Aura had been sick, the blessing of the Galanis line and the ability to take dragon form passing to Kellian instead. He hadn't thought much in his young age about how that had affected Aura. Instead, Kellian was so excited to show him his powers, shifting into a rather small white dragon that grew as he did. The rumors were based around the old faith that one who was born into the blessing would take form, there was no other option. So when Aura fell sick, few of the older folks had whispered about a cursed princess, and what it meant that the gods skipped her, leaving her without her birthright. It had been so many years since anyone had whispered of such things now. Nox tried to push away the thoughts and focus on the white haired princess in front of him, setting a palm on her shoulder.

"Fate is a fickle beast," Nox began, "but you, you are strong and brave, you possess the wisdom of the kings and queens before you. You take such great care and time into your people. You, Aura, are the princess fated to The Hollow. You are meant to be as you are." Aura simply nodded to him in reply, slowly squaring her shoulders, standing up and reaching her full height. The queenly air about her returning quickly. She brushed off her dress and turned on her heel.

"We have work to do," She stated, unrolling a few maps that Esmeralda had brought from the libraries. The maps were crusted on the edges, darker spots smudged some ink, but the layout of the Evanthian royal court lay before them. Large stone walls surrounded the castle and royal court. The gates opened twice a day, in the mid morning and before dusk. Marketers came in and out, stocking stalls with produce and other items to buy. Similar to their own markets in The Hollow but absent of any items of the magical variety. Those were found in the shadows of the night, markets that happened on the outer village streets, not within the walls of the Evanthian castle. This was where they would enter, securing a cart and setting up a stand in the royal markets on mid morning opening of the gates. They would have till sunset to be back, with their people, and sneak out under the guise of merchants leaving the royal walls. That gave them mere hours. Aura unfolded another map, let her hand glow with light, holding it up to the map, this one was a blueprint of the castle, the light sprites had painstakingly sent information back and forth and made a rather precise map of the castle by sneaking in unseen with their ability to disappear to the human eyes.

"Here is where we enter, I have a connection in the outer village here where we can procure a cart and clothes." Aura nodded along taking in the information.

"We can collect clothes and hide them in the cart to help disguise our people," Aura noted.

"Ember will join us, her sister is in the palace as we speak and she has other sprites ready to help us along the way." Nox pulled a candle to his side of the map.

"You'll need to cover your hair," Nox said, glancing up at the princess. "White hair is rare beyond The Hollow and can draw unwanted attention."

Aura's face tightened at the suggestion. Her long, white hair was not just a part of her identity but a symbol of strength and power among the Galanis women—a legacy she revered, much like the way her mother had worn it, as immortalized in the paintings. Without a word, she shifted her focus back to the details of their plan.

It was simple: traverse the land beyond The Hollow, infiltrate Evanthia, break into the castle, rescue the prisoners from the Mad King's dungeon, and return home.

Nox felt a thrill surge through him at the prospect. This was the kind of real mission he had longed for—a chance to make a tangible difference for his kingdom. He saw the same spark in Aura's eyes as they strategized, a fiery determination that mirrored his own. This was where she truly belonged, and he could sense the excitement coursing through her as they mapped out their path to freedom and justice.

CHAPTER 8

Aura

I t was morning when Aura found Kellian in one of the studies the next day. He was dressed in royal garbs, a golden embroidered brown leather tunic and a tied belt around his waist. His hair was swept back into a bun, clean and precise. He looked every bit of the king he would soon be.

"We have located the woman who sent the elixir's and threats," he said, not looking up as she walked into the room. She let out a sigh, waiting for the next bit she didn't really want to hear.

"She will be tried for high treason against the crown."

"Kel." Aura walked forward, placing her hands on the wooden desk he sat in. Her gauzy blue sleeves of a formal dress draped around her, flowing into billowing skirts and a tie around her neck. She loved this dress, and was not planning on getting dressed up for bad news today. She had council meetings to conduct, court members to meet with, a training class to be reassigned while she was gone.

"It is done. Mae was let go, she and her family under watch to make sure everyone is safe. I will not stand for threats in this kingdom, especially to my family. The court will meet on the morrow," he said, finally meeting her eyes.

"Rule fairly, but kindly." She nodded. Fendiah would say as such if he were here but he was still in the northern Isles, at the dragon council. It could be days, weeks, or months till he returned, they had no way of knowing. But her brother ruled fairly, as he was taught. He always placed kindness first in their sacred land.

"Always," he replied sternly, then shifted his expression into something lighter. "Why are you dressed up for the day?"

"I'll be on the road for goddess knows how long, I'll miss my nice things." She smirked with a twirl. "Additionally, I have meetings today, I'll leave notes for you when I am done."

"Thank you sister." Kellian smiled. "I am proud of you, you are so much like our mother, more and more every day." His eyes were ever so slightly watery, only few knew the signs of an emotional Kellian, he was so quick to wear a stern and stone faced expression. But she could see it, the crease on the corners of his eyes, the way the light was glimmering off his golden eyes a little too much. He cleared his throat and the emotion was gone as fast as it came.

"Are you ready for your travels?" He asked, changing the subject. Aura gladly accepted the change, and fell quickly into explaining the plans her and Nox had concocted the night before. Kellian said once they were back to the edge of The Hollow, he and Ameline and Kyeria would meet them just past the border, and escort them home. No one knew of this plan inside the castle but their small inner circle of trusted family. There was no time to send word to Fendiah, and ultimately the siblings did not want to, since Fendiah had drug his feet on rescuing the trapped people for years. Aura was ready, she could do this and the excitement gnawed at her throat. She finally had the chance to prove herself to her grandfather, the king.

The sun was casting small shadows, as it hung low in the sky, along the path of Aura's mothers gardens. She walked the space in a quiet solace and asked the goddesses and gods for their favor, to protect her on her journey. The day had been busy, her eyes were heavy and tired. A good night's rest was needed before the long journey. They would travel across the Ash Mountains, a path she knew well, past the Great Lake where she had met Kyeria and through the same side Kyeria had entered, the Eastern border that touched Evanthian lands. The forest went on for some time before villages began, according to Kyeria. Nox had made quick work of sending messages to his people outside the barrier. One in Levin, a small river side village a days journey from the barrier's edge, and another in Ancher where they would get a merchant's cart and begin the journey to the castle walls. The trek to Ancher would take five days in total if they rest sparingly.

Aura was dawning her travel clothes, a pack on her back as she walked the familiar path past the gardens and to the back path to Nox's house. Her hand reached for the cool metal of the door, and it opened for her easily.

She found Nox in his kitchen, warming a soup on his stove and muttering to himself.

"All packed?" He asked, as she crossed through the doorway.

"Mmhm," she hummed and dropped the pack to the ground. They needed to pack light as they would be traveling on foot for most if not all of the journey.

"I made us a warm meal, our last before the dried meats and bread for the next while." Nox motioned to her to grab a bowl he scooped the soup into. She did so easily. The shift in them was evident, after only a few nights of staying with him and she was comfortable here. She sat cross legged on a couch near a wooden table he had set up near his fireplace.

"How are you feeling about the journey?" Nox asked, sitting next to her. She nodded into her soup, a big helping going into her mouth making her groan on first taste. His eyes met hers, amused.

"Goddess above, who knew you could cook like this?" She hastily took another bite.

"There's plenty more." He chucked in response. "We leave before first light, I have received back word that horses will be waiting for us in Levin."

"How do you know so many people?" Aura asked.

"I made friends rather easily." Nox shrugged.

"Of course you did." She scoffed and was met with a half hearted glare. His hair was cropped short again, no longer falling in front of his eyes or nearly touching his shoulders. His usual scratchy short beard was gone as well. She was oddly fond of his longer hair, and found herself missing the pieces that drifted down and got in his eyes.

"I like your long hair." She noted out loud.

"Hmm," he muttered, "it'll grow plenty over the journey. Then you can run your hands through it again, like you like to."

Goddess above, give her strength. That smirk could make her walls fall in an instant. A fact that she hated about herself.

But her strength gave out quickly, as he moved towards her, took her finished bowl from her hands without breaking eye contact. He placed it on the table and moved his arm past her, leaning into her.

"Unless you like this better and you just don't want to admit it," he said, taking her other hand and placing it on her cheek. Her hand glided over his soft skin and she didn't fight the movement, the closeness, or the overconfidence of Nox. No, she melted right into it, because her damned body was traitorous. They spent the night tangled up in the other, skin pressed to skin, roaming hands and mouths. It was comfortable and normal for them now. She was comfortable here, without the sweet words, only using their hands to communicate with each other. Not one sweet nothing muttered to the other.

Morning came too quickly. She heard the birds singing outside, their songs drifting in through the open window. The barracks were quiet, no one was awake as the sun was hours from rising. But the night birds were her sign. She pushed herself off Nox, annoyed at herself even sleeping so closely to him. Closely, was of course, an understatement. Aura had woken, her arm and leg wrapped around Nox, her head resting on his chest and his arm wrapped around her, holding her to him. She was weak when it came to him. *She hated it.*

"Get up." She shoved his shoulder and pushed herself up on the mattress. He groaned, blue eyes cracking open and drinking her in. She rolled her eyes, not wanting to know what thoughts were littering his mind, because simply put—they did not have time for that.

"Let's go," she said, pushing off the bed and redressing in her training clothes as the base, a light linen skirt tied to her waist with a wrapping ribbon. She secured her leather corset, tied up her boots, and clipped a brown, and rather boring, cloak around her neck. She walked over to the fire place, embers long since died out and reached into the ash.

"What—" Nox started but clamped his own mouth shut as she took ashes into her hands and pressed them into her hair, using a small mirror he had to cover her white hair, turning it a muddy grey and black.

"There," Aura announced when she was done, washing the soot off her hands. Hands on hips, she stared at Nox expectantly. He looked dazed, gorgeous blue eyes trained on her.

"Well that is different," he finally spoke.

"You said I needed to cover my hair." She shrugged.

"And now you'll smell like a fireplace," he grumbled, pulling on his own clothes, pushing on boots and slinging his pack around his shoulders. He didn't say another word, only walked down the stairs and out the back door, expecting her to follow.

They walked in silence till the sun crested over the mountains, announcing the morning with the songs drifting through the air of the morning birds that lived in the mountains. Ember was due to meet them at the lakes but that was still a ways away.

"So you don't like dark hair on me?" Aura asked, smirking as they climbed another boulder.

"I do not care the color of your hair, princess," he grumbled.

"You know," she hummed to herself, "you're going to have to call me by my name out there, not princess or your highness."

Nox only glared at the rock beneath his feet. He had slipped up and called her name just the other day while reassuring her after the information about the woman who called her cursed and tried to poison her magic with an elixir. It was so rare for him to use her given name, that she could count it on one hand over the last twenty years it had happened. It was always, your highness, or princess. Sometimes even, Ror, when he really wanted to make her mad.

Oh, no.

"Whatever you say, Ror." Nox smirked, looking back at her and holding out a hand to help her over a few tall rocks. She glared hard, threw all her energy into the glare even.

"Goddess above, of course you pick that." She wasn't sure when he began the nickname, but she had never liked it. She loved her name, it was picked specifically from her mother, a family name, the last queen Ophelia's own mother had been named Aura.

"Why not my actual name?" She grumbled, swatting away his hand and climbing over the rocks herself.

"Might be caught." He shrugged and walked ahead.

Aura got used to staring at his backside until they reached the lakes. It was odd to see him out of uniform, no red cape or chainmail on his muscular form. Instead, he wore a simple linen shirt and trousers. He looked like any given villager, but the thin fabric held tightly to his muscles making Aura even more annoyed.

The view, she had to admit, was not bad.

A flutter of light flew past them then paused in front of them, just as the trees broke apart to reveal the Great Lake.

"Hello!" Ember said happily, her hair was flowing around her small body and she wore a brown leafed dress with a small corset around her waist.

"My sister, Nessa, sent word that our people are not in the dungeons, they have their own rooms actually, in the far west end. Our plans may need to change a little, as there is a ball the night we are set to arrive, and the prisoners will be there." She shook her head sadly. "The Mad King seems to like to use them as trophies, has the witches perform during the balls."

Aura shuttered at the thought. "Change of plans then." She nodded. "I guess we're going to a ball." She smirked. Nox looked at her with uncertainty but she didn't leave any space for argument, simply walked ahead of them towards the border.

"And," Ember spoke up again, pulling a ring from her bag she had slung across her. "Esmeralda sent me with this, it will alter your appearance," she noted, tossing the ring to Aura. Aura smiled, *no more covering her hair in ash, thank the goddess.*

Aura slipped on the ring, Nox's expression looked startled and Ember only smiled. Aura wished for a godsdamned mirror in these mountains. She wondered how deeply her appearance had changed, and wanted to walk back to the Great Lake, to see her reflection in the lake. But they hadn't the time, and with the change of plans, they had much to figure out on their journey.

Ember flew near Nox, as they went over the information they both knew, planning a new entrance into the castle. They would still enter as merchants during the day, but would sneak into the ball disguised as Evanthians and sneak the prisoners out to safety. By the time they neared the edge of the barrier, Aura took a steadying breath. She had never been beyond The Hollow borders, only within and safe. But this was her chance to be something more. The magical barrier glittered where it ended, the light reflecting along it. Ember smiled and flew past them, going through the barrier first, Nox motioned for Aura to wait, for him to go first. She glared at him at the assumption and instead pushed through before he could.

A coldness washed over her, making her bones feel itchy and odd. She shuddered at the lack of magic in this land, the difference that such a small step could be. When she turned back, expecting to see Nox, she saw only trees and the beginnings of a mountain. Her breath hitched, *where was he?*

Only a second later, he appeared before her, as if she blinked and suddenly he was there.

"What—" she started. But then familiar blue eyes and bulky stature was in front of her again.

"You can't see past the border from the outside. Only on the Evanthian border side, however. Esmeralda and Kyeria reinforced this area after the beast was banished," he explained. She sighed and nodded, turning to the light sprite by her side.

"Ready?" she whispered to her old friend. Ember nodded, determination clear on her features and her light shifted, only a reflection of her surroundings, Ember all but disappeared. Only a small fraction of light reflecting notified Aura of her presence. She felt the air move from Ember's wings as she flew closer to Aura's ear.

"I'll stay hidden, but I am here," she whispered to Aura.

Hours into their trek, Nox paused and decided to make camp far from the main path. They set up a small fire, and ate their dried meats in silence for dinner. Aura's body was sore, muscles aching. She was used to training and fighting, but climbing through the Ash Mountains, then walking a forested hillside, had not been easy. Nox rolled out a bedroll in the small tent, and motioned towards it,

"Rest, I'll take first watch." His voice was low in the silent forest. Barely above a whisper. The fire had been extinguished, and only the moon was providing them light now. Aura held out her hand, making a small light appear, dancing around her fingers in three plumes.

"Mind if I sit? I will not be able to sleep," she asked quietly. His chin dipped in a nod, signifying a yes. They sat against the sturdy thick base of a tree. Aura wondered what the breeze was saying as it blew past them, missing her friends already.

"Are you worried?" Aura's voice was barely a whisper as if not wanting to even put the words out into the world. But she couldn't help it, her body was racked with tension, anxious energy filling her muscles. She didn't love the last minute change of plans.

"It will be fine," Nox said, laying a hand on the ground, he tipped his head back against the bark of the tree and stared through the branches into the sky.

"Who do you know in Levin?" Aura asked, changing the subject.

"Someone my mother was close with, she is trustworthy and kind," Nox sighed into the night, "but, you will go by Ror. From here till we are back. I do not wish to risk any information about you getting into the hands of the Mad King. We get in, get our people, and get out." He tilted his chin, meeting her eyes then glancing at the three tendrils of dim light bouncing around them.

"No more magic, it's outlawed here, and would draw too much attention."

"We're in the woods, far from a path or a village," Aura argued.

"Nonetheless, I do not wish for royal guards to appear and drag us into the dungeons of the Mad King." His tone was slow and serious, a tone Aura had heard often when he spoke to the soldiers, but never, if not rarely, to her. She held her jaw closed, holding back her reply and snide remarks on the tip on her tongue.

"Like you would let them." Aura smirked. "Why did it have to be Ror?" She sighed and let her head tilt back onto the bark of the tree as well.

"I like it." He shrugged. Aura found herself biting back a smile.

"You're getting soft on me, Captain."

"Never," He replied quickly with a bump of his shoulder, the humor again drifting away. He looked to her, eyes dark. "I am no Captain here, only Nox. We are not the people we are back home," he paused, the air drifting around them, the leaves of the tree shaking gently, "We cannot be them."

"I've always wanted to go on a mission outside of the borders," she whispered into the night. "Ever since I was young, I wanted to do more, be more." The night seemed to accept the truths, swallow them up into their silence. An owl cooed in the distance.

"You have always been more," Nox whispered back, letting his own truth into the night. They sat in that silence, in those truths. Feeling the freedom to speak those words outside of The Hollow's borders, in this new unknown land, where they could be Nox and Ror, not a princess and the captain. She let the light drop, let only the moon be their light again. The light poured back into her fingers as she tapped them on her thigh. She could feel the warm gaze of Nox, watching.

 *Nox* 

The dense forest loomed around them as they continued on the winding journey to Levin, its shadows deepening as dusk quickly approached them once again. The air was thick with the scent of pine and earth, and the occasional crack of a twig underfoot seemed unnaturally loud in the stillness. Nox moved with practiced stealth beside Aura. They had been traveling for three days in disguise, their true identities hidden beneath layers of falsehood and secrecy as they embarked on a perilous mission to rescue their people.

Aura, with her midnight colored hair now hidden beneath a plain hood, kept up with Nox and his stark pace through the woods. Aura's eyes were sharp and her movements precise, something Nox had always admired in her, something that had made her such a skilled fighter. But Nox could see through the façade of her practiced indifference; he knew the mission was wearing on her, this need to prove herself, to be something for her kingdom. It pained him to see her so burdened.

Aura and Nox trudged into the village of Levin after three days of travel. The journey had left them weary, the terrain unforgiving and the weather unkind. Dust coated their worn disguises, a stark contrast to the pristine clothes they had worn on their mission's outset. The village itself was a patchwork of quaint cottages, each with smoke curling lazily from chimneys.

The sun was beginning to set, casting a golden glow over the humble village. Aura's eyes were drawn to the modest stone cottage at the edge of the village, its thatched roof and flower-lined windows a welcoming sight. They approached with a mix of relief and apprehension, their disguises—a simple traveler's garb—doing little to mask their exhaustion. The door creaked open as they reached it, revealing an elderly woman with silver hair and kind eyes. She looked up from her evening chores with a warm, inviting smile.

"Welcome, travelers," she said, her voice soft but resonant. "You've arrived just in time for supper."

Nox gave her a weary smile. "Thank you, ma'am. We've been on the road for days and could use a place to rest."

The woman stepped aside, ushering them into a cozy, well-lit interior. The scent of freshly baked bread and roasted vegetables filled the air, a stark contrast to the travel-stained smell that clung to them. She led them to a wooden table where a hearty meal awaited.

As they sat, Aura noticed the woman's discerning gaze linger on Nox. There was something familiar in her expression, a flicker of recognition that Nox seemed to catch as well. He hesitated, then spoke.

"Do you—do you remember a woman named Elara?" he asked gently.

The woman's eyes widened slightly, and a wistful smile touched her lips. "Elara? Of course, I remember her. She was a dear friend—such a kind and courageous soul. It's been many years since she's left us."

Nox's gaze softened. "She was my mother."

The woman's face lit up with a mix of sadness and joy. "Oh, how lovely to hear her memory spoken of. She was an incredible woman, and I remember her fondly. She always spoke of you with so much love and pride, when you were just a little one"

Aura watched the exchange with a mix of curiosity and respect. She could see how deeply Nox was affected by the woman's words, a tender expression settling over his features as he absorbed the connection to his mother.

The woman busied herself with serving the meal, her movements filled with a grace that belied her age. The table soon filled with the rich aromas of home-cooked fare—roasted meats, vegetables, and a fresh loaf of bread. As they ate, the conversation turned to stories of old, with the woman sharing anecdotes of the village and its history. Nox listened intently, occasionally contributing his own recollections of his mother, the two finding a shared solace in their memories.

After supper, the woman led them to a small but comfortable guest room, adorned with simple furnishings but exuding warmth and comfort. The bed was modest but inviting, and Aura and Nox settled in with a sense of gratitude. The elderly woman checked on them one last time before retiring for the night. "Rest well. You'll need your strength for the journey ahead."

With that, she left them to their rest. Aura and Nox exchanged tired smiles, the exhaustion of their journey mingling with a quiet sense of contentment.

They lay side by side, the soft sounds of the village outside a lullaby to their weary minds. They would be setting out at first light, traveling five more days to the next village. The path would be long and arduous, but for now, they allowed themselves the luxury of rest.

When the morning sun peeked through the window, casting a gentle light on their faces, they prepared for the day ahead. The horses— borrowed for their journey—were ready and waiting, their coats gleaming in the early light. With a final check of their supplies and a heartfelt farewell to the kind woman who had offered them sanctuary, they mounted their horses and set off, the road stretching out before them.

The adventure was far from over, but the brief respite had rekindled their resolve. As they rode into the horizon, the village of Levin faded behind them.

The days blended seamlessly into one another, punctuated by moments of quiet solitude and bursts of shared laughter. The rhythm of their journey allowed space for ease and connection. Nox watched as Aura gradually relaxed, shedding the sharp edges of her usual demeanor. Her typical jabs and quick retorts softened, revealing glimpses of her true self beneath the hardened exterior.

He marveled at the transformation, seeing her genuine smile and hearing her unguarded laughter. The walls she had built around herself began to crumble, and in their place, he found a warmth that was both surprising and deeply moving. Nox struggled to keep his own emotions in check, but it was becoming increasingly difficult. The softer version of Aura, vulnerable and real, was disarming him in ways he hadn't anticipated.

His own facade of indifference was slipping as well. The pretense he had maintained around her was unraveling, giving way to a burgeoning sense of affection. This newfound ease between them was a revelation, a refreshing shift from the guarded interactions they once shared. Nox couldn't ignore the truth any longer: his heart was irrevocably entangled in this delicate and intimate connection.

As they reached a secluded clearing, Nox stopped and signaled for her to do the same. He could see the fatigue etched into her features, the slight tremor in her hands as she adjusted her cloak. They had been avoiding conversation, each lost in their own thoughts, but now, with the forest around them still, Nox felt an overwhelming need to break the silence.

"Ror," he began, his voice gruff but gentle, "we need to rest for a moment."

She glanced at him, her expression guarded. "We can't afford to waste time," she replied tersely, though there was a softness in her voice that betrayed her exhaustion.

Nox sighed, stepping closer. "Just a brief rest. You're pushing yourself too hard." Aura turned to face him, her eyes flashing with a mix of annoyance and something else—something he could never quite name but always felt like a sliver of hope.

"And what would you know about it, Nox? You've always had your duty, your purpose. You don't understand what it's like to be..."

Her voice trailed off, and for a moment, the air between them was heavy with unspoken words. Nox's heart ached at the distance she maintained, the walls she had built up. He had longed to bridge that gap, to show her the truth of his feelings, but she had always seemed so distant, so determined to push him away.

"Perhaps you're right," Nox said softly, taking a step closer. "But there's something you should know, something I've been wanting to say for a long time."

Aura's gaze met his, a flicker of curiosity behind her guarded eyes. "What are you talking about?"

Nox's breath hitched as he searched for the right words, his heart pounding in his chest. "I've been by your side for years, and I've seen you at your best and your worst. I've watched you fight, lead, and even struggle. And through it all, I've..." He paused, swallowing hard. The words felt both heavy and liberating. "I've admired you, Aura. From the very beginning, I've been in awe of you. It wasn't just about my duty or my oath—it was about how you've always been more than just a princess to me. You're strong and courageous, and... you're everything I've ever wanted."

Her eyes widened, and for a moment, the hardness melted away, replaced by something vulnerable and raw. "You... you can't mean that," she whispered, her voice trembling. "You've always been so—" She trailed off, unable to find the right words. They drove each other insane, completely and utterly wild. In words and touches and every moment in between. The annoyance, the softened hate, it was normal for them, a given. It was comfortable. She knew where she stood. "I thought—"

Nox stepped closer, his hands reaching out to gently touch her shoulders. "I've been that way because I thought you hated me," he confessed, his voice filled with a mix of relief and sadness. "I thought if I played the game, it would be easier for you. But the truth is, I've never hated you. I've always admired you, loved you more than I ever allowed myself to admit."

Aura's eyes filled with tears, and she looked away, her emotions too overwhelming to contain. "I thought you hated me too," she admitted quietly. "I pushed you away because... because I didn't want to be hurt if you didn't feel the same, it was easy to assume we hated each other, but these last few days..."

Nox's heart ached at her words, and he gently turned her to face him. "I've never hated you. I've only ever loved you, even when it was the hardest thing to do."

The clearing was silent but for the distant rustle of leaves, and for the first time, they were truly alone—free from the roles they played, from the masks they wore. Nox cupped her face in his hands, his thumbs brushing away a stray tear that had escaped her eyes.

"Aura," he said softly, "we're about to face a dangerous mission, and I need you to know that my feelings for you have never wavered. If you'll have me, I want to be by your side, not just as your protector but as someone who would burn the world down if you asked me."

Her gaze softened, her tears mingling with a smile that spoke of hope and longing. "I-I want that too," she whispered, her voice barely audible. "I want you by my side."

With a shared, silent understanding, they closed the distance between them, their lips meeting in a kiss that was both tender and fervent. The forest around them seemed to pause, the weight of their unspoken feelings lifting as they embraced. In that moment, the danger of their mission faded, replaced by the undeniable connection they had fought so hard to conceal.

Together, they faced the uncertain path ahead, their souls intertwined—a guiding light in the darkness.

CHAPTER 10

Aura

Aura was still reeling from Nox's confession. From her own heart that felt like it would leap out of her chest at the words. She had been fighting with herself for so long, but her heart was always his. A place where she felt calm and secure, where she could truly be herself. They had traveled on a hidden trail, far off the main one of merchants and travelers. Riding as far as they could before resting the horses and themselves under the cover of the dense forest.

They would arrive in Ancher soon, only a day or two journey left of this last leg. The gothic Evanthian castle would be before them sooner than she was ready for. Esmeralda had warned Aura of the whispers of The Red King of Evanthia. Whispers said he had descended into madness and cruelty.

The sun hung low on the horizon, casting long shadows through the dense forest. Aura walked through the clearing, her mind drifting in the quiet warmth of the afternoon. Her gaze fell upon the delicate glow of a light sprite hovering near the edge of the trees. It pulsed softly, as though carrying a message.

The light sprite darted forward, stopping inches from her face. "For you, Princess," it chimed, its voice like the whisper of bells. Aura extended her hand, and the sprite dropped a letter, shimmering faintly with the insignia of The Hollow.

She frowned, recognizing the seal of her brother—the prince. But why would he send a letter through a light sprite, especially here, when they were so far from the capital?

. . .

Aura broke the seal, her curiosity piqued, and unrolled the parchment.

Aura's fingers tightened around the letter, the paper crinkling under the pressure. Her heart thudded painfully against her ribs as specific words sank in. *Assigned? Commanded?* Her brother had assigned Nox to her side, it had not been a choice of his own will or heart?

A sick feeling rose in her chest, twisting her stomach into knots. She had believed that their connection had been born from something real, something pure. And now, to discover that he had been ordered to be by her side—it made her question everything.

She turned sharply on her heel, her breath quickening as she marched back toward the camp. The fire crackled softly in the distance, and there was Nox, sharpening his blade with calm precision, his eyes lifting the moment she entered the clearing. He smiled, a brief warmth crossing his face as he rose to greet her.

But she wasn't here for smiles.

She threw the letter at his feet, her voice tight. "What is this?"

Nox looked from the letter to her, his face hardening slightly as he bent to pick it up. His brows furrowed as he read the contents. When he finished, he remained silent for a moment, his jaw set in a grim line.

"You knew," Aura said, her voice low but trembling with emotion. "All this time, you've been my guard—because my brother ordered you to be? You are with me not of your own free will, but of what? Convenience?"

Nox raised his gaze to meet hers, a storm of emotions in his eyes. "Aura, it's not—"

"Not what?" she snapped, stepping forward. "Not what it looks like? I thought—" She paused, struggling to keep her voice steady. "I thought we meant something to each other. But now, I find out you were following orders?"

His face softened, and he stepped closer, though she recoiled slightly. "No, Aura, listen to me. Yes, your brother assigned me as your guard. It was my duty to protect you. But my feelings for you—what grew between us—was never a part of that duty."

Aura's eyes narrowed, her disbelief clear. "And yet, you never told me the truth. How am I supposed to believe you now?"

Nox's voice grew desperate as he reached for her hands, though she pulled them away. "Because it's the truth. Aura, you have to understand —I'd follow you anywhere. I would lay down my life for you, not because of some order, but because you mean everything to me."

She stood there, her chest heaving, her mind racing with conflicting thoughts. "You were supposed to protect me, and yet you kept this from me?"

Nox's expression was pained, his voice low. "I didn't tell you because I didn't want you to think... that my loyalty was tied to a command. It's not. I swear to you, Aura, my heart belongs to you. I'd die for you. I'd kill for you. Not because it's my duty, but because I love you."

His words hung heavy in the air, and for a long moment, neither of them spoke. Aura's heart wavered, caught between the betrayal she felt and the depth of Nox's raw sincerity. His eyes pleaded with her, and despite the hurt, she could see the truth in them—the man who had held her on all those quiet nights, who had whispered promises of love into the darkness, wasn't just fulfilling an order.

She swallowed hard, her voice softening just a little. "Then why didn't you tell me sooner?"

Nox lowered his head. "I didn't want to burden you with it. I was afraid... afraid that if you knew, it would make you question everything between us. And now, I see I was wrong for keeping it from you."

Aura looked away, blinking back the tears that threatened to fall. She didn't know whether to scream or collapse into his arms. The weight of the revelation crushed her, but somewhere beneath the hurt, she could still feel the love they had built. After what felt like an eternity, she finally spoke, her voice barely above a whisper. "I don't know if I can forgive you for this... not yet."

Nox nodded, his voice gentle but unwavering. "I understand. I'll be by your side, not because I was ordered to, but because I chose to. I choose you over anything else in this world or the next."

Aura slept restlessly that night under the stars. Nox had leaned against the trees, keeping watch the whole night. They had not switched, she had not offered for him to rest, she simply let her frustration brew and fester. His face was solemn when she gazed over at him the few times she flipped over. The fur blanket was warm around her. The horses tied up to the nearest tree. She let herself be angry, let her heart mourn and feel it all until morning. When the sun broke over the horizon she squared her shoulders, dusted off her clothes, remade her pack, and walked over to Nox. He looked worse for wear. Dark clouded eyes, the lack of sleep evident. She glared at him as fiercely as she could, walking up close enough for their chests to touch. She tilted her head up, to look at him.

He was so much larger than her, she forced herself to not feel small. Then she shoved her hands into his chest once. Then twice. Letting out a small guttural umph.

Nox saw the walls around Aura's cracking, saw her forgiveness setting in. The smirk lazily appeared over his mouth was evidence enough. He knew her, knew her heart and her mind. They had been through too much at this point. Together.

She crossed her arms and glared again, lips turned down with great effort.

"I am still mad at you," Aura grumbled. Nox only nodded as if to say, *as you should be.*

Then she grabbed the front of his linen tunic, pulling him to her. She reached for him, dragging him down to meet her. Her lips collided with his in a desperate plea.

She was so mad.

But she knew this, knew that hatred and anger was what fueled them from the beginning. And while they had grown past that, the anger turned to annoyance, then to respect, then to admiration and now to love.

"I love you too, you fucking idiot."

As they arrived in Ancher, the sun was setting, and the last golden spirals of light gave the village roofs and cobblestone streets a warm, golden hue. Nox dropped off the horses at an old inn on the outskirts of town, as directed from the kind woman in Levin. They continued on foot, hoods covering their faces as they walked through the town square. A market was starting to set up, carts being rolled out.

A night market.

Nox's keen eyes scanned the surroundings, ever alert despite the relaxed demeanor he held. Aura, her royal poise hidden beneath a simple cloak and tunic, walked beside him, her eyes wide with curiosity and excitement.

The town was picturesque, with charming houses and a bustling square. It wasn't long before they arrived at a modest, ivy-clad house.

280

The front door creaked open before they could even knock, revealing an elderly man with a bushy beard and a broad smile.

"Nox! By the stars, it's been ages!" The man's voice was booming with genuine joy.

Nox grinned and embraced the man. "Good to see you, Galen. This is Ror, my..." he hesitated, thinking quickly, "...my traveling companion."

Aura stepped forward, offering a warm smile and a polite nod. "Pleasure to meet you."

Galen's eyes twinkled with amusement. "A pleasure indeed. Come in, come in! I've been dying for some good company. The tavern's not far from here, and I've got a feeling tonight's going to be a good one."

They followed into the house, which was filled with the comforting aroma of roast meat and freshly baked bread. The evening meal was a lively affair, with Galen recounting tales of his younger days, and Nox chiming in with his own stories, each embellished with enough exaggeration to make the tales entertaining.

After dinner, they made their way to the local tavern, a bustling place with a low ceiling, wooden beams, and the familiar sound of clinking mugs and boisterous laughter. The tavern's interior was warm, with a crackling fireplace that added to the inviting atmosphere.

As they entered, the chatter and laughter of the patrons seemed to swell, and Nox led Aura and Galen to a table in a corner. Aura's eyes sparkled with amusement as she took in the lively scene.

"Well, this place has more character than a royal ball," she said, her voice low to avoid drawing attention.

Nox chuckled. "And considerably less etiquette. Just how I like it."

Galen winked and signaled to a passing waitress. "Three ales and a plate of the finest sausages you've got!"

Aura nudged Nox playfully. "Is this how you treat all your guests, or am I getting special treatment?"

Nox leaned closer, his voice teasing. "You're getting the special treatment. I've got to make sure you're properly introduced to the joys of the common folk."

Galen chuckled heartily. "And trust me, they'll make sure you have a memorable time. You're with the right people for that."

The ales arrived, frothy and golden, and the sausages followed, sizzling and fragrant. They clinked their mugs together, and Nox lifted his in a toast. "To old friends and new adventures."

Aura grinned and raised her mug. They sipped their drinks, the warmth of the ale spreading through them. Galen wandered off, talking to other villagers near the bar. Nox leaned back, a playful glint in his eyes. His voice low, "So, how's the life of a commoner treating you so far?"

Aura laughed, the sound bright and clear. "It's a refreshing change. No courtly intrigues, just good food, good drink, and good company."

The night continued with laughter, songs, and a friendly game of dice with the locals. The tavern's atmosphere was infectious, and the worries of their mission seemed to melt away, if only for a few hours. Aura and Nox reveled in the anonymity and the camaraderie, their usual roles of princess and knight replaced by that of carefree travelers.

"I think this might be one of the best nights I've had in a long time," Aura admitted, her voice soft but filled with contentment.

Nox looked at her with a genuine smile. "You and me both."

He clicked his mug against hers, his eyes meeting hers with a tenderness that spoke of deeper feelings. "To us, and to whatever comes next."

The laughter and music continued around them, but for a moment, it was as if they were in their own world. Aura felt the anxiety of the rest of the mission bubbling up inside of her, but instead took another swig of her ale, pushing it back down.

Aura pushed herself up from her seat, and walked to the bar to get another drink. As she waited, she felt a presence behind her—someone too close, invading her personal space. She turned to find a burly man with an unsettling grin, his eyes glinting with a predatory gleam.

"Why don't you join me for a drink?" he slurred, his breath heavy with the scent of ale and something more unpleasant.

Aura took a step back, trying to keep her voice steady. "No, thank you. I'm waiting for someone."

The man's grin widened, and he stepped closer, pressing his body against hers. "Come on, don't be like that. You look like you could use some company."

Aura's heart raced as she tried to move away, but the man's hand shot out, gripping her wrist with a forceful grasp. Her eyes scanned the room for Nox, but the crowd and the dim light made it difficult to see clearly. Anger rose as she struggled to free herself, her voice rising in annoyance. "Get your hands off me, before I remove them from your body!"

Nox, who had been engaged in a conversation with Galen at a table, noticed the sudden commotion. His eyes immediately locked onto Aura's figure, a drunken male with hands on her, and his expression hardened. He stood up, his movements quick and purposeful as he made his way across the room.

In a swift, powerful stride, Nox reached the man, his presence commanding attention. "Get your hands off her," he growled, his voice a low, dangerous rumble.

The man looked up, his grin faltering as he saw the fury in Nox's eyes. Before he could react, Nox grabbed him by the collar and yanked him away from Aura, sending him stumbling backward. The man crashed into a nearby table, knocking over a pitcher of ale and scattering patrons.

"What's the meaning of this?" the man spat, trying to regain his balance and composure.

Nox's reply was a punch to the man's face, a brutal blow that sent him reeling. The tavern fell into a stunned silence, the laughter and music fading as onlookers watched the unfolding scene with a mix of shock and fascination. The man tried to rise, his hand going for a weapon hidden beneath his coat, but Nox was quicker. With a fierce determination, he grabbed the man's arm, twisting it behind his back and slamming him against the wall. "You think you can just touch people like that?" Nox's voice was a harsh whisper, full of anger and a promise of more pain if needed.

The man struggled, his face contorted in pain, but Nox's grip was unrelenting. Nox delivered a series of precise, powerful blows, each one designed to incapacitate rather than kill. The man's attempts to fight back were feeble and quickly overpowered. With a final, punishing punch to the jaw, Nox sent him crashing to the floor.

The tavern erupted into murmurs and gasps, and Galen, who had been watching with a mixture of worry and approval, stepped forward. "That's enough."

Nox, breathing heavily, glared down at the man, who was now curled up on the floor, groaning in pain. "You're lucky I'm in a good mood," Nox spat, his voice dripping with contempt. "Stay away from her. And don't come back."

He turned to Aura, who had watched the scene with wide eyes, her face pale but resolute. She took a hesitant step towards him, her gaze filled with gratitude and concern. "Are you alright?"

Nox's expression softened as he approached her, his anger giving way to a deep, genuine concern. "I'm fine. Are you?"

Aura nodded, though her hands trembled slightly. "Fine."

Nox gently cupped her face, his touch tender as he searched her eyes for any sign of lingering distress. "I'm sorry. I didn't mean for things to get out of hand, but I couldn't stand to see him touching you like that."

Aura managed a small smile, placing her hands over his. "I would have slammed his body into the table same as you, but I thought we were trying to lay low, Nox."

Galen approached, offering a reassuring nod. "Let's get you both out of here. Before the lot of you attract any more trouble."

Nox nodded, a protective hand on Aura's back. The patrons of the tavern slowly resumed their conversations, the excitement of the altercation giving way to the usual revelry.

The moon hung low and heavy in the sky as Nox and Aura made their way back to the inn Galen directed them to. He left them with a bag filled with clothes for them, their new disguises. That of people of the court. Aura was rather excited to get rid of these travel and dirt ridden clothes and put on something fit for a ball.

Now, as they settled into the quiet comfort of their rented room, the weight of the evening's events seemed to press heavily on them. The room was dimly lit by a single oil lamp, its flickering light casting gentle shadows on the walls. Aura sat on the edge of the bed, her fingers brushing against her disheveled dress as she tried to steady her breath. Nox stood a few steps away, his knuckles still stained with blood and his expression a mixture of concern and lingering anger.

He approached her slowly, the fierce protector softened by the tenderness of the moment. With careful movements, he crouched in front of her, his gaze never leaving her face. His hands, rough from countless battles, were surprisingly gentle as he cupped her cheeks. The contrast between his strength and his tenderness was both comforting and disarming.

"Aura," he began, his voice a soft murmur that seemed to resonate with both regret and affection. "I'm sorry. I should have—"

She placed a hand over his, stilling his words. "I am fine, all is well." And she felt it as so, she wished to go back and punch the idiot drunk herself.

Nox shook his head slightly, the intensity in his eyes giving way to a deep, heartfelt sincerity. "You're my moon, Aura. In the darkest of nights, you're the light that guides me. You're strong, more than you know. And I couldn't stand to see you hurt."

Her eyes softened, and she reached out to touch his face, her fingers brushing over the bruised skin of his cheek. He leaned into her touch, closing his eyes for a brief moment as he savored the connection between them.

When he opened his eyes again, "I would rip the world apart, piece by piece, to get you back, my moon."

Aura felt her insides warm, her heart flutter. She hadn't known it to ever flutter except here with this man who had always been so stoic, so easily to throw back sharp jabs with her. This side of him, this gentleness was so at odds with the bloodied knuckles and even his words. And she loved him for it.

CHAPTER 11

Nox

The gothic castle loomed above the darkened landscape, its spires piercing the night sky. The air was cold and heavy with the scent of damp stone and distant incense. The castle's grand ballroom was alive with opulence and decadence, its high ceilings adorned with cobwebs and gilded chandeliers that cast eerie shadows on the walls. Laughter and the clinking of glasses mingled with the haunting strains of a string quartet, creating a discordant symphony of celebration and foreboding.

Aura, dressed in an elegant gown of deep blue velvet that contrasted with the bright scarlet of the ballroom's typical guests, moved gracefully through the crowd. Her eyes, now keen with both determination and affection, searched for any sign of the kidnapped witches and fae. Nox was transfixed, wholly by her. The blue of the dress was almost a perfect match to the blue of his own eyes. With her deep raven colored hair instead of her normal white locks, she was a vision, even with her appearance altered by her enchanted ring.

Nox was dressed in a dark, refined suit, his usually rugged appearance masked by a careful façade of noble elegance. He had spent a lifetime at court, he knew how to act his part. His sharp eyes scanned the room, alert for any hint of danger or the whereabouts of their captives.

The two made their way through the throng of guests, exchanging subtle glances. "Stay close," Nox murmured, his voice low but urgent. "We need to blend in while we find them."

Aura nodded, her gaze sweeping over the masked faces around them.

She spotted a cluster of guests gathered near a grand fireplace, their conversations animated and their masks glittering in the dim light. "There," she whispered, "we should start with that group. It's possible they've seen or overheard something."

As they approached, Aura and Nox engaged in polite conversation with the guests, their voices low and their demeanor casual. Aura caught snippets of conversation about the kidnapped witches and fae, fueling her resolve. The guests were discussing the "new additions" to the mad king's collection, hinting that the captives were kept in the castle's dark dungeons, not to be brought out till midnight.

Nox's gaze flicked toward a hidden door behind a tapestry. "That's likely where they're being held," he said. "We need to find a way down there without drawing attention."

The ballroom's grandeur seemed to mock their stealthy mission as Aura and Nox slipped through a concealed doorway behind the tapestry. The narrow, dimly lit corridor was a stark contrast to the opulence of the ballroom. Their footsteps echoed softly on the cold stone as they made their way down winding stairs, leading deeper into the castle's bowels.

"Follow my lead," Ember's soft voice whispered to the two of them, appearing with her manipulated dull light in the staircase.

The air grew colder and more oppressive as they descended, the walls growing darker and more foreboding. At the bottom of the stairs, they reached a heavy iron door marked with arcane symbols.

"This is it." Ember nodded towards the door.

Nox produced a set of lockpicks, working with careful precision until the lock clicked open. The door creaked slowly, revealing a dank, shadowy dungeon. Ember moved them through the dark labyrinth, her dull light guiding them. They came across a sleeping guard slouched in a chair and Aura pulled a potion from under her skirts, courtesy of Esmie. She wafted the potion under the guard's nose, ensuring he took a very deep sleep and would not wake any time soon.

Inside, Aura's eyes adjusted to the gloom, and she spotted the captives huddled in a corner of the cell: two witches with tattered robes and a fae woman whose ethereal beauty was marred by the grime of captivity. The fae woman's eyes widened as she saw them, hope flickering in her gaze. A small flame cupped in her hand to keep them warm. Aura marveled at the magic, so akin to her own but burning like fire rather than her own white light.

"We're here to rescue you," Aura said softly, stepping forward. "Can you walk?"

The fae woman nodded, her voice trembling. "We can, but the guard—"

"The one posted was taken care of, and I swiped these." Aura pulled out a heavy metal ring with a large silver skeleton key, sliding it into the lock on the dungeon cell, the old metal creaking as she pushed it open. The two witches stood and rushed to her.

"You are an heir," one of them whispered, her voice raw and scratched. The witches looked nearly identical. She knew her golden eyes gave her away to anyone from The Hollow. Only that of the Galanis line had golden eyes.

"Yes, I am Aura." Aura smiled gently, holding her hand to her chest. "Let's get you home."

"Princess!" The small girl gasped.

"Thank the goddess." The boy sighed and helped the girl next to him up from where they had been in the corner of the dark cell.

"I am Eamon, this is Selene." The boy introduced himself, his dark hair was scattered down his neck, his skin pale and a golden rune wrapped around one arm. The rune matched the other witch, her hair the same ebony color as the boys. The pair of blue eyes bore into Aura's.

"About damn time," the Fae woman muttered, stepping forward. She was older than the witches, a scrunched brow and a flicker of light next to her.

"That's Zephyra," Eamon muttered. The twins stayed close to the other, seemingly keeping themselves small. Aura tried not to shutter at the sight, at the terrible things they must have endured.

"I told you they were coming!" a small voice broke through the cold dungeon. The light shifted and a light sprite appeared.

"Nessa." Aura nodded, seeing Ember's sister.

"Your Highness!" She bowed and fluttered around the witches.

"There's a hidden tunnel down the east end," Nessa's soft voice drifted to them, relaying the information and layout of the dungeons. Aura felt a sigh of relief at this part, the sprites had worked tirelessly to do their part, and it was irreplaceable.

Nox interrupted, his gaze alert as he scanned the dungeon. "We need to move quickly. I'll lead. Aura, make sure they stay close."

The group moved cautiously through the dark corridors, but their progress was interrupted by the sudden clamor of approaching guards. The sound of clanking armor and harsh voices grew louder.

"Hide!" Nox hissed, pushing the captives behind a stack of crates as he and Aura took cover in a shadowy alcove. The guards' lanterns bobbed closer, their voices echoing off the stone walls.

Aura and Nox exchanged determined glances, their hands brushing briefly—a silent promise of support. As the guards passed by, Nox readied his sword, and Aura prepared her magic, keeping the glow so faint to only guide them. When the guards were out of sight, they resumed their escape, moving swiftly but silently through hidden passages and secret doors. The belly of the castle was a labyrinth, but Nessa's familiarity with its intricacies guided them efficiently.

The dungeon's chill clung to the air as Nessa and Ember led the rescued captives through the shadowed stone corridors. The two young witches, their expressions a mix of hope and exhaustion, followed closely behind. The fae woman, with her dark skin and void-like black eyes, was last, her presence a stark contrast to the dimly lit surroundings.

A faint light signaled their escape, but as they neared the castle's outer walls, their way was blocked by a group of armed guards. Nox stepped forward, his sword flashing in the dim light. "We'll need to fight our way through," he said, his voice firm.

Aura nodded, her hands glowing with a soft, ethereal light as she prepared her magic. "Stay close." Zephyra held out her hands, her dark skin was slightly glowing. Aura could see now her eyes were almost black, void of color. Zephyra shifted to be in front of the twins.

Protecting them.

Their escape route was nearly in sight—a secret exit concealed behind an ancient, rusted door. But just as they approached, the clatter of armor and the harsh clamor of boots on stone signaled the approach of soldiers. The hallway ahead was now occupied by a group of heavily armed guards, their eyes scanning the area with grim determination.

Aura's heart raced as she assessed the situation. Her fingers hummed with the excitement to dig her daggers from where they were strapped to her thigh under her gown. Her power was begging to be used, flooding through her. Nox stepped forward, drawing his sword with a swift motion. "Stay back and protect the captives," he instructed the witches and the fae woman. "We'll handle this."

Zephyra, her eyes gleaming with a deep, otherworldly void, nodded resolutely. "I'll provide cover," she said, her voice calm yet fierce. The soldiers, unaware of the imminent threat, continued their patrol, their faces obscured by their helmets. Aura and Nox readied themselves, exchanging a final glance of silent determination.

As the soldiers turned toward them, Nox moved first. With a powerful thrust, he engaged the nearest guard, his sword a blur of steel. Aura followed, she struck with precise, fluid movements. Her blade sang through the air, cutting through the guards' defenses with lethal accuracy.

The fae woman stepped forward, her hands raised as flames began to dance around her fingertips. With a fierce gesture, she unleashed a torrent of fire that surged down the corridor, the flames scorching the guards and forcing them to stagger back. The heat was intense, the fire crackling with a primal energy that seemed to pulse with her own power. Aura had never seen anything like it, her void eyes and fire that came from the fae the way the light came from her own fingers.

Aura and Nox fought with a coordinated grace, their movements a blend of strength and agility. Aura's strikes were sharp and relentless, while Nox's swordwork was a fluid counterpoint, each swing clearing a path through the enemy ranks. Together, they created a deadly dance of steel and fire, their actions synchronized in perfect harmony.

The twin witches, standing back with their eyes closed in concentration, began to chant in unison. Their voices wove an intricate spell that conjured a swirling vortex of wind and debris. The vortex lashed out, pushing the soldiers off balance and disrupting their formations. The witches' magic acted as a barrier, providing vital cover for Aura and Nox as they pressed forward.

One of the soldiers, attempting to flank them, was met with a sudden burst of flames from the fae woman. The fire leaped from her hands with an explosive intensity, engulfing the soldier in a blaze that sent him crashing to the ground.

As the battle raged on, the soldiers' attempts to regroup were thwarted by the relentless assault. Aura's blade cleaved through armor, while Nox's sword struck with precision, each blow incapacitating a foe. The fae woman's fire magic continued to burn with an unyielding ferocity, creating a barrier of flames that kept the remaining soldiers at bay.

The witches' magic was a whirlwind of energy, their spells striking with pinpoint accuracy. They summoned bolts of lightning and gusts of wind that blasted the soldiers back, their combined power a formidable force that turned the tide of the battle.

Despite their numbers, the soldiers were no match for the coordinated assault. As the last of the guards fell, Aura, Nox, and Zephyra stood amid the debris, their breaths heavy with exertion. The corridor was now littered with fallen foes, the flickering flames of the fae woman's magic casting long shadows on the walls.

The witches, their faces pale but resolute, approached. "Is it safe?" one of them asked, her voice trembling but hopeful.

Aura nodded, her gaze still scanning the area for any remaining threats. "For now. We need to move quickly before more guards arrive."

Zephyra's eyes returned to their usual void-like calm as she extinguished the last of her flames. "Let's go," she said, her voice a soothing contrast to the chaos. "We're almost free."

With a final glance at the fallen soldiers, Aura and Nox led the way to the secret exit. The passage beyond was narrow and steep, but it promised freedom from the castle's oppressive grasp. The group moved swiftly, their steps echoing with a sense of both relief and lingering tension.

As they emerged from the dark, confining dungeon into the open air of the night, the stars above seemed to shine with a newfound clarity. The castle's ominous silhouette loomed behind them, but their escape was complete. They had fought through adversity and emerged victorious, their bond strengthened by the trials they had faced together.

Nox and Aura breathed heavily, their faces smeared with sweat and grime. The captives, though shaken, were unharmed.

"Let's get out of here," Nox said, glancing toward the castle's gates.

They made their way through the castle's darkened outdoor grounds, finally reaching the outer wall and the eastern gate. They straightened their backs, Aura swiping a couple of glasses of ale on an abandoned step and handed them to Zephrya and Nox. Zephyra smirked immediately, catching on to Aura's thought. *Act drunk.* If they were simply party goers drunk on the night's delights they could slip out amongst the crowd. Zephyra brought a beaming smile to her lips and lifted her cup,

"To good fortune!" she cheered, Aura cheered with her, and Nox raised his glass. Zephyra fake stumbled into another couple, grabbing a shawl from a table nearby. The lights were getting brighter, tables strewn across the grasses, flickering candles and flame around them. The night of revelry from the ball was far into chaos. Zephyra laughed and pushed the shawl back to the witches, then eyed a coat hanging haphazardly along a wall, people laughing and drinking nearby. Eamon noted her glance and moved so quickly Aura hardly caught it before he was donning a rather nice courtiers jacket. It was too big for his malnourished frame but he tugged his sister into him. Covering the both of them. Zephyra slung her own shawl over her shoulders, a black lace and fur combination. The three of them had successfully covered their tattered clothing, enough to blend in with the crowd. They made there way closer and closer to the gates.

"We will cause a distraction, you go through first while the guards eyes are on us, then we will follow," Nox ordered lowly. Zephrya only nodded, shuffling the twins closer to her. She hummed a tune and engaged them in conversation. Selene stayed quiet, eyes downcast, but Eamon smiled widely to match that of the fae woman. Her hair she had let down before they came into the courtyard, covering her ears from sight.

Nox turned to Aura. "Follow my lead, Ror." He smirked. She eyed him suspiciously but nodded all the same. The music from a band on a small stage was loud, people cheered and drank all around them. They walked closer to the gates, her heart beat matching her with each hurried step. She took a breath and settled herself, her hands tucked into her pockets, her magic wanting to be let free.

"My Lady!" Nox practically shouted and stumbled his steps pulling Aura with him. "You have bewitched me, taken my heart with your beauty, it is unmatched," he declared. People began turning, watching the scene unfold.

"I cannot breathe without you, I wake with your lips on my mind, I fall asleep dreaming of your"—He looked around with a lopsided smile

—"I'm sure the people could guess." Bellows of laughter surrounded them. Nox dropped to one knee before her. The breath wholly left Aura's lungs.

"Put me out of my misery, my love, be my wife, bear my children, be my future." His voice was deep and loud, making sure everyone's eyes were on theirs. Aura tried to bite back the smirk, she brought her hands to her mouth covering it and jumped up and down,

"Yes! Yes! A thousand times yes!" she exclaimed. Much to her own surprise, Nox pulled out a red ruby ring, surrounded by two smaller dark stones on either side. He held it out for her. She stared, wide eyed in response, nodded her head with a smile, and Nox slipped on the ring. Nox rose from his feet, grabbing the silks of her dress and pulling her to him. Hands on either side of her face, eyes wide.

"A fucking ring?" she bit out, keeping the smile in place. He kissed her, then pulled back,

"Grabbed a souvenir from the ball room, you like it?" He smirked back at her.

"You are insane," she whispered before laughing and falling into his chest and hiding her face. He lifted a fist to the sky and cheers and bellows surrounded them once more. They had shoulder taps and congratulations given out to them as they walked through the gates easily. A guard, shouting after them to "have a fun night."

The dawn was breaking as they emerged from the castle's shadow, the first light of morning casting a golden hue over the landscape. They found Zephyra, Eamon, and Selene waiting down a street from the gates. Together, they fled through the forest, leaving the gothic castle behind, its dark silhouette fading into the distance.

As they reached safety, Aura and Nox shared a look of relief and triumph.

"You are a wonder, *wife*," he whispered as he pressed a kiss to the top of her head. Aura smirked and held up her hand adorned with her new ring.

"It does look rather nice." She smirked and wiggled her fingers under the moonlight. Zephyra spoke in hushed tones to the twins, calming them. They found food for them as they had not eaten in two days, learning the food was doused in something that subdued their magic. Once Nessa had informed them that they were being rescued, they gave up the food. But the two young witches looked frail and Aura worried for them. They found their stashed bags and quickly ate some rations before heading into the forest.

Days went by, they stopped to rest when they could. Nox and Aura guided their people through the paths they had come through, back to their rightful home, back to safety.

In the grand hall of Hollow's Castle, a thousand candles flickered like stars pulled down from the heavens, casting their soft glow over vibrant banners. The Hollow's crest embroidered in golden thread flowed in the night's breeze. The air hummed with quiet anticipation, a symphony of murmurs and the intoxicating perfume of freshly bloomed flowers. Petals, delicate as whispers, lay scattered across the marble floors, polished to reflect the night's splendor. It was a night of celebration, a royal wedding unlike any other, where Prince Kellian stood at the altar with Kyeria, his soulbound.

Princess Aura, radiant in a gown of silver that shimmered like the moon's reflection on still water, stood beside Nox, her own soulbound partner. Polished royal armor adorned his body, a red cape flowing from his back dignifying him as Kellian's second in command. His ocean eyes, always so steady, were alight with admiration as they watched the scene unfold before them. Kellian and Kyeria's hands were intertwined like the roots of ancient trees, as they stood at the altar. It spoke of a love deep and unspoken, forged through time. Aura's heart swelled as her gaze fell on her brother, Kellian, standing tall and proud. He was draped in royal armor, dragon scales glinting with a metallic sheen, a white cape flowing at his own back.

Beside him, Kyeria stood in serene grace, her emerald eyes reflecting the pulse of the earth itself. She wore a gown woven from the forest's own colors, green and gold, the very essence of life and magic swirling around her. Flowing sleeves with golden embroidered vines wrapped up her arms, ending in cuffs at her wrists. The back of the dress cut low, gathering at her waist and flowing down into an endless train of emerald. Together, they were a portrait of unity—fae and dragon, earth and flame—two souls intertwined in a bond as ancient as the gods and goddesses.

The ceremony unfolded to the soft, enchanting notes of fae melodies, notes that seemed to float through the air, wrapping the hall in a spell of peace and joy. Aura felt a tear slip down her cheek, not of sorrow, but of pure contentment. Turning to Nox, she whispered, "Look at them, they are truly perfect together."

Nox, ever the silent one, allowed a rare smile to cross his lips. His gaze found hers, dark eyes reflecting the light she brought to his life. "They are," he murmured, and though the words were simple, the meaning behind them was vast as he squeezed her hand three times signifying three words—*I love you*. She was his moon in an endless night sky, the constant that guided him through all. In the same way, Kyeria was Kellian's sun, a bright and constant reminder of life and magic.

Next to them, Esmeralda, the royal witch whose wisdom had guided the kingdom through its darkest days, watched with quiet pride. She was absent of her normal deep maroon wardrobe, instead wearing a silver shimmering gown to compliment Aura's own. Her hair was braided and twisted back away from her face, golden gems adorning many strands all pulled into a twist of curls at the nape of her neck. The twin witches rescued from the dungeons of Evanthia stood by her side, their expressions full of wonder, honored to witness such a moment. Once, they had been lost, their magic misunderstood and feared. Now, in The Hollow, they were celebrated, their power a beacon of light, as all magic was cherished and regarded here on this sacred land.

Zephyra, once a force of untamed magic, had found her sanctuary in the Dragioner Forest, her flame now a steady warmth, no longer wild but still fiercely powerful. She and Aura had worked together to understand both their magics, the flame and light so akin to the other. Zephrya was still a mystery to many, keeping to herself, and yet to reveal her true background. Nonetheless, the heirs had granted her safe haven here in The Hollow, as they had Kyeria. Zephyra had saved and stayed with the young Hollow witches, Eamon and Selene, in the clutches of the Evanthian King. She had protected them with her own life, despite hardly knowing them. And for that, Kellian and Aura had offered the safety of The Hollow, a home and a land where she could exist in whatever capacity she wished.

As Kellian and Kyeria exchanged their vows and sealed them with a kiss, the hall erupted in applause and cheers, a chorus of joy that echoed through the castle. Aura and Nox joined the celebration, their hearts full, overflowing for the love that had bloomed in the hearts of the newlyweds. The night unfurled like a storybook, with dancing, laughter, and tales shared beneath a sky full of stars that seemed to shine brighter than ever before.

In that moment, bathed in the glow of the moon and the lanterns strung throughout the castle, it felt as if the universe itself was rejoicing, cradling them all in the warmth of its embrace. For Aura and Nox, for Kellian and Kyeria, and for all those who had gathered in The Hollow's sacred land, it was a night of beginnings. The battles of the past, the sorrows and struggles, were now but memories, woven into a tapestry of joy that would carry them into the future and what was yet to come.

And so, as the stars watched over them and the laughter spilled into the deepest hours of the night, a quiet promise filled the air—a promise of brighter days and unshakable bonds. They had all found their place in this world, and they lived happily ever after.

THE WINTER WITCH

part four

four years later

Under the Willow Tree

Beneath the willow's shade, she sits,
a young witch cradling the weight of the unknown.
The soil beneath her; her home—
rich in magic, hums with secrets,
yet something deeper stirs in her veins.

Old journals, worn and whispering,
reveal the pull of distant Isles,
where her ancestors wait,
scattered like forgotten echoes.

The magic in her blood is restless,
tugging her from the only world she knows.
She rises, leaving the Hollow in silence.
The path unfolds before her,
her fate no longer waiting—
but hers to claim.

CHAPTER 1

The Witch in the Library

I n the tallest spire of the Hollow's grand library, where the shadows danced like phantoms and the scent of old parchment lingered in the air, Esmeralda Winters sat by the fire. Her figure silhouetted against the flickering light, an array of necklaces adorned her neck. The library, a labyrinth of towering shelves and ancient tomes, was her sanctuary—a haven where she could lose herself in the pages of forgotten lore and the warmth of her cat's contented purring. She sat on the first level of the library, it was quite extensive, going down for many floors with older texts as it went. An enchanted candle stick sat next to her. Intricate golden stems held a long candle. It never dimmed, never blew out or melted, bound by a spell to stay lit - *always.*

Mittens, a black ball of fluff with eyes that gleamed like emeralds, lay curled next to her, a constant companion through the long hours of reading and researching. Esmeralda stroked the cat absentmindedly, her gaze fixed on the open book in front of her. The text was a relic, its pages yellowed and delicate, and its script written in a coded language that twisted and turned like the branches of the frost-covered trees outside. An open journal next to her, helping her cipher the code.

Esmeralda's thoughts wandered as she traced the intricate symbols into her journal. At just twenty years of age, she was the last Winter Witch of her kind, a title that carried both pride and a weight of solitude. Her Gran, who had raised her in the hidden kingdom of The Hollow, had passed away years ago, leaving behind a collection of diaries that had become Esmeralda's guide and mentor. Through those pages, she had learned the intricacies of magic, unraveling secrets of the craft that had shaped her life and her destiny. How to make potions and master her ability at healing.

The warmth of the fire contrasted sharply with the cold that pressed against the library's windows. It was a peculiar sensation, one that reminded her of her own dual existence. Esmeralda was a product of both the world of her Gran's teachings and the royal lineage she had been thrust into when her life changed irrevocably. The Hollow's royal family had taken her in after Gran's passing, and she had grown up alongside the heirs—Kellian and Aura.

Four years ago now, Kyeria had wandered into The Hollow's enchanted embrace by a twist of fate, her magic being from the same goddess that blessed the magical border around the land of The Hollow. Running from people set on ending her life because she was Fae in a land that despised their kind. The Hollow, however, was a place that had people from every corner of the realm. Even that of those below the realm in the Shadowfell. Fate had led Kyeria here, and had been the soulbound to Kellian when he was still a prince. Now, Kellian and Kyeria were the King and Queen of The Hollow. Protecting the sacred land of the dragons. Kyeria was the first dragon rider to exist in the last decade. Her bonded dragon, Ameline, was a fierce protector. Esmeralda spent endless hours with her in the caves, talking about the history of the land and swapping folklore. Ameline had known of the Winter witches, Esmeralda's family line. Had even gone as far to gather more information for her from the other Dragons.

Esmeralda loved her home, loved this land. She felt the pull of the magic here, felt her Gran's presence here long after she passed. She spent most of her time in the library or in the potions tower that all her ancestors had used. Now Esmeralda was teaching Selene and Eamon, the twin witches Aura and Nox rescued from the Evanthian dungeons. The twins' arrival had altered the dynamics of the kingdom, adding new threads to the intricate tapestry of the Hollow's fate. Two young souls that Esmeralda had taken under her own wing, and grown rather fond of.

She felt her life a tapestry woven from the threads of her Gran's teachings, the royal family's stories, and her own quiet longing for a place she could truly call her own. Though she was cherished and cared for by the royal family, she often felt like a quiet observer in a world that spun around her with dazzling complexity. As she turned a page, her gaze fell upon an ancient map sketched in faded ink, depicting what looked like The Hollow in its early days.

Symbols on the map represented forgotten magics and long-lost realms.It looked decidedly familiar, almost shaped in the same way as, what they knew now, the Isles. Esmeralda's fingers hovered over the map, tracing the paths, and around what was within the borders of The Hollow, the vast Ash Mountains and the Dragioner Forest. It wasn't long ago now that Aura had defeated the Shadow beast that had slipped through a crack in their realm from below. The beast was a Helian of the worst kind, eating away at magic, at the magic that fueled the borders, keeping the lands of The Hollow a secret from the outside world. To the East was a world without magic or fae, outlawed and punishable by death. Aura and Nox had saved a set of twins and an otherworldly fae woman from the dungeons four years ago now. Zephyra had quietly molded into life here in The Hollow. The court offered her a place to live in the castle, just like the twins. But once she knew the twins were safe she gently declined, living now on the outskirts of The Hollow, checking in from time to time. The twins, however, stayed in the castle, close to Esmeralda, they all took turns helping the twins with lessons. Magic from Esmeralda and Kyeria, sword wielding from Aura, sword making from Nox.

As Esmeralda riffled through the letters on her desk, she realized the last one she had sent by messenger sprite over a week ago had gone unanswered. Which was unlike Zephyra. While the fae woman liked to be in the secluded part of the forest, she also loved written correspondence and her letters frequented Esmeralda's desk. Esmeralda finished up her last batch of potions, two healing elixrs and a calming draft. Tying them around with twine and attaching them to her belted corset.

Outside, the wind howled through the forest, its voice a reminder of the ever-present chill. Esmeralda took a deep breath, the cold air mixing with the warmth of the fire. She glanced at Mittens, whose eyes were half-closed in blissful contentment. With a final pat, Esmeralda closed the book, and left the tower. Headed out the gates of the castle and towards the Dragioner Forest, determined to see her friend.

It was almost the Winter Solstice. The chill in the air was bone deep now, winter had begun early this season. She could feel the chill nipping at her skin through the warm fur she had around her shoulders over her wool cloak. The red cloak was her own personal stamp of identity. She had worn one since she was young, her Gran making it for her. The one that donned her shoulders now and had once belonged to her Gran herself. She tucked away her childhood one in storage, ready to one day pass it on to the next Winter Witch.

Esmeralda, lost in her own thoughts, almost missed the song on the wind sweeping her dark curls into her face. Kyeria had taught her how to listen to the wind. While it didn't speak to her like it did to her fae friend, Esmeralda learned how to see the signs, when the breeze was not just a breeze but a signal, when the magic was buzzing enough in the air to spark awareness. A branch cracked from behind her, stealing her own steps. She turned to look, seeing nothing but a moon lit dirt path behind her. She shook off the feeling of being followed and continued on her way, guided by only the moon.

Crack.

"Show yourself" Esmeralda commanded, holding up a stone she had imbued with Aura's light magic to light dark forest.

From behind a shadowy tree, stepped a familiar figure clad in shining armor and a sword strapped to her side.

"Lia." Esmeralda drawled, "why are you following me?"

"It is my job." Lia replied simply. She spoke the truth, Lia had been assigned to Esmeralda as her personal guard at the beginning of the year. Esmeralda in turn had spent an entire year evading her bodyguard at all costs. She was like a dark cloud following her everywhere. Her jet black cropped hair was show of that enough. Lia stood stoically, like a blank wall.

She hated this. Hated being followed. Hated feeling like a Child. Esmeralda was now twenty years of age, she had grown up here in these lands and she knew the forests in the dark as well as she did in the light. She did not under any circumstance need someone following her and frightening the animals along the way. Now none of the wild sprites, Esmeralda had become so fond of would come out and join her.

"I am simply going to visit Zephrya." Esmeralda explained trying to stay upbeat. She hated that Lia made her feel this way, hated hating. Esmeralda was the positive one, the sunshine and rainbows one, the goddess damned happy one.

"And I am accopanying you."

"You do not *need* to" Esmeralda said with a tight smile.

"It is commanded by his Highness, the King, that I follow you where ever you may go, to keep you safe."

"I am plenty safe, I grew up in these woods, the birds, the sprites, the wild animals they all know me." Esmeralda huffed, "they do not, know you. Which actually probably makes this more dangerous." she finished, crossed her arms, and began to lean against a tree trunk feeling rather self assured. Esmeralda however miscalculated how close said trunk was and stumbled backwards before catching herself and her cheeks turning a dangerously bright shade of red.

Lia pointed a look at her.

Esmeralda turned on her heel and continued walking.

It had been another turn of the moon since that night in the woods. Zephrya had been fine, simply enjoying her days exploring the forest. Esmeralda had left contented that her friend was okay, promising to bring her baked goods the next time she saw her and that was that.

The morning sun filtered through the tall, ancient oaks surrounding the castle, dappling the stone courtyard with golden light. Esmeralda sat cross-legged on the cool stone steps, her nose buried in a weathered leather-bound book. Her chestnut curls spilled over her shoulders, catching the soft breeze that carried the scent of lavender from the gardens. She had been here for hours, lost in a world of faded ink and cryptic prose.

"Your Highness, if you don't eat, I will force you to take a break," a sharp voice broke her concentration.

Esmeralda looked up to find Lia standing a few feet away, arms crossed and a faint scowl tugging at her lips. Dressed in her usual dark leathers, Lia looked every bit the intimidating guardian Kellian had appointed. Her steely gray eyes scanned their surroundings before landing back on her charge. She had become rather outspoken these last few weeks - most likely tired of Esmeralda trying to evading her, only to be found curled up with a book in the highest towers of the castle.

"That's outside of your responsibilities," Esmeralda replied, her voice light but distracted as she turned another page.

Lia's frown deepened. "Your physical wellbeing is my responsibility."

She stepped closer, her boots echoing in the stillness of the courtyard. "What's so important that you've forgotten basic human needs?"

Esmeralda hesitated, her fingers brushing over the delicate handwritten lines of the diary. She didn't like Lia, but she had grown accustomed to her constant looming presence, she tried not to giggle when Mittens hissed at her, even offered her tea just the other day. She was trying at least. But it was a piece of her Gran—a woman she barely remembered but who had left behind whispers of a life far beyond the confines of The Hollow, and she honestly was itching to share what she had found with basically anyone.

"This," Esmeralda said softly, holding up the book. "It's Gran's diary. I found it in the old library last night."

Lia tilted her head, her expression softening just enough to betray curiosity. "What does it say?"

Esmeralda's eyes lit up, and for the first time that morning, she set the book down on her lap. "It's not just a diary—it's a map. Gran wrote about places she traveled to before she came to The Hollow, places I've never even heard of." She traced the delicate script on the page. "She mentions people—relatives. I think she was trying to leave me a trail to follow."

Lia's lips pressed into a thin line. "Outside The Hollow?"

Esmeralda nodded eagerly. "Exactly. I need to know more about where I come from. Who I come from."

Lia's jaw tightened, and she straightened to her full height, her hand instinctively resting on the hilt of her sword. "You're talking about leaving the kingdom. You know that's not exactly encouraged."

"I'm not asking for permission," Esmeralda said, surprising even herself with the firmness in her voice. She stood, holding the diary close to her chest. She was tired of being told what she could and couldn't do. "I'm going, Lia. With or without anyone's approval."

For a moment, Lia said nothing, her gaze fixed on Esmeralda. The witch's determination was apparent, but so was the spark of vulnerability beneath it. Lia had sworn to protect her, even if it meant guarding her through the reckless decisions she occasionally made.

Finally, Lia let out a long, resigned sigh. "I'll come. But only because someone has to keep you alive while you chase down your grandmother's secrets."

Esmeralda beamed, a smile so bright that it almost made Lia forget the storm of doubt brewing in her chest.

CHAPTER 2

Off on a Quest

The royal hall of The Hollow glimmered with soft, otherworldly light, the glow of enchanted lanterns casting long, gentle shadows across the room. Esmeralda stood just outside the double doors, her hands clasped tightly around her grandmother's diary. Her heart thudded in her chest. She knew what she wanted to say, but talking to Kellian and Kyeria about leaving their home, filled her with dread.

She knew they would respect her choices, but she looked up to them nonetheless, and wanted their approval. Kellian and Aura, his sister, had been her only family growing up, after Gran passed. They were her chosen family. Who had loved and cared for her when she needed it most, who had stayed with her those awful nights after Gran passed. Aura would sit in the library with Esmeralda to keep her company, they all checked in daily regardless of any royal duties. They surrounded her with love, and she hoped wanted to leave The Hollow, to look for her ancestors didn't diminish how thankful she was to them.

Taking a deep breath, she pushed open the doors.

Inside, Kellian and Kyeria sat on their respective thrones, though "thrones" was a generous term for the intricately carved chairs that looked more like extensions of the living wood around them. Kellian's bright golden eyes, sharp as ever, softened when he saw her, and Kyeria offered a welcoming smile, her long copper hair cascading over her shoulders like sunlight.

"Esmie," Kellian greeted warmly, rising to meet her. "You look like you've been scheming. Should I be worried?"

Esmeralda smiled, stepping further into the hall. "Only a little."

Kyeria laughed softly, gesturing for her to come closer. "Tell us what weighs on your mind."

Esmeralda gripped the diary tighter, the aged leather grounding her. "I found something. Something that might help me understand where I come from." She opened the book carefully and held it out to them. "It's Gran's diary. She wrote about her life before The Hollow—about family beyond our borders."

Kyeria leaned forward, her silver eyes scanning the pages. Kellian stood beside her, his brow furrowing as he glanced over her shoulder.

"Your grandmother was always a bit of a mystery," Kellian murmured. "Even to us."

"That's why I need to follow her trail," Esmeralda said, her voice steady despite the nerves coiling in her stomach. "She left clues about our family—about my family—and I can't ignore them. I've already spoken to Lia, and she's agreed to come with me."

Kyeria looked up sharply, her expression unreadable. "You mean to leave The Hollow?"

Esmeralda nodded. "I do. I know it's not what you would have chosen for me, but this isn't just about curiosity. It's about finding a part of myself I've never known. I promise, I've thought this through."

Kellian's lips quirked into a half-smile. Esmeralda continued, "And it's not a decision I'm taking lightly. Lia had agreed to accompany me, so you don't have to worry."

Kyeria closed the diary gently and placed it on her lap. Her gaze, soft yet piercing, met Esmeralda's. "We'll always worry. It's what we do. But this decision is yours to make."

Esmeralda's chest flooded with relief, but Kyeria had not finished.

"Know this, though: the world beyond The Hollow is not as forgiving as you might hope. There are those who would see your magic as a threat—or worse, as a prize. Lia is strong, but even she can't shield you from everything."

"I understand the risks," Esmeralda said firmly. "But I need to do this. For Gran. For myself."

Kellian stepped forward, placing a hand on her shoulder. His gaze was warmer now, the worry receding just enough to let pride shine through. "Then we won't stand in your way. But we expect letters.

Regular ones. And if you run into trouble, you come straight back here. Understood?”

Esmeralda grinned. “Understood.”

Kyeria rose from her throne, gliding over to her. “Your grandmother would be proud of you, Esmeralda. And wherever this journey leads you, know that you’ll always have a home here.”

Esmeralda felt her eyes prick with tears, but she blinked them away, hugging the diary close. “Thank you. Both of you. For everything.”

Kyeria placed a warm hand on her cheek, pulling her into a tight hug. “May the stars guide you, my dear.”

As Esmeralda left the hall, her heart felt lighter, though a flicker of fear still lingered in the back of her mind. The path ahead was uncertain, but at least she knew she wouldn’t walk it alone. Lia would be at her side. And no matter what, The Hollow would always be her home.

CHAPTER 3

Moonlit Lake

The gates of The Hollow loomed tall behind them, their ivy-clad ironwork shimmering faintly with enchantments. Esmeralda stood at the threshold, her satchel slung over one shoulder, the diary clutched tightly in her hands. Beside her, Lia adjusted the strap of her sword sheath with her usual stoic efficiency, while Mittens, sat perched in a cozy travel basket slung across Esmeralda's other shoulder, tail flicking lazily. She had brought everything she needed— a wolf bone dagger she had carved herself a few years ago, a custom made sword from Nox, some extra potions and herbs. She had it all. Aura had taken them time to refresh her on how to wield the sword that had been her eighteenth birthday present from Nox. Nox had a pension for blacksmith work, now only making few pieces for his loved ones while also being the Captain of the royal army. He had made her one out of steel, it was light and strong, intricate carvings on the top made the hilt feel more like a staff, and tiny deep maroon gemstones lined the middle of the hilt. Esmeralda loved it. Aura and Nox had waved goodbye early this morning, a glassy eyes princess sent whisps of light towards her since the light had barely crested over the mountains.

The early morning air was crisp, carrying the scent of pine and the faint hum of magic that always lingered in The Hollow. For a moment, Esmeralda hesitated, glancing back at the only home she'd ever known.

"You're not backing out already, are you?" Lia's voice was low and steady, with just a hint of teasing.

Esmeralda turned to her with a small smile. "No. Just... saying goodbye in my own way."

Lia nodded, her gray eyes scanning the road ahead. "Well, let's get moving before I change my mind about this whole thing."

Mittens meowed in protest, as if seconding Lia's grumpiness, and Esmeralda laughed softly. "Don't listen to her, Mittens. This is going to be an adventure."

The cat yawned, unimpressed, curling deeper into the basket.

The first stretch of their journey led through the dense woods surrounding The Hollow. Though Esmeralda had walked these paths before, they felt different now—more alive, more mysterious. Every rustling leaf and distant birdcall seemed like a whisper of encouragement, or perhaps a warning. The snow was falling lightly around them, but the chilly air only made Esmeralda more excited.

"Do you even know where we're going?" Lia asked after an hour of silence, her tone dry.

"I have a good idea," Esmeralda replied, pulling the diary from her satchel. She flipped to a page where her grandmother had sketched a crude map. "Gran mentioned a place called Moonlit Lake. It's supposed to be the first stop on this journey. Something about the water holding memories."

"Memories?" Lia raised an eyebrow. "Sounds ominous."

"Or magical," Esmeralda countered, her eyes sparkling with curiosity.

Lia shook her head but didn't argue further. Instead, she kept her hand near her sword hilt, scanning the trees for any sign of danger.

At the far end of the edge they stopped by a familiar stone house. Smoke was drifting into the canopy of leaves from the chimney. Snow surrounded the small cottage, small Cronus flowers blooming through the snow along the stone pathway. A familiar dark haired woman stood at the doorstep, next to her two smaller figures. Zephrya greeted them with a warm smile,

"Best wishes to you, dear." She said pulling in her friend for a rare show of affection. Esmeralda squeezed her friend tight before looking to the twins with glassy eyes. Eamon and Selene stepped forward. Selene looked withdrawn as she did when she felt emotional, she was strong and stoic. Much like the grumpy guard who was watching from a distance. Eamon on the other hand, threw himself into Esmeralda's arms with glassy eyes.

"Don't die." He whispered into her ear. Esmeralda pulled away with a smile,

"Nothing of the sort!" She insisted. "I'll write as soon as I can, be good," she turned to Selene, "both of you. Keep up with your lessons while I am gone and practice." Esmeralda tried to keep herself from shedding tears but her vision became watery faster than she would have liked. She quickly brushed away a stray tear. Zephrya nodded to her as if to say, *I've got them.* Leaving them felt like leaving a piece of her heart behind. She send a final wave goodbye before following a few paces behind Lia through the wood, till the cabin could no longer be seen.

As the day stretched on, the dense forest began to thin, revealing glimpses of rolling hills and distant mountains. The sun hung low in the sky, casting golden light over the landscape.

Just as Esmeralda was beginning to relax, a low growl broke the stillness.

Lia froze, her hand flying to her sword. "Stay behind me," she ordered, her voice sharp.

Esmeralda stepped back instinctively, clutching Mittens' basket close. The cat hissed, its fur bristling.

From the underbrush emerged a pair of shadowy creatures, their eyes glowing faintly red. They were wolf-like but larger, their forms unnaturally elongated, as if something had twisted them into darker versions of themselves.

"Night wolves," Lia muttered, drawing her blade. "They shouldn't be this far south."

Esmeralda's heart pounded, but she forced herself to think. "What do we do?"

"You do nothing," Lia snapped. "Stay back."

One wolf lunged, and Lia met it with a swift strike, her blade gleaming as it cut through the air. The creature yelped and retreated, but the second wolf circled closer, its growl deepening.

Esmeralda set the basket down gently, whispering to Mittens, "Stay here, okay?" The cat gave her a wide-eyed look that seemed to say, *What do you think I'm going to do?*

As Lia engaged the second wolf, Esmeralda closed her eyes and reached for her magic. She could feel it thrumming beneath her skin, warm and restless. Summoning a spell wasn't second nature to her yet, but she couldn't let Lia fight alone.

"*Lux ignis!*" she shouted, thrusting her hands forward.

A burst of golden light erupted from her palms, blinding the wolves and forcing them to retreat with pained howls. They disappeared into the woods as quickly as they'd appeared, leaving behind only silence and the faint smell of singed fur.

When the danger had passed, Lia turned to Esmeralda, her expression equal parts impressed and exasperated. "That was reckless." It was true, bursts of magic deep in the forest only attracted trouble. Kyeria had warned of using magic sparingly not to attract attention. She had told of how outside The Hollow and Isles, magic was not accepted but rather feared.

Esmeralda shrugged, a sheepish smile tugging at her lips. "It worked, didn't it?"

Lia shook her head, but there was a flicker of amusement in her eyes. "Just don't make a habit of it."

Mittens meowed loudly, as if to remind them of his presence, and Esmeralda scooped him back into the basket. "You're welcome," she teased the cat, scratching behind his ears.

"Let's keep moving," Lia said, sheathing her sword. "I'd rather not wait around to see if they come back."

Esmeralda nodded, the diary tucked safely back in her satchel. As they resumed their journey, the weight of the encounter lingered. She could have reached for her sword, or even dagger, but it was like her magic was begging to be used, sparking at her fingertips, it had felt so easy, so right.

Moonlit Lake was just beyond the golden northern gate, which was the edge of The Hollow's magical border. Esmeralda felt herself taking a deep breath, steadying herself and marching ahead.

The night was still, save for the soft rustle of leaves in the trees behind her. Esmeralda stood on the shore of the lake, the water before her a perfect mirror to the star-dappled sky above. The moon hung high, its silvery light bathing everything in a soft glow, making the world feel both dreamlike and tangible. The air smelled faintly of damp earth, and a chill caressed her skin, the coolness settling deep into her bones as she prepared to cast her spell. She had read over the spell a dozen times, the night before. Committed the elegant scrawl of her Gran's handwriting on the aged journal to her mind.

In her hands, Esmeralda held the lock of her grandmother's silver hair, carefully bound with a black ribbon. It was a piece of her grandmother's life, something she had never let go of, and now it was meant to help open the past. She clasped the silver cuff she always wore, a gift from her Gran—an heirloom passed down through generations, in her other hand. It was warm against her skin, though the surrounding air was not, as though the cuff itself held a piece of her family's magic, a conduit to what had come before.

She whispered the incantation softly to herself, feeling the words reverberate through her chest:

"Luna memoriam, aperi mihi,
Flumina noctis, vitae sigilli,
Speculum aquae, veritatem tene,
Praeteriti cordis imaginem da me."

Her breath caught in her throat as the words left her lips, a rush of energy filling the space around her. The water before her began to ripple, faint at first, then growing more pronounced. The moon's reflection seemed to stretch, twisting, as if the lake itself was waking from a deep slumber. She felt it—like an electric pulse racing through her veins, a tingle that started at the back of her neck and traveled down her spine, igniting every nerve in her body. The magic was ancient, full of power, and it flowed through her with a warmth that was both familiar and odd at the same time. She felt her heart beat faster, an unspoken connection to the lake, the moon, and the memory she sought.

A sharp gasp escaped her as the lake's surface began to shimmer. The reflection of the moon flickered like firelight before it twisted into something else entirely. Slowly, the water began to form an image, one that rippled into focus with an almost haunting clarity.

It was a small, dimly lit bookshop, rows upon rows of shelves lined with dusty, weathered books. A heavy scent of parchment and ink wafted toward her, and the faint crackling of fire echoed in the distance. The warmth of the shop contrasted sharply with the coolness of the lake's surface, making her feel as though she had stepped into the memory herself. She could hear soft murmurs of voices—whispers that felt distant, like fragments of forgotten conversations.

Esmeralda's breath hitched. She knew this place. It was a shop from her grandmother's past, a memory she had never spoken of, but one Esmeralda recognized instantly. She could almost feel the weight of the books, the presence of someone—perhaps her Gran—browsing the shelves, running a finger along the spines of volumes long forgotten. She focused harder, willing the image to focus.

In the corner of the reflection, she saw the flicker of a town street—cracked cobblestones, a lantern hanging crookedly from an old sign that read *The Gilded Quill*. The town was unmistakable. She had seen it on the map in her grandmother's diary, tucked away in the margins near an ancient sketch of a hidden path. The name, *Draketon*, was written in fine, delicate ink, and it sent a rush of excitement through Esmeralda's chest.

She knew where it was. *She knew where to go next.*

The memory shifted, the light from the lake's reflection fading as the image dissolved back into the water, leaving Esmeralda breathless, the pulse of magic still humming through her skin. The silver cuff at her wrist seemed to vibrate with a faint energy, and she realized the memory had left a piece of itself within her—something she could carry forward.

For a long moment, Esmeralda just stood there, her hand still held out over the water, her heart pounding in her chest. The memory of the bookshop was fading, but the knowledge it had unlocked—of *Draketon*, of the town with the crooked lanterns and the scent of old books—was alive in her now. Her grandmother's past was no longer an enigma. It had a place, a name, and a path she was ready to follow.

Lia stood behind her, unease written on her face. She had always shown such emotion around magic. Esmeralda always found it rather ironic that she was assigned as a bodyguard to a witch. She turned toward Lia, "I know where we're going next," Esmeralda said, her voice steady, though a thrill still ran through her at the discovery.

Lia raised an eyebrow, glancing from Esmeralda to the water, then back at her. "Draketon!" Esmeralda announced, "there is an old bookstore, one Gran talked about in her diary."

The journey had only just begun, but Esmeralda could feel the weight of it now, the pull of the past woven tightly with her future. She had unlocked the first memory, and it was more than just a clue—it was a calling. She was closer than ever to uncovering the truth about her family. And with the lake's magic still coursing through her, she felt ready to meet whatever lay ahead.

The sun hung high in the sky, casting a warm glow over the countryside as Esmeralda and Lia stopped to rest beneath a towering oak tree. The air was rich with the scent of wildflowers, and the gentle rustling of leaves in the breeze created a peaceful symphony. Esmeralda sank onto the soft grass with a sigh, Mittens curled up beside her.

"This is nice," Esmeralda said, stretching her arms over her head. "A moment of calm for once."

Lia leaned against the tree, her arms crossed and her ever-watchful gaze scanning their surroundings. "Too nice," she muttered. "Peace like this usually means something's about to go wrong."

Esmeralda rolled her eyes, plucking a blade of grass and twirling it between her fingers. "You're exhausting, you know that? Can't we just enjoy the quiet without imagining disaster?"

Lia's lips twitched in the hint of a smile, but her tone remained firm. "Quiet is when you prepare. Speaking of..." She pushed off the tree, looking down at Esmeralda with a serious expression. "We need to talk about your training."

Esmeralda groaned, flopping back dramatically onto the grass. "Lia, not this again. I already know how to fight!"

"Do you?" Lia raised an eyebrow, crouching beside her. "Because throwing spells from a distance isn't the same as defending yourself when someone gets close. What happens if your magic fails or you're caught off guard?"

Esmeralda propped herself up on her elbows, meeting Lia's gaze with a stubborn look. "I can handle myself. I'm not helpless, Lia."

"No, you're not," Lia agreed, her tone softening. "But there's a difference between being capable and being prepared."

There was a beat of silence, broken only by Mittens' tiny snores. Esmeralda sighed, brushing a stray curl from her face. "Fine. What's the plan, oh wise and battle-hardened warrior?"

Lia smirked, standing and offering a hand to Esmeralda. "First, we find a clearing. Then, I show you what you're really made of."

Esmeralda took Lia's hand, allowing herself to be pulled to her feet. "You're awfully confident for someone about to be bested by a witch," she said, her voice teasing.

"We'll see," Lia replied with a wink.

The clearing they found was shaded by a canopy of trees, dappled sunlight dancing on the ground. Lia handed Esmeralda a wooden practice sword, her own already in hand.

"Start with your stance," Lia instructed, circling her. "Feet apart, knees slightly bent. You need to be balanced, ready to move in any direction."

Esmeralda adjusted her footing, mimicking Lia's posture. "How's this?"

"Good. Now grip the sword properly. Tight enough to hold control but loose enough to adjust."

Esmeralda nodded, following Lia's guidance. She held up the sword, feeling its weight in her hands. "I feel ridiculous."

"You look ridiculous," Lia quipped, earning a glare. "But that's the point of practice. Better to feel ridiculous now than dead later."

"Charming," Esmeralda muttered, her lips twitching despite herself.

Their sparring began slowly, Lia guiding Esmeralda through basic strikes and blocks. Each clash of their swords sent vibrations up Esmeralda's arms, a stark reminder of how different this was from wielding magic. While she had had basic training in wielding a sword, she preferred her magic or a dagger. This felt unnatural to her.

"Move your feet," Lia called, sidestepping one of Esmeralda's swings with ease. "You're too rooted."

"I *am* moving!" Esmeralda shot back, her frustration bubbling.

"Not fast enough." Lia feinted to the left, then tapped Esmeralda's shoulder with the flat of her sword. "Got you."

Esmeralda groaned, lowering her sword. "You're infuriating."

"And you're improving," Lia said, her smirk softening into a genuine smile. "But you're still thinking too much. Fighting isn't about overanalyzing—it's instinct. Trust yours."

Esmeralda paused, her sword slack in her grip. "I'm not sure I know how to trust my instincts," she admitted, her voice quieter. "Magic is apart of me, and extension of my own soul, but this— this is so different."

Lia stepped closer, resting a hand lightly on Esmeralda's shoulder. "You do. You just haven't realized it yet. You've made it this far, haven't you? That wasn't luck—it was you."

The weight of Lia's words settled over Esmeralda, warm and steady. She looked up, meeting Lia's gaze. For a moment, the world seemed to fall away, the only sound their steady breathing.

"I'll try," Esmeralda said finally, her voice soft but resolute.

"That's all I ask," Lia replied, stepping back and raising her sword again. "Now, come at me like you mean it."

This time, when Esmeralda lunged, there was no hesitation—only determination. The clash of their swords echoed through the clearing, and somewhere in the midst of strikes and parries, Esmeralda realized that fighting, like everything else on this journey, was something she didn't have to face alone.

CHAPTER 4

The Enchanted Bookshop

The cobblestone streets of Draketon were narrow and winding, flanked by crooked houses and the faint glow of lanterns that flickered like ghosts in the growing dusk. Esmeralda had always imagined the town would be quaint, but seeing it in person filled her with a sense of wonder. Each corner held something new—old magic, old buildings, old stories. Snow covered the roofs, the roads were dusted with the powder as well. Winter had set in here in Draketon.

At the edge of a narrow alley, tucked between two weathered stone buildings, they found it: *The Gilded Quill*, the bookshop from the lake's vision. The sign creaked in the wind, its gilded lettering almost unreadable beneath years of wear. Esmeralda's heart raced as she stepped inside, her eyes immediately drawn to the countless shelves that stretched from floor to ceiling, each one laden with dusty tomes and scrolls that seemed to hum with a magic all their own.

The shop was small, but the air was thick with the scent of old paper and ink, mingling with the faint aroma of dried lavender that reminded her of The Hollow. Everything was bathed in the warm glow of dim, flickering candles, and the floor creaked beneath their feet as they made their way deeper into the store. A soft bell jingled above the door as they entered, but no one came to greet them.

Instead, a figure emerged from behind a stack of books—a tall, thin man with wild, white hair and spectacles perched precariously on his nose. His robe was patched in several places, as if he had lived a hundred lifetimes in its fabric. He eyed them both, his sharp, inquisitive gaze flicking over Esmeralda with a knowing, calculating look.

"Can I help you?" The shopkeeper's voice was raspy, but kind. His eyes narrowed as if sizing them up.

"We're looking for information," Esmeralda said, her voice almost breathless. "About my family. About the bloodline of the Winter Witches, they lived in The Hollow."

The shopkeeper's expression shifted, a flash of recognition crossing his face before he quickly masked it. "Ah, the Hollow, you say? Not many come searching for that these days. You're in the right place, though." He gave a small, amused chuckle. "Everything you seek is hidden somewhere here, if you know how to find it."

He gestured for them to follow as he shuffled deeper into the store, his movements quick and precise despite his age. Esmeralda glanced at Lia, who was already on edge, her eyes scanning the shadows of the shop, alert for any sign of danger. But Esmeralda could feel the pull of something different here—a quiet, pulsing magic that drew her forward. The soft pitter padder of Mitten's paws on the hardwood flooring as he brushed against the spines on the lowest shelves.

The shopkeeper led them to a narrow aisle in the back of the shop, where the shelves seemed to be filled with more than just books. There were old relics, trinkets, and scrolls, each one emitting a faint glow. The man's bony finger ran along the edge of a shelf before he reached up to pull down a heavy, ancient tome bound in dark leather.

"This," he said, handing the book to Esmeralda, "is where your family's story begins."

Esmeralda took it reverently, her fingers brushing the worn surface of the cover. She could feel the weight of it, not just in her hands but in the air around her. This book, it seemed, held more than history—it held a secret.

As she opened the first page, a delicate, yellowed parchment fluttered out, revealing a page of intricate family trees. The sigils of ancient families were marked carefully, their names written in elegant script, some faded, some barely legible. Esmeralda's heart skipped a beat as she spotted her family's name at the top of the tree—*The Winter Witches*.

Her eyes darted across the page, tracing the lines, following the branches until they landed on something that made her breath catch.

There, at the very heart of the family's history, was a sigil—an ancient emblem, half moon and stars intertwined, glowing faintly with a silver light. It was unmistakable. It was hers.

"This is it," Esmeralda whispered, a thrill running through her veins. She traced the sigil with her finger, feeling its magic pulse beneath her touch. "This is the symbol. The mark of my bloodline."

Lia, standing a few steps behind, let out a quiet breath. Esmeralda glanced up to see her watching, her arms crossed, though there was an unreadable look in her eyes. "What is it?" Esmeralda asked softly, her voice hesitant.

Lia's gaze flicked back to the book, then returned to her. "I thought... I didn't know it would mean so much to you. Seeing it." Her voice was quieter now, more thoughtful. "I didn't understand before. But I see it now."

Esmeralda's chest tightened with something she couldn't quite name—relief, maybe, or a deep, aching gratitude. She hadn't expected Lia to understand so soon. She hadn't expected this quiet, intimate moment to settle so naturally between them. The moment was interrupted by a crash. Turning Bothe Esmeralda and Lia saw Mittens, sitting haphazardly on a stack of books, next to him, fallen dusty books. The shopkeeper grumbled towards the cat who ran back to Esmeralda with wide eyes.

"I need to find where this sigil leads," Esmeralda said, her voice firmer now. She turned the page, searching for the next clue, the next step. "This is just the beginning."

The shopkeeper, who had been watching them both with a quiet smile, cleared his throat. "The sigil you've found is not just a mark of your family. It is a key. There are places in this world where the sigils have power—places where your bloodline once stood, where secrets were buried."

Esmeralda looked up, her heart racing. "Where do I find these places?"

The shopkeeper tilted his head, eyes gleaming with a knowing light. "That is a question only you can answer. But this book," he gestured to the tome in her hands, "will guide you. If you know how to read between the lines, it will show you the path."

The enchanted bookshop, with its winding aisles and whispering books, felt like a new beginning. Esmeralda was bursting with excitement as they left the bookshop. Knowing that sigils could be keys and this land's magic feeling so familiar, like Gran had walked these very streets long ago.

The warm glow of the morning sun filtered through the trees as Esmeralda and Lia made their way down the cobblestone street, their steps in sync with the bustling life of Draketon. The town had a sleepy charm to it, like an old, cozy sweater that had been worn and loved for centuries. The buildings were crooked but inviting, each one carrying its own story. The air smelled of baked bread and honey, mingling with the earthy scent of freshly watered gardens and the distant chirping of birds.

As they rounded a corner, Esmeralda's gaze was drawn to a little shop tucked between two larger buildings—a small bakery, its windows fogged with warmth, a gentle cloud of sweet, yeasty smells wafting out the door. A sign above the door read *The Cunning Crust*, its lettering curling whimsically as if it had been scrawled by a mischievous hand.

Esmeralda paused, smiling to herself. "Let's stop here, gran mentioned a bakery in her diary."

Lia, who had been walking with a wary air, stopped beside her, casting a skeptical glance at the bakery. "A bakery? You're telling me the next clue in this grand family mystery involves pastries?"

"Not just pastries," Esmeralda said with a wink. "Magical pastries."

Lia raised an eyebrow, her lips twitching slightly at the corners. "You know, I think the spellbook might have left that part out."

Esmeralda chuckled, nudging her with her shoulder. "Trust me, Lia. There's something about this place that's more than just flour and sugar."

The door chimed as they entered the bakery, and the warmth enveloped them immediately, the sweet scent of cinnamon, vanilla, and butter swirling around like a welcoming embrace. Behind the counter stood an elderly woman with a wide smile and hands dusted with flour. Her wild silver hair was tied in a loose bun, and her glasses perched low on her nose, giving her a perpetually amused look.

"Ah, customers!" The woman's voice was as warm as the oven

behind her. "Come in, come in! Don't be shy! You've caught me in the middle of a batch of my famous honeyed lavender scones. Would you like to try one?"

Esmeralda's stomach growled in agreement before she could answer. "I'd love one!" she exclaimed, stepping forward.

Lia lingered at the door, her arms crossed, eyeing the shop's contents with suspicion. "I'm not much of a scone person," she muttered, but the woman's smile was so wide and kind, it was hard to resist.

"Trust me, my dear," the baker said, offering Lia a knowing look. "These scones are a treat for both the body and the soul. Especially if you're looking for something...extra."

Esmeralda shot a glance at Lia, whose skepticism was slowly melting away. "Extra?" Lia raised an eyebrow, clearly intrigued despite herself.

The woman gave a little wink and a mysterious smile. "Oh yes, we specialize in pastries that hold secrets. Come, sit, and I'll tell you about them."

Lia let out a quiet huff but eventually relented, taking a seat at one of the cozy wooden tables near the window. Esmeralda followed, her excitement bubbling over as she waited for the next clue to unfold.

The baker placed two scones on the table, their golden-brown tops dusted with a perfect layer of powdered sugar. "Eat first, then we talk," she said with a sly smile.

Esmeralda couldn't wait. She took a bite of the scone, and immediately, a wave of warmth spread through her, as though the magic in the bakery was slipping into her bones. The flavor was sweet and floral, the honey perfectly balanced with the delicate notes of lavender. She closed her eyes, savoring the taste. "This is incredible," she whispered.

Lia, finally giving in, took a small bite of her own scone. Her eyes widened, and a small smile tugged at her lips. "I'll admit... that's better than I expected." Crumbs littered the curve of her lips and Esmeralda reached out a hand, using her embroidered handkerchief and wiping away the crumbs. Lia was left wide eyed and speechless at the gesture.

The baker chuckled at the exchange. "You've got a good eye, young lady," she said to Esmeralda. "Now, let me tell you why you're here."

Esmeralda set down her half-eaten scone, her curiosity piqued. "We're looking for information. About my family. A sigil—something that connects us to an ancient bloodline."

The baker nodded slowly, her expression becoming more serious. "Ah, the Winter line. It's been centuries since anyone came looking for them, but I've heard the whispers." She leaned in slightly, lowering her voice to a conspiratorial tone. "They say there's a place, an old stone circle in the hills outside of town. The sigils of your bloodline can be found there, hidden under layers of earth and time. But you'll need more than a map to find it."

Esmeralda's heart skipped a beat. "What do you mean?"

The baker leaned back in her chair, her hands clasped in front of her. "The sigils won't show themselves easily. They need a key. Something personal. And for that, you'll need a special recipe—a recipe from the Winter family. But," she paused, her eyes twinkling mischievously, "I'm afraid it's not one I can just give away."

Lia narrowed her eyes. "And what does it cost?"

The baker's smile was as sweet as the scones. "Oh, nothing too difficult. Just a small favor. You'll know it when you see it."

Esmeralda leaned forward, trying to suppress the thrill that was bubbling up inside her. "What kind of favor?"

The baker tapped her chin thoughtfully. "Well, if you can track down a particular herb—the golden iris—I might consider it. It's said to only grow on the highest peak in Draketon's hills, but I'd say the journey will be well worth it. My old bones just don't work like they used to"

Esmeralda nodded eagerly, ignoring the low groan and permeant scowl from her bodyguard. "We can do that."

The baker grinned. "Good. Then we have a deal. Bring me the golden iris, and I'll give you the recipe you need. But be warned, it's not just any herb. It has a peculiar magic of its own. If you're not careful, it'll slip away when you least expect it."

Lia let out a breath, looking out the window. "Of course. Because why wouldn't this be more complicated?"

Esmeralda chuckled, reaching for her purse. "Don't worry, Lia. It'll be fun. I think we might even make it into a little adventure."

Lia glanced at her, and for the first time, there was a softness in her eyes—a flicker of something like trust. "You've got a funny way of making everything sound like fun," she said, her voice seemed like it had less of an edge.

Esmeralda smiled at her, feeling a warmth settle in her chest. "Well, it's more fun with you here. Besides, I think you're starting to enjoy this whole quest thing a little more than you admit."

Lia huffed but didn't deny it. "We'll see how much fun you think it is after we climb that mountain."

Esmeralda laughed, the sound light and carefree. "Deal. But you have to admit, you're getting soft. I can see it."

Lia's lips twitched, and she gave Esmeralda a side-eyed look. "Watch it, witch. I'm still the one keeping you safe."

"Of course you are," Esmeralda replied with a wink. "Now, let's go find that golden iris."

And as they left the bakery, the warmth of the scones still lingering in the air, Esmeralda couldn't help but feel that this journey, with all its puzzles and challenges, was exactly what she needed—and, just maybe, what Lia needed too.

CHAPTER 5

The Golden Iris and
the Tiny Dragon

The path to the peak was as winding and picturesque as one could imagine—a hidden trail that twisted through dense woods, past streams that sang their quiet lullabies, and under trees whose branches formed natural arches overhead. The air was crisp, and the scent of pine mingled with the earthy notes of damp leaves. The journey itself felt like a story from the old tales, one Esmeralda had always dreamed of living but never quite expected to experience.

Lia, ever the stoic protector, led the way with purpose, her boots crunching softly on the forest floor. Esmeralda followed, a lighter step to her walk, her eyes scanning the landscape, taking in the serenity of the world around them. Mittens, as always, trailed behind them, his small, fluffy form weaving in and out of the underbrush, clearly enjoying the freedom of the wilderness, chasing insects as they walked and scaling the rocks.

"Do you think we'll find it?" Esmeralda asked after a while, her voice soft, the quiet of the forest settling around them. The climb had been hard, and they had been searching for quite some now.

Lia glanced back over her shoulder, her brow furrowed but her tone more relaxed than usual. "We'll find it," she said, her confidence unwavering. "The bakery wasn't wrong about the herbs being here. We just need to find the right spot."

Esmeralda smiled at the quiet reassurance in Lia's voice. There was a softness in her eyes today, one that hadn't been there before. Maybe it was the mountain air or maybe it was the journey itself, but Esmeralda felt the distance between them shrinking with every step.

The sun was beginning to dip low when they finally reached the peak. The view was breathtaking, the valley below bathed in the warm hues of dusk. And there, nestled in the crook of a rock, was the golden iris—its petals a vivid, glowing yellow, catching the light of the setting sun and shimmering as though dusted with stardust. It was as if the mountain had been waiting for them, for this moment, for the flower to bloom just in time.

Esmeralda knelt down, her heart fluttering. "It's beautiful," she whispered, reverence in her voice.

Lia nodded, her usual guarded expression softened by the scene. "We should hurry. The light's fading, and we need to get back before it gets dark."

Together, they carefully plucked the golden iris, wrapping it in a cloth to protect it for the journey back. Mittens, curious as ever, sniffed around the flower but didn't seem overly interested, instead choosing to bat at a fallen leaf that caught his attention.

By the time they returned to *The Cunning Crust*, the sky was painted with the deep purples and blues of twilight. The warm, golden light from the bakery windows beckoned them inside, and the scent of freshly baked goods filled the air once more.

The baker was waiting by the door, her face lighting up the moment she saw them. "Ah! You've done it! You actually found it!" she cried, her arms thrown wide in exaggerated joy.

Esmeralda laughed, holding up the golden iris like a trophy. "We did, with some effort. But I think it's worth it."

The baker's eyes gleamed. "Oh, it's more than worth it! Now, come, sit! You've earned a treat. These, my dears, are my special jellie pastries. Made just for heroes like you."

Esmeralda and Lia settled at the same table as before, Mittens hopping onto the chair beside them, his little fluffy paws resting on the edge. The baker set a tray of golden pastries on the table, their crusts lightly dusted with sugar and their centers oozing with bright, fruity jelly. Esmeralda could already feel her mouth watering in anticipation.

"These," the baker said with a wink, "are the most magical pastries I've ever made. They're said to make your dreams come true, so let's see if they work for you."

Esmeralda took one, savoring the burst of sweetness as the jelly dripped slightly from the pastry's center. "This is divine," she said, her voice muffled by the pastry in her mouth.

Lia, ever the skeptic, hesitated but took a bite. Her eyes narrowed, and then, as if she hadn't expected to be so impressed, she gave a small, approving nod. "I'll admit, these are good."

As they ate, the conversation between them became lighter, more relaxed. For the first time in a while, there were no heavy thoughts about duty or danger—just the shared joy of a simple, sweet moment.

But as Lia lifted her pastry for another bite, she misjudged just slightly, and a small glob of jelly dripped onto the front of her tunic. She cursed under her breath, looking down at the stain with frustration.

Esmeralda, always quick to help, reached into her pocket and pulled out her handkerchief. "Here, let me help."

Without a word, she gently dabbed at the stain, the fabric soft against Lia's skin. Lia froze for a moment, and for a heartbeat, the world seemed to pause, as if the air itself held its breath. Esmeralda's heart fluttered in her chest, and she couldn't quite explain the warmth that bloomed in her chest, the closeness she felt in this simple act.

"Thanks," Lia murmured, her voice softer than Esmeralda was used to hearing it.

Esmeralda's smile was soft but genuine. "Of course."

Just then, Mittens, who had been perched on the edge of the table, leaped from his spot and landed with a small, frantic scramble onto a shelf of ingredients. A few jars wobbled, and then, as if in slow motion, one tipped over, spilling its contents across the floor.

Esmeralda turned just in time to see Mittens' form blur as he stumbled into the jar, and with a bright flash of magic, the little cat was gone.

In his place, a tiny, wriggling creature now stood—small and black with scales that glistened like midnight, wings fluttering weakly as he looked up at them with wide, confused eyes.

Lia froze, her mouth open. "Is that...?"

The baker erupted into a laugh so hearty it filled the entire room. "Oh, it's just a temporary side effect. Happens sometimes when animals get into my magic ingredients. Don't worry. He'll be back to his normal self in a few days, or weeks, one can never really know, but eventually!"

Esmeralda stared at the tiny dragon now sitting on the floor, blinking up at them with his tiny, cat-like eyes. "Mittens..." she breathed in disbelief.

The tiny dragon opened his mouth and let out a tiny puff of smoke, his wings flickering with excitement. Esmeralda couldn't help but laugh. "I guess it's true what they say—curiosity killed the cat. Or... turned it into a tiny dragon."

Lia, who had been trying to suppress her amusement, couldn't help but chuckle at the sight. "Well, this won't be a problem at all!"

The baker wiped a tear from her eye, still laughing. "Indeed. A little dragon is an excellent companion, I must say. Quite fitting for a journey such as yours."

Esmeralda reached down and gently scooped the small dragon into her hands, cradling him as she would a kitten. "He's going to be impossible to explain to anyone, isn't he?"

Lia smirked, her eyes still soft with amusement. "At least no one can say you don't have a good story to tell."

With a soft sigh, Esmeralda smiled down at Mittens—the tiny dragon now nuzzling her hand. "I think we might just be getting the hang of this whole adventure thing."

CHAPTER 6

The Sigil and the Mini Dragon

The next morning, as dawn painted the sky with soft hues of pink and gold, Esmeralda and Lia set out once more. The tiny dragon —still very much Mittens, despite his new, scaled form—was nestled in Esmeralda's coat pocket, his tiny head poking out from the folds of fabric, his eyes wide with curiosity. His wings twitched every now and then, and every so often, a tiny puff of smoke escaped from his little mouth. He was undeniably adorable, but the reality of the situation was not lost on them: Mittens was now a miniature dragon for who knows how long on this strange, unpredictable quest.

The baker had, of course, offered them a warm breakfast before they departed, but both women had been too eager to leave. The sigil they sought—the mark that could link Esmeralda to her bloodline—had been promised to be nearby. In fact, the baker had mentioned it briefly when they were discussing the golden iris the previous evening. "I think you'll find it," she'd said with a knowing smile. "There's a place not far from here where the sigil is hidden. You'll know it when you see it. "Trust your magic, young witch."

Lia, ever pragmatic, was already mapping out their route, though she couldn't resist glancing occasionally at the tiny dragon nestled against Esmeralda. "I still can't believe he's a dragon. A *tiny* dragon, but still. How are we supposed to explain that?"

Esmeralda's lips twitched with a smile, her fingers gently stroking Mittens' soft back. "I'm not sure. But I think he's growing on me. I mean, it's not every day you find out your cat's a dragon. At least he hasn't burned anything substantial—yet."

The words were barely out of her mouth before Mittens let out a tiny, mischievous puff of fire, as if on cue. Both women stopped and stared at him, but he only blinked innocently, his wings fluttering. He let out a puff of smoke, and stared at it curiously as it floated on the wind.

"He's lucky he's cute," Lia muttered, but her lips quirked up slightly.

After a few hours of walking through the lush woods, they finally reached a place marked by an ancient, weathered stone archway, half-buried under creeping vines. It was clear the place had been abandoned for ages. There was no sign of life, save for the soft rustling of leaves in the breeze.

Esmeralda nodded, her heart beginning to race. She could feel the pull of magic in the air, an almost tangible presence, as though the very ground beneath her feet was holding a secret.

Lia stood a few steps ahead, her senses alert, eyes scanning the area with the practiced wariness of someone who had spent her life being prepared for danger. "Are you sure?" she asked, voice low.

"I can feel it," Esmeralda said, the magic was thrumming under her feet, the wind was blowing by. *This was it.*

As they stepped past the stone arch, they entered what appeared to be the remnants of an ancient garden. The ground was overgrown with moss, and scattered across the area were broken statues and forgotten relics. But among them, nestled against the trunk of a great oak tree, was a stone slab. It was half-hidden by the thick roots of the tree, but the sigil was unmistakable—etched deeply into the surface, glowing faintly under the canopy of branches above.

Esmeralda's breath caught in her throat. The sigil was beautiful— intricate, spiraling, and undeniably familiar. She could feel its power, the connection to her bloodline, like a thread pulling her closer to her ancestors.

Lia stepped forward and gently brushed aside the roots that had grown over the slab, revealing it more fully. "This it?"

"Yes," Esmeralda said softly, kneeling down to inspect the sigil. Her fingers brushed against the stone, tracing the shapes with reverence. It was then that something remarkable happened.

The sigil pulsed with a warm, golden light, and Esmeralda's vision blurred for a moment, the air around them crackling with energy. She gasped, her hand falling away from the stone as if it had burned her, though it hadn't.

"What's happening?" Lia asked, her voice tinged with concern, looking to her hand for any signs of damage.

"I—I don't know," Esmeralda stammered, her heart pounding, rubbing at her hand. But as the light swirled around her, something shifted in her mind. A memory, vivid and sudden, unfolded before her like the pages of a forgotten book.

In her mind's eye, she saw the old, familiar faces of her ancestors—smiling, proud, and standing in a circle around an ancient altar. The sigil was engraved in the stone, much like the one before her, and Esmeralda felt a wave of recognition wash over her. This was her family, her bloodline, and their legacy.

But there was something more. A name. A place. The town from the map.

Vornwick.

Her fingers trembled as she straightened, the memory fading as quickly as it had appeared. "I know where we need to go," Esmeralda said, her voice steadying. She met Lia's gaze, her eyes bright with determination. "Vornwick. That's where the next clue lies."

Lia raised an eyebrow, her lips quirking up. "Another town? Is it on a map?"

Esmeralda nodded, determination flickering in her gaze. "It is. And it's the next step in this journey."

Lia let out a soft sigh, her stoic demeanor cracking just enough to reveal a hint of exasperation. "Then let's get moving, before that little dragon decides to torch something important."

A small laugh escaped Esmeralda, light and airy against the forest's quiet backdrop. She stepped closer to Lia, her pace aligning with her bodyguard's steady stride. As she did, their hands brushed—a fleeting, unintentional touch that sent a warm ripple through Esmeralda's chest.

Neither pulled away immediately, and for a moment, the air between them felt charged, their shared silence saying more than words ever could. Then, as naturally as it had happened, Esmeralda shifted her hand back to cradle Mittens, her smile lingering as they continued down the path together.

Mittens, who had been squirming in Esmeralda's coat pocket, let out another tiny puff of smoke. He was becoming more and more animated as the morning wore on, his little dragon wings flapping with enthusiasm soon and flying beside them.

As they began their journey toward Vornwick, Mittens fluttered around before he perched on Esmeralda's shoulder. The little dragon let out a soft, contented chirp, and Esmeralda smiled, knowing that with every step they took, they were one step closer to uncovering the truth of her family's legacy.

CHAPTER 7

Heart to Heart

The night had fallen quietly around them as Esmeralda and Lia sat beside a crackling campfire. The woods around them were thick with the scent of pine and earth, the firelight dancing across their faces, casting long shadows on the ground. Mittens, still perched on Esmeralda's shoulder, let out a contented chirp as he curled into a small ball, falling asleep.

Esmeralda looked at Lia, who was silently sharpening her blade, the rhythmic scrape of steel on stone breaking the silence between them. The firelight illuminated Lia's profile—strong, stoic, yet there was something else there now. Something softer that Esmeralda couldn't quite place, but she felt it growing. It had started to happen slowly, a change that had unfolded between the quiet moments and shared glances on their journey.

The wind whispered through the trees, and Esmeralda found herself chewing on the edge of her lip, the words forming in her mind but hesitant to spill out. She had been thinking a lot lately about the bond she was forming with Lia—the quiet moments, the flashes of warmth that were always followed by a guarded look, as though Lia was constantly holding herself back. But why? What was she hiding?

"You've been quiet tonight," Esmeralda finally said, breaking the silence. Her voice was soft but steady. "I wanted to ask you something."

Lia's gaze flicked up, her expression neutral, but she didn't stop what she was doing. "What is it?"

Esmeralda hesitated for a moment, trying to find the right words. "I... I don't know. You've been different, lately. Not just with me but in the way you look at things. I can feel it. And I—" She stopped herself, not wanting to push too hard. "I guess I just want to know what's going on in your head. I know you've been my bodyguard this past year, but I can't help but wonder... what do *you* want out of all of this?"

Lia paused mid-swipe, her hand resting against the stone for a moment before she exhaled, her shoulders stiffening just slightly. She set the blade down with a quiet clink and then turned her full attention to Esmeralda, her gaze softer now, thoughtful.

"I never planned for this," Lia said, her voice low but carrying a weight of unspoken truths. "I never planned to follow a young royal witch around on a journey like this. Hel, when I first took this post, I didn't think it would be so much about *you*... I thought it would just be about duty. Protecting someone from a distance, making sure they were safe and sound."

Esmeralda blinked, surprised at the vulnerability in Lia's voice. She had never heard her speak so openly, and the words made her heart soften. "But it's more than that for you, isn't it?"

Lia nodded, slowly, her eyes dropping to the campfire as though it held all the answers. "When I was younger, I always dreamed of being in the royal army, fighting beside the royals of The Hollow. I wanted to be a soldier, part of something bigger than myself. I wanted to protect— *really* protect. The royals, the kingdom, the people. I saw them as... as symbols of strength, the heart of our land. And I always believed that's where my place would be. Standing by them, keeping them safe."

Esmeralda watched her, fascinated by this side of Lia she had never known. She had always thought of Lia as an enigma—serious, guarded, but never fully understanding why.

"But life doesn't always turn out the way you expect," Lia continued with a faint smile, though it didn't quite reach her eyes. "I finally was old enough for the army and I was assigned as your bodyguard. And honestly? I didn't expect much. I thought it would be boring. But then... then I started seeing you for who you are—not just some princess or royal figurehead, but someone who actually *cares* about people. About *your* kingdom, even when it seems like everything is against you. I see you and how fearlessly your protect and love your people and family. I've watched over this last year, the way your visit villages, how much you have helped the twins. I didn't expect this quest, or to ever leave The Hollow. I didn't expect the magic, let alone being around it this much, but most of all I didn't expect you being so *you*."

Esmeralda's heart tightened in her chest, a warm surge of something fluttering in her stomach. She reached out, brushing her fingers over Lia's hand—an unspoken gesture of solidarity, of understanding.

"I never knew any of that about you," Esmeralda whispered, her voice soft but filled with gratitude. "I just thought of you as my bodyguard. But hearing you say all of that... it makes me feel like I understand you better."

Lia's gaze flicked up, meeting Esmeralda's for a moment before she gave a wry smile. "There's not much to understand. I'm just here to do my job."

Esmeralda shook her head, a small, knowing smile tugging at her lips. "That's not true. You're more than just your duty, Lia. You've become my friend. You've helped me see the world differently, especially when I was lost or unsure. And... I don't know if I could do this without you."

Lia's expression softened slightly, and for the first time, Esmeralda saw a glimmer of something she hadn't noticed before—a trace of warmth in her eyes. "I never thought I'd be following you around like this," Lia admitted. "But I'm glad I am. I'm glad it's *you*. I'm glad I'm with you on this quest, even if it's not what I imagined."

Esmeralda's heart swelled. "I think I'm glad too," she said, her voice barely above a whisper. "I'm glad we're doing this together."

Lia exhaled, a gentle, almost relieved breath, and for a moment, the silence between them wasn't heavy or awkward. It was a shared understanding, a quiet moment of connection.

Then, with her usual wit, Lia broke the silence with a smirk. "Well, if we're going to keep going on this quest together, you should know one thing."

Esmeralda raised an eyebrow, intrigued. "What's that?"

Lia leaned in slightly, her voice dropping into a teasing tone. "I'm not going to let you get us killed by some ancient magic or stray dragon fire. So, you better be prepared to listen to me when I say *don't touch anything*."

Esmeralda laughed, a genuine sound that echoed through the night, warming her from the inside. "I think I can handle that, if it means keeping us both alive."

Lia smirked. "Good. Because I can't babysit a *mini dragon* and you at the same time."

Esmeralda smiled back, her heart feeling lighter.

CHAPTER 8

To Vornwick!

The days were passing by in a quiet rhythm, the steady crunch of boots against the earth the only sound besides the soft chirp of birds and the rustling of leaves in the wind. Esmeralda had always loved the forest, its stillness, its secrets, and the way the light seemed to dance through the trees in soft, flickering beams. But now, it felt different—almost as if the woods themselves were a witness to something new, something unspoken between her and Lia.

The journey to Vornwick had been slower than Esmeralda had anticipated, but the pace felt right. It allowed her to savor the moments of silence between them—moments where words were no longer necessary, where they simply existed together in the quiet of their shared company.

Esmeralda glanced at Lia, who was walking a few paces ahead, her back straight, eyes scanning the path ahead. It wasn't that Lia was distant, but there was something about the way she moved that gave off the sense of a soldier always on alert, always prepared. Yet, Esmeralda had noticed that over the course of their journey, Lia's posture had softened, her steps less guarded. There was something more open about her, as though she were letting down the walls she'd built so high over the years.

And Esmeralda... well, she was beginning to notice things about Lia she hadn't before. The curve of her jaw when she smiled at something unexpected, the way her brow furrowed when she was focused, the briefest flicker of vulnerability in her eyes whenever Esmeralda caught her off guard.

It was hard to ignore the way her heart would flutter in her chest when Lia smiled at her—like a warm gust of wind on a chilly day. Or the way her voice, so steady and unflinching, could somehow make Esmeralda feel like everything was going to be okay, even when the future seemed uncertain.

She shook her head slightly, pushing those thoughts aside. She couldn't afford distractions—not when she was this close to uncovering the truth about her family. She couldn't let herself be distracted by... feelings. Not now.

But even as she tried to quiet her thoughts, her gaze kept drifting back to Lia. Her shoulders, the way she moved, the subtle but undeniable pull between them.

"You're quiet," Lia said suddenly, breaking the silence, her voice light but with a hint of amusement.

Esmeralda blinked, startled from her thoughts. She hadn't realized how lost in them she'd become. "Sorry, I was just thinking."

Lia smirked, glancing over her shoulder with a raised eyebrow. "What, did you get lost in your own head again?"

Esmeralda laughed, the sound coming easily. "Maybe. It happens sometimes."

"Good thing I'm here to pull you back out," Lia replied with a wry grin, the teasing edge to her words almost making Esmeralda's heart skip a beat.

The playfulness in Lia's tone was a stark contrast to the stoic figure she had once been, and it warmed Esmeralda more than she cared to admit.

As they continued on their way, the landscape began to shift. The towering trees started to thin, giving way to rolling hills that stretched toward the horizon. The air grew sharper, fresher, and the scent of distant sea breezes began to linger in the air. Vornwick was close—she could feel it.

Esmeralda quickened her pace to catch up to Lia, who had already fallen into a natural rhythm with the road. "So, what do you think Vornwick will be like?" she asked, hoping the casual question would distract her from the stirrings of her heart.

Lia's eyes softened for a moment, her lips curling into a faint smile.

"I've heard it's a quiet town. A little isolated, but beautiful. The kind of place where everyone knows everyone's business, but they still keep to themselves."

Esmeralda chuckled. "Sounds a bit like the The Hollow. Although sometimes everyone seems too wrapped up in their own things." She sighed, being so much younger, she tended to not be as involved as she wished she could be in Royal duties. While she wasn't a royal herself, growing up with them, and helping around the castle and with the villages had given her a purpose.

"That's because you're royals," Lia teased, her tone light. It was common for people to group Esmeralda in with the Royals, to hold her with the same respect and awe as them, but she didn't always feel it. Lia looked at her, a thoughtful glance, "I imagine that's a bit of a different world."

Esmeralda hesitated before responding. "I don't think I've ever felt like a royal," she admitted softly. "Sometimes, I feel like I'm just pretending to be someone I'm not. Like the weight of my title is just a costume I have to wear. But I'm not sure what I'm supposed to do with it. I'm still trying to figure that out."

Lia's expression softened, and she slowed her pace until they were walking side by side. "I think you're doing just fine," she said gently. "You've got a good heart, Esmeralda. You're not pretending. You're just... learning. And that's okay."

Esmeralda felt a small blush creep up her neck. "I've always felt like I was supposed to have it figured out by now," she confessed. "I was supposed to know what kind of witch I was, what kind of leader I would be. But I don't. I've been searching for so long, and sometimes it feels like the more I uncover, the less I actually know about myself."

Lia nodded, her eyes fixed ahead as she spoke. "I get it. I've spent my whole life wanting to be something, wanting to be *someone*—a soldier in the royal army, to stand beside the royals and protect them. But then, life happens, and you end up in a different place. A place you didn't expect, but a place where you learn things about yourself you never knew."

Esmeralda smiled softly at Lia, her heart swelling with something she couldn't quite name. It wasn't just the quiet, reassuring words that comforted her—it was the way Lia said them, the way she was always there, steady, when Esmeralda needed her the most.

"I didn't expect to end up here either," Esmeralda murmured, her voice barely above a whisper. "But I'm glad I did."

Lia's gaze flicked to her, and for a brief moment, their eyes locked in an unspoken understanding. Neither of them said anything, but the silence between them felt like a quiet promise—a recognition of something deeper, something that had started to bloom on their journey, something neither of them had expected.

As the sun began to dip behind the horizon, casting the world in hues of pink and gold, they continued on toward Vornwick. Neither of them spoke much after that, but the air between them hummed with an unspoken connection, growing stronger with every step.

When they finally reached the town's outskirts, the lights of Vornwick twinkled like stars against the darkening sky. The journey had led them here—together—and as they ventured into the town, Esmeralda felt a sense of calm wash over her. No matter what came next, she knew that this bond between her and Lia, however it would unfold, was a part of her journey now.

CHAPTER 9

The Grand Library of Vornwick

As they walked into the quaint town, Esmeralda felt overwhelmed, unsure of where to go. But then there it was a golden beacon of a sign. The Grand Library of Vornwick.

"Of course!" She pointed to the wooden sign, reaching out and dragging Lia by the hand.

The Winter Witches were known to be scholars, they all held the histories of The Hollow as well as cared for the magic of the land. *This had to be it,* Esmeralda thought.

The ancient doors of the Grand Library creaked open with a sound that echoed through the towering stone halls. Esmeralda could feel the weight of history pressing in on her as they stepped inside, the air thick with the scent of parchment, ink, and the unmistakable tang of magic. Shelves stretched up into the high, vaulted ceilings, each row filled with books of every shape and size, some old and tattered, others gleaming with new enchantments.

"This place is incredible," Esmeralda murmured, her voice filled with awe as she ran a finger over the spine of a nearby book. The pages practically hummed with energy, like they were waiting to be opened.

Lia nodded, but her focus was on the rows of books, her sharp eyes scanning for any sign of danger. The walls of the library, though beautiful, seemed to conceal countless secrets. Esmeralda was already lost in the magic of it all, her mind swirling with thoughts of her family's past, and the answers she was hoping to uncover. But she knew that finding what she needed here wouldn't be easy.

The library, after all, was known for its enchanted shelves. Books appeared or disappeared based on the seeker's desires, but that didn't mean they would be found easily. The shelves were a labyrinth in their own right, a maze of magic that only the most skilled witches—and the most stubborn—could navigate.

"So," Esmeralda said, pulling herself back to the present moment as she turned to Lia with a grin. "Any idea how we're supposed to find a specific family tree in all of this?"

Lia crossed her arms, her expression as stoic as ever, but Esmeralda could see the faintest hint of amusement in her eyes. "I'm guessing you're not going to let me do all the work?"

Esmeralda laughed. "Not a chance."

Together, they wandered deeper into the maze of shelves, Esmeralda's eyes darting from book to book, her mind racing with possibilities. Mittens, always a curious companion, was darting between the aisles, his tiny wings fluttering by. Then suddenly, the padder of cat paws on hardwood made her head turn. There was mittens, back in fluffy cat form. She turned to tell Lia.

Suddenly, a loud *click* echoed through the library.

"Mittens!" Esmeralda called out. She turned to see the cat pawing at a small lever hidden behind a row of books, his tail twitching with mischief.

"What did you do now?" Lia muttered, stepping forward to gently nudge Mittens away from the lever. But it was too late. The sound of stone grinding against stone reverberated, and the floor beneath them shifted.

Esmeralda gasped, stumbling as a section of the bookshelf slid open to reveal a hidden staircase leading downward. The air was colder now, and the shadows seemed to stretch longer as they peered into the darkness below.

"Well, that's not ominous at all," Lia said dryly, her hand instinctively going to the hilt of her blade. "Welcome back, Mittens."

"Come on, don't be such a pessimist," Esmeralda teased. "Besides, if we're lucky, this might lead us straight to the records we need."

Lia shot her a sidelong glance. "Lucky? Nothing about a dark ominous stairwell to who knows what feels lucky."

But Esmeralda's excitement was contagious, and after a moment's hesitation, Lia followed her down the narrow staircase, Mittens trotting ahead as though he knew exactly where he was going.

The staircase spiraled downward, and as they reached the bottom, they found themselves in a small, dimly lit chamber. The walls were lined with ancient relics—gilded frames, faded tapestries, and delicate scrolls piled high. It felt like they had stumbled upon a hidden sanctuary, a forgotten corner of the library where the oldest secrets were kept.

"Is this...?" Esmeralda trailed off, her eyes wide as she spotted something that made her heart leap. There, in the far corner, illuminated by the soft glow of floating candles, was a family tree carved into the stone wall.

Her fingers trembled as she approached it, tracing the intricate lines that formed her lineage. Her heart skipped when she saw the familiar name of her bloodline: *The Winter Witches*. She followed the branches of her family tree, her eyes scanning for more familiar names, but then—

She froze.

Beside her family name, there was a break in the lineage, a sudden shift in the pattern. The name changed, and next to the Winter Witches, there was the name *Willow Witches*.

A shock ran through her, a jolt of recognition mixed with excitement. Esmeralda stepped closer, her eyes narrowing at the sigil next to the Willow Witches' name. It was different from her own family's sigil, but there was something undeniably familiar about it— something that spoke of an ancient connection. Her fingers gently touched the sigil, a soft warmth curling through her as though the symbol itself recognized her touch.

"Do you see this?" Esmeralda whispered, turning to Lia, her voice a mix of wonder and awe. "The Willow Witches... I think they're connected to my family. I've never heard of them before, but they must be."

Lia's eyes softened as she studied the family tree, her gaze lingering on the unfamiliar name. "Maybe this is why you've been feeling so drawn to this quest," she said quietly.

Esmeralda smiled, her heart swelling at the truth of Lia's words. "I think you're right."

She paused for a moment, taking in the gravity of the moment. "The Willow Witches..." she repeated softly, almost as if testing the name on her tongue. "I have to find them. I have to know more."

Esmeralda's heart fluttered at the quiet sincerity in Lia's voice. She looked at her bodyguard—her companion—and for the first time in a long while, she didn't feel so alone in her search.

"Thanks, Lia," Esmeralda said, her voice soft. "I don't think I could do this without you."

Lia gave her a small smile, her expression slightly teasing. "Well, you'd probably get yourself into more trouble without me."

Esmeralda grinned, her spirits lifted by Lia's dry humor. "True. But that's why I'm glad you're here."

The sound of Mittens meowing echoed from across the chamber, and Esmeralda turned to see the little black cat batting at a loose scroll with his tiny paws, then raced ahead of them up the stairwell and back into the main library hall. As she stepped toward him to fetch him, she felt a weird magic as she passed the final step, landing back into the library hall. She looked up.

Mittens... wasn't a cat anymore.

Instead, he was sitting in front of them with a small puff of smoke and a soft, inky black tail. He blinked at them with wide, green eyes that gleamed with mischief—and then he let out a tiny, dragon-like growl.

"Mittens?" Esmeralda gasped, her eyes wide.

Lia's mouth quirked into an amused smile as she crouched down to get a better look at the tiny creature. "Well, guess he's back to dragon form."

Esmeralda bit her lip to hold back a laugh as she knelt beside her now-mini dragon. "I—how is this even possible?"

The little dragon let out another soft growl, its wings fluttering as it tried to puff out a small cloud of smoke. Lia leaned in closer, her eyes sparkling with mischief.

"Well," Lia said with a grin, "it's a good thing this library is full of strange magic, right?"

Esmeralda chuckled, reaching out to gently pet the tiny dragon. "I think we've found another clue—the magic of the library must have broke through his spell from the jelly pastery."

The little dragon purred in response, nuzzling her hand affectionately.

"Well," Lia said, standing up with a shrug, "I suppose we'll figure it out eventually. But for now, I think you have a family to find."

As she gazed at Lia, who offered a faint smile of her own, Esmeralda felt a warmth settle in her chest. Maybe—just maybe—this was where she was meant to be. And with each passing day, that truth seemed to grow stronger.

CHAPTER 10

The Willow Witches

The journey to the northern end of the Isles had been long and arduous, the wind growing colder with each passing mile as the sea mist thickened and the shores grew more rugged. Esmeralda's heart was light, though, fueled by the anticipation of finally uncovering the last piece of her family's story. The clues had led them here, to a remote village nestled at the foot of ancient cliffs, where the land seemed to hold the whispers of centuries.

The village was small, a peaceful place of simple homes made from stone and timber, each one adorned with vibrant tapestries that fluttered in the crisp sea breeze. There was something timeless about it, as if it had existed for as long as the land itself. The people here moved with purpose, their faces marked with the serenity of those who lived close to nature and magic. Esmeralda felt an immediate sense of belonging, as though this was where she had always been meant to be.

Lia, ever watchful, was by her side as they walked through the village, her eyes scanning the surroundings. Despite the calm atmosphere, there was a quiet tension in her posture, a reminder of how much danger Esmeralda had faced on their journey.

"You seem... different here," Lia remarked, her tone softening as she looked around, taking in the warm glow of lanterns hanging outside cottages and the faint sound of singing in the distance. "Like you've found your place."

Esmeralda smiled, her heart swelling. "I think I have."

They were led deeper into the village, where a large circle of people had gathered around an ancient willow tree at the center. Its branches stretched wide, its leaves shimmering with an otherworldly glow. This was the heart of the village—the source of its magic, and the namesake of the Willow Witches.

As they approached, Esmeralda felt a pull in her chest, a quiet hum of magic resonating from the tree. She had never experienced anything like it—there was something ancient and powerful about it, as though the very earth beneath her feet was alive with stories waiting to be told.

The matriarch of the village stood before them, her age impossible to guess, her silver hair flowing like a river down her back. Her eyes were deep and wise, the same shade as Esmeralda's own, and when their gazes met, a spark of recognition flickered between them. This woman was family.

"You've come," the matriarch said, her voice warm and welcoming. "I knew you would."

Esmeralda's throat tightened, emotion surging in her chest. "I didn't know what to expect," she whispered, her voice breaking. "But I think... I think I've found what I've been searching for."

The matriarch reached out, pulling her into a gentle embrace. "You are home, child."

Esmeralda let the words wash over her, feeling the weight of them sink into her bones. She had spent so long searching for answers, and now, standing here among her relatives, she realized that the answers had been waiting for her all along.

As they sat around a fire that evening, the village elders shared stories of Esmeralda's ancestors—the Winter Witches who had once roamed the land, their magic intertwined with the cycles of the seasons. The elders spoke of how her family had come to this land, adopting the name *Willow Witches* as a homage to the great willow tree that had become their sanctuary.

Esmeralda listened intently, captivated by the tales of her ancestors, of women who had worked with the land, cultivating herbs and healing magic, of witches who had used their knowledge to protect the people of the Isles. The more they spoke, the more Esmeralda felt a deep sense of connection to the land, to the traditions, and to the women who had shaped her bloodline.

"I never knew," Esmeralda said softly, her voice thick with emotion.

"I never knew this part of my family, this magic. It feels like a whole world has opened up to me."

"You are part of it now," the matriarch said, her gaze filled with pride. "And you are welcome here, always."

Esmeralda's heart swelled. For the first time in her life, she felt truly seen—not just as a royal witch from The Hollow, but as part of something far older, something that stretched back through generations.

As the evening drew to a close, the matriarch handed Esmeralda a weathered grimoire, its pages yellowed with age. "This belonged to your great-grandmother," she said. "It's yours now. Use it well."

Esmeralda took the book in her hands, her fingers tracing the worn cover. The weight of it felt comforting, as though she had been given a gift that was meant for her alone. She glanced at Lia, who stood a little farther off, watching the proceedings with a quiet smile.

The night was growing late, and after a long day of stories and bonding, the villagers retreated to their homes. Esmeralda and Lia were invited to stay in a small cottage near the base of the willow tree, its hearth already glowing with warmth.

As they sat by the fire, Esmeralda's heart felt lighter than it had in years. She glanced at Lia, who was watching her with an unreadable expression. There was a softness in Lia's eyes, a tenderness that hadn't been there before.

"I think... I think I've found everything I was looking for," Esmeralda said softly, her voice barely above a whisper.

Lia's eyes flickered toward the door, her hand tightening around her mug of tea. "What does that mean for you now?"

Esmeralda hesitated, the weight of her next words hanging in the air. She had found her family, her lineage, but the road ahead was not so simple. She had a place here, among the Willow Witches, but what did that mean for her life back in The Hollow?

"I don't know yet," Esmeralda replied. "But I think I'm starting to understand that family isn't just about bloodlines... it's about the people who make you feel like you belong."

Lia's eyes softened, and for a moment, the distance between them seemed to vanish. Esmeralda felt her heart beat a little faster as Lia leaned in slightly, her voice low and sincere.

"I never thought I'd be here, on a journey like this, with someone like you," Lia said. "But I'm glad I am."

Esmeralda smiled, her heart fluttering in her chest. She felt captivated by Lia as she spoke. "Me too." She replied in almost a whisper against the night sky.

The fire crackled between them, casting flickering shadows on the walls of the cottage. And in that quiet moment, as the world outside seemed to hold its breath, Esmeralda reached out, her fingers brushing Lia's. The touch lingered, soft and tentative, and then, without another word, Esmeralda leaned in, her lips brushing against Lia's in a kiss that felt like the culmination of everything they had been through together.

It was gentle at first, as if they were both testing the waters, but when Lia's hand cupped Esmeralda's cheek, deepening the kiss, Esmeralda's heart soared. This was something new, something that felt right.

When they finally pulled away, both of them breathless, Esmeralda's heart thudded in her chest. She knew that this moment marked the beginning of something neither of them had expected.

As they lay together on the couch, wrapped in the warmth of the fire, Esmeralda's thoughts turned inward. She had found her family—the Willow Witches. But now, the choice loomed before her: stay here, where she felt a deep connection to the land and its people, or return to The Hollow, to the family she had made with the twins, and the life that had started to feel like home.

CHAPTER 11

The Heart of the Willow Witches

The days in the village stretched out like a warm, comforting blanket, wrapping Esmeralda in a sense of peace she hadn't known in years. The mornings were crisp, filled with the sounds of birdsong and the soft rustling of the willow tree's leaves, and the evenings were alive with the glow of lanterns and the laughter of villagers. Esmeralda spent much of her time immersed in her family's history, pouring over the ancient texts the matriarch had given her, but there were also moments—quiet moments—spent with Lia.

The two of them would wander the village's herb gardens, where the air smelled of lavender and thyme, and the earth was rich with magic. Lia, though still reserved, had continued to soften in Esmeralda's presence. Her smiles had become more frequent, and her eyes lingered just a little longer on Esmeralda, as if she were allowing herself to take in the person Esmeralda had become. The invisible walls between them had come crumbling down, shedding hour by hour. Stolen kisses during walks to meals in the great hall, Lia pulling on knitted mittens onto Esmeraldas hands to keep her warm in the cold weather. Walking hand in hand through the snow around the village. Talking late into the night, and then doing it all over again.They had fallen into an easy routine.

They spent evenings by the fire, Esmeralda with her grimoire and Lia sharpening a dagger or polishing the hilt of her sword, the steady rhythm of their actions creating a comforting harmony between them. Sometimes, Esmeralda would hum softly as she read aloud from her great-grandmother's grimoire, and Lia would listen, the flickering firelight catching in her eyes.

It was during one of these nights, with the wind howling outside and the warmth of the hearth surrounding them, that Esmeralda picked up her quill and began writing.

Dear Kellian and Kyeria,

I miss you both terribly. I never expected to be so far from The Hollow for so long, but this journey has been... life-changing. I've met my relatives here in the Isles, among the Willow Witches. They practice a form of magic that feels deeply connected to the land, and I feel more at home here than I ever thought possible. But I must admit, I feel torn.

I promised to mentor the twins, and though I've found family of my own, I can't shake the feeling that they need me. I think of them constantly, of the promise I made to help them with their magic. But I also know I've found something here—something that could be the key to helping them grow. I'm writing to Zephyra, who knows the twins well. Perhaps she can offer guidance.

I hope to hear from you soon.

With all my love,

Esmeralda

She sealed the letter, her heart heavy with the weight of her decision. The village had become a place of healing, of connection, but it was impossible not to miss the twins. She had made a promise to them—to help them unlock their potential, to be the mentor they needed. But this place, with its deep connection to magic and the land, could be the perfect place for them to grow. The Willow Witches had their own way of teaching magic, one that was as natural as the herbs they cultivated and the land they tended. Perhaps this was the future she had been searching for—not just for herself, but for the twins, too.

Lia watched her carefully as she folded the letter, her voice soft but steady. "You're torn," she observed. "Between two places that feel like home."

Esmeralda nodded, feeling the truth of Lia's words settle in her chest. "I don't know what to do, Lia. I made a promise to them. But here... I feel like I've found something deeper, something I didn't know I was missing."

Lia leaned forward, her gaze intense, but there was a softness in her eyes that made Esmeralda's heart flutter. "You can't force yourself to choose between the two," Lia said gently. "It's about where you feel your magic is calling you to be. And the twins, they'll understand. They've always known you've had something special within you."

Esmeralda took a deep breath, the warmth of Lia's words wrapping around her like a comforting cloak. "I think you're right," she said. "I need to listen to my heart. To the magic inside me."

Lia reached out, her hand brushing lightly against Esmeralda's. "Then, listen carefully. You'll find your way."

The next day, Esmeralda penned a letter to Zephyra, pouring her heart onto the page. She told her everything—the beauty of the village, the warmth of her newfound family, and the uncertainty she felt about leaving The Hollow. Zephyra had been with the twins since they were young, and Esmeralda trusted her wisdom above all else. She needed Zephyra's advice.

When the letter was sent off, Esmeralda turned her attention back to the village, trying to push aside the worry gnawing at her. She didn't want to rush this decision, but she knew something inside her was shifting.

Over the next few days, as Esmeralda spent time with the villagers, she realized that this place, this home, could offer the twins exactly what they needed—an environment rich with history, filled with people who understood magic in its purest, most natural form. The Willow Witches lived in harmony with the earth, their magic rooted in the plants they grew and the land they nurtured. It was the perfect place for the twins to learn, to connect with their own magic in ways Esmeralda had only just begun to understand.

And as she spent more time with Lia, something else became clear. The quiet moments they shared, the laughter they exchanged, the way their hands brushed together as they walked through the village—it all felt right. Esmeralda had been searching for her family, for answers, but what she had found was something even more precious: a connection that was both grounding and transformative.

One evening, as they walked along the edge of the village, the setting sun painting the sky in shades of pink and orange, Esmeralda reached out, her fingers brushing Lia's. Lia turned to her, her expression unreadable for a moment, and then a small smile tugged at the corner of her lips as she intertwined their hands.

"You're thinking too much again," Lia teased, her voice light but with a warmth that made Esmeralda's heart skip.

"I can't help it," Esmeralda replied, her voice soft. "There's a lot on my mind."

Lia stopped, turning to face her fully. "You don't have to have all the answers right now, Esmeralda. Sometimes, it's enough just to follow what feels right."

Esmeralda smiled, her heart swelling with affection. "And what if what feels right is here, with you?"

Lia's gaze softened, and for a moment, the world around them seemed to fade. "Then I'll be here, with you."

Esmeralda leaned in, her lips finding Lia's in a soft kiss, one that felt like a promise. A promise to stay, to find their way forward together.

The kiss lingered, tender and slow, and when they finally pulled apart, Esmeralda's heart was light and happy.

In that moment, the decision she had been so afraid to make didn't feel so impossible anymore. She would find a way to bring the twins here, to this magical place where they could grow and learn, and perhaps, in the process, she could find her place in both worlds—the world of her roots and the family she had made with Lia.

In the morning a sprite arrived with a letter from Zephrya, Esmeralda greedily ripped it open with her wolf tooth dagger she kept on her belt.

Dearest Esmeralda,

I received your letter, and I understand the weight of what you are carrying in your heart. The pull between your past and your present, between duty and desire, is never an easy thing to navigate. But I've known you for many years now, and I know you are not one to shy away from the hard choices. You are a woman of deep conviction, of wisdom beyond your years, and you will find your path.

You ask where you should be, where your magic belongs. Let me tell you this: your magic has always been intertwined with your heart. It is not bound by the walls of The Hollow or by the bloodline of your ancestors—it is tied to the very land that calls to you, to the people who understand you, and to the connections you've made along the way.

Your magic will tell you where it feels most at peace. And right now, I know that peace can be found in the land where the Willow Witches live. Their connection to the earth, to the herbs and the plants, to the cycles of nature—it is a harmony that will resonate with the deep magic within you. Your family, both by blood and by choice, is there, Esmeralda. And while it may not have been the home you expected, it is the home that calls to your soul.

As for the twins, they need you—of that I have no doubt. But they also need guidance in a way that will help them unlock their full potential. I believe that teaching them where the magic of the Winter Witches originated could be the most powerful way forward. They will grow here, under the same sky and the same stars that your ancestors did, and their magic will bloom in ways that The Hollow may not have been able to nurture.

I would be honored to bring them to you, if you decide this is the right course. They would be in good hands, and I know that, with the support of the Willow Witches and the love you carry for them, you will teach them in ways that will shape them into the powerful witches they are destined to be.

Listen to your heart, Esmeralda. It has never led you astray.
All my love,
Zephyra

CHAPTER 12

Friendly Advice

Esmeralda stood beneath the ancient willow tree that anchored the village, its gnarled branches stretching toward the sky like an open embrace. The roots of the tree dug deep into the earth, and in that moment, she felt a pull—one that mirrored the connection she'd been searching for her whole life. The village around her buzzed with the quiet hum of daily life: women and men weaving herbs into bundles, children playing by the stream, the low murmur of elders telling stories in their small stone cottages. This was where she was meant to be.

Lia stood beside her, her gaze soft as she watched Esmeralda take it all in. It had been a week since they'd arrived, and in that time, Esmeralda had been overwhelmed by a sense of peace she hadn't expected to find. It was as if the land, the people, the very air here understood her. This was home, not just in the literal sense, but in the deep, spiritual way she'd always longed for.

Lia, ever the protector, stood a little apart, her arms crossed as she surveyed the surroundings. But there was something different about her now—less guarded, more present. The tension between them had eased, and the quiet moments they shared in the village had woven a thread of understanding between them. Esmeralda had noticed the way Lia looked at her sometimes, the softness that had begun to slip past her usual stoic exterior. It made her heart flutter in ways she hadn't expected.

"Do you think it's foolish?" Esmeralda asked, turning to Lia, her voice tentative but sure. "To stay here, I mean. To make this my home."

Lia gave her a thoughtful look, her arms uncrossing as she finally took a step closer. "I don't think it's foolish. I think it's brave. It's what you've been searching for, Esmeralda. All this time. You don't have to explain it to me, but if this is what your heart needs... then I think it's where you belong."

Esmeralda smiled softly, touched by Lia's support, by the quiet understanding in her words. "It's just... so much. To leave behind The Hollow, the twins, all that I thought I was meant to do." She glanced at the distant horizon, where the last light of day glimmered across the rolling hills. "But here, I feel like I'm standing on the edge of something... a future I've never allowed myself to dream of."

"I see you, Esmeralda Winter, for exactly who you are. It has been an honor to watch you here, among your people. To watch you bloom," Lia's voice filled with affection.

Esmeralda felt heat rush to her cheeks and looked down to her hands. Lia reached out a hand, tilting her head up to meet her gaze.

"trust yourself."

Esmeralda sighed, feeling the weight of her thoughts settle in her chest. The village, the Willow Witches, this land—this was where her magic had truly come alive. She could feel the threads of her ancestry weaving through the very air around her, and it was here, with these people, that she could learn, grow, and teach in ways she had never imagined. She had found her roots, not just in blood, but in spirit.

"I've made my decision," she said quietly, her voice steady. She turned to face Lia fully, her expression resolute. "I want to stay here. I want to learn more about my family, about the Winter Witches, and what this place can teach me. I feel like it's time. And... I've decided to ask Zephyra to bring the twins. This is the place where their magic should be nurtured, too. It's where they belong."

Lia's eyes softened as she reached out, resting a hand gently on Esmeralda's shoulder. "You're doing the right thing. The twins will flourish here, just as you will."

Esmeralda exhaled, feeling the decision settle into her bones. It wasn't just the pull of her ancestors or the magic of the land that had led her here; it was the deep, resonant truth that her heart had whispered to her all along: this was where her future began.

As the sun dipped below the horizon, painting the sky in shades of violet and gold, Esmeralda took a deep breath, preparing to write her letter to Zephyra. Her heart was full, and for the first time in a long while, she felt the weight of her choices lift. This was where she was meant to be. And with the twins coming to join her, her family, both the one she had found and the one she had chosen, would finally be complete.

Later that evening, after a dinner shared with the villagers, Esmeralda sat at the small wooden desk in her cozy cottage, quill in hand. The quiet of the village settled around her, the only sound the soft rustle of leaves in the wind and the occasional hum of magic in the air.

She began to write, her words flowing easily as she poured her heart onto the paper.

Dear Zephyra,

I have made my decision. I want to stay here, with the Willow Witches. This village, this place, feels like home in a way I never knew I needed. I feel a connection to it—one that my magic recognizes and calls out to. I want to learn more about my ancestors, about the Winter Witches and the land we came from. There's so much here for me, and I know it's where I'm meant to be.

As for the twins, I feel in my heart that this is the place where they can truly unlock their potential. They will be safe here, and they will grow into the powerful witches they are destined to become. Please, bring them here. I know this is where they belong.

I look forward to being reunited with them, to sharing this new chapter of my life with them—and with you.

With all my love,
Esmeralda

CHAPTER 13

A funny little thing called love

The days in the village seemed to stretch on, each one blending into the next like the slow, steady rhythm of the seasons changing. But within that peaceful flow, something beautiful, something deep, was quietly growing. Esmeralda and Lia hadn't spoken much about it—there was no need. They simply *felt* it, like an undercurrent that tugged at them both when their eyes met, or when the world around them grew silent and still.

The morning light filtered softly through the leaves of the willow tree, casting delicate patterns on the ground. Esmeralda and Lia sat side by side, preparing herbs in the cool shade. The scent of lavender and rosemary filled the air, mingling with the earthy fragrance of the village.

Lia, usually so meticulous and reserved, had relaxed into the rhythm of village life. Her hands, always so steady in their movements, moved with grace now as she worked beside Esmeralda. Every so often, their fingers brushed, and though neither acknowledged it, a warmth lingered in the space between them.

"You know," Esmeralda said, breaking the comfortable silence, "I've never seen you look so... content."

Lia glanced at her, a soft smile curling on her lips. "Maybe you're rubbing off on me."

Esmeralda laughed lightly, her heart fluttering at the sound of Lia's unguarded tone. "I'm not that good of an influence, am I?"

"I never said you were," Lia teased, her eyes gleaming mischievously.

"But you do make it easier to forget that I'm supposed to be keeping you safe."

Esmeralda's heart skipped a beat. The warmth between them flared, and her cheeks warmed with the quiet affection that had been growing in her chest. She looked down at her hands, pretending to focus on the herbs, though her mind was caught in the space between them.

"Well, I'm glad I'm not *too* much trouble," she said softly, unable to keep the playful edge out of her voice.

Lia's gaze softened, and there was something in the way she looked at Esmeralda—a tenderness that had always been there but now felt more pronounced. "You're never trouble, Esmeralda."

Their eyes met again, and for a moment, neither could look away. The unspoken words hung in the air, and Esmeralda could feel her pulse quicken.

She swallowed, her voice barely above a whisper. "I'm glad you're here."

Lia's lips twitched in the faintest smile, and she leaned in just slightly. "I'm glad, too."

After a long day spent walking the forest trails in the snow with Mittens, back to his original form, trailing along behind them, Esmeralda and Lia sat together on a large, moss-covered stone by the river. The water babbled gently over rocks, and the sky was painted with the warm hues of sunset. They had jumped in the river, spending the last hours of light in the water together.

"I used to dream about adventures like this," Esmeralda confessed, her voice quiet as she dipped her toes in the cool water. "But I always thought it would be different—more dramatic, more dangerous, you know? The kind of thing you read about in stories. I never imagined it would be like this. Peaceful."

Lia chuckled, her voice low and smooth. "We're still adventuring, Esmeralda. Just... in a quieter way. "

Esmeralda leaned back, her head resting against the stone, and for a moment, she let herself simply *feel*—the warmth of Lia's presence beside her, the gentle ripples of the river, the soft chirping of birds in the distance.

"Do you think," Esmeralda began slowly, "that sometimes... the world works in quiet ways? That we don't always notice until we're here, in the middle of it?"

Lia's gaze met hers, and for a heartbeat, Esmeralda saw something flicker in her eyes—something more than just the protective shield she usually wore.

"I think you're right," Lia said softly. "Some of the most important things don't come in loud, obvious ways. They can be soft and just as powerful."

Esmeralda smiled, her heart swelling with a warmth she couldn't quite name. It wasn't love yet, but it was something close—something that felt like a promise, like the quiet unfolding of a future they hadn't fully realized. She rested her head on Lia's shoulder, and they stayed like that, letting the time pass them by.

A few days later, as they prepared for dinner in the village hall, Esmeralda was setting the table when she caught a glimpse of Lia through the window. The evening light cast a golden glow around her, highlighting her strong, graceful silhouette as she carried in bundles of herbs from the garden.

In that moment, Esmeralda realized just how deeply she had come to admire Lia—not just as a protector or a companion, but as a woman, a person whose strength and resilience had carved a place in her heart.

Lia's eyes met hers through the window, and there was something in the way she looked at Esmeralda—something soft, something knowing.

Esmeralda felt her breath catch in her throat, her pulse quickening. She hurried to finish setting the table, her hands trembling slightly. It was a moment of clarity—of realization. This was where she wanted to be. Not just with the Willow Witches, but with *her*. With Lia.

That night, after dinner, they sat outside under the star-filled sky, the air cool with the promise of autumn. Mittens curled up contentedly on the grass, his little black form a silent witness to the quiet shift between them.

"You've been quiet," Lia said, turning her head toward Esmeralda. "What's on your mind?"

Esmeralda hesitated for a moment, her fingers tracing the edge of her glass. "I was just thinking... how lucky I am."

Lia raised an eyebrow. "Lucky? In what way?"

"In this moment," Esmeralda said softly. "With you. Here. I've never felt more..." She trailed off, " Like I've finally found something that feels right."

Lia's expression softened, and she leaned in just a little, their shoulders brushing. "I feel the same way."

Their eyes met, and for the first time, there were no walls between them—only the quiet understanding that had grown between them, unnoticed, over the course of the week.

And in that moment, with the cool night air around them, Esmeralda knew. She didn't need words, didn't need to explain. What had begun as something tentative, something unsure, had blossomed into something steady, something true.

"Lia," Esmeralda whispered, her voice barely a breath, "Will tou stay?"

Lia's eyes softened, and without a word, she reached out, her fingers brushing Esmeralda's cheek. "I go, where you go." Her hand tugging Esmeralda to her, their lips colliding. With the moonlight shining down upon them, the snow beginning to fall and the soft sounds of the forest beyond the sleeping village, they lost them selves to each other. Leaving lingering kisses, soft and slow.

In the silence that followed, under the willow tree, in the heart of this village, they found something they hadn't known they were looking for.

A home.
Together.

The Knight & Her Witch

I
n the whispering winds of a shadowed glen,
    A witch and her knight met again and again.
One with the stars in her dark, woven hair,
The other with armor, a heart laid bare.
They wandered through forests, through mountains, through mist,
Each step a new story, each glance a soft twist.
The witch with her secrets, her magic untold,
The knight with her courage, a heart made of gold.
By moonlight, they'd talk of the paths they had crossed,
Of battles they'd fought and the things they'd both lost.
The witch would enchant with a touch of her hand,
The knight would protect her, a fierce, steady stand.
Through rivers they rode, through the thickest of fog,
The witch found her heart in the silence, the slog.
And the knight, ever steadfast, in the storm's cruel embrace,
Found love in the softness of her lover's grace.
For journeys aren't just the miles that we roam,
But the souls we encounter, the places we call home.
And the witch, with her magic, and the knight, with her fight,
Found love in each other, in the dark of the night.

E.R. Maggetti is writer of cozy fantasy who brings a touch of soft romance and fantastical magic to the world of fantasy. With a love for creating enchanting worlds and captivating characters, E.R. weaves tales that will transport you to new realms and leave you spellbound. When not writing, you can find E.R. lost in a book, drawing or walking on the beach with her family and fur babies.

What's Next?

Follow along @authorelliana for updates and new book announcements.

E.R.Maggetti also writes contemporary romance under the pen name, Elliana Rose.

Other Works by Elliana

Sparks Fly Series

- For The Thrill of It All - Elliana Rose
- Heart Racing - Elliana Rose
- Until The Lights Go Out - Elliana Rose
- Fall Into Me - Elliana Rose

Acknowledgments

Where do I even begin? If you were to ask me this time last year if I thought I'd be published by this time next year, I would have spit out my Dr. Pepper. I have been making up stories since before I could write, let alone hold a pen. My mother would write sentences along with my drawings and staple the pages together to create a "book". Between that and making fairy houses in the leaves and sticks, it makes sense I landed here, making up stories about magical worlds.

I knew the first book I wanted in the world where fairies fluttered by, a beautiful golden castle, and a world that looked like what the fairytales in my head looked like. In The Hollow, is where my mind has always gone, to a beautiful land where people of every kind were loved and accepted. Kyeria is my soul character. She has faced so much in her life, littered with trauma, but she herself is soft and so strong. I always wanted a character like her, and writing her was healing for me in many ways. On the opposite side is Aura, the perfect character I love to read. She's fierce and badass and takes no ones shit. But as I wrote her, as her story began, she was so much more. Her own demons of not being enough plagued her, and accepting love and care from someone was her own personal battle. I love these characters like they're my own children, which I know many authors can attest to. Novella one was for me, a soft love about finding your person in a turn of serendipity. Novella two was for you, the badass princess, the forbidden love affair and the gorgeous dark haired knight.

So first and foremost; thank YOU, dear reader. For believing in me and my fairytale. For cheering me on while I drafted and being apart of the bookstagram community that makes my heart all warm and fuzzy.

Thank you to my amazing writer friends, and the chaos writer group chats who put up with all my 'how the heck do you self publish' questions. Thank you to my sweet friends who let me talk out my ideas before they ever formed into The Hollow.

Thank you to my soulmate, Kassandra Tate for being my number one supporter since day one when we were little babies in High School talking about out fan fictions (lol). You inspire me daily and I wouldn't be the writer I am today without **you**. To my Ferris, Kalina Tyne, for being apart of every aspect of the first novella, helping me form and perfect Kellian and Kyeria's stories.

Thank you to my amazing cover artist and author friend Ashley Jurgens for making my art dreams come true!

Thank you to my amazing editor, Kay Morton for taking such care of these characters. For being a validating voice in the void of drafting. For having belly laughing worthy comments about Nox and Kellian. I am so so thankful for you - and I am so sorry for all the spelling errors you had to endure.

Thank you to my sweet family for being my loudest most fearsome cheerleaders, who never let me give up on my dreams. For the hundreds of 'proud of you' texts + love you texts while I went into my writing hole. To my mom and dad for fostering a creativity in me from the the second I was born. For always telling me to reach for the stars. To my mom for listening to me explain my plot by plot ideas, and lending me her wonderful home to have a (free) mini writing retreat where I got the BULK of The Hollow written. To my dad, who has been telling me stories forever, who I watched make his own stories, covering the dining room table in post cards of his screenplays, putting a camera in my hand and saying, "go create." I love you, I love you, I love you.

To my sweet Husband, Kyle. God, I love you. You are the blueprint. The real life book boyfriend. The one who has seen me through every phase of life, who has sat with me in my dark times and my bright times. Who taught me I can do anything I set my mind on, and that he would be right by my side while I do it. Hey you married a published author!

Thank you thank you, I cannot wait to have more stories in this world, there is so much more to come!

xoxo - Elliana